ICE PICK
A novel

Donnie Dale

A
Novel
Press

Ice Pick

978-1-938968-01-3

A Novel Press
Printed in the United States of America

www.DonnieDale.com

Cover photo: Alyx Alaina Schwarz
Cover design: Paula L. Johnson
Author photo: Skye Moorhead

To my parents:
Floyd Donovan Dale and Ethel Angie Dale

1

HE GETS HIS DESSERT

He cut wedges of bloody steak with a long blade gently folded out of a worn pocket knife and stabbed them into his mouth dripping. He washed them down with loud drinks from a hip flask he had taken from his pocket when he sat at the table. He wasn't the biggest human in the cafe. He wasn't the prettiest, with a head as shapeless and brown as a roast. When he tilted up to breathe past a chew of meat, though, there was always an eye to meet his. Eyes went to him. Eyes went off him. He didn't seem to notice.

She noticed him. Hers were two of the eyes. Wanda couldn't figure what it was. His oblivious eating? That long hair that hung over his face like a shredded blanket? She could hardly take her eyes off him, as if he were some kind of performing artist working in blood and whatever was in that pewter flask. Her friend Pauline, sitting on the red leather bench across from Wanda, kept glancing over her shoulder to see what it was that drew her away from their conversation.

Finally Pauline saw him. They both watched for the length of one long chew, two long breaths. That cock-of-the-walk, I'm-eating-here expression, that's what it was. Pauline swung her head back and set her mouth.

"You stop that, Wanda." Then Pauline looked back at him again. You had to.

"Ha ha ha ha ha ha ha ha!" This Donovan laughed so loudly at something, holding his head back and cheek pursed so food wouldn't fly out. It solidified his position in the room, no doubt. Donovan Daley was his name.

"How can you laugh at all that?" Joseph, his companion and his brother, asked quietly. Trying to calm him down. He was younger and smaller and rounder of head than his drunken brother. He sat across from him like an admiring assistant to a magician on a stage. Sober and crafty-eyed as a child's pony. "We're in the middle of a depression."

"Didn't we start drinking during Prohibition!" Donovan yelled. "Didn't we find California in the middle of the Dust Bowl!" He looked around the room for corroboration.

Sure, it was the yelling, partly, that drew her eye to him. Everybody looked over again, waiting for something to happen. Something would. They just knew.

"We're gonna get rich in the Great Depression!"

Chuffing out another big laugh, the man exploded backward in his bench seat. Lodged against the window as if blown there by his own wind. It was like a Heh Heh Heh from a giant, but he wasn't that big. The couple seated on the bench behind him, though, rocked from the force of the blow to their common seats.

"Fine, you got me there," Joseph said softly. He seemed to know it was no use trying to calm his brother. Cheap forks clanked on thick china in the little café that occupied the corner of the street. Cooks raised their voices back in a kitchen that boiled with beef smoke and gravy steam. One peeked out and reported back to the others what was going on out there in the world of eaters and yellers.

"Hard liquor not sucked out of a Mason jar!" Donovan yelled, taking a quick pull from his flask. "Oranges picked from the field! That ain't gonna put a smile on your face? We made it outta there!"

Mary, the wide-bodied owner of the cafe, came over. Stood as solid as a corner column on a grandiose porch, hands on hips and hair heavy with grease dangling out of a limp net.

"Hey, Donovan. Gimme a drink a that." She laid a meaty hand on his shoulder until he handed over his flask.

"Careful with that, it'll loosen ya up," he said, lifting his eyebrows at his brother. They came in here a lot, and Mary was big on joking around.

"You loosen me up," this Mary said. Maybe she was just big on Donovan. Tossing down a shot and whisking the cap back on and tossing him the flask and winking and taking off for the kitchen. Donovan settled back in his seat, grinning. He was damn sure loose.

"You boys about finished, ain't ya?" said a voice.

Donovan looked up. The lead bull in a dirty crew of three men who shuffled up to their table stood gazing down at their nearly empty plates. Good natured enough. Joseph looked up. Good natured enough. Wanda Kitchen looked over. Everybody seemed good natured enough.

But Donovan didn't answer. Joseph squirmed, looking only at his brother. He didn't look at the men again, he looked at his brother.

The three men held fast at the brothers' table. The plates had only the red, gnawed Ts of t-bones and the sallow yellow cobs of corn left. There was a lot of thin blood and blood serum pooled on the plates.

"We got dessert yet," Donovan said without looking up again. It was the first time he had spoken softly. He lowered his head and inserted a toothpick between thick lips and looked straight into his brother with those bloodshot eyes. You could tell he wasn't going to pay any more attention to the man.

"We'll wait, no offense," the big man said. He looked over at Joseph, who shook his head sadly.

The seats were benches. Donovan skidded across so quickly he was standing in the crew leader's face before the man could back up. There might have been contact.

"We don't mean nothin', pardner. Just lookin' for a table."

Wanda Kitchen barely caught the flash of Donovan's fist. There was a fleshy pop. It could have been a dropped baked potato. The big man went to the floor. The second man went to the floor. It was hard to see how. The third man got caught up in the legs of his downed friends, and he went to the floor. He jumped back up, and he went to the floor again not of his own accord. He hardly had time to raise his arm in self-defense. Every time someone went to the floor there was a sound like tough beef being tenderized with a mallet.

From Wanda's side of the room it looked like the men were diving to the floor so they could roll around there. Playful-like. They seemed to be slithering around in the aisle like kids playing snakes or horsie, trying to get up but not really.

Diners at nearby tables leaned away. Fluids had flown out at them from the men's faces. Donovan scooted back into his seat. Balled into the corner next to the window, the way he was before. His face had hardly changed. More red in it, maybe. That's all.

"You jakes smell like turpentine," Donovan said offhand. He took another swig of the flask he'd left on the table as the men played on the floor together. "Ought to wash off when you come off a goddamn oil rig."

Joseph, his damp-eyed little brother, stood out into the aisle and sternly delivered something of an instructional lecture to the men who were gathering themselves up from the floor. "Don't say a word when he's drunk. He's a mean drunk, and I don't mean maybe. When he's stinko you best just scoot on outta here if you—"

The big leader man, his brown clothes smeared with the indelible smudges of the oil fields, had his pride at stake. The patrons could see that. Joseph stepped back. He could see that. Wanda could now see that he hadn't been on the floor voluntarily. The mark on his face where his forehead met his left eye roared with anger.

He leaned into the table to have a word. There was a split second where the room thought it might go okay. Then his head snapped back and he walked backward rapidly about ten steps and collapsed halfway into the kitchen, raking sugar and salt from the counter as he flailed for balance.

Wanda was half out of her seat. Pauline twisted around at the clink of broken glass. She had been facing the wrong way and was trying to figure why patrons were deserting the cafe. "What's going on?" she kept asking Wanda. Who was watching so intently she forgot to hear her.

Donovan fired out of his seat. He jumped up on his table and stood there, one foot in his plate, which broke. He slipped, almost fell, regained his balance, and turned to address the audience.

"Damn you and the oil rig you rode in on!" he said to the two men leaving the vicinity and, Wanda felt deep in her soul, to the world in general.

She was on his side immediately.

Wanda liked men who worked out matters of the world in a highly physical way. He wasn't a real big man, but he had a nasty way of operating his body. Like some movie actors could really gangster-light a cigarette and just immediately make you want to go home with them? This man had a stylish and efficient method of gangster-lighting his body.

He jumped down from the table, into the aisle. Landed crouched with scarcely a shock even from that height. His little companion was trying unsuccessfully to restrain him, pulling on his arms from behind. Couldn't hold him.

The other two men were halfway to the door as Donovan pursued. Not that they were reluctant to go. Their facial gestures. Fear-driven. Yet the drunken fool refused to relent. He chased them through the door, a square-cut man, and stood holding it open and taunting them.

"Ya can have the goddamn table when I'm done with my cake!"

He stood holding his dessert in one hand. Balanced amazingly. A huge piece of chocolate cake on a tiny plate. Turning just in time to greet the owner of the cafe.

"Donovan! Getcher big ass outta here before I brain you with this skillet!" Mary yelled.

The big stevedore of a woman came at him with the cast iron. He reached out and gently wrested it from her with his free hand and asked her to return to the kitchen. It was like a man lovingly taking a toy from a naughty child.

"Nobody's rootin' me outta here till I've finished, Mary. Sorry 'bout that."

There was the noise of many shoes. Donovan looked over her shoulder and saw the police pouring in the door. He gently moved Mary back behind the counter and out of the way. He studied the matter for a moment and then sat down at his place and braced himself.

Using his name as if they had seen him before, pulling up alongside his table, the policemen made entreaties. Although he seemed to know one or two of the coppers personally, he refused to budge from his chocolate cake. They helped the oil worker up and out. Carried, basically. Finally they ordered Donovan up with the deep voices of men accustomed to compliance.

He wouldn't move. He forked a bite of his dessert. Mary made a tremendous cake, apparently. He bunched his shoulders and chewed on it stolidly, drunk as hell and his face set the way drunken faces solidify into a peculiar ugliness. Chewing a little off-center.

"Sit down, sister," somebody said behind Wanda. She was standing in the aisle, fascinated. She could tell from the drunk's accent that he was one of the dust bowlers. The police had mistreated them for years. That was her first concern. For the drunk. In any crowd, the one who stood out was the one for her.

"I'm not your sister," she said, whirling on a businessman in a bowler. By the time she turned back there was a major eruption occurring on the other side of the room.

She was alerted to it by a policeman. The copper rolled by her, doing a reverse double somersault with a lot of backspin. How he got over in her aisle, she couldn't see or even guess, the physics of it were so unlikely.

There was a sudden surge of blue-black wool uniforms to that end of the room. Tables scunched out of place as the cops shoved in with hips and shoulders.

"I ain't leaving...till I've eat...my dessert!"

Coppers dropped in the aisle, also sounding like baked potatoes. More potatoes came in. The reputation of the police here was tarnished, one might say, and the sympathies of the diners mixed. They were sick of the drunk, but they had been sick of the police for years. Finally they grabbed him, the mob of policemen did, and the table came loose from its moorings and the red and gray oilcloth ripped and everybody fell into the aisle.

Three or four of the cops got him down, a smothering effect, and they smacked him whenever a hole in the pile opened up. No room for a good hit. Coppers were hitting coppers and breathing like milk cows asked to run. There was no movement finally except a lot of heaving of lungs on the part of everyone. Much energy was being expended just to hold Donovan down.

Finally something of a breathy discussion. A mutter about what to do with him on the part of a skinny little sergeant. They jerked Donovan upright and were about to carry him out. When a big mitt came out of the middle of the scrum. Grabbed the half-eaten piece of cake off the bench, where it had tumbled. And pulled it squished between his fingers back inside the pile.

As the pile moved by Wanda she could see a bloody face in the center chewing as best it could on the cake. Happy as a lark in spring the way a drunk will get.

"Hang on a second," Wanda told Pauline.

She got up and went for the door behind them.

"Beware a them coppers," Pauline said. "Their dander's up."

Wanda was already outside. They had got the paddy wagon backed up almost to the door. Four coppers shoved and pulled on him, but the drunk had his hands braced against the door of the van.

He was so strong they couldn't dislodge him no matter how they whacked on his arms and pulled on his fingers. Finally the sergeant lost his patience. He pulled a sap the size of his fist from his back pocket.

"Sorry about this, Donovan," he said. Only half sincerely.

"Don't do it, you big ape!" Wanda yelled. Ever since Flint, ever since Detroit, ever since Akron she hadn't trusted a policeman.

Not even a glance at her. The sergeant sapped the drunk. The man's head made a sound like a melon being struck with a 34-ounce bat, and he collapsed like an accordion at the end of a song. With a little whimper and a shush of air.

"Did you see that?" Wanda yelled to the crowd that had gathered in the dimming, halo-lit Los Angeles evening. She was dancing around the outskirts of the skirmish, poking men on the arms as they craned their necks to see into the fray. She pointed accusatory fingers at the coppers. But the folks were gathering and enjoying this. Nobody else said a word. This saved them a nickel they would have paid for the flickers.

"Take him to the stationhouse," the sergeant told the other cops. They were all wearing faces like primitive masks, wooden and carved and puffing from the effort of folding Donovan's collapsed body into the van.

"You see? That wasn't necessary!"

This little bull sergeant gave Wanda the evil eye. "Get lost, sister. 'Fore I run you in too."

All right, if there was one thing Wanda Kitchen couldn't stand, it was when a man called her sister. Her feeling was, they're not her brother and she's not in any way their relation. She would not be thought akin to this kind of mindlessness in any way. It set her off something fierce.

She was just starting for the cop when somebody tugged her from behind. She spun mightily to give whoever it was what-for.

"Wanda, don't. It's just some drunk," Pauline said.

Well that set her off too. That's what's wrong with the world, isn't it? Wanda thought. It's not just some drunk. It's not just some strike-breaker. It's not just some hobo. It's a man. This is what the people who run the world, the people who caused all this, don't understand. A man's a man, and he deserves his chance, his place, a place to cut loose. It's the men with fire in them who get muscled away in paddy wagons. The ninnies stand around like these men were doing here, taking in the sideshow, running the world with paddy wagons, policing it with saps.

It was a way of thinking she had. It wasn't new to this era, to the summer of 1938. But it was new to her and she was enjoying it immensely, this way of thinking. Free and true. Clear and objective, born of chaos and catastrophe, she was fond of saying.

But by the time she turned they had slammed the doors of the wagon. Half the cops piled in. It started up with a cough of smoke and a grinding of gears. Wanda pulled loose from Pauline and ran to the last two cops, who stood there rubbing injured jaws and shoulders as the paddy wagon pulled away and into the dark.

"Where will they take him?" she asked. "And don't call me sister."

"Over to Highland Park," one said. "You might as well forget about him, sister. He's in for it."

All she could do was shake her head. These bootlicks were as dumb as cattle lowing in the fields. She and Pauline went back inside to help Mary clean up the place.

"Wow, that fellow was out of his head," Wanda said, reaching broken china out from under chairs and tables as patrons stood back and waited for their lives to settle into the orderly and complacent again.

"Just being Donovan," Mary said. "Bless his fool heart. He always gets his dessert."

"My god, you're awfully forgiving."

"Ah, he'll be back in the morning. Pay for everything and apologize like hell."

Now the little guy who was with the drunk came over and apologized for him. His brother. He didn't look much like him, especially in his round little face or his dark eyes. Mary introduced him as Joseph.

"Aren't you going to go see to him?" Wanda asked. "Bail him out?"

"Nah. Give him a chance to sleep it off."

So that's how Wanda Kitchen came to meet Donovan Daley. She would always think it sounded odd, a runaway Jewish socialist from Minnesota going nuts for an Oklahoma cowboy slash ice man. She could only say it was the way the world worked in this turbulent new era, where the serfs in Russia and the working stiffs in America rose up in unison. Where the Nazis in Germany achieved solidarity with the fascists in Los Angeles. Where a cowardly world of intolerance and shame met face to face with the polyglot and disconcertingly happy disharmony of the city of the angels.

Where Wanda Kitchen, a Jewish socialist union organizer, stood up for Donovan Daley, an Okie with a taste for hard liquor and blood. She had to laugh, because despite her attempts at rationalizing it with philosophy it was a physical thing, really.

2

WHAT DO YOU WANT?

When it became the law in Germany that a Jew couldn't have sex with an Aryan, that's when Wanda felt she had to step up to the plate for somebody like Donovan. Simple as that. Call it philosophy. Sure, call it lust. Call it that force that he had, the kind of force she had seen in the movement, the kind of force required to spin this crazy planet backward like a top.

After all, it was a sex force as much as a world force, wasn't it? That was her theory, anyway, a theory she worked on.

The man wasn't looking very forceful by the time she got down to the Highland Park stationhouse to bail him out. Cops, bristly in their wool, curious as to her intentions, took her through a hallway to a block of massive cages, looking her up and down with their big oligarchic faces as they held doors open for her.

He was lying in his cell in a sheen of vomit and snoring through blood clots in his nose. Pauline turned her head away from the sight. Wanda had tears in her eyes. He was so bruised, so beat up. She had seen it before in Detroit and Akron and even the Flint sit-down. She had seen the "running of the bulls" when the General Motors goons attacked the boys with hickory clubs and lengths of pig iron. She had seen the Pinkertons swarm around a corner dressed like businessmen and set upon a group of men warming their hands at a fire barrel. She'd seen the blood, smelled the vomit, helped set the bones. She had been there shortly after the little steel massacre in South Chicago.

She counted them men, the real men. The ones who stood out in the rain for a week with guns in their faces protesting toward a common cause. What were these other animals, the ones with the guns and truncheons? Who needs a railroad bull, a uniformed strike buster, a company lackey?

Any chippie can have one of them.

So Wanda paid the twenty-five dollars for Donovan's bail and the coppers dragged him out into the anteroom and dumped him onto a wooden chair at her feet. He was half-unconscious, almost tipped off the chair but caught his balance and sat perfectly stabilized. Finally he stirred.

Sat up somewhat straight.

Opened his eyes and looked around.

Pulled back scabbed lips and smiled a crooked smile over bloody teeth.

"Damn, that's good cake," he said. He licked his tongue out as if he could still taste the chocolate icing on his lips. It must have been long gone, the chocolate, his last pleasurable recollection.

It was his eyes, though. It was his pottery-blue eyes. They were all humor and defiance, not at all the eyes of a man who had been danced on by police boots. These were the eyes of a man who even though he's lost his little pocket war with six or eight coppers still feels he's the one who did the stomping.

"I'm Wanda Kitchen," she said softly.

He stood. Crookedly at first, painfully straightening a broad back until he was at least looking her in the eye. Some kinks in his vertebrae, apparently. He held out his hand. Looked down at it, reconsidered and wiped it on his trousers.

Thankfully, he put it behind his back to hide the thing. It was smeared with dried blood, slices of skin jutting from knuckles that had smashed against the cutting edges of teeth.

"Hullo."

"Hi."

"Who's your friend?"

He looked at Pauline, and such a pang of jealousy clobbered Wanda right there on the spot that she felt a blush creep up her chest. Even though she realized he wasn't flirting with Pauline, or picking her over Wanda. He was just courteous. He was that, too.

These men from the South were awfully fine in that regard, was Wanda's feeling on that. Odd, because even though she had befriended, tutored, doctored and fucked them, she had come to think that men were a scourge. South and north, west and east, they were just as traitorous as they were necessary. This was a contradiction that she had not fully resolved.

"This is my roommate, Pauline."

He nodded. "Donovan," he said.

He turned back to Wanda. It was those studious blue eyes, then, that got her. A little crinkle of a smile line that downturned a bit. Something so fetching about that asymmetrical eye. But that blue, off the charts of Jewish travel, tasted like saltwater in her eyes.

"I thank you for footin' my bail. I'm gonna pay you back."

He headed for an interior door, as sideways as a car with a broken chassis, and it was there, already, so early in their relationship, that she realized she would have to fight so hard to control this force. Sometimes you don't know what draws you to a lug. A look, a word, a walk. At this moment there was even an inkling to leave, part company now before she could be frustrated or threatened or whatever it was she would be by this oversized personality.

But of course, as the history books would show, she didn't.

"Where are you going, cowboy?" she asked. "The door's over here."

"Clean up a second. I'll be back, don't you worry." So he gave her that look. He may have even known why she was there. He may have seen through her right there. This prohibition against Aryan sex and how it was playing with her.

And my god, when he came out of the restroom his face was washed clean, his hair slicked back past a horseshoe hairline, and his walk almost straightened out. For the three minutes he was in there Pauline was giving Wanda the crinkle-eye, the okay-you-did-your-duty, let's-get-out-of-here-while-the-getting's-good eye.

But when he came out all slicked up Pauline saw what Wanda saw from the start.

Donovan Daley was a man of medium height but a little thick in the neck and waist. There would someday probably be an old sepia photo of him hidden in the history books of Los Angeles, as a working stiff pouring concrete on an endless skein of new streets, maybe. His arms were a bit long and his hair a jumbled pale brunette of indeterminate ethnic origin. But his head was pure sinister for a woman. Not gorgeous, he wasn't. But he had a twinkle to him, and a solidness, and a sinisterness.

Not a wholesomeness. But who cared, that wasn't what Wanda Kitchen wanted.

Those eyes slashed over at the cops as he went to collect his belongings, and they looked back at him as an equal. They had beaten the shit out of him but he was letting them know he was the winner. Wrongly so, but even the ones who might have retained a grudge accepted this information graciously. One of them even tipped his duty cap in generous sarcasm.

The desk sergeant gave him his wallet, a pocket knife, a handful of coins, a bloody and dented straw hat and a huge ice pick. The sergeant pushed the pick reluctantly across the desk. It might have been a foot long, honed to a pin at the end.

"Pretty nasty thing to be carrying around," the sergeant said.

"Ice man," Donovan said. He dropped the pick into a special little leather sheath on his belt she hadn't noticed before. The threesome headed for the door. "Had it made special. Last a hundred years," he called back to the man.

"You carry an ice pick with you to a restaurant?" Wanda asked. For want of anything better to say.

"Never know when you'll need to flake off a little something."

"Good thing you didn't pull it," the desk sergeant muttered. "They was ready to plug you right there. Lucky they didn't, way I hear it."

"Yeah, and lemme tell you...." Donovan was about to stop in the door and say more, but Wanda and Pauline shoved him outside.

Pauline flipped her a precipitous, big-eyed glance and a subtle little shake of her long hair behind his back. Get out of here now, the glance said, get away from him. She didn't approve, Paula didn't, and never would.

Donovan stopped on the sidewalk of the busy street and turned on them. "Who are you, now?"

"Wanda, Wanda Kitch—"

"I mean, who are you? How come you to pull me out of the slammer? Not that I ain't grateful, mind ya."

"I don't know. I was just in the restaurant, we were, Pauline and I, and we saw how the cops treated you. Roughed you up, see. Overstepped." My god, she was stammering. Wanda Kitchen never stammered. Wanda Kitchen never dissembled. This drunk. Was he worth it?

He looked right down into her for so long she knew how this was going to work out if he wanted it to. There was a tug at her insides, the insides that she liked to tug. Those insides.

"Had it coming, the way I acted. How's Mary's place? Hope it ain't tore up too bad."

"She said you'd be in in the morning with some restitution."

"Restitution."

He held the word there, looking it over. He examined her very closely. He looked down her body, at her clothes, at her breasts, at her shoes, at her toes through her shoes, at her body through her clothes. Lord she could feel him pinching her nipples.

"Restitution." Odd. How he seemed much more curious than carnal, and how carnal she felt.

"Is that a big word for you?" She couldn't help herself.

A moment of consideration, of détente. But he let off this smile. He had a big, wide mouth, lips a little thick for his face. His smile jumped right up into his eyes.

"Sort of. But I can handle it. What I mean to say is, what do you want?"

For a second she thought he was going to call her sister and if he did she'd spin on her heels and leave him right there on the street in front of the stone stationhouse, its façade as rugged as the Indian dwellings she had visited on her way west. But he didn't. That sealed it, because she knew she didn't want to be his sister.

"Nothing," she said. She lied so badly she was sure he could see that too.

3

JUST A CONCERNED CITIZEN

Donovan Daley could see that this woman was a little obsessive. She bailed him out of jail, though, she was a friend. Especially when his own brother wouldn't lift a finger.

The women helped support him when he got woozy on the way to her car. Wanda offered to take him to her apartment to clean up. That was a risk for a woman to take. Donovan recognized that. It was a lawless time, an era of trunk murders and decapitations. Women turned up missing. Men turned up dead. This whole city had turned up from somewhere and was having trouble cleansing itself of past deeds. So everybody suffered, as from some sort of universal sin of origin.

She lived over in Silver Lake not far from his ice route. Pauline said she didn't want any part of this, she could see how it was headed. So Wanda dropped her off at a friend's house and drove on. A knot on the back of his head throbbed so hard when he bent over he almost hit the dashboard of her old Packard from the sense of faintness it brought him.

"I've got to stop, please ma'am," he said all of a sudden.

She pulled over and he stumbled out into a field of vegetables and puked on them. Looked like carrots. The vegetables, not the puke. That looked like cake mix. Then he stood spraddled and pissed so weakly he didn't even know when he quit. It was alien and adulterated piss. It smelled like the smell of weeds after you've pulled them up and got their juice on your fingers, noxious and heady.

He eased back into the Packard and apologized. He wasn't feeling good anywhere all of a sudden. The kidney punches maybe, or maybe he had a concussion. She was leaning over his way as if she had been looking out the window watching what he was doing.

"Fine, I'm fine," he said, and she started the car. "Just fine."

They got to her apartment building at what seemed like three in the morning. He had puked so much he was almost sober. That didn't mean he felt good.

It was a bunch of little rooms stacked like layers on a cake, about five feet from the street. The cake ran back to the end of a long lot. Dirt driveway, dirt back lot, newborn weeds high in the soft headlights of the Packard. He could almost smell them. He thought he was going to have to throw up again but it passed.

"We have to be quiet. My landlord is an Aimee Semple disciple, and he's death on men in these apartments," she said. She was referring to the woman preacher that was all in the news.

Her flat was at the back end. They parked the car and tiptoed down there, scuffling in the dirt, she tugging him along faster than he wanted to go. She pointed to a second-floor apartment, and they went up the wooden stairs. His head throbbed like a steam thrasher started up in a confined space.

Worse, having become something of a ladies' man since he left the ranch, he was beginning to rue his condition. Too damaged to feel the effects of this fine looking woman. She switched on the light in her living room. Her single room. It was the first time he had registered a good, sober look at her. His vision was blurred before, the harsh light of the police station stabbing and blinding.

Wanda Kitchen was about five-two in a black and white polka dot going-out-to-dinner dress. She had a head as oval as an olive, and it was all frighted up with frizzy hair and dark eyebrows. She had what he would have guessed was an Indian nose. Like it had been busted in a fight and reset by an amateur. It was as narrow as a ridge of the San Gabriel Mountains, which had been eroding since the Precambrian he knew from the geology he had been reading. There was sort of an outdoors look to her skin. Smooth as flood water in a deep stream and tan like that. If he didn't know better he would think she was one of those Crow Indians from out his way. You marry a Crow to a white and you get Crow offspring.

If she was beautiful, you would have to study her for a moment to determine why. She had a natural oval gemstone of a face, lustrous but unfaceted as if it had just been unearthed and scrubbed clean. She had a funny accent, too. He couldn't place it. He knew he shouldn't talk. He was part Choctaw, and everybody said the Okie boys had a funny accent. A Choctaw Okie from the woods, you couldn't understand him at all.

Her eyes. They were gold. Eerie gold. Like orange blossom honey in a jam jar he saw at one of these roadside fruit stands so common out here. Two little honey jars.

"Now you gonna tell me what's going on?" he asked big round gold eyes.

"I'm just a concerned citizen, trying to see that other citizens get a fair shake."

Uh huh. That's real likely, he thought, though he didn't see any henchmen waiting behind the curtain with lead pipes. She wasn't threatening, a woman thin of limb, neck and waist. She leaned in front of him and poured water out of a pitcher into a wash basin. She had a white towel draped over her arm like a barber.

Sitting in one of her two kitchen chairs, he could see there was no kitchen as such. The place was one room with a little gas stove at one end and a bed at the other. Dirty pans were on the stove and a lot of dresses were piled on the bed as if somebody had sorted through them for something to wear.

"Take your shirt off."

The minute she set about working his head with that rag he forget to ask anything else. He was trying not to yell. The woman scrubbed at him from brain-box to breadbasket. And started talking. She could really talk.

"Stop your squirming. I've cleaned up a lot worse than you."

"Yep. Yep." Tears clumped in his eyes.

"I cleaned up the boys at Flint, and nobody knows this but in thirty-four when I was organizing in the Arkansas delta there was violence on those poor farmers and sharecroppers. Oh, there was violence. It took me right back to when my father was in the mines. One day he staggers home from work, something wrong with him."

"Yeah? Ow."

"He had a broken collarbone after a timber fell on him in the number two tunnel. There weren't any safety procedures or emergency supplies, you see. But that's not the worst of it. On his way out of the mine, seeing he was injured, the son of the mine owner fired him on the spot. Before he could even see a doctor! Use them up and get rid of them when they're hurt!"

He began to think she was not paying a lot of attention to what she was scrubbing. His ear hurt like jumping Jesus and she was looking off out the window while she gabbed. He took her hand, gently, the way he took the skillet from Mary, and got the rag away from her. He really felt she was going to kill him with it, if a man could be killed by a washrag.

"What do you do, Wanda?" He let go of her and her arms dropped to her side. She got a look about her. A look of astonishment that everybody who didn't know her would have said was cynical.

"I'm a union organizer. I told you."

"You a red, are you?"

"I'm not a red, I'm a socialist. We're just asking for what's right for the people."

"See, I was in the mines. Out in the Mojave. There was a strike."

"You what?"

"Come in as a replacement."

She whirled and threw the rag against the wall and turned on him. He was still watching the wet rag as it slid to the floor. What a woman, was all he could think. Where was this thing going to end?

"Strike breaker? You were a strike breaker!"

"I didn't know. We were just hired off the highway."

"Carried on the backs of American laborers! Boy, did I misjudge you!"

"It was work."

"Yeah? Where else did you work?"

"I worked on Hoover Dam," he said proudly.

She leaned over at him. "Did you know over 200 workers died at that dam? That we know about. They were denied union representation, they were worked to death. I don't even want to hear the name Hoover from your lips, that killer."

"Hey, it was a hell of sight when we finished it, that dam was."

She grabbed his shirt off the floor and threw it in his face. All of a sudden she was standing across the room. He lurched to his feet as fast as he could and put his shirt on. More than a little confused. Everybody knew that if you found work in the depression, you took it.

"A dollar's a dollar when you're flat busted," he said. Not too loud, though.

"This is a degenerate man chinning at me."

She was still across the room, but she was leaning over at him, throwing some hissy words. Looking fetching doing it, though. Her polka dot dress clung to her every move and mood.

"I am so sick of you people. Scabbing off the workers who have fallen ahead of you. Walking on their poor backs. I am so sick of these drifters from the middle-west, so ignorant they're digging for gold in the pants pockets of the industrialists. I'm sick of these helpless little actresses getting palsy walsy on Mr. Goldwyn's couch. I'm tired of the stupid sweater girls with nothing but boys and phone numbers on their brains."

She started pacing along the opposite wall. As if she had forgotten him.

"It's just so maddening, these college boys in their striped shirts and fur coats drinking out of their girlfriends' shoes and hitting the jazz clubs while their fathers are stripping the nation. I'm tired of the shop girls waiting for their louse of a boss to give them a tumble and take them out of their ordinary existence. I'm sick of the preachers lightening the pockets of the palookas and promising them God and prosperity are just a short prayer away, put a dollar in the collection plate why don't you."

Moving toward the door, he was afraid to say a thing now. He experienced a light-headedness and sort of careened away from the chair for a step. Recovered. Got his boater off the couch. It had spatters of blood on the brim.

"Much obliged for your help, Miss Kitchen. You got a phone I can use to call my brother? Our neighbor has the phone, but she'll take a message."

"I don't have a phone. Did you know the phone was invented in the same year as Custer's last stand?"

"I beg yours?"

"The same year. That tell you anything about the chaos of industrialization?"

He got the door himself. She didn't make any sense at all. He was starting to worry that maybe she had a gun. Sometimes these radicals got violent.

"I didn't know that."

"Seems kind of a prophetic juxtaposition to me, the way times are going."

"Thank you once again. I didn't know about no strike. I just wanted to work."

He got out the door. Halfway down the stairs. "I'll get your bail money back to you," he called when she came out the door.

"All right, come on," she said. She had her car keys in hand and she passed him going down the stairs. He limped badly and had to stop once. "Watch your step."

So without another word they got in her car and she hit the foot starter and fired it up. She pulled out of the dirt driveway scrambling rocks and dust.

They rode along quietly. He pointed her north and then east onto Melrose, until they got over near Highland and he said "Here." And pointed the direction to her, north toward the hills. There was a town being built out here around the movie industry, but he liked the rural feel of it. And it had a cute name. Hollywood.

"This is a nice place," she said when she parked in front of his duplex.

Her voice had gone soft again. He couldn't figure it out, these modern women. Hell, give him a sweater girl any day. You can fill a sweater? You could talk his kind of talk.

"Come on in, if you want," he said, though. Out of obligation, or hope. "It's late."

He could swear she looked like she wanted to. Even after all she said.

"Give me your number, I'll call you."

"I don't have a phone, remember." She looked at him as if he were a twenty-foot mine timber that had fallen on her and trapped her there.

"Where you work."

"I don't like to use the phone at the union hall."

"Tell me where you work, I'll pick you up after."

"Not if you're a damn scab, you won't."

"I ain't no scab. I work where there's work."

She pulled something out of her purse. Fast. Mad fast. It was as dark as the inside of a mule out here, but she wrote out something.

"I sure liked the way you busted up those coppers," she said, more quietly yet. "What did you do that for?"

"I wasn't finished eating."

She couldn't seem to find any fault with that reasoning. "Pick me up at six." She forked over the address.

"This that union?" He held it up high, trying to find some light.

"Yeah, does that bother you?"

"Not me."

He opened the door and got out of the Packard. It was a '35, the one with the turtle back, and from his side it looked like it had been in a couple of wrecks. The door didn't slam right. He finally got it, and when he bent over to look in and say thanks she ripped out of there.

She liked him, he could see. Hard to say why. He'd seen it before, though. There was no accounting for the craziness of city women.

4

RUCKER'S HOUSE

The day started way too early. Donovan felt his bones had been broken and reset crooked in the night. His head felt like it had been removed for repair and put back on sideways. His back was sore its entire length and breadth.

But the ice men started early, and instinct took over when Donovan felt his brother roll out of bed. They had grown up getting out of the house before daylight on the ranch, but today he could barely peel his peepers open. In fact, only one opened on its own accord. He pried the other loose from the seepage that had welded it shut.

"At's what happens when you get stinko on a weeknight." Joseph stood looking down at him in disgust, buttoning his shirt with short, stubby fingers. Then he turned on all the lights in the apartment, just to see his brother shrink in pain.

It was still dark when they got to the plant. A line of square panel trucks was already muttering in the yard. Gas and oil fumes in the air from a rowdy bunch of Chevrolets and Packards and Hudsons. A crew at the big bay door loaded the trucks with blocks of ice. It was so warm the crystals coming off the blocks when they knocked together melted in the dirt immediately.

They loaded twenty-four three hundred pound blocks, scored in increments of twenty-five pounds, into the brothers' old Double A Ford. Joseph pulled the canvas cover over the open back and threw the tailgate up and latched it. He went to the cashier's cage and signed for them.

Donovan sat in the driver's seat thinking how weird this Los Angeles was. There was generally not much wind in this country. Even when the fog came in it didn't come in on the wind. It just walked in from the ocean. The heat did too. From the desert lands east of them. By the time they pulled onto Sunset and made their way into Silver Lake there was ice water dripping behind the truck. Even welcome work seemed tedious in such heat, but Joseph had a favorite topic of conversation.

"You gonna try out that Mrs. McCants today?" Joseph asked him. They had eaten their breakfast out of greasy paper bags he had packed with biscuits and ham the night before, and he curled up against the door ready to go to sleep again.

"Ain't having nothing to do with Mrs. McCants," Donovan said.

He veered off at Hyperion and made their first stop. It was almost light. He peeled himself from the wheel and got out like a cat with a broken back. Put on his heavy leather uppers, which kept melt water from soaking his shirt. Didn't even look at Joseph, he knew he wouldn't get any sympathy.

He took his ice pick and expertly chipped off a twenty-five along its score line and it bounced off onto the tailgate. He threw the tongs on the block and arched it over to his back and here he went. Joseph chipped off the next block and strode across the street, lugging it two-handed like a man with a limp.

This work always amazed Donovan. Going in people's houses. It took some getting used to. Some houses had little doors built into the wall so the icebox could be accessed from the porch. Most didn't.

"Ice man!" he yelled. But not too loudly in case everybody was still asleep. He walked in the unlocked side door.

The first house was as quiet as sleep-breathing. Donovan hauled the twenty-five in the kitchen door and stepped over some wooden kids' toys and, as quiet as he could be, clicked open the icebox door. He slid the block onto the top shelf. There was talking in a back bedroom, but nobody came out.

Marking the twenty-five on the scorecard on the wall, he scooted out of there before they could catch him. A lot of people were out of work, and they had nothing better to do than talk. That lost time would catch up to the brothers around mid-afternoon when the sun was like a hotplate.

By mid-morning, when he got to Mrs. McCants' and Joseph crossed over to the Steadmans', the street boys were out, running after them in their short pants. They had their pocket knives out and chipping away, the little dickens.

"Sling us a flake, Mister!" And when the ice truck stopped the boys were on it as quick as mice. Climbing up the back and sucking ice chips on the tailgate, scattering before the ice men got to them, circling closer when they left. As persistent as crows on roadkill.

"You boys got yours you better hightail it," Donovan yelled back at them as he trudged toward the house. But they knew he wouldn't come back, not with a block on his back.

"Come on in, Donovan!" Mrs. McCants yelled. Her face bloomed at him in the kitchen window. Sure enough by the time he got in the door she had her robe open and a tit swinging half out while she stirred an egg in a skillet.

The baby was in its chair as always and smiled at him almost as big as its mommy did. She was a snowy-faced thing in her first year out of the birth. Donovan shot the twenty-five in the box. She got there while he was still down on his knees. Leaned in over him and got a bottle of milk off a shelf.

"Oops, excuse me," she said, taking her time, clinking bottles around in there. Strawberry hair swung by his face. She moved back and smiled down at him all hot-faced like a cat licking cream off the floor.

Donovan stood and watched in appreciation. Sometimes you just had to. The woman bent over the toddler feeding him bites of boiled oats. Her robe swinging like curtains. Everything opened up wide as she reached in her pocket.

"I've got your fifteen cents right here." She reached halfway across the table to hand the nickel and dime to him. Showing him all she had in the way of milk production.

"Thank you." You had to be brief in these instances, but oh the appreciation.

"I'll bet them leathers is quite hot," she said the way she had done probably five times this month. "You want to take them off and rest in the shade a spell? I can't believe they make you wear them wool clothes like that."

She stepped over to adjust his leathers. It was all a man could do to keep her wedding vows for her. Donovan without a woman for two months, too. Her robe had fallen half off her shoulders by now, the way heavy fabric will on a woman who doesn't care.

He brought himself back out of it. Brushed by her and eased out the door. He lifted the nickel and dime as a thank-you, the wool rubbing him hard in the crotch of his trousers the way wool scratches a sensitive spot.

"Maybe next time," he said as he eased the door closed. He wouldn't, though. She was married, and the Daley boys, after the breakup of their mother and father, had a thing about that. It was a hard thing to have in this city, but they had it.

Joseph waited by the truck. "Yeah?" he said. "What did she do today?"

"Half naked, she was, that woman."

"Ha!" Joseph would snort and carry on in indignation, but there was a lot of curiosity about Mrs. McCants from a young man who listened to the preachers one after the other on the radio every Sunday. He was much too young for women in a mental way.

"Let me ice that side of the street next time," he said as they pulled away.

"You don't need any a that trouble," Donovan said. Grinding the gears of the Ford on up the hill.

Then it was the Rucker place. His favorite.

The Franklin Hills had layers of houses like a spiral cake, and the truck was up at the top where the swells built the big ones. You could see right downtown from here and all the way over to the Hollywoodland sign on the ridgeline where houses were being built clear into the mountains. Nobody could believe anybody would live that far out, but construction was leapfrogging the farmland and snaking up into the canyons.

Donovan parked the Double A and took the pick out of his holster and chipped off some flakes and flung them to the kids following. Joseph helped him get the first three hundred skidded out and balanced on the tailgate. Just looking at it was a chore. A three hundred pound block of ice was like picking up a desk filled with lead. Donovan got under it and got his leathers adjusted. Even a little crease under that weight would cut like an axe.

He readjusted the tongs on it and swung around under and bent his knees and it was up. It wasn't friendly, from the look on Donovan's face. But it was up.

"Get me a 'nana, willya brother?"

For some perverse reason he liked to stand a while under a three hundred. It reminded him what you had to set your shoulder to in the world.

"You can't eat a damn banana with that up," Joseph said. But he was already hustling over to the truck to get one. He knew Donovan would stand there until he did. He ate half a dozen bananas a day. They kept him going between meals. Joseph fed it to him while he stood there, water starting to sluice off his leathers, the cold of the blue block of ice eating into his shoulder as a couple of kids looked on in wonder.

Still chewing, he headed for the stairs leading up to a large house elevated and half hidden from the street. Joseph stood watching him waddle along till he was sure he had it. Then he hoisted a twenty-five and went to the other side of the street.

There were forty-three concrete steps and Donovan studied every chip and grease spot on them as he fought his way up. He could see dress shoes as he got halfway. Rucker was at the top of the stairs waiting for him. As usual. All he could see at first was his feet, then his legs, then his chunky barrel chest and a puffy, rigid face with a Havana jammed in it. Off behind him, waiting in the driveway by his Pierce-Arrow, was a little guy named Whitaker. His security man, bodyguard. These oil cheats needed that.

"Some say three hundred pounds is too heavy for a man to lift," Rucker said studiously, taking the cigar out as Donovan went by. He was grinning a silly smile out from under a snaky Henry Ford mustache. "That's what they tell me, but I tell them old Bananas proves it wrong every day."

"What're you grinnin' at, then?" Donovan asked as he plodded on, careful to see what stance his security man took. Not that it mattered. You couldn't stop to chit-chat. Melt was coming off him like lather from a horse.

"You. Humping that block of ice. You better get it in the box or pretty soon it'll be two hundred pounds. Have to dock your pay."

Try it, Donovan thought as he stumbled around the back to the kitchen door. He was picturing the oil man's head on one of the damn silver platters on display in his kitchen cabinets. Millie his maid saw him and had the door open. She was a bit of a snoot too working for old Rucker but at least she would turn a hand. The man had the biggest iceboxes on his route except for the markets.

She flicked the latch and opened the specially-made icebox for him. Donovan angled around and worked the slab just so, inching it in there. If it got to the floor, he had long ago determined, he was leaving it melt there beside that big six-burner gas stove with all the fancy nickel plating.

"Hear you ice boys tried to unionize," Rucker said as Donovan headed down the steps for the other three hundred.

Donovan didn't answer him. He couldn't figure why the oil man took such an interest in his travails every other day of the week. The man had refused to let him bring the ice truck up the driveway. Would obstruct it, he said. He just seemed fascinated that somebody—and not a big man, either--could carry a block that big.

This Whitaker sauntered over to see what was going on. He had coal-black hair and the dainty facial skin of a gambler or nightclub singer, somebody who worked all night and slept late, far out of reach of the sun.

Both men looked up under the ice man's cap now that they were close. To see why he didn't answer. There were marks, definite marks, on Donovan's face.

"What happened to you, lose a fight?" Rucker said.

Donovan was poised on the steps, catching his breath. They heard voices, one of them a woman's. They looked down at the street below.

"Who's that woman?" Rucker asked.

Wanda Kitchen stood there beside their ice truck talking to Joseph. Donovan forgot about Rucker and went down the stairs.

"Hi," Wanda called.

"Morning," Donovan said. Damn, she looked awfully fine in sunlight. That frizzy hair just lit up. Funny how she carried her thin shoulders so straight, like a man carrying a pack.

"I thought I would come see you at work. It was my lunch time."

"Good. I'm glad you did."

"I always wanted to see how the ice business worked."

"Look all you want. Get a good idea of how not to do it. Right Joseph?" Donovan whacked his brother on the shoulder. He didn't answer, though. Joseph wasn't much good around women if you put him next to one.

"Did I accuse you of being a scab last night?" She tilted her head over to gaze into his eyes.

"Nah."

"You're a worker, I can see. I didn't know if I was too hard on you."

"Joseph and me, we got the best jobs in the world."

"We're told Consolidated Ice House has 240 ice plants and over 4,000 routes in the state." Joseph was drawn out. He was awfully proud to be working. They had come from a state where it seemed everybody was looking for a job and none were to be found. "She's got unlimited future, ice does."

"People have to keep their meat and beer cold, right?" Wanda ventured.

Donovan followed Joseph's eyes down. The little brother was staring. She was wearing pants. The women was wearing trousers, could you believe it?

"How far do you have to go today?" she asked.

"A piece. We finish this route about dark." He nodded to Joseph, who skidded the other three hundred out onto the tailgate. "I'll be right back."

The second block was always heavier. Donovan got under it, veered off, righted himself, and heaved one foot up after the other on the steps. He only made about twenty risers before he had to blow. He didn't even look up at Rucker, but he knew he was up there in his pinstripe London-cut gabardine suit with the gold tie and the matching tie tack made out of a sizable gold nugget. Ready to go to work. Donovan guessed he was providing the day's first entertainment.

"Didn't work, did it?" the man said. Finally Donovan looked up at him. "Organizing."

"They made us independent contractors," Donovan huffed up at him. He got his foot positioned so as to make that next step. Once you got moving it was all right. He passed him chugging air like that old Model T his father had years ago when he was a boy.

"I heard the Okies were just bindlestiffs pretty much all of them," Rucker said, sneaking into the kitchen of the back house behind him. Donovan got the three hundred stuffed in the box and quickly shouldered out the door.

"Oh, good morning, Donovan," Rucker's wife said perkily. She stood outside, a tall thin woman dressed in white.

Donovan said "Morning, Lilly," perkily himself, and turned to Rucker. Who was just beaming at him like a real estate salesman. Whitaker came in behind him. He propped his coat open so Donovan could see the butt of his revolver.

"I don't know any a them hoboes," he said to Rucker, still puffing like a horse coming over a hill. He tipped his cap to Lilly. Who handed him a fresh cinnamon roll still warm from the oven.

"Damn reds soon'll be taking over the country," Rucker said. He looked to Whitaker for backup. Whitaker didn't respond even with his eyes, which remained on the ice man. Donovan had seen this man around town, is how he knew his name. And reputation. He took a step closer to him. So if he drew that revolver, Donovan would feed it down his throat like a coil off a cinnamon roll.

"Not if I can help it," Donovan said. "But any man helps me work for a dollar instead of a dime, I'm for that man. Thanks for the bun, Lilly."

He tipped his cap good day to the wife on his way down the steps. She waved back. So did Millie. Lilly and Millie. Rucker and Whitaker, he didn't even look back at them.

"Hey, Bananas!" Rucker called out. "When you gonna come work for me in the oil fields?"

He didn't even stop. "Too messy. Oil belongs in a car, not on a man."

"Yeah? You're wet all over. Ain't he, Eddie?" He was talking to Whitaker.

"We could use a man like you," this Whitaker said softly.

"That's what the women all say, too."

Not stopping. He could hear them laughing back there.

Down at the truck Joseph and Wanda were waiting. Joseph nervous. He leaned back against the quarter panel nonchalantly but one leg jittered almost out of control.

"You stay out of his way," Joseph said. Jerking his head up at Rucker. Wanda looked a question at them.

"Joseph thinks one of these days I'm gonna take old Rucker down."

"You keep your distance unless you want to end up on a slab."

"I'm tempted, too. Jump on his back and ride him face first down them stairs like a sled. See if that cigar comes out his ass."

For some reason Wanda wasn't surprised at this outburst. This apparently was a violent man. Yet, he wasn't scary at all. He seemed, in fact, somehow endearing and gentle. He had a rollicking motion in his walk that she loved to watch.

"Rucker?" she asked. "Not Charles Rucker?"

He held out the cinnamon roll and pulled it into three pieces and gave her and Joseph their sections. He got the water bottle out of the truck, and they washed it down drinking right from the mouth. She did too. She didn't seem to be offended by this.

"That's him."

"The stock swindler?"

"Hasn't been proved," Joseph said. Donovan just snorted. Wanda outright laughed.

"If there's that much smoke…"

"Big ol' fire someplace," Donovan said.

They all turned to look up at the top of the stairs. Rucker and his man had returned and were up there watching them. Talking about them. Donovan and Wanda laughed again. Joseph didn't have anything against oil people the way his brother did.

"Now I know what you do," Wanda said. She walked around their rickety ice truck, eyeing it suspiciously, though she had seen a thousand of them chugging around the county hauling milk and bread and vegetables door to door.

"You want to ride with us?" Donovan asked. "It'll keep your milk cool."

She just stood and pondered him for a while. He was awfully forward for a bohunk. "Some other time. I'll see you tonight." She got in front of him. Shook his big hand. Shook Joseph's little hand.

It was a long day for the ice men, and when it was over they headed home, one unsold twenty-five pound block of ice skidding around in the back. They liked to go back along Melrose, past the studios. The Gower, the Paramount, the Raleigh. Hoping to see Cagney or Lillian Gish come out. Joseph didn't care so much for the pictures, but Donovan said he'd pay a silver dollar to catch a look at Edward G. Robinson with a gat in his hand.

They had a double they were renting over on McCadden in Hollywood because they liked the rural atmosphere. With its mountain background it was very different from the Panhandle of Oklahoma. It was a cute little stucco neighborhood. The builders were really testing the limits of concrete, using it on walls, archways and beside enclosed entries with wrought iron gates. Their double's white stucco was as smooth and washed as skin.

They had to go around to the side door to get in. The family that rented the front unit got the street view. They got the back yard. A big oak tree out there was where Donovan liked to go after his bath and have a few beers before he went out. This shade in the summer was pretty good living, and that's where he was half an hour later.

"You're not drinking another one, are you?" Joseph asked. Finished with his bath, he came out back shirtless with a glass of water. He was so pale it looked like the stucco people had whitewashed his little bald chest.

Donovan sat in a spring chair and ignored him. In fact, there were four empty beer bottles there. He liked to replenish the fluids he'd lost on the ice route, and he didn't feel like explaining that.

"You still going out with that woman tonight?"

Donovan's mouth tended to show a bit of sag after a few drinks, and it sagged now. The shade was so good. He could sleep. But he had hurried Joseph through the day so they could finish early, and he wanted to go see this Wanda. Wanda Kitchen. What a name.

"Darn tootin'," he said. He wanted to get in her kitchen.

5

PERILS OF PAULINE

She didn't know why, but all afternoon Wanda expected to see him again. She knew he was limping around delivering ice, thinking his narrow little high-plains, café-brawling thoughts. But back in the union hall in downtown Los Angeles she kept looking around as if he might show up there at two in the afternoon. Or three, or four.

But there was only Pauline and Mike. She didn't know what it was about men. When you met one it was like having your monthlies. They were always in the back of your mind and you just had to deal with it and change the bandages until it was over.

Wanda Kitchen was a union organizer with the ILGWU. She traveled around the country organizing. Not the workers, which was difficult, but the unions. Which was even more difficult. She had been through some of that nasty stuff with U.S. Steel and Ford Motor Company and General Motors when she was young and learning "the struggle." She had graduated to the garment workers, trying to set up new locals and patch up old locals that had pulled apart a little at the seams from the muscular contractions common to organizations that tested the soul.

Like the International Ladies Garment Workers Union in Los Angeles. It was a going concern at one time but fell into disrepair. Not because the shops threw them back, but because the Reds had taken over. They became radical and unyielding. They wanted to build the revolution their way.

Wanda couldn't believe it. The Reds didn't want to let Mexicans in, but Mexican women were half of the work force in this city. They didn't want to let the Italians in, who could be loud and troublesome. They didn't even want to let in the Molokon Russians, tall, stately blondes who were very quiet but also could be headstrong and difficult. Shoot, let's face it, she thought. Everybody is difficult. Which is why you have a union in the first place.

So she was in the union hall, an empty little brick storefront downtown with some chairs set up at one end. All they needed was about thirty chairs, things were so bad. She had invited Donovan to pick her up here for a reason. Any man who could be a scab, even unwittingly and for the intention of feeding his family, needed some indoctrination.

Plus. Something deep inside her took pride in these old union halls. Even empty, they rang of brogans and harsh voices thumping off the walls. Full, they shuddered like a concert hall full of tubas and trombones. She wanted him to see her here. In her place.

A union hall was so basic. Old wood floors with the shine trod out of them. The high ceiling as if it were built as a church, which it was to her. They were analogous to some essential but purely functional part of human anatomy. A throat, perhaps.

Because what would come out of them was a voice, rising from a body of men and women. She loved it when the old hall filled and there was the sudden thrust of voices in extremis, protesting, philosophizing, extemporizing. Trying to rearrange the important stuff of their lives. Her life.

One problem, she had found when she got here, was that men had mostly taken over the local. All the members were women, the cutters and pressers and machine operators trudging in here after a 12-hour day hunched over a little sewing table, their eyes still full of polka dots and inseams. They were the heroes, their Latin or Eastern European or Chinese faces tired and reeking of tragedy.

But the men got to be boss. There was Mike, the president, a flinchy little Irishman who apparently had an illness that had no name and spent half his days in bed. There was Israel, a well-meaning New York Jew with too much internal dialogue going on in his head. They were both borderline Reds, but they weren't the problem.

The women began coming in with their hair still pinned up from work and their hems dirty from dragging across dusty dressmaker shops. Just as the ladies shuffled quietly to their seats, imbued with both a native defeatism and a learned union optimism, here came Donovan. He was on time and scrubbed down, wearing a coat and bow tie and a derby. Mike went over and intercepted him. No worry. This guy had Mike pumping his hand and smiling and pointing to her across the room. He walked over.

"Miss Kitchen," he said.

"Mister Daley."

They stood there a minute. Perusing the crowd. Taking the respective temperature readings that a man and woman in this situation might take. Of the crowd. Of each other.

"Sorry about Mike. We have to make sure who you are. Because of the spies. The Merchants and Manufacturers Association is after us in a big way, the way the Iron and Steel Institute was back east. The way the –"

"That's okay. Your meeting over?"

"Just starting."

He looked her head over, starting at the eyes and moving around the head and ending back at the eyes. It seemed he got it. Why she wanted him here. He smiled as big as he could out of a face gone a little crooked from fists and truncheons.

"I'll wait outside," he said. He had a black eye, and the back of his noggin was overweighted like a balloon with a weak spot.

"No, have a seat. Did you get off work early for me?"

Grinning a little yes, he took a seat in the back row. Pauline and four or five others, a couple of men among them, grabbed the front seats. The garment workers filled in between, tiny dark women and long lithe women and ruddy-faced stubby women, their faces as scrubbed as possible. They were wearing the dresses they made at home after making dresses at work all day. A couple of them brought babies, balancing them on their hips the way college girls balance books.

As soon as Mike called the meeting to order, Pauline started up.

"Mr. President! A procedural matter. I think we should have more women on the board. This is a travesty of the international women's movement."

"Okay, Miss Posner. But don't you—"

"Don't you interrupt me. I've got legitimate procedural matters to discuss. And the local is broke, besides." Pauline, with her narrow, flushed face, was much more animated than she was at the café the night before. Her cheeks reddened like those of a painted figurehead on an old schooner in the harbor.

"Well if you would let us get to the minutes we could proceed."

"Why can't you see how important it is to look to the Russian women as an example? Mr. Stalin has given them their entire freedom. There's a revolution, and it's passing us by."

And so it went for a long while. The trouble was, Wanda had learned, the old Needle Trades Industrial Union was disbanded a while back, and those members, doctrinaire communists, had gravitated to the ILGWU.

Their whole rationale was to convert these "treacherous" socialists to the hard line, the Soviet line, and that's why Wanda was here. To set things right between the Reds and the Pinks.

"Pauline!" Wanda yelled. Pauline turned back to where she was sitting beside Donovan.

"I have the floor, here," Pauline said. This was the time of night Wanda called the Perils of Pauline.

Wanda said, very carefully, "We all see what you're doing. There's no excuse for it. If you don't like this union, you should quit and join another. Form your own. Don't try to ruin our attempt to help these women gain their rights. They work hard, they don't want to come in here and hear us arguing social philosophy."

Donovan had never seen anything like it. Her voice was pretty calm, but there was fire in it. Everybody picked it up. Everybody in that dark room, man woman and child. There were further fireworks. This Pauline didn't give in. A couple of her friends spoke up. Men from back east, judging from their accents. Reds too.

It was all about "international brotherhood" and "the solidarity of the working class" and "the people's rights to collective bargaining from a position of strength" and that. It meant nothing to Donovan, who sank lower and lower into his chair.

But a couple of the garment workers got some backbone and spoke up for Wanda. She rallied and said that they didn't care a damn about international this and international that. What she wanted was for these sewers and cutters to get a fair wage and a 10-hour workday and a full half hour for lunch. She wanted a lot. Nobody got that.

"They're women with a future, women with vision, women with talent and dreams," Wanda said, and by then everybody in the room was screwed around in their seats looking at her. "Frankly, I don't care if they're for or against Stalinist agrarian reform or the long march of the proletariat. I want them to be able to earn a living wage."

Afterwards, the garment workers shyly eased near to Wanda and shook her hand and overcame their shyness and hugged her. They got tears in their eyes. She oohed and aahed over their babies. They talked about organizing the workers in their shops. Quietly, as if somebody might be looking over their shoulders.

Nothing was ever resolved in these union deals, Donovan had seen that in the mines out in the Mohave. You've just got owners and workers locked in one feud after another. Always over money. So he kept out of all that, just pulled his weight and pulled his wages. You were better off that way.

He waited for her outside, and Wanda finally came out with Pauline. The troublemaker. "Look here, Hollywood's the fashion center now," Wanda was saying. "Women across the country are following what Garbo and Lombard are wearing. We should take advantage of the fact that these new sportswear lines are being designed and sewn right here." The two stopped beside Donovan. "We have leverage."

Both women looked at him. Kind of smiles on their faces. Like they never had a cross word to say to each other. Women. Ain't they a kick? He never had anything but a couple of hand-holding girlfriends in Oklahoma. He understood after a while that you don't get to know a thing about them in that kind of a deal. Her family kills a chicken for you on Sunday, and everybody's on his best behavior. Until he got in their clothes he never had any idea what they really thought or wanted. That's when it got scary.

Different with Wanda. He understood that right up front. She said what she thought.

"I want to just instill some idea of fulfillment in those women," she said as they drove among the tall brick buildings of downtown. He had taken the Red Line here so he could drive home with her. "And a sense of responsibility in the world. When those two factors meet amicably, we'll have something like a sensible arrangement. A real social contract."

That was over his head. He jounced along trying to hold still. The pain of his injuries was worse today. He noticed some places on his body he hadn't noticed since the time his horse threw him on the ranch three years before. Ribs, shoulder blades, places like that talking to him.

"Where we going?" he asked after a while. They were headed south. Away from their parts of town.

"Dinner."

Soon they were out in the boondocks again. He had been down here once or twice, not on any business he'd care to talk about with her.

"Niggertown?"

"Negroes. Please. The best food in the county, and you get great music, too."

He'd never seen so many Negroes in one place as in this Club Alabam. It was a big building with little square tables and a round stage with a band playing all get-out. There was a palm tree in a pot to one side, and a mezzanine from which black couples chatted and looked down on the dance floor.

There were only two white couples in there. Donovan and Wanda were one of them. Guided by a waiter, she waltzed right over to an empty table and sat down in a flock of Negroes who all looked to be wondering where these people came from. And she looked around at them. Smiling.

No, she didn't waltz over. She boogie woogied over, wiggling around like that, because that was what the band was playing. Donovan didn't know what his face was doing. He had nothing against the…Negroes. Who cared about any of that?

6

BOOGIE WOOGIE GIRL

Oooh, Wanda loved a dance floor. There was something wicked and energizing about it, all waxed and glowing and slippery as ice, feet moving so frantically across it, as if compelled by happiness itself. And she hated an empty space on a dance floor.

Club Alabam wasn't empty, it was jumping. But most people were eating stolidly, and there were open spaces on the floor. These offending vacancies enticed her with some sort of witchy magic syncopated by the chop-chop swing tunes ringing around her. The honk and squeal of the sax went right into her.

"Dance?" she asked, her face swaying over the cutlery. Her shoulders danced in anticipation, enticing him, her invitation enhanced by the dancing candle on their table.

Donovan shrugged. In an inviting way.

So they finished ordering and she reached over and got him up. Funny man, he seemed to have no knowledge of this music. But oh, he could dance the boogie woogie.

He glanced at the feet of the other dancers. Getting the beat from their spit-shined shoes and the mood from their expressive black faces. The two-toned oxfords around him tapped so smoothly, slipping and sliding on the waxed wood, that there was only a woodwind sigh from those fifty hard soles. Black horn players swayed, glistening under the lights, cheeks puffed on trombones and trumpets. Sweat flew as they flung themselves side to side.

And off he went, his feet moving like lightning, throwing his legs out, doing the bump, his face all studious. She could tell that his body still hurt from the night before, but he'd had a couple of drinks. All injury seemed forgotten, all hurt forgiven.

Her kind of man. Pretty soon he was throwing her over his shoulder, between his legs, twirling her outward into the crowded floor.

Bumping her butt against other butts.

Reeling her back to hug in tight and spin around again.

She thought her skirt was too long to fly up past her hips, but there it flew. She did the twirl, she did the flying Dutchman, her legs were up in the air and over his head. He had his lip jutted out in a pugnacious jokey-face at the surrounding jitter-buggers. Black people looked at him like he was a crazy man and smiled so big that Donovan smiled back. As if they all really could have meant it.

Mean it! Really really mean it! she thought. Her brain was just scandalously loose. It was her goal to be as wild as the Negroes, and now they seemed pretty sedate in comparison to what was going on in her head.

The song ended. At least two people slapped them on the back and laughed to the rafters at the sheer exuberance of it all. For some obscure reason some of these people liked to see whites sneak into their club and jostle elbows with black folks. Who could conceive of such a thing, after all?

"The boogie woogie man," she said breathlessly. They trotted over and hit their seats with a bang.

"Boogie woogie girl," he said, cocking his head naughtily. "This ain't your first time."

"We always went to the clubs in Harlem and St. Paul and Chicago. I saw Jimmy Yancy and Lux Meade up there. I don't know this band, but they're good. They're all good."

My god it was hot in there with the lights and everybody dancing. She had sweat skittering under her arms and down her sides clear to her underpants. Donovan went quiet after a while, and she noticed he was eying the other white couple across the dining hall.

"Somebody you know?"

"Yeah."

It was unusual for him to be so still. So stilled. He didn't want to say anything more, it seemed. He tucked into his steak with some vigor. She did the same with her ribs. But after a minute of watching him glance she couldn't contain herself.

"Who is it?"

"The guy's Eddie Whitaker. That guy on my route today."

"Uh. Yeah, so?"

"The security man for old Rucker. Charles Rucker."

"Oh, yes." She refreshed herself on him. "The oil man."

Donovan blew a derisive razz. "Oil man! He don't pump oil, he don't drill oil, he sells oil. Oil he don't own. Fake oil."

"Snake oil." They laughed at that.

"Three hundred pounders, he takes. Two every other day. Bustin' my back. Won't let me drive up the back, either." They ate some more meat and rice. He was really looking hard at this man, though.

"Security man?"

"Enforcer. Goon."

"Rucker. That's the bigshot who's selling shares in that new oilfield down in the south bay, isn't it? You send him some money, someday he'll find oil?"

"Yeah, and maybe he won't."

"There's oil everywhere in this California."

"But maybe he don't own it."

Donovan looked over at Whitaker. Who was looking at him now. The man had a sweet gaze, so very peaceful and sweet.

Something about it Wanda didn't like. That sweetness. Just the way there was something about Donovan's she did like. That bitter sweetness. Maybe that was why she didn't like this Whitaker. The boogie woogie man's sweetness didn't like this other sweetness, the way eating honey was so much better than eating sugar. It was woman's work to find the good sweetness amidst the bad sweetness, and she felt good about her success.

"Don't you love this whole thing," she said. Her eyes skittered off and around. There was a 10-piece orchestra playing, and what do you know, right after she polished off her spud, here came a song slow and easy.

"That's my song! Donovan, that's the boogie woogie girl's song!"

"Come on," he said.

He held his hand out for hers. She came around the table for him. That boy had seen her love of this song, oh he had seen it right in her face.

She curled into him. She pressed into him. Stomach to stomach. She tucked her head into the sweet spot at his neck. She ran her arm up and around. She could feel his big mitt circling her, and off they stepped, so lightly she knew it wasn't just the cocktail she'd had or the three he'd had.

No doubt, they had lift together. His big left hand felt like a bunch of rough wooden pegs in her right, but his grip was easy and secure and it relaxed in the sway and play of their bodies. She burrowed her giveaway face farther into his white shirt until the bow tie tickled her nose.

After the song was almost done he said, "What's it called?"

"'After Glow'."

She whispered because of the mood of the band. But she could feel him pull his head back and look down at her. She kept her face buried.

"How's that sentimental for ya?"

"Oh, you know."

After a while she looked up at him. She realized he didn't know how an afterglow would have some meaning, that innocent fighting boy. The song ended, and he took her hand and tugged her back toward the table. They had to split over a table in their way, but kept fingers touching and the couple sitting there just ducked and laughed. Funny man, how he seemed so ornery and worldly, his hair falling over his eyes when he looked at her.

"Good clarinets up there," he said, at a loss.

"I love a good tenor sax best of all."

"You ready to go?"

He was counting out the tab, throwing an extra dollar down for the black waiter who had hovered in deference to the white people. More than he made in a day, she guessed. Don't worry, she was taking notes.

Over on the other side of the room a big group of white men came in, making a show and a stir. They looked around and rushed to this Whitaker's table. Raucous, they yelled at him and his girl to get out of this dive and go uptown. "Let's blow this damn Central Avenue!" one yelled. "Sunset Strip, and how!" yelled another. They looked like cops and talked like frat boys.

The white men hauled the couple out with them, good riddance, Wanda thought. They shoved blacks aside as they stumbled back to the door. Nervous eyes all around. Resentful eyes, watchful eyes, hateful eyes on this tidbit of insolence.

"I'll be right back," she said.

She let Donovan sit and be the only white man in the room while she zigzagged among the tables to the restroom. She tinkled, she listened to what the colored girls were saying about their men, their jobs, their lives. She was a little high from her cocktail. But she got enough to see how lively and lovely their lives were, too. That was part of her job, she thought, seeing how everybody lived and loved. She obtained clues so she could make it all better.

They exited the club, Donovan and Wanda, waving to the people they had danced around, and no sooner were they outside than they were barricaded by this mob of white men shouting for their cars. They had valet parked and couldn't get their automobiles back fast enough.

"New red Cadillac!" one shouted, waving his arms. Colored boys of 14 or so ran here and there trying to get it settled. "Black Olds, boy!"

Wanda glanced at her man and something in his face looked very leery as they moved outside. He watched everything, the men's loud guffaws, their way of taking up the whole entrance so black folks had to scoot around close to the wall to get in. Whitaker was in there, more quiet and patient than the others.

Several coloreds also waited for their cars, accustomed to being shoved to the back row even at their own clubs. Wanda was about to push through when a little black man and his wife squeezed by the crowd. At the last second a close-cropped whitehead was shoved by his friend, and he stumbled drunkenly into the black man. Who dodged away apologetically the way he would do in this situation.

"Watch yourself, boy."

The big white man appeared angry at him. Not at his friend for shoving, but at the black man for being in his way. All the white faces turned, as if on cue. Wanda's stomach shuddered. It all looked like such a pretext, one of those senseless unravelings in the hard way that men played.

"Get the hell out of the way," the man said. He grabbed the black man by the jacket. A hat flew off. Got quickly trampled by a couple of other whites.

The black man's wife stepped forward. "Excuse us. We didn't mean nothin'."

"Look out, there, Sugar Tits," the pusher said, leering.

"Say, now," the black husband said.

"Oh, I'm sorry, Rastus. Didn't mean no disrespect to your hootchie."

"Hey, Lewis," one of the other white men called, "that ain't Rastus. That there's Sambo."

"Aw, I'm sorry, Sambo," this Lewis said sarcastically. "I didn't recognize ya."

As blacks pressed in to see what had happened, white arms roped them out. "Back off, here." "None a your business." "Get him, Lewis." They'd all been drinking a lot, Wanda had seen it before. Since childhood. A calf singled out for the slaughter.

She eased around the back side to get out of the way, despondent. These muscle plays were hopeless. She felt for Donovan's hand. But it was gone.

"He ain't doin' nothing, let him off," she could have sworn she heard Donovan say. She looked around, and he had that big old friendly grin on his face. "Colored boy works with me."

"What's that you say?" A couple of white burr-heads butted in toward him. Whitaker, the security man, stayed back. He watched with that peaceful face.

"I just know the guy, he's all right." Donovan reached down and got the black man's fedora. Brushed it off with a bunch of meaty fingers. "Here ya go, Melvin."

The man took it, bobbing his head right and left the way the Negroes did in strife of this sort, confusion coming from all angles. He didn't seem quite sure who was on his side, if anybody. It could all be a trick.

"Thank ya, sir, thanks be."

Donovan put his arm around this Melvin's shoulder and walked him into the door of the club. "How ya doin', Mary?" he asked the black man's wife. "Them kids doin' okay, now? They over them sniffles?"

The black woman nodded. The couple disappeared inside. Donovan popped back out, adjusting his coat. Drawing close, he looked the biggest loser, the stumbler, in the neck.

"He didn't mean nothin', citizen," Donovan said all false-friendly like. Wanda was starting to think this man didn't care a thing about his health and old age.

"Looks like you got some black eye there already," big man said. "You don't want another one, you and your nigger friend too."

"Pop him one, Lewis," one of the others yelled. Donovan didn't say a thing. Wanda was praying, though. And, praise be, her prayer was answered.

Big man reached to shove Donovan away, and there was a chopping sound like a nose structure going back deep into a skull. Her man's fist was so quick there was no time for anybody else to react. Big man Lewis recoiled, dropped to his knees, trying to get the breath to say something, snorting like a lame horse down there, spraying blood.

But Donovan was just looking at the rest of them. Oh, her man, it was those eyes. They were killer-blue. Wounded somehow, yet killer too. When she looked at them her knees went weak.

So did theirs, apparently.

"Whaja do that for?" said one bleached-out bozo, very offended now but leery. He was looking for moral support from his comrades, the way such people do. But they hung back, afraid of this kind of unexpectedness. A couple of them looked to Whitaker for advice, assistance, insight.

The black people in the area had moved aside to make room. They hadn't seen precisely this kind of activity before, and it was frightening how bad the white men could go. Even with each other.

"Man's outta line with my friend," Donovan said simply. "You get him to a doctor real quick and set that nose, he'll be good for work tomorrow."

He gave them another five seconds to consider his words. Maybe it took ten seconds, one of those little eternities. The man down at Donovan's knees was snuffling blood out onto the sidewalk and trying to suck air in through his mouth and trying to say goddamn. It came out "da dum." When he saw that nobody else was going to attempt to be dangerous, Donovan reached down and jerked the big man to his feet.

"There ya go, pardner."

He dusted him off a bit. More for show than effect. He glanced over at Whitaker, who didn't acknowledge with even a glance. He struck the big man on the sides of his arms in a comradely way of saying toodle-oo, took Wanda's hand, and off they strode, her heart whamming away like a jackhammer removing a bad stretch on Los Angeles Street.

"Here." She gave him the keys to her car. "I'm shaking too bad."

He opened the door for her and off they went. He didn't say anything. They plowed through traffic up Central until he could catch some through-roads to the north side of town. He was thinking of her, she was thinking of him, her eyes stabbing out at passing light shows.

They were up in the Wilshire district before she could think what to say. It was about 10 at night. Donovan leaned over against the door as he drove with one big hand. He looked sleepy, ready for bed.

"Where do you know that guy from?" she finally asked.

He looked over, eased out of his thoughts. "What guy?"

"That Negro man?"

"I think I saw him over on my route. Drives a vegetable wagon or something."

"You didn't know him?"

He shook his head. "I don't know any nig...Negroes in this town."

He pointed right and left at the next intersection, asking which way to go. She pointed left. She said to aim for his house. She could drive home from there. She would take him anywhere he wanted to go.

7

SKUNKS AND SAINTS

This Wanda didn't know what a man's life was like out in the working world, even if she was a union organizer. There were harsh rules and you've got to stick up for what's yours, was Donovan's recipe.

It was that way in the schoolyard when he was a muddy-faced ranch kid coming into May on a buckboard and he had to fight the town kids. It was that way on the highway through the Southwest, when he had to fight the anti-Okie bigots and scam artists. It was that way in the mines of Arizona and the Mojave, where he fought over whiskey and slights. It was that way in this big town. Except here, he fought for fun. He was home, he could do that.

Sure, he considered himself to be the nicest guy in Los Angeles County, but there was a right way and a wrong way to approach it. If you approached it with pride you had to fight for it.

It sure got Wanda loosened up. On the way to his place she scooted over and collapsed onto his arm as he drove up to the double. He had to rouse her when he parked, she was so relaxed. They went inside, march-stepping, they were so close. She was on him like a waistcoat. Not saying a word. Hoping he hadn't hit that man for her sake, to impress her, but not caring if he had.

He had. He didn't like to see anybody get pushed around, but he wouldn't have stepped in if it hadn't been for Wanda. He hoped and prayed Joseph was out to dinner or something. It was the first time he had said anything resembling a prayer in fifteen years. But no. Joseph sat in the living room waiting for him. Reading one of his business improvement magazines. Donovan and Wanda even had to separate and one sit next to the brother on the settee. Her.

"Oh, you should have seen him," Wanda started up, voice gruff with emotion. Donovan tried to warn her off, but she slogged through the whole story. Joseph could hardly believe it. He had a small face for a Daley, and his blue eyes perked right at her.

"He would have taken on the whole lot of them," Wanda finished.

"And you wasn't even drunk?" Joseph asked him.

"No time, dancing so much. We had us a good old time."

"That for a nigger, too," Joseph said.

Okay, this woke Wanda up.

"Negro, you mean?"

Donovan saw that coming, her little tic.

One thing you had to recognize about brother Joseph. He had a particular set to his mind. Donovan, he described himself as a pretty open-minded fellow. He would look around, he would accept something or move away. Joseph, he was the Daley with the hard head.

"Nigger," he said real firmly. "I ain't met a Negro yet. A negroid person is a nigger."

"Uh huh," said Wanda. Recognizing one fact. The Okies might have been disadvantaged, but they didn't feel they were the low folks on the totem pole.

Joseph turned right away to his brother. See, he was a real loyal hand and a hard worker, but he had that set to his mind. Unusual for such a young man, in Donovan's experience. Even for ranch boys, who were all hard headed. Joseph stared at him, his mouth squenched to one side, and then got up and retrieved something from the bureau.

Donovan took the opportunity to catch the look from Wanda. Joseph came over to him, and Donovan didn't want to take the letter he held out. Knowing what it was.

"Mama wrote." Joseph tapped him on the hand with it.

Donovan recognized the stationery with the little red two-cent stamp on it. After some tapping on his hand he took it. He fished it out of the ripped-open envelope.

There was the usual stuff about how hard it was back home. His mother attacked his father again, as she did in all her letters. They arrived one a week. She reminded him that she'd lost the ranch, and that the McCalesters that own the bank bought the whole place at auction for $325. She put that in every letter. She said the boarding house wasn't making any money yet. But she was sure it would.

"Same old thing." Donovan stuffed the letter back in the envelope with the curlicue handwriting on it and sailed it across the room to Joseph.

Who was perched against the dresser, his leg jittering. The letter whirled around and landed at his feet.

He got that set to his face. He wouldn't turn his eye off Donovan. He swooped the hair back off his face. All the Daleys had that long straight hair, some brown, some black, some blondish. There was some Indian blood in there from their mother's side.

Joseph would never admit that, Donovan knew. He didn't like Indians, either. He didn't like much of anything that wasn't pure white.

"That skunk's fouled everything up," Joseph said.

"She's doing all right."

"That woman's a saint. I ought to go back and help her out."

"Yeah, I bet she could use a free dishwasher at the boarding house."

Wanda wasn't following, though she did pick up a note not only of disagreement but sarcasm on Donovan's part. Joseph looked pointedly at her.

"Wanda, could you excuse us a second?"

"Sure." She didn't move, though. Was she supposed to get up and go outside? She was mad, anyway. Donovan hadn't known her long, but he could tell by the ramrod-straight attitude of her head when the woman was mad. You'd better be able to tell when a woman's mad in this world, he knew, or you're sunk from the start.

Finally Joseph got up from the settee and waved his brother into the kitchen. Donovan pardoned himself. He was wishing he had thought to get her out of there before all this.

"That skunk ain't sending her any money at all," Joseph whispered loudly.

"What's it matter? We send her a check every month."

Wham. Joseph whammed the flat of his hand against the door. He was not a pacing kind of man, normally. Or a hitter. But now he started to walk it off.

"It's not right!" he said. "What he did!"

Wanda stuck her head in, looking to see what the pounding was all about. She couldn't see much, and the thought occurred that Donovan might be hitting him.

"Everything all right?" she said. Joseph shut up tight as a man's flies, as their father might have said. Donovan was thinking he needs himself a girl, Joseph does. He's packed a little tight in there.

"Here's what happened." He knew telling Wanda this would anger Joseph. "Our mother and father got a divorce here a couple years ago. It's throwed the whole family outta kilter."

"She doesn't need to know any of that," Joseph said very emphatically.

"Some of the kids, the older ones that left a while back, they sided with Father. The younger ones, that grown up more with Mama, they taken her side."

"None of her business, this woman."

"We lost the ranch. Drought. The cattle dried up and died, wheat did too. My dad's out here. Mother got herself a partnership in a boarding house in Woodward."

"She wouldn't care about any of this."

"That's where me and Joseph differ. He goes with Mother, I go with Father."

Donovan didn't know why he was running off at the mouth like this. He hadn't talked about it to anybody. Except Joseph. Who talked about it angrily in terms of skunks and saints.

"Our little sister Mazie is still back there. Joseph keeps wanting us to go back and help. I say we're doing more good here where we got jobs. There's not a dime to be had in Oklahoma, and if there is, the bank men snatch it up and hide it in their pocket."

"Damnit, Donovan. The world doesn't care about our problems, but you should think of your mama. You were the eldest. She always favored you."

Joseph had a petulant cast to his face. Keeping his eyes fixed on his brother the whole time as if the secret could be retracted along this line of sight.

Donovan threw his hands in the air. He got his glass off the counter and filled it with water from the faucet. He remembered how they had no faucet on the ranch. There was a well, and you went to the well, rain or snow. Then one day the dust half-filled the well. There was no more water. He liked very much this idea of the faucet.

He offered Wanda a drink. This Los Angeles was a good place to drink water. He loved the pure idea that you could reach up and snatch a lemon off a tree and make lemonade in a second if you had a dime to buy a bag of sugar.

"We only have two glasses," he said. She took a drink out of his glass. "So. What do you think of the Daleys now?"

"I'm sorry to hear it. That doesn't happen with Jewish couples," Wanda said. "My parents, they'll just stick with each other until one drops dead of stubbornness."

This was the first either of the men had heard of this Jew thing. Joseph acted like somebody had stabbed an ice pick into his neck. He squirmed his head. He turned right and then he turned left to get away from the pain.

She was just smiling as if she didn't know she was a Jew. Though by now some inkling of the issue was breaching. Joseph looked at Donovan.

"That's a Jew you're courting?" he said. "A goddamn sheanie?"

"Oh, is that the way," Wanda said. Her face went red in streaks from her neck to her hair.

"Hold off," Donovan said, putting his arm out so she didn't attack his brother. She leaned that way hard and she had surprising strength.

"You're sparking with a damn member of the traitor race."

Joseph wouldn't let up. As for himself, Donovan was a little taken aback. Not that it mattered. Her being of the Jewish persuasion. He had no idea. He had heard the word intoned like this, like a sneer or the punchline to a joke, all his life. But from Joseph it didn't sound so conversational. What was a Jew, anyway? Joseph knew something, apparently.

"So what if I am. It's none of yours," Donovan said to him. He was still trying to figure out what it meant. He'd heard of them, Jew people, but it was like having a wolverine come into the living room or something. You've heard of them, you didn't even know what one looked like, and now all of a sudden one's here.

"So that's the way it is in here." Wanda spun on her heels and headed for the front door.

Donovan took off after her, quick on his feet. Joseph came around the settee and tried to grab his arm, but Donovan didn't care what he thought. It was a trait of his. He didn't care what anybody thought. What was a Jew anyway? Something to be scared of? This little frizzy-haired girl? Whoever heard of such a thing?

8

WHAT'S A JEW, ANYWAY?

It was impossible to know, of course, when and where these situations, these people, would crop up. Anywhere, obviously. Any time. They lurked out there. She was the mouse, they were the cats. It was their house. They could pounce at any time.

Running out of that house, she wondered if she mentioned her Jewish parents to them just to get this kind of information back. Sure, she did. You had to test. She was always doing it.

She tried to get in her car, but suddenly Donovan was there ahead of her. He leaned on the door and blocked her. That was a mistake, because she hated it when anybody impeded her progress. Especially a man. She fought the door for a second. She couldn't even wiggle it. She pulled at his arm for a second. He moved less than the car.

"I'm sorry about that," he said.

She looked up. She saw in those eyes that he was. This was surprising. This was wholeheartedly surprising. Her spirits just leaped up.

"See," she started. She was almost in tears but she blinked it all away because she wouldn't allow that to happen. "I know there are filaments running through society. These filaments can gather energy and grow larger, or they can start big and taper off. Like tree roots pushing through the ground. But it's a given that humans have this life force, this movement through society. Through history."

She whirled, almost into his arms, he was standing so close. He wouldn't interrupt her. She could see from the first time she saw his face that he knew something was troubling her. As far back as the jail that first night. She could see that he saw past her and into her, even if he had no idea what she was talking about.

"But it's what the roots carry that's important. It's not what color the roots are, or what tree they come from. Do they carry nutrients or do they carry toxins? That's it. Do they nourish or do they poison? Are you with me?"

He nodded. His brother, this evil little Joseph, hadn't emerged from the house. It was a good thing. She might set upon him. She certainly would not have let herself say these vulnerable, silly things the way she was doing here. Tears came when she saw how Donovan was sticking by her, she just couldn't blink that rapidly. Was he that naïve, that he didn't know what a Jew was? Or did he just not care? She had carried Jew with her like a steamer trunk filled with iron all the way across the country, and if he didn't care, that was something.

"See, there's the brother love, and there's the lover love. And it's the lover love that's fun, but it's the brother love that's so important. To society. We need both. But a country, a world, runs on brother love. You don't have it? You have China versus Japan, you have France versus Germany, you have Spain versus Franco."

Feeling she shouldn't—it was a risky moment for her—she hugged him. She just needed somebody to clutch at that moment. She could go find another Jew, another black, another Mexican, they were all the same in the roots.

But for some reason she trusted this man. This damned Aryan. But there was nobody else to trust, and you had to trust somebody after all these years of losing ground in every nation on Earth. Didn't you? He was certainly giving her free rein.

"It's these tribes, these organizations, these perverted governments, that can wring the essential humanity out of us if we're not careful." They had gotten in the car. She said this as he was driving—she turned over the keys, she was shaking again. "Individual to individual, we make do with each other, but as soon as we identify with some group…. There's some fanatic, there's some rogue idea. Some evil concept that wins out. You know what I mean?"

Yes, he did. Or nodded that he did. When he listened he looked so meek, she thought. He seemed to be cogitating every word and every letter of every word. Ruminating the words as if they were bites of chocolate cake.

"The individuals stop being individuals and start being mobs. They hate. Why would somebody hate me?"

He had no answer to that. He couldn't imagine.

At Mary's café they beat on the locked door and the owner let them in.

She was still cleaning up after a hard day, but she could see they were in a crisis. So Donovan helped her wash the last dishes and clean the countertops because her help had had to leave early. Wanda followed them around with a cup of coffee in her hand, talking about it.

"Ideas, that's all we've got. We're a nation of ideas." She moved aside for the string mop he whipped back and forth. A surprising man. If there was any little job that needed doing, he jumped right in. "If those ever run out or go bad and we turn to simple tribalism and consumption? We're no different than the serfs, the slaves. Our president will be no more than the czar, the kaiser, the king. We're done, finished."

He nodded along with her. Taking cues from Mary, who had no idea what this woman was talking about either. He wiped down the last dirty table as Wanda followed him from chore to chore.

"Why does everybody care about the Jews so much? Mary, do you care what the Jews are doing every minute of the day?" Wanda tried to hold Mary's eye as she dodged around behind the counter refilling ketchup bottles. Mary waved her hand at her dismissively. She was falling asleep on her feet. Finally she just put her hands on the lunch counter and blew a strand of hair out of her eyes.

"Naw, I don't care. They'll go to hell or heaven, I'm sure. Like the rest of us."

"You go on to bed, Mary," Donovan said. "I'll finish up here."

He shooed her to the back of the café, where there were steps leading to an upstairs apartment. After she struggled up the stairs he came back along the counter, watching Wanda watch him come along. He cleaned the grill with a long spatula, racking the lard to one side where it could be used to fry the eggs the next morning.

Drawing himself a cup of coffee, he finally settled across from Wanda at a table. The floor creaked above them for a few seconds, then all was quiet.

"Getcha more coffee?"

She shook her head. Tired of her own tirade.

"All that what you was sayin'? About tribes?"

She nodded her head.

"My father taught me that early-on. We used to sell cattle to the government for the Indians, and they'd kill them from horses. The way they did buffalo in the old days."

"Really? Bows and arrows?"

"Rifles. And one day my dad heard some soldiers talking about them savages. And he real quiet-like lit into 'em. Told me, don't let me ever hear you calling somebody somethin' you don't know firsthand about."

"Where did Joseph find all this hatred about the Jews?"

"I don't know. He grew up with my mother, after I'd left home. He's better educated than me, he finished high school. But she was full of bile by then."

"It must have been nasty. The divorce."

"Then as soon as Joseph come out here he just got all beside himself. He's been stewin' like a steam boiler the whole time."

She took a sip of his coffee. Not really wanting the coffee as much as the sharing. It was difficult for her, now that she had calmed down, to know what to say.

"Where you from, Wanda?"

"Minnesota. Since I left home I've lived in New York, Detroit, Atlanta, St. Paul. A lot of places. Too many places."

"I wouldn't of guessed Kitchen was a Jew name." He couldn't even think of a Jewish name, but knew they contained gold and berg sometimes. Once Joseph had told him they were sneaky, those people, because they could be all around you with deceptively neighborly names like Lewis and Miller.

"My father changed it when he came to this country. Kirtschner, it was, in Hungary. Trying to be a normal American, or pose as one."

"Hungary. There's Jews in Hungary?"

"Oh, yes. I forgot. You don't know about the Jews."

"I've heard them mentioned." This got a laugh.

"Funny man. I'm a real disappointment to my family, not becoming a nice mamele. But I got this fascination with the Anglo-Saxon-Teutonic-Nordic-American phenomenon. The energy, the dominance, the potential. For good or ill."

"I never thought about it."

"Maybe it's like playing with fire. Or like running into a burning house."

"You're the kind wants to save people. How come you left home?"

"You ever heard of Gertrude Barnum? Pauline Newman? Rose Pesotta?"

"Nope."

"Unionists. Feminists. Radicals. Socialists. You know how there's supposed to be a honeybee that flies out and finds the honey and goes back to the hive and tells the others?"

"Yeah?"

"I don't want to be the queen bee. I want to be that other bee. The messenger bee, the activist bee. Whatever you might call him."

"Her. All those bees are female."

"See? There you go."

They laughed. But her face went sober. "See, I've been in cities where I've seen tycoons in raccoon coats get out of chauffeured limousines and walk through a line of two hundred destitute men waiting to apply for one job sweeping floors. I've seen society dames in taxis drive through a crowd of threadbare shop girls slogging home from work. I've seen farmers watch their land and belongings being auctioned off to a bunch of bankers in tailored suits. This California, it's booming. You don't see the cruelty so much, but even here the people who have are making it off the people who don't have."

They studied each other's faces. Why had they been so drawn to each other's faces and heads and bodies, she wondered? Why were they so content to sit here—at 11:35, by the new Coca-Cola clock humming on the wall with its electric tail hanging down—and discuss Jews and other tribes so freely?

Again they tried her apartment. They drove in quietly, lights out, trying to not wake the landlord, whose apartment was the first on the street. Her window was dark, so they both were hoping Pauline was out. But as soon as Wanda pushed the door in, Pauline's head popped up from the sofa.

"Who is it?" Pauline yelled.

Wanda thought these damn Reds, they never went out and had any fun. The most Pauline would do was gather comrades in some gloomy room full of smoke and avidly praise Stalin's relocation programs.

"It's just me," Wanda said.

"It's not just you," Pauline said, peeking at Donovan before they could back out of the door. She pulled her nightgown tight.

There was a road that angled up into the hills of Griffith Park that he knew how to find at night, don't ask him how he knew. Donovan drove again because now her hands were really shaking. She was delicate that way, some vulnerability rising to the surface.

He parked on a dirt turnout and pulled the hand brake on the Packard. When he shut off the motor of the well used car it was like a rolling steel barrel clattering to a rest. Everything was dark except the lights scattered in patches in the valley, and even that was quiet.

"Look, there's a premiere or something," he said.

By leaning a bit they could see two spotlights in Hollywood crisscross and knife across the low clouds. The rest of the valley was a vast, mottled smudge of dark and light. Even downtown, off to the left, had only a few office windows lit. Capitalists staying up late counting their wins and losses, she imagined. Farms and empty lots blotted in square segments of utter darkness.

"Sorry about Joseph," he said.

"I know." She rolled her window down.

"Feels funny sitting in the passenger seat of my own car," she said by way of a lame excuse for scooting over next to him. He casually put his arm around her.

"We weren't raised that way. Joseph and me."

"What did you do when you were kids?"

This perked him up. He told a boyhood of riding ponies after straying mama cows. He talked about flights of ducks and geese clouding the skies over the North Canadian River as they came in to light on the water. He recalled spending most of his childhood with an old single-shot .22, with one bullet his grandfather gave him every day to get a goose or duck for dinner, and the slap of the shot as it scared up a dense phantasmagoria of birds over the river.

"What about you?"

So she told him about a little girl holding her mother's hand and walking on a concrete island in a vast water. She told him how these Hungarian refugees moved around the country looking for work and kinship. She could recall playing in the woods with a homemade doll when her father worked in the mines in North Carolina. She played with the same doll on the streets of New Jersey and Ohio. By the time she got to Minnesota the doll was worn out and she was a permanent cooking helper for her mother. The Kirschners, the Kitchens, settled into a life of work and the Judaism they weren't allowed to have in peace in their homeland.

"How come you to leave home?"

"Same as you."

"Family?"

"Yes. And no. Just me. Restless." She cuddled in close to him, unsure how she could feel such kinship. "The Jews have a vast collective memory, and it usually consists of this sentence. 'The worst can happen.' I didn't want to be part of that anymore."

"Excuse me, but what do Jews do, anyway?"

"Everything under the sun. What do Okies do?"

"Everything."

"So there, then."

"You showed me, huh." He laughed. She laughed. She snuggled in tighter.

"I just couldn't stand that structure. That rigorous male structure. Temple three days a week, bar mitzvahs to go to year after year. The you-have-to-do-this, the you-have-to-do-that. No backtalk, no sass."

"I can see that. You're all sass."

She sat up for a second and scanned his face. Couldn't find any malfeasance implied in that. But she didn't snuggle in again for a minute.

"My father. He would talk about these great social movements going on around the world. But he wouldn't let us get out and join them. 'Just let the dust settle a few years,' he would say. My family acquired all these clothing stores across the Midwest, and we were every one of us way too busy being successful to take part in the rest of the world's struggles."

"How many stores?"

"There are probably twenty now. Every now and then somebody will write and say we just opened a new branch in Osh Kosh or Omaha."

"You still in touch with your folks?"

"I write. My father's still mad at me. Calls me that rebellious girl. He says it was the influence of the Roaring Twenties, when everyone played too hard and loved too many. To his way of thinking it led to moral decay. Jazz and gin mills, that's all he saw in it. I saw the freedom, the yearning to turn society on a dime."

She turned on the seat so she faced him squarely. "Wasn't it just a new way of looking at your fellow man? A new way of moving on the dance floor? Those sexy picture shows? Maybe the twenties changed us, but won't people in the future say the thirties changed us, the sixties changed us?"

He shrugged and nodded. Didn't seem so sure. The twenties were pretty blatant.

"It's the way life is. You left home too," she reminded him.

"Yeah, but our family fell apart, and the dust blew in from the fields. We stuffed rags around the windows and doors, and you'd wake up in the morning and still have dirt in your mouth. You'd eat, there would be grit on the table, in your grits."

"And here we are."

So he leaned over and kissed her. It was a peck, really, no more. She allowed it, but no more. She seemed to be studying the issue in some depth, by the look on her face.

"I think I should get home."

"Yeah, it's late."

"I didn't mean I'm sorry you did that. It's just real late."

"I'll get me another one soon."

"You're awfully sure of yourself," she said. Smiling. He smiled too. They were just smiling away at each other. Awfully altogether sure of themselves.

9

POOR BONNY PRINCE ALBERT

It was Sunday, then. Even the ice men had the day off. The meat and the milk would have to rely on the last little lump of ice until Monday.

They had decided they would go to Muscle Beach. Wanda wanted to look at the muscle men. They would be very modern and go eat at that new automat cafeteria downtown. They would go see a movie. It would be a full day.

What they didn't count on was Joseph. "I've never seen the muscle men neither," he said. He had a lost, whiny expression on his face. As Donovan had explained to Wanda the day before, his brother had a peculiar set to his mind. He was smart, and a hard worker, but he couldn't be derailed once his mind was made up.

So off they went on the long trek to the ocean, the three of them. They took her car. The brothers hadn't gotten around to buying a car yet, and the trolley was too far.

"You buy this car from a Jew automobile dealer?" Joseph said from the back seat. He thought he knew how to cause trouble for the couple. Donovan gave his brother a look, and Wanda gave Donovan a look. She didn't even want to see Joseph's face, but apparently they were stuck with him.

Santa Monica was beautiful. The pier was crowded with strollers and fishermen. A breeze blew pelicans across the scene. There were a thousand people in drab bathing suits on the beach. Kids were in the water, leaping. Negroes were on their side. There was somebody on a big board paddling around in the water and then trying to stand up on it. That got a laugh from everybody. Donovan bought ice cream for Wanda and Joseph, who was a bit of a tightwad.

When she saw the muscle men and the weightlifting equipment she ran across the sand toward a human pyramid they were building. The brothers followed more slowly. Everybody down here was sunburned except for ones who wore their hats. There was a pyramid of men in their bathing suits, their bare legs spread for balance, standing on each other's shoulders and grinning for an appreciative crowd of dozens.

To one side, other muscle men clanked iron weights on rugs on the sand, lifting them up and throwing them down as if in disgust. Then smiling for more onlookers lined up there. One yelled, "We need a woman for the top of the pyramid!"

Before she could even think, Wanda leaped out in front. So did four other women. The weightlifters picked a beautiful little curly-headed blonde. Wanda stepped back.

"Shoot," she said, kicking sand. "I wanted to go up there."

"What for?"

"I don't know, for the view. What do you think of those skimpy little suits?" She pointed to the muscle men's tight bathing shorts. Little dormant penis heads poked at the material. He didn't even answer. He had on his best suit and bow tie, as did most of the men. With Panama hats and boaters. The older ones had walking sticks to help get them across the sand.

The weightlifters explained to the blonde how to get up on the pyramid. The men arranged themselves three-wide on the bottom row, two in the middle. The woman climbed up, taking their hands. She stood on two shoulders for a second, wobbly, ready to fall. For an instant she was still, a crooked grin on her face. The men handed her down, trying not to touch her private parts.

"Anybody else?" they yelled. This time only two women stepped forward. Wanda was one. The men picked the other, a curtain-hair blonde. This time Wanda came back mad.

"What is it with the blondes?" she asked, her face in Donovan's as if he had been the one to choose.

He shrugged. After the pyramid, the men took the blondes over to the weights to show them how to do curls and squats. Being very facilitative the way men can be around women. Everything was agonizingly innocent, the muscle men striving so hard to be appreciated.

"Somebody want to come in here and try to lift this?" yelled one of the muscle men squiring blondes.

He was a little guy, but the blood vessels fairly popped through the tight skin of his thighs and biceps when he demonstrated a clean and jerk. It was like he was embedded with roots under his skin. The bar had two big weights on each end labeled 100, plus some smaller weights. He pressed it up, straining mightily with his cheeks puffed out, and threw it down as if in disgust. Then smiled to applause all around.

"Aw, that's a fraud," Donovan said.

And before anybody could stop him he strode out there to the little guy. Everybody laughed a bit at the audacity. Donovan did a little jig in his suit to demonstrate his sense of humor. He was about the same size as the little guy, who wasn't so little after all.

Donovan reached down with one hand and grabbed the bar. He got his legs under him and jerked it up and got under it and threw it over his head. Then he threw it down on the rug as if he was disgusted with it. It clanged like a train linking up.

"I coulda told 'em," Joseph said. "That brother a mine can pick stuff up."

The muscle men were still talking about him when Donovan led the other two off to get cream sodas. He took Wanda's hand. Wanda hugged into his arm as they struggled through the sand.

They drove all the way back downtown to a Hill Street cafeteria. They finally found a parking spot blocks away. The automat was a big room full of tables with a wall of little windows over to the side where they could choose their food. Meat, starch, vegetable and dessert all framed in the windows like paintings.

Donovan and Joseph walked up and down the little windows like hicks straight out of the badlands. They got in everybody's way, the Sunday-off men with their slickly parted hair and the floral women in black pumps. Finally Wanda had to rein them in and show them how to get a tray and pick courses for their meal. Donovan paid for everybody again, $1.25 total. He was spending money like crazy.

"You get enough?" he asked Joseph. The little guy's tray was loaded with dishes. Everybody got the famous lemon pie. Joseph was flustered by the pretty clerk at the counter, who looked at him as if he was a hick.

"I think I'm going on home after this."

"We could drop you off," Wanda said. As nonchalantly as she could muster.

"I'll just take the bus." And he asked Donovan for the fare.

After eating, Donovan and Wanda, free at last, walked south out of the cafeteria, and Joseph walked west. There was more lift in their feet now. "Joseph's a little tight with a nickel," Donovan explained. "Five times as tight with a quarter," Wanda said. They laughed all the way to the car and cranked the windows down to let out some of the heat.

But they looked at her watch and it was only 1:30. The movie they wanted to see didn't start until 6:00.

"Have you seen the advertisements for those model homes out east?" she asked.

"Out east?"

"San Gabriel Valley. They looked so cute in the paper."

"Let's go."

It was a long drive on new paved roads, other Sunday day trippers clogging the lanes with old black cars, and the air was fuzzy with dust and haze. She drove, he slumped in his seat, content to watch. They told jokes and laughed. They pointed at odd sights and laughed. They looked at each other and laughed. Sometimes they just sat there looking straight ahead and broke out in laughter for no reason. One wouldn't have thought that citrus groves and alfalfa fields were so inherently hilarious.

The model homes were in a flat area between the monstrous San Gabriel Mountains to the north and some smaller hills to the south, surrounded by vineyards and flower fields. The land for about fifty acres around had been scoured and there was a pall of dust even though the earthmovers were off for the day.

They turned left at a large promotional billboard at Running Springs Road. Little two-bedroom houses with big windows seemed to have sprung right out of the disturbed soil. Many were still under construction down at the end of the street, just stacks of sticks with potential customers parading in and out and touching things.

The office lawn, along with its big sign announcing AFFORDABLE HOMES RIGHT HERE, was strewn with "starlets" in bathing suits pretending to mow, rake and water the grass. All four of them were blond. Two platinum, one normal, one dishwater.

"I guess every house comes with quiff," Wanda said behind her hand. He laughed and they went to look at the model homes. The quiff waved at them as they went by, little doll-faced jackals. When they walked up to the model they liked best, the Glenwood West, he was already joking how there wasn't a glen or a wood for twenty miles. It was a yellow house with white trim and the black number 1620 running down a porch post.

Inside, she went completely quiet. There was a yellow kitchen and two bedrooms so small the model beds almost filled them. She was stunned.

She had the new-house look on her face.

"Wouldn't it be nice to have a little house like this?" The cynicism had gone right out of the little radical's body. This took him by surprise. She stood transfixed by a print on the living room wall. Two little girls frolicking in a field of flowers.

"Live way out here? You'd do that?"

"Sure. Pay for it on the monthly plan."

Tentatively, he said, "You could plant some fruit trees in the yard. A big old avocado tree. I love them things."

"And what about in here? Build some shelves over there and put my books on them so I could see them all. Cook on an electric range. Have your friends over to discuss Sinclair and Mulholland. I'm so sick of not being able to find my books."

"Uh huh," is all he could say. The only book he had was the Blaster's Handbook, a manual on how to apply dynamite to stumps and mine tunnels.

The salesman was in the bathroom showing some country folks how to use the flush toilet. He was a man scarred by the smallpox all the way up his neck and cheeks. His forehead and nose were as smooth as Mexican tile, but like a lot of survivors he looked like he had been up to his eyes in pox. A flock of gawkers strolled by, going room to room, and suddenly Wanda foresaw it all. The streets lined with trees, the lawns all needing mowing, the rooms filled with kids.

"And you could have a vegetable garden," she said, recognizing his continual need for food.

"This place already has iron pipes with town water, can you believe it? Your ice box would be filled with ice made from good water."

She was dancing around some other house hunters to keep in eye contact with him, and they all smiled at her enthusiasm.

"You could keep a dog here if you put up a fence," he said.

"You could have a house dog."

"A dog that lived in the house?" What a thought.

She jogged over to the bedroom door and pointed in. "Little kids, when they got bigger we would have to add on another room, because a boy and a girl would want separate bedrooms."

"A boy and a girl," he said, amazed at the thought. But even more dazzled by the realization that she had said we. We would have to add a room.

The poxed salesman came up behind them, gaudy in his plaid burgundy and white sports coat, and said over their shoulder, "Room for more bedrooms. Working class dream you got here."

Donovan and Wanda were struck by the words. She had a vision of her garment workers ensconced in these little houses, raising their children in this kind of scrubbed and secure future.

But the salesman was taking a closer look at Donovan's face. "That's quite a shiner you've got there, fella. You trying to punch somebody in the fist with your head?" He commenced laughing hilariously at his joke.

Dragging Donovan out the back door before he could get mad, Wanda went all the way around the house and looked in every window. As if she were a mother peeking to see if her kids were playing nicely, a neighbor prying on village family life.

In the car he drove this time. Her hands were shaking again. She was quick to embark on emotional flings that disturbed the equilibrium. Not always in a bad way. She could easily be disturbed in a good way.

They went back by the northern byroads, up through Pasadena and Glendale. She was quiet, and leaned on him. It was still early. He pulled off before he got to the Los Angeles River and found a little dirt road that went down to the water.

They sat in the car for a while in the shade of an ancient cottonwood tree whose leaves trickled in the breeze. He got a big bunch of bananas from the back seat and they stripped a couple off and ate them. They drank water he had brought in one of his glass jugs. She said it was getting late for the movie.

"Wait a minute," he said.

He got out and she got out and he opened the trunk and pulled out a couple of guns. A rifle. A pistol. She stood looking at them in his hands.

"Whenever I get out and around I like to do some shooting."

Still she just looked down at them. Not as if the guns were abhorrent to her. More as if they were strange creatures from Australia or Borneo, never seen alive before. She reached down and touched the revolver, ran one finger over its cold, cylindrical flesh. As if indeed it were of some unique evolutionary line.

"Shooting?"

He shoved the pistol in his back pocket, put the rifle in the crook of his arm. Pulled out two boxes of shells. They walked down to the river, a flood-scoured depression with a thin stream chuckling around rocks at the bank nearest them. There were some old tires and cans caught in fallen tree limbs and moss. He jumped over the stream and she followed. Mystified.

Donovan picked up a rusty red tobacco can, carried it over to the foot of the far river embankment between willows and cottonwoods. He set the can on an exposed root. Walked back. She had to turn and follow him back. She didn't even understand the principle, that you stood over here and shot at something over there.

"Here." He handed her the green box of pistol shells. He took cartridges from the other box and loaded the rifle's magazine.

"Springfield thirty ought-six. Cut the stock down from a military rifle. You've got your post sight up front, your blade rear sight, bolt action." He pulled the bolt back and jacked a shell in from the magazine smooth as a flywheel working a piston.

She looked up into his blue eyes as if catching God in the middle of a miracle. His face was as open and strong as western light. Hers as complicated as European history. But he had guns. Nobody could touch her now.

"Wait a minute, wait a minute." He was going way too fast for her.

"I thought all you Reds were gun-totin' revolutionaries."

She glanced up. "Socialist." She took the rifle as he held it out to her. "What do I do with it?"

"Hit that can."

She looked at the can. It was a hundred yards away. She hadn't realized they had walked so far.

"I can barely see it."

"You know how to hold it?"

Seeing the consternation in her face, he took the rifle. Slipped off the safety with his thumb. Raised the rifle. WHOOM! It discharged so loudly and suddenly that she felt her face had been slapped. The sound knocked her backward two steps. Maybe there was some kind of wind associated with the discharge. Her hands flew up to protect her face.

She opened her eyes in time to see the can settle down again. Now it lay on its side. A big whiff of dust swirled behind it where the bullet had scuffed.

"Go check out Prince Albert."

Hesitantly, a little scared, she walked over and looked at the can. Prince Albert had a hole right through his mustache, and there was a jagged exit wound on the other side of the can.

"You hit it! The bullet went all the way through the can!"

"Set it up again!" he shouted. "Put some dirt in it!"

She did that and returned to his side. He had the rifle perched on his hip, the barrel up in the air. She looked at it with some interest. As if she were seeing potential beyond her normal scope of things.

"Give me it."

He handed her the rifle, helped her get it settled against her shoulder. She looked really out of kilter and off balance there in a light green dress. He adjusted her. Got her front foot forward and her front elbow under her hand.

WHAM! Surprised she had fired, she looked up from her sights. He looked worried.

"Be careful with that trigger. That bullet'll carry a mile or more. You could kill somebody in Burbank."

She thought about it. They were in Glendale and she could hit somebody in Burbank? She looked at the can. It was still sitting there. There was no dust. "Where did I hit?"

"I don't know. You were high. We might have to leave town."

"Really?"

"Just kidding. Here."

He got around behind her. Settled her in again. Pushed her head down over the rifle so she could see both sights. "Line it up." He squeezed in tighter, his cock against her hip. He had to use mind control over it to keep it down.

"Post in the middle of the blade with the can on top of the post."

"Like this?" The barrel waved around like a diving rod.

WHAM! She looked up and let the heavy rifle swing down. There was some dust off to the right.

"Not bad," Donovan said. He grinned at her. "You almost hit it. That's a hard shot."

He took the rifle and levered another cartridge in. The empty shell came flicking out and he caught it out of the air with his quick right hand and put it in his pocket. He swung the gun up and leveled it and fired. WHAM! He perched the rifle on his hip again.

"You missed it!" she said, laughing out loud.

"Oh?"

Running this time, she picked up the can. Prince Albert had a hole in his neck. The dirt was still in there. It was a mystery to the city girl how all this happened. It seemed impossible. Donovan came up behind her.

"Here." She jumped. The noise, the danger. "Let's try the pistol," he said. They stepped back a bit, and she examined this new piece of curious machinery.

He pulled a latch on the top of the pistol and pushed a button on the side and it broke in two and the barrel swung down. Exposing five holes in the cylinder. He began taking bullets from a box and sliding them into the holes. He left one empty.

"Okay. Smith & Wesson, shoots an S & W .38 cartridge, you put four in and leave the cylinder under the hammer open for safety. Watch."

He pulled back the hammer and swung the revolver up to almost level. BAM! He fired at the can from about 10 yards away. The can lurched to one side. She just looked up at him with a face born again in revelation. She started to go get the can, but he stopped her and told her about never going out in front of a shooter, and he opened the cylinder again and then said to go ahead.

She found another hole in Prince Albert. Who was pretty shot up and unrecognizable. "Looks more like the Archduke Ferdinand," she said. "That's the one—"

"I know who it is," he said.

She resettled the can. Stepped back. He handed her the pistol. "Same idea. Line up your sights. Target on top of the sights."

BAM! The can fell right over.

"Got him," Donovan said. Grinning big.

"I did it!" Wanda shouted. She kept her stance. Pulled the hammer back. BAM! The can skidded along the ground, its dirt emptied out. The prince was dead for sure.

She ran after the can, waving the gun wildly. Picked up the can and waved it around. How could she be this excited? She spun on her heels, arms signaling touchdown. But Donovan was suddenly behind her, grabbing the dancing pistol and holding it up high.

"You could kill somebody. You remember you still have a shell in there?"

"The prince is dead," she said. Oh, she had a thought process going. A very heightened thought process. "From an uprising by the proletariat. Poor Bonny Prince Albert."

On the drive downtown they took back routes through Glendale and Chinatown at dusk. They were in a hurry to catch the show. They both loved the flickers, he the Dead End Kids' crazy antics and she "Love Is On the Air" kind of romances with Ronald Reagan. They parked on a back street and ran all the way to the Million Dollar Theater on Broadway.

"The Adventures of Robin Hood" was playing, and they got in just as Errol Flynn showed up, racing into Sherwood Forest on his horse. She took his hand and pulled it over onto her leg. Just rested it there. They ate snacks one after the other.

He liked the sword fighting and when Robin put arrows in Sir Guy's henchmen's chests. She liked it when Olivia de Havilland as Maid Marion came in and gave with the big brown eyes. He guffawed as the merry men commenced swinging on vines. She poked her tongue out at the cowardly Sheriff of Nottingham. But got quiet every time Robin talked of injustice and protecting women and children from the ravages of the usurpers. As Robin wrapped up the castle with some rip snorting good swordplay, Donovan was already out of his seat and easing toward the exit.

She stood watching the credits. Transfixed. He had to go back for her.

"You ready?"

"That's what I want to do."

"What?" He looked at the screen. People's names scrolled down. Everybody else in the theater had left, and a kid in a uniform came in and starting picking up trash.

"Strike a blow for mankind."

"It's just a movie."

"Is it? You mean we don't believe in Robin Hood?"

He didn't really have an answer for that. "I guess it's not just a movie," he finally said. Just for her.

"There, see?" She took his hand.

This time their search for a cozy spot had a more serious tone to it. They drove to her place, but her Aimee Semple-worshipping landlord was standing out front watering the dirt in the dead of night. They drove right on by.

"Pauline would be home anyway," Wanda said. She was driving again, even though her hands were now shaking. She was driving fast.

"Joseph too."

They headed for Mary's café. They caught her just turning the lights off. When they banged on the door the lights came back on.

"We just want to get a soda pop," Wanda pleaded.

"Lock up when you're finished, kids. I'm going to bed."

Mary trudged back into the kitchen and upstairs. As soon as her footsteps had settled, the two turned out the lights and drew sodas from the fountain and retired to the darkest corner booth. It had a circular seat. They scooted in, arms locked around each other. Not saying a thing.

Soon she was drinking from his soda and he from hers. Then they kissed the strawberry and root beer sweetness from each other's lips. Then they lay back, half curled on the seat. Then he unbuttoned her blouse. Something in her, something in him, was going nuts, as if their internal clocks had raced ahead of the clock clanking away on the wall.

"That feels so good," she said as he pushed her soft little brassiere up over her soft little breasts. When she raised her arms he stopped dead. She was shaved clean as a newborn in her armpits. He'd heard of this, but it was raw to see.

She started on his shirt. Impatient and rough. A button flew off and rolled down the aisle. A three hundred pound block of ice couldn't break that button free, but she did. Nobody even looked for it.

Skirt and trousers were a problem in the booth. They slid out and stripped in front of each other so fast they seemed to be jitterbugging. Headlights from cars on the street skipped across them enticingly. They looked and looked at each other, so serious with faces all askew, scanning everything.

Kneeling, she did something to him that he had never even heard of. Then he laid her down gently on the seat and did something to her that she had wanted for months. Then they worked really really hard for a short while. Then he suddenly pulled out and a heated stickiness spread across her belly and he apologized and clawed a handful of napkins from a dispenser and wiped at her until she was clean.

Then they lay back exhausted and listened to Mary again squeaking the floorboards above them. They grabbed their clothes when they heard her open the door at the top of the stairs. "Did you kids get your pop?" the woman yelled.

"I got mine!" Wanda yelled back. Giggling into her hand.

"Me too! Go to bed, Mary!" Donovan yelled. He had to bury his head in her breasts to keep from laughing out loud.

"Ga night!"

"Ga night!"

"I better get dressed," Wanda said.

"Forget it," he said. He got up above her again and the headlights flashed on his black eye and crazy hair. He looked like a murderer with a big smile. They threw their clothes aside and repeated everything just to make sure they had it down right.

THE NIGHT THEY HAD REVELATIONS

Three months later. They woke in the dark at the same time every morning in the double, and so they did today. After two solid months of living together, she still couldn't sleep past four o'clock. Sometimes she woke at three just to have a piece of him before he went out on his route. The sound of him stropping his straight razor in the bathroom would act like an alarm clock, and sometimes she would catch him with shaving cream still on his face and make a mess of it all over the sheets. After he left she lay in bed until sunup, thinking too hard, whereupon she fell asleep again and woke up just in time to get to work late.

She was so marinated in sex that she could barely wait to get home. She was so proud of herself. The hell with thwarting Hitler, she loved the hell out of this wild Okie gunslinger.

Donovan was exhausted. But he couldn't be happier with the Jews. He was a man who had always worked and played hard, but this was the first time it seemed to be carrying him where he wanted to go and loved to be. He started up the Model A and clattered down Melrose as fast as the low-geared truck would go for a mile and picked up Joseph, who was standing on the side of the road in front of the house where he rented a room. Shivering in the chilly air.

"Morning."

"Yup."

They didn't have a lot to say to each other. At the plant Joseph bundled up in the corner of the truck working the morning red out of his eyes as the loaders rocked the truck dropping in the three hundreds. They drove to their route a little dispirited.

Mrs. McCants still yelled for Donovan to come in as she worked to make breakfast in the kitchen. But her robe didn't fly open anymore. She could sense that the ice man wasn't titillated or fascinated the way he used to be. "He probably found himself a girlfriend," she would tell her little boy after the ice man left.

At Rucker's place Joseph loaded him up with a three hundred, and the oil man was waiting at the head of the stairs. Ready to go to work but needing his morning diversion.

"Hey, Bananas! How's that Jew girlfriend?" Rucker said as the ice man plodded uphill, one step at a time. Donovan's legs seemed leaden. He stopped alongside anyway.

"What do you know about my girl, Rucker?"

He glared at the man in a way that anybody who knew him or knew of him would take as potentially harmful. Rucker, though, seemed to have no sense of self-preservation. Besides, he had his man Whitaker, who stood waiting beside the muttering black and green Pierce-Arrow, making a little drawing on a pad of paper and looking up occasionally.

"Oh, I have my ways. I know a lot about your life. Bedding down with the Jews, flirting with the union, loving up the niggers. No offense to you, of course."

Donovan was about to put down the three hundred. He would risk the gun, but he realized he would never get the block up again. He decided to deliver the ice and come back and see what this was about. He went around to the kitchen and got the block in the box. It had a bulge of ice at one end, and the door of the box wouldn't close. Donovan swiftly took his big ice pick from its holster. Chipped twice at a crucial fault line in the block and lifted away the bad corner.

He shoved the block all the way in and closed the door and put the excised corner in the sink. Lilly came in and said good morning and gave him a ripe peach. For the twentieth time he wondered what a good woman like this saw in Rucker. A grifter with a con man's heart and a coward's mouth.

"Donovan, we won't need ice the next time. We're going out of town for a couple days," she said.

By the time he got around to the stairs again, Rucker was getting in his car, Whitaker holding the door open for him. Whitaker went around to the driver's seat. The big car roared down the driveway. Rucker waved farewell out the window.

"Son of a bitch," Donovan muttered before he got the other three hundred.

"I dislike that mug very damn much," he said to Joseph, who was in

the driver's seat and waiting when he got back the second time. Donovan
shed his leathers, plopped into his seat and got a banana from his stash
on the floor.

"He's not so bad," Joseph said.

Donovan looked surprised. "Where you know old Rucker from?"

"Oh, I don't know. I've seen him around."

His big brother peeled a banana and watched him maneuver on the
hilly street. Park in front of the next delivery. "Your turn," Donovan said,
and Joseph got out and tonged a fifty and lugged it into an old craftsman
house with a gull-wing porch. When he came back, Donovan was still
looking at him.

As the ice truck started down the hill a Helms Bakery truck came inching up the incline. At the wheel was a man Donovan thought he had seen
before. As he got closer, he could see that it was the black man from Club
Alabam, the one he had saved from Whitaker's crew. The man raised his
cap in deference as he went by.

"What you saying hi to these people for?" Joseph said.

Donovan didn't even answer. He had no use for Joseph at the moment.
The more his brother said he shouldn't, the more he liked the black folk.
That was the way his mind worked. Since he had installed Wanda in the
double, and Joseph had left in disgust, their relations had become a little
stilted. He didn't see him at night anymore.

"You heard from Mama lately?" he asked.

Joseph reached behind the seat and retrieved an envelope. Donovan
could tell by the distinctive cursive lettering, huge and open and childlike,
that it was one of their mother's. He took it but didn't open it.

"What does she say?"

"Read it."

"I'll get car-sick."

"That skunk's living in California. He thinks he's going to team up
with us, and Mama's warning us to keep our distance."

Donovan had known for months that his father was in Los Angeles
County. He had talked to him on the phone. He had a notion that he, the
eldest brother, might be the one to reconcile this family. But really, he
knew better. Three other brothers were scattered all over the country and
didn't want to see the mother. Joseph and two younger sisters still at home
didn't want to have anything to do with the father.

"He's your father."

"Yeah, and she's your mother." A scolding tone that Joseph used more and more. He had the accelerator down on the Model A, and she was coming off the hill pretty fast anyway.

"Better watch the road here," Donovan said, grabbing hold of the door as his brother barely slowed through the stop sign and whirled right onto Hyperion. Swerving and narrowly avoiding a smashup with a big Cadillac full of swells.

"Goddamn!" Donovan yelled. By then the Cadillac had receded into the distance. Two of the people in there leaned out the windows and yelled back at him, holding onto their hats. When Joseph stopped at his apartment and got out, Donovan scooted over to take the wheel. Ground the floor shifter into gear.

"Wasn't our fault they broke up," he said to Joseph, who stood there just off the road waiting for him to go. "We ain't the only ones."

"Doesn't make it right."

"You beat yourself up over it, all you'll get is beat up," Donovan said as he let the clutch out easy. "You know what Will Rogers said, 'I never met a man I didn't like.'"

"Yeah? What about Rucker? You don't like him."

"Hell with Rucker."

As he went down Melrose he again looked for stars among the people pouring out of the Raleigh and Paramount lots. He fancied he would see Errol Flynn, maybe in that funny green Robin Hood hat with the feather sticking out of it. Then he remembered that he was under contract to Warner Brothers, and anyway, he would come out hidden in a chauffeured car if he came out at all.

Wanda came baby-stepping out to greet him as she always did. She already had her houserobe on. A cup of coffee in hand.

"Hi."

"Hullo, there."

They couldn't restrain themselves from banging into each other with a hug. The couple demonstrated their relationship all over the neighborhood. Everybody on the street knew everything about them already. They were just as transparent as the old married couple farther up the block who beat each other and screamed out of windows at bedtime.

As usual, once inside, they kissed and fondled for a minute, getting a read on the direction their love might take in the next few minutes and hours and days. She had his heavy wool shirt off and was lifting his undershirt over his head. He sagged onto her, play-acting exhaustion.

She laughed. "Okay, get yourself a beer and I'll meet you out back."

He took two bottles of beer from the ice box and went out the back door. They had two old spring chairs back there on the accidental lawn. The sun was still up over the back fence, so he moved the chairs under the shade of the big oak. He loved to sit in that dense shade and listen to birds and squirrels sifting around for food in its droughty leaves.

Wanda came out with a plate piled high with hunks of cheese and bread and cut-up carrots. She set it on the grass beside him, but he grabbed bread and cheese before it got to the ground.

"Thanks, babe. How'd it go for you today?"

"We picketed old Jacobs' shop. It was very exciting, we had forty women out there with placards. The police came."

"You convince 'em to go union?"

"We got them to talk about it. And I think we've got a majority, if it comes to a vote."

"I'm gonna cook you some steak on the grill tonight." He took bread and cheese and disappeared it.

"You're tired."

"Not as tired as I will be when I get finished with you."

She got out of her chair and came over and sat in his lap. The steel of the chair groaned. She kissed his chewing lips, which held still for a second so she could hit them.

Leaning back, Wanda looked him over. This was about the only thing in the world that could make him uncomfortable. Sector by sector, she looked over his face, which she now found so compelling. His mouth and nose were too big, but somehow when he smiled, as he did now with a big goofy grin, everything came into proportion.

"What are you lookin' at?"

"Big old you."

"Quit it, then. I want to look at you."

"You can look all you want."

He looked and looked, then ate some more hunks.

"I'm goin' out tonight," he said.

"You're what?"

Now she really leaned back and examined him.

"I don't have to explain it. Sometimes I need to go out by myself, is all."

He picked up the second of the beer bottles he had brought out. He tipped it up and drained about half of it. He had a stubborn Daley set to his face. He didn't get it often. When he was drunk. And when he wanted his way. He was a completely agreeable sort most of the time.

She struggled up off his lap and went into the house. He finished the beer and got up and went into the house. He got steaks out and grilled them over a little firepit he had created in the back yard. He used wood that had fallen off the oak tree, and when it burned down to coals he toasted his steak and let hers go another ten minutes.

He fished the potatoes out of the coals. They were black and streaked with ashes. Three of them. He put two of them on one plate with the bloody steak, one on another.

They sat outside and ate, the spring chairs bouncing as they cut at the steaks. He had hacked off chunks of butter and put them on the sliced potatoes, and there were peeled carrots too and a big hunk of lettuce on each plate. She wouldn't look at him.

"I like to make up a plate for you," he said softly.

She said nothing.

After they ate it was dark. He tried to say something to her, but she didn't want to talk and went into the living room. He understood how she felt and was sorry about it.

She read at her stacks of books for a while. He picked up a book and tried to read it. But his mind scrambled back and forth from the book about a guerrilla waiting to blow up a bridge in Spain. The guerrilla's thoughts weren't as compelling as his own.

As she read, skipping from book to book to check facts and the continuity of ideas, a peculiarity of hers, still ignoring him, he put down his novel and went into the bedroom and went to sleep. At half-past midnight he woke up, and she was asleep beside him, still dressed. Lights still on. A book by Karl Marx was open beside her and one by Jean Jacques Rousseau lay as if it had flopped closed.

He carefully got out of bed. He pulled a little cloth bag out from under some old clothes in the closet and turned off the lights and left the house. Drove away as quietly as he could in the ice truck.

He parked down on Hyperion and took out the little bag. Removing a long-sleeve black shirt from it, he changed into it. He took out the Smith & Wesson and checked the loads and put it in his belt.

There was something else in the bag, and he folded it and carried it in his hand. He slowly walked up the hill in the darkness that was always umbrellaed by the lights of the city, past all the houses he had iced that morning.

Tired when he first drug himself out of the truck, he oddly enough felt

more and more energetic as he topped the hill. He was a young man working a physical job for long hours, but a jolt of energy came into him like
a shot of whiskey.

Walking just past Rucker's drive, he slipped off the street and into the
landscaping trees. Up the steep-sloped lawn, manicured in the moonlight.
He did something with the folded-up thing, ducking his head to do it.

At the house he sat on the front porch a minute and rested.

When he lifted his head and looked out on the yard in the moonlight
he had on a black mask, like the one the Lone Ranger wore in the picture
shows. It looked hand-fashioned. He seemed a movie actor who had just
come off the set for a breather.

When he got up off the porch he went right to the front door. The ice
pick appeared in his hand. He inserted the tip into the lock of the door and
messed with it until he could turn the knob.

In the living room he quickly pulled the door shut behind him but left
it unlatched. He stood there for a long time. Listening. After a while there
was a woman's cough from way back in the silence of the house.

Slowly he began to ease to the center of the house. He made no sound,
his breathing was easy. As if he had done this before.

It took him a while to ease across the huge living room. The Ruckers
had Victorian tastes. Curvilinear couches and love seats littered the room,
and huge paintings of earls and lords hung on the walls behind them.
Thick rugs of dense design silenced his deliberate footfalls.

Across the dining room and its creaky wood floor. Through the kitch-
en, where he acknowledged the huge ice box he cussed every other day of
the week. Into a hallway.

There was a den off the hall. The masked man slipped into it. Again
stood still for a minute. Two. He went to a huge desk with an ornate lamp
and pictures in frames sitting on it.

Donovan opened a drawer of the desk. Bent low in the dark to look
into it.

Closed it. Tried to open another and finally got it with his lockpick.
Looked through it by bending close and shuffling papers.

He removed something from that drawer. Impossible to see what it
was in the darkness, which was dampened only by lazy moonlight sifted
through gauzy curtains on a huge window.

Out of the den now. Back into the hallway. Which creaked, but only
casually. Like a thin branch scritching the siding of a house in the wind.
Again he stood silently for a minute. Anyone watching him would have

acquired night vision by now. Would have seen that the eyes behind the mask peered unblinking at a door at the end of the hall.

He knew he shouldn't, but he moved toward that door. When the floor scritched he stopped and rested for some moments.

A two-inch opening in that bedroom door drew his hand. He slipped his hand in and slowly pushed the door inward, an inch at a time. The door was absolutely silent on its hinges.

Coughing suddenly erupted from the room. Donovan shoved the door inward using the coughs to mask any sound and sifted one foot into the bedroom and then the rest of his body.

Standing in the half-open door, he looked at a figure tossing on the huge bed. A woman. He adjusted his head so both eyes could focus. The woman lay half-naked on the sheets, twisting now in an attempt to get back to sleep. When she turned he could see half of her face. It was Millie the maid who lay on the huge master bed.

Her head snapped to. She sat upright as if prodded and looked, alerted by a sound, at the half-open door.

It was empty.

"Mr. Rucker?" she said softly. She covered her naked breasts with one arm and leaped out of the bed. Running for the door. Running down the hall. Into another bedroom at the far end. She slammed that door behind her.

On the front porch Donovan sat breathing deep. As he sat he swung his legs off the porch like a boy in a swing. There was a nonchalance to him, as he took off his mask and folded it, and he looked up at the moon in the clear sky with no more care than a little boy in a swing.

He pushed himself off the porch and hustled down the sloped lawn to the street. Emerging from the landscaping, he looked both ways down the black asphalt. He walked down the middle of the street like a lord in his own garden and descended the hill.

When he parked the ice truck at home he shut off the motor and coasted the last few yards. He was quiet going in the door of the house and quick to bed.

Wanda lay apparently just as he had left her. Distinct on white sheets in near darkness. He put the cloth bag in the closet. As he lifted his shirt over his head he emerged to see her sitting up. Looking at him.

"Tell me about it, why don't you." Her voice had a note of resignation. Of determination to get this over with. "See, I've gone through this before. Going out late. Coming in early. All that stuff."

"No, babe. It's not –"

"If that's it, let's just get it over with now." Amazingly calm, she got up and switched on the light and strode to the closet. Swiped the clothes aside and plucked the cloth bag off the floor in the corner. She spun around and turned it upside down over the bed.

The revolver bounced across the bed. Then the mask floated out. Along with a folded wad of ten dollar bills with a rubber band around them.

Her eyes could not interpret this evidence. Slowly she picked up the mask. Unfolded it. Placed it across her cheekbones. When the eyes looked at him they seemed to be grasping at this page of his storyline.

"I do it once a month or so," he said, standing there with his shirt off, a slab of a man whose skin was yellow under the light bulb. "I stopped it after I met you. I'll quit it for good if you want me to."

She put on the mask and settled it in place. She took the rubber band off the bills and unfolded them. She counted them. Slowly.

"There's eight hundred dollars here."

She picked up the pistol. She had the pistol in one hand and the money in the other and of course the mask on her face. He had the distinct feeling she was going to ask for his black shirt next.

"It's from Charles Rucker. It's oil scam money. It's been got illegal, is the way I look at it."

"Are you crazy?" she asked him. But in a contemplative, not an accusatory, way.

Wanda threw the gun on the bed, the money on the bed, where it spread wide. She took his arm and pulled him into the living room. She led him to the couch in the dark and sat him down and sat beside him. She still had the mask on.

"How long have you been doing this?"

"I see these people on my route. They're living high. They're the swells, fat on oil, and it ain't all gotten in the right way. It's only oil people."

She just looked at him. In the dark he could barely see her eyes, because the gold was gone and they seemed black and unreachable. And then there was the mask to contend with. She seemed to like it, the mask.

"See, my parents' ranch in Oklahoma had oil under it. And the bank beat them out of it because of the dust bowl. And went in with some wild-catters and now Mama and Father are broke up and suckin' hind tit. While the oil men, hell, they're living in grand style. So every time I see one of these big shots rolling in it, I like to take a hand."

This was more than he had said all day. In the dark her hand sneaked over and closed on his. Patted it as she thought about all this. Out the window to the side yard the limbs of trees were frozen still by moonlight. Like a photograph not properly developed.

"This is truly a revelation to me. What do you think you are, Robin Hood?"

"No. I got the idea from the Zorro pictures."

"Zorro? Zorro! Oh my god. You are simple. Do you think you're Zorro, then?"

"Not him, neither. Just the mask, is all."

"Well maybe you are. Maybe you are Zorro. Robin Hood. It's an idea that's taken hold, hasn't it. It's that kind of era."

Now he didn't say anything. He could have pointed out that he wasn't giving the money to the poor. He could have explained that this hatred was something he didn't like to live with. He could have tried to get her to understand that he might even shoot somebody if they caught him. If it was the right person who caught him. He might have told her that a man who came out of the Dust Bowl with nothing on his back but a dusty coat might do most anything under duress.

He might have told her that a little heart-shaped watch that he had given her, on a gold chain that made it a nice necklace, and told her that he had bought at Sears & Roebuck, had been pilfered from one of those houses.

But he didn't tell her any of that. Truthfully, he felt a little ashamed of himself. She wore the necklace all the time now, and he just couldn't tell her how bad he had been in this regard.

"You're giving them the razz," she said. "The oil grifters."

"You might say."

"We'll give that money to a good cause. A worker's fund or orphanage."

"I was saving for a car."

"You want to ride in a car bought from ill-gotten gains? Bought from the money of people duped by false advertising and exaggerated claims that they would get rich?"

He thought about it a while. "Yeah." He'd never thought of it that way before. It was the night they both were having revelations.

"I'm also saving for a mine."

She took off the mask so she could see him better. And he could see her better. "Mine? What kind of mine?"

"Gold mine. Little claim I staked when I was in Arizona. Before I came here. It's just waiting down there for me to develop it. Small operation, one or two people could do it just fine. It's assayed out, I just need a grub-stake to get it going."

She thought about it a while. Shrugged her shoulders.

"Can we give some to the poor?"

"Sure."

"Okay, then. What kind of car you want?"

HITLER AND THE BOYS

Joseph walked into the big hall and liked what he saw. It was all very orderly and organized. A row of brown shirts stood on stage, their ties crisp and the knots all on the same level as if the men had been selected solely by height. Their hair combed to one side across their foreheads. The hall was full of seated citizens of the Republic. Up high above the stage on one side was a swastika made out of wood, painted red and mounted on the wall by a couple of nails.

On the other side was a portrait of Adolph Hitler. Joseph thought he looked very chancellorish and inspiring in his uniform.

Taking a handbill from one of the two uniformed guards at the door, Joseph found a seat in the back of the Deutsches Haus hall. He was just in time. The hall had filled, and a man he recognized as a leading business-man of Los Angeles strode to the front of the room as if leading his people out of slavery. He spoke so loudly he didn't even need the microphone that was there for him. He stood to one side of it.

"The time has come to show we are real Americans. No more Jews. No more Africans. No more of these brown masses swarming from the southern border."

Wild applause. Joseph applauded and relaxed. He exchanged a glance with the man next to him. A very white man who applauded so hard the sound almost hurt his ears. He looked at Joseph as if asking to be ap-plauded for applauding so hard.

"Fight this overthrow by the murky races!" the speaker said, stepping right and left in tall boots his trousers were tucked into. He had a natural-born speaker's talent. "Support immigration laws! Buy gentile! Employ gentile! Vote gentile! Boycott the movies, which are rife with Jewish pro-paganda! Hollywood is the Sodom and Gomorrah where Jewry controls vice, dope and gambling! The very evils of our enlightened society. It's all gone to communists and Jews, and believe me. They are one and the same thing. There will never be a mixed-breed Los Angeles if I have any say about it!"

After the speech there was a little marching drill by the brown shirts, who gave the funny stiff-armed salute to Hitler's image at the end. Everybody in the audience stood and gave it, too.

Joseph did too. He didn't care. It felt kind of good. Heart-warming, you might say. His whole body felt full of ideas and of the belonging to ideas.

Another speaker came to the podium and talked about the coming war in Europe. "Notify your government representatives that you want America to stay out of this war!" that speaker shouted. "Let old Hitler and the boys handle it!" Joseph didn't pay much attention to him. He wasn't interested in Europe, and the speech was too long.

Finally there was a prayer to end the meeting. Everybody said amen and gave each other self-satisfied smiles and milled around eating homemade cookies and drinking punch off a side table. Refreshments were provided by the Bund Auxiliary, according to a little sign next to the punch bowl. Joseph nodded to everybody and walked by the desserts but was too nervous to take anything. He was a little more sunburned in the face and shy than everybody else.

He was about to leave, but a man came up to him. "Welcome," the man said and stuck out a beefy hand. "I'm Charles Rucker."

"I recognize you."

"You and your brother deliver the ice."

"Yessir. Glad to meet you."

"Did you hear about that nigger quarterback over in Pasadena?"

"Jackie Robinson. All over the sports pages."

"They shouldn't allow it. That deprives a good white boy a chance to play."

"Right, right," Joseph said.

Rucker smiled big, dressed in a pinstripe suit. He liked sounding people out and forcing them to come down on one side or the other. He put one of his trademark cigars in his mouth. Lit it with a wooden match. Sucked and sucked. Finally it caught and made a little popping noise.

"And what about this Jewess old Bananas is running around with?"

"Bananas?"

"Your brother. That's what I call him. Eating those bananas."

"Oh yeah, he eats five or six of them a day."

Joseph moved aside to let the uniformed brown shirts march out the door. Most of them were of high school age. Tall and thin and handsome and black-haired, most of them. There were a couple of older men, too. Joseph wondered for a moment why they weren't blond.

"He living with that woman?"

"Yeah, he is, sad to say."

"That's pitiful, a man like him can't get any kind of quim but a Jew."

"Donovan? He can get him any woman he wants. He's had plenty."

"He has? Hootchie man, is he?"

Joseph just looked at him. As if he didn't understand the concept.

"You don't…want him…to be a bad example," Rucker said between sucks on the big rolled Cuban. "To our youth."

Joseph didn't know quite what to say to the man. Maybe he was awestruck that such a figure would notice him. So Rucker went on.

"You being a good supporter of the American fuehrer, I'm going to tell you a little secret. You know that Long Beach is loaded with oil, don't you. Your name is Joseph, isn't it?"

Joseph nodded. "Yessir. I heard that."

"My company, Beach Oil Management, is developing one of those fields. Big project. There's so much oil down there it's seeping into people's houses. Just coming through the floorboards."

"No fooling."

"Nope. Now some people look down on the Okies. Try to stop them at the borders, even. I am not one of those people. I believe in providing every man an opportunity to better himself. It's America's way. Bootstraps. Pull 'em up." He sucked hard at the recalcitrant weed.

Rucker paused to see how this information was being received. This ice man seemed a little backward. Sometimes they made the best troopers, though. People with a quiet, hidden determination to right the world.

"I fully expect a car to end up in a tar pit, just like the elephants out there in La Brea. Just sink out of sight in crude oil. Now here's what I'm doing. I'm cutting in a few of the choicest people here…"

He swept his arm around at the crowd at the German American Bund meeting. There were probably two hundred in the room, not counting the marching brown shirts. They were out in the hall practicing their salutes and yelling Heil! Heil! in unison.

"…and we're selling them shares. Selectively. There's just not room for everybody to get in. Can't everybody be rich. It's not the way it's done. You familiar with common stock?"

"Not so much."

"This is very much the same. We're selling shares in the oil field. Four bits a share. Chance to get in on the ground floor. See the skyscraper go up. We're already paying back cash dividends and high interest rates to the early investors. There's risk, oh yes, but there will be substantial bonuses at the end, oh yes indeedy. Now I've got industrialists and politicians begging me for shares, but I'm making special offers to friends of the fuehrer."

"I'll pay some thought to it. Thank you, Mr. Rucker."

"Next time you come by the house, come on up. Old Bananas, he's the only one can carry them three hundreds, isn't he."

"Only one I know of."

"That brother of yours, he needs to get his head straightened."

A man in a hundred dollar suit and ten dollar slicked-back hair came over. Inserted himself between them and addressed Rucker. He cut red-necked Joseph right out.

"Brother Rucker. How are you this fine morning?"

"Good, good. What are you up to, Preacherman?"

"Excellent. I wanted to tell you how much I enjoy the advertisements for that stock offering. 'Put your money where your oil is. This is such a big gamble, it's a cinch.'"

"We've got a slick agency handling that. They really put a hammer lock on a man's thinking."

"I hope you don't forget the Kingdom Temple when you're counting your millions. You can't go wrong buying a few prayers, can you?"

Joseph took the opportunity to sneak toward the door. He came for the communal feeling and the patriotic fervor, not the glad-handing that occurred later. He wanted to get away from the Kingdom Temple man, who last time had hounded him so unmercifully that Joseph finally dug in his wallet and gave him a dollar. Just handed him a whole dollar.

"Come see us!" Rucker yelled at Joseph as he neared the door.

"Who's that little feller?" this Preacherman asked.

"Nobody," Rucker said, turning so Joseph wouldn't even see his mouth move. "Goddamn Okie."

On the street by the parking lot, where Joseph had to go to catch the bus, Whitaker stood conversing with a couple of mugs. He had one foot up on the bumper of the Pierce-Arrow as if it belonged to him. Not likely. This was the Metropolitan Town Brougham, every inch gleaming. When Joseph went by, they shut up and turned to watch him go. There wasn't a sympathetic eye in the crowd.

The next morning, Joseph and Donovan were both worn out. They took to their route like dogged old hunch-shouldered horses, which they would have seen pulling ice wagons up these very streets not fifteen years ago. That's how fast the automobile had come in. But being motorized didn't seem to help the mood of the brothers' day.

Skidding two blocks of ice out onto the tailgate about eleven o'clock, they looked exhausted. They hauled ice into houses on opposite sides of the street and got in and moved the truck up to a vacant lot for an early lunch. It was grassy where they ate, and there was shade under the trees overhanging from the next yard.

The Helms Bakery truck came up the hill, and Donovan flagged the driver down. The big truck rolled to a stop, smelling like a morning kitchen. A familiar black man was driving.

"Mornin'," Donovan said. Grinning at the Helms uniform. The sparkling white shirt and purple bow tie looked funny on the little black man.

"Mornin'." The delivery man killed the motor and sat looking at him. "My real name's Boniface Fish."

"I beg yours?" Donovan was taken aback. He squared his head around so he could see the man better. Oh yes, it was coming back to him.

"At the club that night. You called me Melvin. I know it was just a play-act, but I wanted you to know. You can call me Bony, everybody does."

"All right, Bony." He reached up and shook the black man's hand. He didn't know why. He didn't care about him one bit. "What ya got in day-old?"

"We got cakes and donuts left over." The man just stared down at Donovan as if he didn't know what to make of him. The ice man glanced over at Joseph lying in the shade chewing his lunch.

"Gimme one a them applesauce cakes. I love them things."

The black man named Bony went into the back of his truck. He was so little, the truck didn't even move as he walked around in it. He came out with a rectangular cake wrapped in a paper sack. He handed it to Donovan, who fished a dime out of his pocket and held it up.

Bony just looked at the dime. Then looked at Donovan.

"You go on ahead," he said.

"Say what?"

"You did something for me, I don't know why you did it."

"That night? Aw, ferget it." Again he proffered the dime. He knew what day-old cost, he bought it all the time. "I don't want your accounts to be off."

The black man just studied him. There was no way in hell he would ever take a dime from this man. He would get down out of this truck and fight him before he would take his money. He studied him because there was a puzzle in that Okie face, and he couldn't figure it out.

"Bony Fish, that's a hell of a name," Donovan finally said. He laughed right out loud. But the black man could see what kind of a laugh it was. Wasn't like the other laughs he got along this street.

"It's something, isn't it?" He smiled, his teeth the yellow-white of old fish bones exposed to the air on a beach.

Finally Donovan put the dime back in his pocket. Stepped back from the truck. The black man was still looking at him as if he had a fly on his nose. The man finally tore himself away. He started up the truck, put it in gear and drove away. Shaking his head.

Joseph looked to be asleep in the shade, but when his brother came over he said, "I don't know why you talk to them people. They're taking up good American jobs."

"Ain't they Americans too?" Donovan said through a mouthful.

"Huh! Rucker says we need to weed out the inferior races."

Donovan broke the applesauce cake in half, examined them carefully and handed the small half minus the mouthful to his brother. "Where do you talk to old Rucker?"

"Down at the Bund hall."

"That Nazi bunch? You crazy? That old Hitler is gonna be killin' people pretty soon." Donovan sounded more irate than he was. Who even thought about such stuff? What happened in Europe was about as interesting as what happened in China. He was just remembering what Wanda had told him. "Probably already is."

"You got to weed out the inferior races. Coons, kikes, wops, idjits. Get all the greasers and chinks out, too."

Donovan collapsed onto the grass beside him. Chewing cake thoughtfully.

"Yeah. And Indians."

"What's that supposed to mean?" This got Joseph's attention.

"You do recall that your mother is one-quarter Choctaw."

"Yeah, so?"

"So that means you'd get weeded out too."

"I don't think that little bit would matter."

"Ha." That's all Donovan could say. He had listened to Wanda discuss international politics and race for weeks, but she had mostly been discussing with herself. He couldn't get his mind around this chaff well enough to talk about it. He was lucky to have come up with the Indian argument. He remembered how even though half the people in Oklahoma had Indian blood, that didn't stop three-quarters of them from back-biting Choctaws and Cherokees and Chickasaws.

"You know what else," he remembered. "We probably got some slave blood in us. Them old Choctaws did a lot of mixing out there in them woodsheds."

"Oh, pshaw," Joseph said. His mouth hung open in shock, a chaw of applesauce cake clogged in there. His big brother only said it to watch him sputter. "That woman's a saint. I don't know how you can talk about her that way." Joseph got to his feet as if ready to fight.

"I didn't say a thing. Only that old Hitler would weed you too, boy, and your mama with you."

This wasn't any kind of racial consciousness or social idealism on Donovan's part. It was more a determination to resist his little brother's ideas. The same reason he helped out that Marvin or Boniface or whatever that black man's name was. Just to be contrary to the dominant opinion. Hell, the Nazis were popular in this town, and many fine citizens were drawn. A recent picnic at one of the parks drew two thousand to hear patriotic speeches. Who cared? Let them waste their time.

In fact, at home that evening, he sat and listened lazily to Wanda rant on about the sorry state of international affairs and the great promise of the New Deal in America, the international brigades in Europe and of course the wonderful developments in Russia with Stalin and his cadres influencing governments all the way to England. Wanda, she liked to help a garment worker move into a nicer apartment, but her larger thoughts were often of the daydream variety.

"It's really not the Charles Ruckers of the world who are the problem," she said as they lay side by side on their old sofa. They both had a bottle of beer going, and her butt was almost off the edge. "We know there will always be people whose main concern is creature comfort at the expense of everyone. The enemy is really people like that bodyguard of his."

"Whitaker?"

"Yes! Yes! He's an ordinary chump like us. The people who side with the swells, who cozy up to them, who slave for them, they're the antagonists. They will destroy any principle to be close to wealth, to have a shot at it for themselves. They come in with feelings for family and nation, and leave with feelings for money and power. This is where the foot soldiers of fascism come from."

They lay there a while, contemplating this. Bored, Donovan began to run his fingers up her stomach to the small swell of her breasts. His hand retraced its route south and she felt the elastic of her underwear give way.

"When are you going to Rucker's again?" she asked.

"We don't deliver there tomorrow."

"I mean at night."

Oh. Now this tickled him. He had thought she would be outraged or offended by his nighttime foray. She was so morally busy. Her head was just rife with ethical issues.

"I oughtn't go back there again. Too dangerous."

Her turn to be tickled. This man, so dangerous in himself, so dominant and committed to his little oil vendetta, had limits? She drew her head back and smiled and stopped his fingers from venturing any lower and took in a suck of beer at the corner of her mouth.

"From the way you described it, there didn't seem to be any problems at all."

"I knew he was gone on a trip."

"Then we just pick a time when he's gone again."

"We? Who's we?"

She smiled. She smiled big. She kissed him lightly with lips tasting of sour hops and sweet insistence. She liked the idea of reversing the flow of money. Sending it from rich to poor. Or maybe it was more to do with the danger of it.

"Me and you. I'm in it too, now."

"Oh no. No you don't. Nowhere near that place." He shot up straight, and she had to catch herself from falling off the couch.

"Ethically speaking, now that I know about it. I'm an accessory. Complicit. I might as well get involved."

"Nope."

He worked himself over her and off the couch, stood up. Forgot even to take that last drink of his beer. He didn't want her in that house, for some reason. He couldn't think what the reason was, but he didn't want her to set foot on that property.

"All right," Wanda said. Standing up and hugging him. "I'll just drive the getaway car."

She was so besotted with love she pulled the clothes off him as delicately and quickly as if changing a baby. He was a baby, wasn't he, with those vengeful ideas of his. She was so tired of the unionists, with their often greedy and hypocritical idealism. This man was so simple and delicious, and dangerous as a cock. She liked ideas like that.

She finally got him wrestled back down onto the couch.

NOTHING'S GOING WRONG

All the days of the ice men were full. But good. They were working. While the rest of the world was in Hard Times. Good was sweat. Good was ache. Good was the rattling of the alarm clock at four in the morning in a world that needed you.

Starting out before daylight as usual, Donovan and Joseph were delayed by a backlog of trucks at the ice plant. There was the puttering chatter of motors in the chilly air as a long line of ice trucks parked and their drivers got out and clanged their doors shut. So the brothers got out too and walked around the ammonia processing facility, where the huge freezing chambers turned out hundreds of three hundred pound blocks daily. The rectangles of ice fell out onto roller conveyors, steaming with frost. Men in ragged coats shunted them to the loading bays with shouts and curses. Like the herdsmen of immovable dumb animals.

There were plants like this all over Los Angeles. Truly there was a future in this bustling, essential business.

An ice route, like a bread or milk route, was a bothersome thing, though. Donovan couldn't sit still over receipts or books. After they loaded up, Joseph took care of the paperwork with a new pencil as Donovan guided the growling truck up and around the Franklin Hills. The older brother had no patience with such things as paper. How much frozen water could he tote. That was his part.

Mrs. McCants didn't answer Donovan's shout, so he barged into the kitchen with a twenty-five dangling from his tongs. He slammed it into the box and was about to leave when he heard her calling him from the back of the house.

"Donovan! Come back here and help me move this furniture!"

He cautiously meandered his way into the rambling house. Suspicious, reluctant. She kept calling to pull him, to guide him. "Where are you?" he yelled softly. "Back here," she shouted back. It was a big house.

He found her naked in a huge bedroom. She faced him, hands on hips, a stern look on her face. He almost leaped backward. Confronted by a big reddish pubic head of hair. Her right foot tapped impatiently.

"You can help me move that bed, can't you?" she asked, a strikingly pretty women all the way down. Her breasts were twice the size of Wanda's, so big it almost seemed they were entire fleshy parts of some larger animal. She was the white of a sidewall tire tinged an Anglo pink in places.

Donovan had a bigger smile on his face than was warranted, given the circumstances. That is, he had immediately determined what course of action he would take, though it didn't wipe away his grin.

"Mrs. McCants, I'm sorry," he said, unable to take his eyes off huge standing nipples aroused by whatever was going on in this woman's head. "You're a married woman, and there's a baby in the house besides."

"Asleep," she said, going to the bed. Crawling across it to her assigned place. "Both of them asleep, the husband and the baby. One with another woman, and the other in its crib."

Donovan stayed in the doorway. His cock was angry at him and hurting, but he stayed put. "Can't do that to my woman," he said. "Can't do that to your husband. See, my mother was unfaithful to my father, and my father was unfaithful to my mother. Who knows who did what first? It was awful hard for the kids. And I determined right up front I wouldn't ever do that to nobody."

Hell. How had that come out of him? He had never spoken of it before. He was ashamed of himself. Still he delayed leaving. The woman looked so good there. So very good there, and there, and there. He could see why picture painters painted so many naked women. He would have too.

Mrs. McCants seemed to understand. Maybe it was the psychology of her own situation that made her appreciate the psychology of his. She got out of bed, a practical woman. She casually slipped on a skirt.

"Thank you for explaining," she said. She picked up a shirt and walked over and kissed him on the cheek and her bare breasts brushed against his arm and she made a little consoling turn, back and forth, to rub against him. "I won't hold it against you, even though I know for a fact that the Invincible Ice man would be a lot more accommodating."

She slipped on her shirt as she watched him go down the hall, finding his way out. She wished she could have him. She'd try again in two days.

Down at the truck, Joseph again asked about Mrs. McCants. He was real interested in her well being, and for a second his brother thought about sending him up there to handle that service call.

"Not home," he said instead. Joseph was just too young to get involved in that situation. The sight of that woman's blush-pink regions would have stopped the young man's heart and tied him up for years. The only things that ruined a susceptible man worse were the horse races and hard liquor. Donovan knew. He had been diverted by all three at various times.

At the top of the hill the ice truck pulled to a stop at the foot of Rucker's driveway. Donovan set the hand brake.

"I'm going up with you," Joseph said. They could see Rucker standing in his pinstripes at the top of the stairs. Checking his watch. Waiting for them.

"What for?"

"Rucker wanted to talk to me about shares."

"In the oil thing?"

"Yep."

Donovan studied his brother's face for a bit.

"All right. Let's go. That might be a good deal for you."

Joseph helped him get the three hundred up. He tried to lift some of the block from behind as Donovan scaled the steps, but he told him that just threw it off balance. They both trudged up toward Rucker and Whitaker, the big brother like a giant followed by an attending elf.

"Bananas!" Rucker yelled as Donovan went by, talking basically to a blue sheet of ice as the delivery man continued on to the house. Joseph stopped in front of Rucker and Whitaker, who looked him over with grins on their faces.

"I want to buy a hundred shares," Joseph said. He pulled a roll of bills from his front pocket. "There's fifty dollars there."

Rucker smiled even bigger. "Now there's a lug doesn't want to lug ice all his life," he said to his man.

"Good investment, oil," Whitaker said, by rote. "Someday crude'll be five dollars a barrel, mark my word."

"Now don't get over-optimistic," Rucker said. "We don't want to scare people off with pie in the sky. Come on in the office, Joseph."

Hauling up the second three hundred, Donovan found Millie in the kitchen. He stopped to talk to her. Fixated by his memory of her in Rucker's bed that night. Wondering even as she chatted about the unseasonably warm weather whether she had any inkling it had been him in the house.

By the time he got back outside, Joseph was standing at the top of the stairs with a piece of paper in hand.

They walked down the stairs together. "Whatcha got there?"

"Certificate for stock. I bought me a hundred shares."

"Hey, Bananas!" Rucker called. "You ought to listen to your kid brother. He's got some sense, that boy does!"

Donovan didn't even look up. In the truck Joseph read the certificate. It looked official, with a 100 in fancy letters in all four corners. Charles R. Rucker's signature big at the bottom right.

"Might as well tear it up now," Donovan said. "You could of got yourself some Standard Oil shares for that. General Motors. Buy a ton of oranges and sell them for twice what you paid and pocket the profit the same day."

Joseph had that set to his mouth. He wasn't even going to reply.

When Donovan told Wanda about it that night, she was so excited. She said they would make sure Joseph got his money back. They would save a hundred dollars out of what they stole.

"We'll sashay in there and get it tonight," Donovan said.

"How do you know Rucker's not home?"

"Millie told me he's going out."

"And who's Millie?"

"His house girl. Maid."

"Look what I had one of the girls make me."

They were sitting at the little painted pine dining room table they had bought second hand. She pulled something black out of her purse. Carefully unfolded it. It was a Zorro mask.

"Aw, shit," Donovan said. He could see the way this was going. "I told you, you're not going in there."

"I know. Just for when I'm driving."

"You can't wear that around town."

"Just for when I'm waiting for you. So nobody recognizes me in the car."

She slipped it on. Goddamn, she looked sexy in it. Black linen, and it had teardrop shaped eye holes with lace trim all around. Miss Princess Zorro.

He leaned right over and gave her a kiss. She responded with that straight-shouldered way she had of moving right into him, taking her shirt off. The sight of her naked except for her mask excited him very greatly. They made love on the couch, then fell asleep draped on each other as if they had melted together there.

He woke her up at one. Wanda squirmed around under the cover he had thrown over her before she bolted upright. Wide-eyed.

"Oh."

Her hands were really shaking by the time they got to the car, and she tapped her fingers on the big wheel constantly. But she insisted on driving the Packard.

"Now look." He leaned over in the darkened car so she understood him perfectly. "I'm not back in ten minutes? You leave. Don't look back. Don't come after me. Don't think twice about it."

"Nothing's going wrong. I can feel it."

"Feel's got nothing to do with it. Another thing. Whether I make it back or not, you drive outta there real nice and slow and normal. Ya got it?"

They wound their way up into Silver Lake and hit Hyperion. After they turned off into the hills he had her drive on by Rucker's place a couple of blocks. The weather had turned cold, and a winter fog had rolled in. It blotted out all light except for a backwash from the Packard's headlights. She turned off the lights and put on her mask.

"Will you take that off, please?" he said.

She did. He got out. He had on his black shirt. His mask was folded in his hand. He closed the car door so quietly the lock barely clicked. He stuck his head in the open window.

"Remember—"

"I know!"

This time he put his mask on as he walked through Rucker's yard. He went to the back door, which exposed him to the guest house in the back. Which was where Whitaker lived. But Donovan didn't want to use the same route twice.

The back door was unlocked. Donovan glanced around. He didn't like that the door was unlocked. But he slipped inside.

Kitchen quiet. Living room quiet. Hallway quiet because he remembered where the creaks in the floor were.

Timing himself, the masked man tiptoed into the den. Approached the desk. He stood listening to the house sleep. Not much moon tonight, so the room was dark. It took a while for the desk to come up in his vision.

It was different. A couple of the family picture frames had been removed. There were a lot of papers scattered on the desk, as if Rucker was in the middle of a project.

Out of curiosity, Donovan stepped close and looked the papers over.

As he squinted against the dark he spotted letters and contracts and indistinct jottings on scratch paper. There was an appointment book with big lettering scrawled in it.

For some reason, Donovan picked up the appointment book. Then he went to the drawer, fiddled it open. As if by magic another wad of ten dollar bills lay in there. Right in the middle of the drawer. Right exactly where the other roll had been.

Donovan grabbed the money. Closed the drawer. Stood listening again in a rush of panic. There was movement deep in the house. Not noise. Movement. He could feel it.

Swiftly he crossed to the big window. Felt for the latch. Turned it. Braced himself and got his hands under the window and raised it quickly and almost silently. Without looking outside he put his feet through the window and draped over and let go and dropped to the ground.

He ran. He ran full speed down the sloped yard even as the lights in the house came on behind him. Every light in the house, and the porch as well. The landscape leaped up at him, half shadow and half light.

A man lurched at him from behind a tree. Donovan hit him so hard with his shoulder that the man never made a sound apart from a huge exhalation of the lungs. The stranger skidded down the lawn on his back ahead of the masked man, who leaped over his unconscious form and hit the street with his legs pumping.

Good, the Packard was running. He could see the tailpipe breathing in the cool air as he ran, and he jerked the passenger door open like a hijacker.

"Gun it," he said to Wanda. "Leave your lights off."

Without even looking at his face she gunned it. The square-back car lurched down the hill, whining like an old dog as it went up through the gears. She had her mask on, and she grabbed and jerked it around so she could see better.

"Turn left here," he said at the bottom of the hill.

"I thought you said we were—"

"Left."

She twirled the wheel left, not stopping at the sign. As soon as they got on Hyperion he looked back. Nobody yet. The street was deserted at this hour.

"Left. Quick," he said.

She twirled left on the first street, between a couple of stores, and rocketed up the shallow slope of a hill.

"Park it." She pulled over to the curb. "Leave the motor on. Pull your hand brake. Take your foot off the foot brake."

She did. Looked at him full of questions. Eyes filling her mask.

"So they don't see the brake lights."

She nodded. They looked through the little rear window back down the street toward the larger thoroughfare. Waiting. My god, they were both panting. Her throat suddenly clotted with emotion and fear. With the realization that something had gone wrong. They sat looking at each other through slits of eyeholes.

Ripping his mask off, he took the Smith & Wesson out of his pocket. He checked the loads and squenched down in the seat until his head was no longer visible from the outside. She took her mask off and did the same.

Down on Hyperion a couple of cars sped by the intersection. Big cars. Their lights and motor noise disappeared quickly. She looked over at him, the whites of her eyes gleaming out of the dark. The Packard putted raggedly. He was sweating so heavily in the cold air that it was dripping off his chin.

"What happened?"

"They were waiting for me."

"Oh shit."

"No longer a problem. Turn it off."

She shut off the engine.

"How much did you get?"

"A wad."

"Damn. What's that?"

She indicated the notebook in his hand. He looked down at it. He had forgotten it. It was still open to the month's jotted appointments and schedules, in a bold, prominent hand.

"I don't know."

They spent an hour parked up the side street and then snuck off toward home the long way around through the back streets of Los Feliz. By the time they pulled into their driveway it was almost daylight.

Donovan immediately got into the ice truck and drove off to work. He stopped and changed into his wool on the way. He was overheated all morning. Inside and out.

THE OIL SCAMMER'S OFFICE

It took two weeks for Wanda to fully appreciate the appointment book. She kept it on the kitchen table and looked at it daily. There was something compelling about it, like the spoor of an exotic and dangerous creature. They were out shopping for their new car when she thought of what it all meant.

"Regular cash shipment. Regular cash shipment. Regular cash shipment," she said loudly, repeating what the appointment book said. "Every Friday, that was the notation."

"What of it?" Donovan asked.

They were standing on the showroom floor of a Buick dealership in the San Fernando Valley looking at a brand new forest-green 1938 66 Series Sport Coupe. It was the one they wanted. So sleek and windswept. They had looked at cars every night over the past week, and that sportster was the cat's meow.

Before Donovan could find out what she meant, a salesman clip-clopped in from the back on the concrete floor. They both turned to greet him. He looked very familiar, a man with severe smallpox scarring to his lower face.

"That Sports Coupe can be had with the self-shifting transmission," the salesman said. "It's a new feature, and a beaut if you're tired of the toil of shifting."

"I like that," Donovan said, peering at the man's deformity. "Don't I know you from someplace?"

"Don't believe so," the man said nervously.

"I've got it," Wanda said. "Did you sell houses out in the San Gabriel?"

The man relaxed. "Yep. Yep. That was me. That tract sold out so fast I had to go to cars. Now this one," he said, turning to the coupe, "is the fighter plane of the lineup. I can tell, you don't want one of those big old bombers."

"That transmission reliable?"

"As winter rain in Seattle. As summer heat in Tucson. Take her for a spin?"

Out on the back roads of The Valley, test-driving it from blacktop to dirt roads between citrus groves, they hummed and hawed over the car. Pretending to not be sure it was this or the new Chevrolet line they were interested in. The salesman sat in the back of the four-seater as first Donovan and then Wanda checked acceleration and braking capacity. They stopped and lifted the trunk, the hood, examining storage space and carburetion.

"She hums nice," Donovan said as they drove on, but when they pulled into the lot, Wanda said, "I like the Chevy better."

"Could of fooled me," the salesman said.

"What'll you take for her?"

"That model goes for twelve hundred. This car right here, it's yours for eleven. Just from me, nobody else, because I like you pair."

They drove off after giving the man nine forty in cash and the Packard. They signed a joint title on it. Old pox-face, as Donovan called him later, asked if they were married. They said no, but they wanted the joint title anyway.

"Regular cash shipment," Wanda said one more time on the way home.

"What's that?"

"It's when they take the cash from Rucker's oil company office and ship it to the bank. Every Friday. End of the week. Probably thousands of dollars in there, knowing old Rucker and that massive ad campaign." She had taken to calling him old Rucker the way Donovan did. It had a slightly pejorative connotation that she liked.

"Yeah, so?"

"Yeah so nothing. I just finally figured out what it meant." She had studied Rucker's appointment book assiduously. Something about it. The thick-ink scrawled notations regarding events and people, the ritualistic rhythm of his scheduling. It was like looking at the scribblings of another species, her own life being so haphazard.

He pulled up beside a newsstand in Hollywood. "I'm gonna get a paper." He walked all the way around the car, admiring it, which was the reason he wanted to buy a paper, just to look at the machine, and when he came back he walked all the way around it again and she was in the driver's seat.

"Let 'er rip," he said.

That was one of the things she liked about him. No male in her family, especially her father, had ever let her take the initiative in anything. She felt like a free woman with this man. He encouraged her to drive and shoot, and he cooked for her too. He seemed to like the adventure of the role reversals. Or he just didn't give a damn.

But as he read the front page of the Times, and as she glanced over and scanned the headlines, her driving grew more erratic. She swerved, almost hit another car, slowed nearly to a stall.

"Whoa," he finally said as she pulled over right there on Highland, barely out of traffic.

"What's wrong?" He looked all around the floorboards to see if something was wrong with the car. She grabbed the paper from him.

The small headline she focused on read NIGHT OF BROKEN GLASS IN GERMANY. She silently scanned the article, ignoring him. When she looked up there were tears in those angry gold eyes, highlighting them, magnifying them. The gold had turned to brass.

"The Nazis have gone berserk. Look." She held out the newspaper to him, disgusted with it. Almost unable to talk.

"I saw that." He hadn't thought much about it, just skimmed the first paragraph before going on to news of the economy. Who cared what went on in Germany?

"Well look, it's a disaster! Thousands of Jews hurt or killed by mobs. You know Hitler put them up to it, don't you! Almost every synagogue in Germany and Austria ruined. Businesses confiscated and given to good Germans. My god!"

She sat behind the wheel looking more and more despondent. Yet even so, more and more irate. Finally she pulled out into traffic again. They weren't far from home, and they got there, to his relief, without damage to the car.

That night he wanted to go out and celebrate the new purchase. Show it off. She didn't. She didn't want to do anything but sulk on the couch. He cooked her dinner, as he usually did. He turned on the radio to listen to Fibber McGee and Molly, their favorite, but it wasn't any fun without her company. He turned it off.

"You want to talk about it?"

He sat across from where she was forted up on the couch, hugging a pillow. Silent way down deep

"You want a beer? Come on, get it off your chest."

He leaned over close to show sympathy. He had learned to do that from previous female experiences requiring tact and subtlety. Which he at one time had had none of. She still wasn't talking. The newspaper lay on the floor, and occasionally she would lean over and read part of it again and huff like a horse disgusted with its day.

"Was anybody you know affected?"

"I want to rob that shipment," she said.

"Rob what?"

"Charles Rucker ships his money to the bank every Friday at two o'clock. I want to steal that money and send it to the relief organizations, the union recruiters, the socialist movement, the shtetls."

"Now wait a minute…"

"You said it yourself. It's dirty money. It's money bilked from people like your stupid brother. Rucker is the one who ought to be bilked."

Listening politely, even calmly, Donovan let out a breath and leaned back away from her. There were some moments of deliberation. His big mouth broke into a pucker as he kissed at the air three times in a row, thinking very hard.

"You know there's a lot more to a stickup than a burglary," he said quietly.

"I would suppose so."

"A lot more."

She glanced up slyly. "You ever done a stickup?" Before she learned of his nighttime forays she had never suspected him capable of such a thing, but she now knew he was. She hoped he didn't take it wrong. She knew Bonnie and Clyde and Pretty Boy Floyd weren't good people, but now she could understand where they came from and why they were so celebrated. Not to mention Zorro and Robin Hood.

"No."

"I hate those people. Those Hitlers, those Mussolinis, those Ruckers."

"Could we give some of the money to the Okies that got run off their farms?"

Now she could barely believe what she was hearing. It was alarming how volatile some of her emotions were. And how much, once they came out into the open, they terrified her. At that moment she hoped he would nix the stickup idea altogether. But he hadn't.

"Sure," she said, shrugging her little square shoulders. "That drought is a Hitler too."

The next day was a Friday. They decided that while he was on his ice route, she would go down to Rucker's Wilshire office in the afternoon. She would "case it" and see what the "setup" was. She specifically used those terms because she had heard them used in the cops-and-robbers flicks.

Dressed in her most casual garb, taking a couple hours away from the union hall, Wanda set up her "stakeout" in a coffee shop across from Rucker's little office building "lair" on Wilshire near La Brea. The oil scammers had an office in a two-story structure with BEACH OIL SHARES! lettered in bright yellow across one window, and she could see it clearly as she drank three cups of coffee and ate a wedge of pie at a little table by the window. The cherry pie blood oozed to the plate, smeared where she scraped up the last bite. Unable to figure out what she was doing there, against all of her principles, she mopped and mopped at the last of the cherry blood and took the sweet tines of the fork to her mouth.

At five till two she took a last sip of coffee, the cup trembling as she set it down on the saucer. She left two dimes on the table. Walked out in bright sunlight and got in her new green Buick. Out on the sidewalk an orange cat sat with one hind leg up in the air licking itself contentedly. She pulled her working woman's hat low over her eyes, slunk down in her seat the way she had seen Bogart do it, and waited for the "subjects" to show.

It was five past two when Whitaker and another man came out of Rucker's building, each carrying a briefcase. It was the man Donovan had punched that night at the club, the goon squad cop. They looked cautiously both ways down the street and got into the Pierce-Arrow parked at the curb.

Wanda watched them out of the side mirror as they pulled away. She started the Buick, fumbling frantically at the key. When the Pierce took off, she jumped the Buick away from the curb. Realizing at the last minute that she was pointed in the wrong direction, she made a hasty U-turn in the next block. She shook her head at how inept she was.

By the time she got headed west the Pierce was four blocks down. It was easy to follow, big and green, with every other little Ford and Dodge keeping its distance as if in fear of it.

Half a mile down Wilshire the car turned right. It lurched up Doheny. The Buick followed. Wanda was crouched so low over the wheel that she looked like one of those hicks just learning to drive a motor and terrified of the road whistling up on her. Halfway up the long Doheny hill the

Pierce turned into a Bank of America parking lot.

Wanda sailed by so fast nobody could have gotten a glimpse of her, she was sure. She must have been going sixty and didn't slow down until she hit Sunset at the top of the hill. And that's what she told Donovan that night.

"They're sure easy to follow."

"Sure, nobody notices because nobody's looking for you," he said. Trying to uncoil her springs a bit. Talking her down. She paced like a parrot on a perch as she related the details of her "stakeout." He put a fresh block of ice in their own box and cooked her steak and potatoes for dinner, and she followed him every step of the way. Talking about this Whitaker and his "sidekick." His "shadow."

"His name's Lewis," Donovan said.

"Yeah, I'll bet he looks out for you," she said, smiling so very big up into his face. "So he doesn't get conked on the nose again."

Her blood was going so fast. She remembered the fight at Club Alabam with distinct pleasure. That win was a harbinger of this next one, a blow for humanity, for the homeless, for the restless, for the done-in, for the weary. For the black, the red, the yellow, the brown. Even for the white, she thought. The little white, the backward white, the weakest white. The hobo, the shmoe, the joe.

Boy, was she wound up. As tight as a new Buick V-8 with the hydraulic valves humming so deep in their steel block. At the same time, she knew they never would pull this "heist." It would just be way too stupid a thing to try.

"So what do you think? Where do we take her down?" Donovan said. He too was just blowing smoke. He also didn't really think they would stick up the payroll. He'd lost any enthusiasm he had for that scale of vengeance. He was humoring her.

"Here's the way it's going down."

She moved in close. Confiding. There was a thin smear of steak sauce left over in the flat of her plate. She began to draw in it with her pinkie finger.

"Here's Wilshire. Here's Doheny." Intersecting lines. "Here's Rucker's. Here's the bank." Dots of white plate stabbed into the sauce.

He almost laughed. She was hunched over her finger-painting. Working a mile a minute. A sudden clash with a new line appearing from off-plate.

"Us. Coming in from Fountain or Third."

"I don't think Fountain goes through."

She licked her finger. He couldn't hold it any longer. He burst out in laughter. Roaring back in his chair, almost knocking over the table as his feet kicked out.

That's hilarious, he thought. The woman really wants to pull a stickup.

14

CRAZY WOMAN WANTS A THOMPSON

The next few days were like that. Tense. Scary-tense. Funny. Ridiculous-funny. She had preposterous plans for running the Pierce-Arrow off the road and hijacking it at gunpoint. She had designs on the money. She had a getaway route.

"Arizona. You want Arizona, we go to Arizona," she said. "Just till the heat's off."

"How do we get the money to the poor from the mine," he asked. Full of humor and condescension. She had actually said the words: "till the heat's off".

"The proletariat and the bourgeoisie are everywhere. I have contacts all over. We can funnel it out."

"Okay, how do we get cash to the bourgeoisie?"

"That's the owners. The proletariat are the poor. Come on."

She looked at him as if he had boils on his eyes. It was a Sunday. They were out in the river bed again. At her insistence. She was practicing quick-loading the guns and shooting at a red Pennzoil can sitting on a rock.

"You may think this is funny, but you better get your head in order."

"Yes, ma'am," he said. He knew they weren't going through with it.

"We've got to buy shells. Six or eight boxes."

"More. In case we have to shoot our way out of someplace." He was really running with this joke.

"Now tell me about Arizona."

He slouched over and sat in the shade while she fired at the can, his back against a big sycamore. Serious of a sudden. "Old gray rock formations. Gold-bearing quartz all through it down in that Oro Blanco district. A lot of ocotillo and catclaw."

"Meeoww," she said, coming over and pawing at him.

"It's a plant, the catclaw. I see you riding through it on the prettiest little roan mare. White face, white stockings."

"Am I wearing a cowboy hat?"

"No, you're right out in the sun. Hair a-flyin'."

"Where are you?"

"I got my own horse."

"What are we looking for, again?"

"It's Bear Valley. We're just going down there to sightsee. Picnic. Right on the Mexican border. Where we can make our getaway if they find us."

"Is there a river?"

"Little stream."

"I want to take my clothes off and get in. Is there anybody around?"

"Just bears and bobcats. I bet there ain't been twenty white men down there in ten years."

"What do we do all day? When we're not picnicking?"

"We work at the mine."

"The Old Soldier?"

"Yep. That's our job. Working that gold. Find that vein. Follow it down."

She whirled. Fired the Smith & Wesson at the can. A big puff of dust flew up in front of it.

"We need a Thompson," she said.

"A what?"

"A tommy gun."

This got his attention. "Machine gun? Thompson machine gun?"

"Darn tootin'."

"Crazy woman wants a Thompson."

"Crazy woman wants a Thompson."

And so it went for days. This kind of foolishness.

But the city was not in the same elated mood, Wanda noticed. There were marches against war in Europe. There were strikes and threats of strikes from the union halls. There were demonstrations against the Okies. For the Okies. The newspapers were full of opinions, against Reds and Okies in the Times, against the Red Squad and the Okie blockade in the Evening News. Reports were that the Germans were going to advance against Poland or Belgium. The Japanese were raping China, and Mussolini was personifying a word which nobody had heard of before. Fascist. There was a new recession in the midst of the Depression, and the Dow was below a hundred again.

The oil companies wanted to drill in the California tidelands, Martin Dies was investigating un-American activities in Congress, Herbert Hoover was denouncing the New Deal and its results, a turtle weighing 1,100 pounds was caught in the ocean and brought ashore to great astonishment, and the Okies mourned their beloved Will Rogers' death in an air crash. Slot machines were being seized from juke joints around the city, Arab nations protested Jewish immigration to Palestine, Nazis were arresting Catholic priests so they could be put in "protective custody," the state of California was proposing a universal health care program that would cover every resident.

And Wanda was busy. The ILGWU struck a shop on Vermont Avenue. It was a small garment shop, producing sportswear for the nation's country club tennis players and golfers, and almost all of its 35 women workers had walked out over pay and hours. Christmas was coming, and they wanted to cut their hours to a twelve-hour day and get off piece work. The owner refused.

Wanda, who had just gotten the shop to go union a few months before, was waiting outside with other union officials when the women walked out. She had picket signs ready. The women walked up and down the sidewalk in a long oval chanting old slogans she had brought from back east. "Solidarity...forever!" they shouted, some of the Mexicans and Russians not even knowing what they were saying. "Workers unite!"

When the Red Squad came in, crammed into three unmarked black police cars, Wanda made a show of resistance but her whole plan was to disband prior to a showdown. Not possible. The cops bailed out, rounded up the fleeing women and forced them inside and sat them at their work tables. The last the union officials saw of the women, the owner of the company and the cops were giving them a stern lecture laced with threats of deportation and jail.

One of the plainclothes officers went right to Wanda. It was Lewis, the man Donovan had punched at Club Alabam. Weeding her out of the rest of the organizers, he and two cops forced her into a car.

"What are you doing?" Wanda said, forced into the back seat with Lewis.

"Troublemaker, ain't ya," Lewis said, settling into the Ford with a large, heavy butt. The bandages were off his nose, but it was still red and swollen from its relocation. His voice had a bit of a honking resonation.

"Where are we going?" Wanda asked. They were speeding through downtown. Headed south.

"You Jew troublemakers, you best get yourselves out of this town."

"So, Officer Lewis, is that your personal message?"

Silence now. The man seemed fairly devastated that she knew his name. His eyes squinted almost shut. He had white hair and eyebrows. Both the cops up front glanced back at him.

"Or is that from somebody further up?" she continued.

"I don't have to take you back. I can do anything I want with you."

Fighting back a sense of desperation, Wanda faced the man. Looked as far into his eyes as she could stomach. "Well, seeing as how forty people saw you spirit me away, and they're going to be wondering where the Red Squad is taking me, I'd say you better do something respectable. If that's within your range of possibilities."

The driver had his eyes on Lewis' eyes via the rear view mirror. A tenseness pervaded the car, hanging on his answer. Finally Lewis nodded to the driver.

They were on South Central. The driver scooted the car over to the curb and hit the brakes and put the car in neutral and sat there fiddling with the shifter. This was not two blocks from Club Alabam. The sidewalks were teeming with Negroes.

"We're watching you," Lewis said. The other cop got out and opened Wanda's door. "You like the bourgeoisie so much, see how they treat you down here in niggertown."

Wanda gladly stepped out. Leaned over to have a word with Lewis from the sidewalk, peering into his window with a victorious smirk on her relieved little face.

"Proletariat. For your information, it's the proletariat I represent." The car roared away and hid her words, and she had to shout the rest. "I don't know why people can't get that right!"

Immediately she turned around. A black man who had heard her comment stopped to stare. There were many people on the street, and every last one of them was Negro. They looked at her with curiosity and alarm. As if fearful of the repercussions of even being near a white woman when she was by herself.

"Sir, do you know where the nearest trolley stop is?" she asked the man.

He politely tipped his boater and pointed across the street and up a block. She thanked him, caught a Red Line car within ten minutes and was back at the union hall in half an hour. All in all, she was disappointed that the police communist busters and union disorganizers were so soft. She didn't even have a good story to tell her colleagues.

"I'll get him," Donovan said that night, though. He wasn't as amused.

"Don't worry about him. It's that whole—"

"I'll get him, I said."

Donovan was drinking. He chewed his food with a vengeful obstinacy and drank beer after beer. The bottles lay on their sides in the mangy grass of the back yard like beaten ten-pins.

By now Wanda knew her man had a vindictive character. No, not that. More that he was just acutely attuned to some kind of severe and hidden inner justice system that could be activated in a moment. She didn't think it had to do with an economic system that put people off their farms and broke up families and scattered them to the dust. It had more to do with some personal memory he wouldn't divulge. She liked it, she could use it, but when she thought of it logically it scared her. It closely resembled the Red Squad system of reasoning and justice.

At that point she changed her mind about robbing Rucker. They had begun to talk less and less about Wanda's idea anyway, and at times like this it seemed a mad, crazy, insane thing to contemplate. And antithetical to her larger philosophies. She didn't tell him this. She would just let it die on the vine.

The very next day, Donovan was called into the Consolidated Ice office downtown. They had left word for him at the ice plant, and he had to send Joseph off alone on their delivery route.

"I'll catch up to you as soon as I can," Donovan told him. Joseph drove away seeming just as happy to be rid of him. They had no three hundreds to deliver until they hit the markets late in the day.

Donovan got off the trolley on Hill Street and walked to the company office with a sense of foreboding. Had there been a complaint? Had somebody seen his ice truck after one of his break-ins? The harried people trudging around downtown, and the hectic traffic of old black cars one behind the other, and the dirty air from the traffic, seemed a sour note. The company couldn't fire him, because he had bought his own route. But they could cancel his contract.

It was a big office, with a lot of clerks in cubicles working straight-backed over encyclopedia-sized ledgers and black typewriters. The sound of keys striking platens and carriages throwing off little bell rings came from all directions. Two slender men in dapper suits strolled nonchalantly out of a side office.

"Come on in, Donovan," said Fred, whatever his last name was. Donovan had met him before, when signing his contract. "This is Art Barnes," the man said, introducing his companion.

In physical conflict he moved as smooth as glass, but at times like these Donovan's brain didn't function well. He bumped into door frames and forgot names as soon as they were introduced to him. His face was falling into frown lines. If somebody would physically threaten him he would perk right up and smile, but this bureaucratic uncertainty was nerve-wracking.

The men took him into a small office. The lettering on the door said REGIONAL MANAGER. They sat him down on a leather chair. One sat behind the desk, the other stood at attention in the door.

"What can I do for you boys?" Donovan asked.

"You know, Donovan, Consolidated Ice started twenty-seven years ago, chopping ice out of frozen lakes in the Sierras," this man said. "We used to haul it down to Oakland and Modesto in wagons, covered in sawdust and burlap."

He looked up at the other manager. Who nodded in affirmation. Donovan didn't need a lecture. Just get it over with, goddamnit.

"This is a big company now."

"With a good reputation. One we like to uphold." They moved around in front of Donovan so they could both confront him.

"I started out in San Francisco with old Harry Ames, who as you know founded this company on a shoestring, and we had one old 1908 Packard truck. Now California has more ice capacity than any other place in the world, and Consolidated is a big player in that."

"Yes, Sir," Donovan said.

"We ice a hundred thousand people, roughly. We ice a fifth of the businesses in Los Angeles. Roughly. Consolidated iced over 150,000 rail cars full of fresh fruit and vegetables last year."

"Yes, Sir."

"Right now we're cooling lettuce out of Palmdale and radishes out of Watts. Our southern division has over a thousand food lockers cooled down. Hell, California is big in ice. The state uses more anhydrous ammonia refrigerant than anybody else in the world."

This time Donovan didn't answer. Goddamn you, just tell me. Odd, bringing a lowly route man in here and giving him a lecture before you let him go.

"So what can I do for you?" Donovan asked again.

"You can become the district manager for North Los Angeles County. That would make us real happy."

Fred stood and came around beside Art. Who said, "You've been recommended to us by everybody who's come in contact with you. Including customers. There's not a man in the company doesn't know how you carry those three hundreds up stairs and into markets."

"You've got a good head on your shoulders, too, Daley."

"This company's always looking for the men to raise up. We'll start you at $325 a month, with a bonus at the end of the year. There's a future here. This is a growing industry."

The other man unexpectedly reached down and plucked the long ice pick from Donovan's holster. "The simple ice pick," he said heartily. "It's the tool of the future."

Donovan was just astounded. He couldn't think of a thing to say, even as the man slipped his ice pick back to him and Donovan stood there holding it like a little curio from the future.

"Can I give it some thought?"

On the way out of the office all the clerks seemed friendlier, all the men in suits appeared to make congratulatory eye contact. On the trolley ride out to Silver Lake, where he caught Joseph just coming down off the hill for the afternoon run, the winter breeze seemed less cold than invigorating. The other riders solid, friendly citizens one and all, ringing the bell and disembarking to their destinations in a reassuring demonstration of a well-oiled civilization.

The brothers finished up their commercial run in the restaurants and markets of Silver Lake a little late. Trying to catch up. For some reason Donovan didn't tell Joseph about the offer, though his brother asked what was going on. Maybe also he didn't want his brother to feel left out.

He told Wanda about it, though. She was very happy for him in a distracted way. The heist was more of an abstract dream now than a goal, but the possibility of it tangled her thoughts in uncertainty. It was hard for her to focus on other futures.

"Are you going to take it?" she asked. "Be no point if we're going to be on the lam."

"I'm thinking about it." His inclination was to take that job. It would mean dressing in a suit every day, though, traveling, setting up ice routes, writing contracts. None of which he liked.

But this heist had become an embarrassing topic, and his dream of having a gold mine in Arizona, bringing him riches and fame, was a pipe dream. Maybe being a manager would be a way to raise up both himself and Wanda. Maybe some little house on Running Springs Road would actually be feasible.

1 5

THE FRIGIDAIRE

It was when Donovan Daley was drunk that he thought he was the most lucid. At least, that was another good excuse to get drunk. He was very lucid the night after his job offer. Or thought he was.

"There's not a goddamn man around here don't recommend me!" he shouted. "Not a goddamn one! They're raisin' me up!"

That was what passed for lucidity. They were walking the streets of Hollywood at dusk. They went up to the boulevard and passed the Chinese, the Egyptian, the Capitan. Which were all lit up, the billboards advertising the latest movies. People were rushing in for shows, out for dinner. There were beggars on the street, but not many. This was the Great Depression, but this was also Los Angeles, the land of opportunity within The Land of Opportunity.

Wanda lagged a bit. When he got red and loud like this she walked so slowly he would have to whirl around and look for her. He was embarrassing. They passed a newsstand, and he stopped to leer at the gossip rags. Hush-Hush, Whisper, On the Q.T. and Confidential. Then he reeled away down the street again.

"Listen up good!" he yelled to a group of people coming toward them on the sidewalk. "Got me a hell of a job offer! Gonna take it, mos' likely!"

The group went on by chuckling to themselves. Donovan turned and hunted Wanda down, took her hand, shuffled his feet until he got in step with her, and they marched like tin soldiers up the street. She had initiated the walk because she wanted him to walk off the booze. They were going out to the San Fernando Valley.

They were going to see his father. Which was why he was drunk, she suspected.

Turning down a side street, they encountered fewer people. He became less boisterous. Almost morose. He had a red-eyed, angry look about his face now. Striding like a horse, he was going so fast she couldn't keep up, now that she wanted to.

A man came up the sidewalk toward them, tipped his hat to Wanda, and Donovan lashed out with a left hook that caught him on the side of the jaw. Down the man went, knocked half silly and rolling around on the concrete. The ice man kept on walking.

"Hey! What was that about?" Wanda yelled. She ran back to help up the struggling man. Dusted his hat off for him. He was on his feet, but his eyes flicked on and off like dying neon.

"Whadya do that for?" the man finally mumbled, rubbing the side of his head.

Donovan started back for him. Wanda headed him off and guided him back toward home. Calling out apologies to the victim, who wobbled up the street like Charlie Chaplin only not as fast or funny as in the movies.

By the time they got in the car—she drove and refused to let him have another beer or take his flask—Donovan was coming down off his high. Getting some of his cheery smile back as she talked to him about movies or sports events that would take his mind off things. Joe Louis, Man O War, anything.

In the Valley he read her directions from a letter written in his father's florid hand. Joseph still passed on occasional letters from his mother, but this was the first from his father. It had come directly to Donovan. It had asked him to come over and have dinner with him.

They drove out from Van Nuys toward distant hills hunkering in the last light of day. It was mostly farmland filled in with subdivisions of little square houses and corner country markets blossoming into towns. They turned right at a hand-lettered sign made from the side of an orange carton nailed to a fence post. Oranges and lemons for five cents a dozen. They headed down a dirt track between lemon groves. There was fruit on the trees, hanging almost white in the headlights like bloated teardrops.

The house was more of a shack in the middle of groves and fruit packing sheds. Donovan sat up straight, sober as hell. The car's lights slid bumpily over aged-black clapboards and corral fences. A decrepit pickup with a dent in the door was parked in the yard, and a single small window of the shack showed light.

They got out in the cold air and knocked on the door. A man opened it who looked something like Donovan, but not much, Wanda thought. He had the thickness of age in his neck and white hair at his temples.

"Hello, Son," the man said. He held his hand out, and Donovan shook it firmly as he had been taught from childhood. But with surprisingly little warmth, somehow. The older man swung the door open for them. A look of confirmed family misbehavior settled into the men's faces, as if they had been through failed reunions before.

"Good," Donovan said. "This is Wanda Kitchen. My father. Donovan Daley Senior."

"Pleased to make your acquaintance, Wanda," the father said. "This is Henrietta."

Now they both noticed a woman sitting over in the corner of the two-room shack. She was a Mexican woman of about forty. Or fifty. Younger than Donovan Senior, but well scuffed by life. As was the father. As he turned in the light, Wanda could see the white hairs growing wild out of ears and his face skin crinkled at all corners and mitred badly by age.

He sat them on some wooden chairs near a pot-bellied stove that was practically rumbling. Fire could be seen through the joints in the cast iron, and his father clanked open a little door in the front and flipped in two sticks of citrus prunings from as far back as he could stand. The house was hot even with the front door open.

"Plenty of wood in this country," the father said. "Something you didn't get in that Panhandle. Used to send this youngster down to the river to scrounge sticks."

"I remember," Donovan said.

"Buffalo chips. Left over from the olden days."

"Hard as rocks."

"Make a good fire, they would. Nothing like a buffalo chip for fuel."

Awkward silence. The Mexican woman got up and stirred something viscous and amorphous in a huge skillet on top of the stove. Beans, it seemed to Wanda, though the evidence was all in the smell rather than the sight.

"Frijoles," the woman said, smiling shyly. She glanced up at Donovan. "Very much you look like su padre."

"Yep, he was the first-born. Most likely to look like me, from what I know now," the father said cryptically. "We're fixing to have some burritos here shortly. Hope you're hungry."

"Yes, we are," Wanda said with as much energy as she could muster.

When she looked over at Donovan, a rigid almost cubist look had come over his face. Not a man to hide his feelings, he was trying to mask them now. Circumstances seemed to have overwhelmed his system of emotional checks and balances.

It wasn't that the crooked board house was so depressing. They all had seen many houses of this ilk, or worse, during the Depression. They had lived in them at one time or another. It wasn't that the people were so disadvantaged. They all had witnessed downfalls greater than this.

It was more how, in Donovan's mind, these signs of downfall were an abject reminder that the family was still unraveling. He hadn't known what to expect, but what he had hoped would be a moderately comfortable reunion with a father he hadn't seen in two years was instead just basically wretched. He knew nothing about the Mexican woman with the pleading smile, but he resented her already.

"While she's finishing that up, why don't you two go on my rounds with me?" his father said.

The three of them went out and got into the old pickup, which rattled like a wheat thresher to start and chuckled and popped as it livened up. They proceeded on a tour of the property. Turned out that the elderly man—hell, he was only fifty, but he just seemed elderly—was the night watchman for a large citrus ranch that was being converted to houses.

"Going to be three hundred houses here!" the father yelled over the clatter of the truck. He turned on a spotlight mounted in the corner of the window, grabbed the handle and swept light over the skeletons of houses in mid-construction. He made a pass along what would apparently be the streets of a new city, up and down, down and back, slinging the spotlight among stacks of lumber and roofing materials.

"They get people stealing fruit, stealing lumber," the father said. "That's why they hired me out here."

Nobody replied. They returned to the house through ultra-dark lemon groves where the spotlight barely penetrated the border rows of trees. They were thinking about this father who had somehow ricocheted off the backside of life and ended up here, spent like a lump of lead that had passed through a body.

They ate beans wrapped in handmade flour tortillas cooked right on top of the stove. The beans were congealed into a semi-solid state. There were carnitas and chiles in the beans. They flipped the tops off strawberry soda and root beer brought in from outside, where the bottles had chilled. All in all it was a tasty little meal.

But Donovan and his father and Wanda ate as if mired in heavy air. Henrietta busied herself around them, lost in some internal cooking behaviorism derived from a culture foreign to them. She was doing her best. Forced more tortillas sagging with beans onto them. Offered more soda pop of different flavors. But they couldn't be dragged from their mental labors by Nehi and pinto beans.

"You ever get any of that oil money off the ranch?" was the only thing Donovan asked his father.

"No, they got everything," the older man answered, limping around the stove hindered by what his son knew was a pelvis deformed by a horse fall twenty years earlier. The bones had shattered and healed funny. "Buddy McCalester was a friend of mine. Bank manager. Now he's farming my land."

"It's a rotten system, rotten to its core," Wanda said, unable to help herself.

"Ah. Nobody cares," the father said. "The dust blew in, and now nobody cares."

Donovan and Wanda left about ten o'clock on legs freshened by the promise of escape. They got in their new Buick guiltily, his father slamming the driver's door and looking in the window at them, proud as could be of this measure of success. Backlit by light from the open door. They sped away as fast as possible. Dodging deer and raccoons and other nighttime travelers of the lemon forest in moody silence.

"Interesting man," Wanda finally said as they climbed the Cahuenga Pass on the way into Hollywood. Maybe it was the brilliant lights of this new city that sparked a little conversation in her.

"Yeah," was all he said. "Used to be."

And they went on down Highland and arrived home this way. Depressed in the middle of the Depression. He drank two beers very quickly and went out in the back yard in the dark for a while. When he came in he said nothing.

He was slow to undress, slow to bed, slow to sleep. Wanda cuddled into him hard-shouldered. Her consoling voice muffled. He wasn't interested in conversation or sex or sleep.

What he found so hard to believe was that his father hadn't mentioned his mother all night. Either to ask about her or to pass judgment on her. Either one would have been more acceptable than this utter obliteration of the family. The father had asked about Joseph, who had refused Donovan's invitation to go out and see him, but not a word about anybody else.

"He couldn't come," Donovan had told his father. Everybody knew it wasn't true, but silently thanked him for saying it anyway.

Donovan finally fell asleep but awoke at two-thirty in the morning and couldn't get back. Something in this woke up Wanda, and she could tell by the tension in his body that he was still upset.

"You want to talk about it?"

"What bothers me," he answered immediately, "is he wasn't no bum. He was a county commissioner, popular in the towns round-about there. He bred horses and was known to always pick a good plow horse or brood mare. Look at the way a horse stood and just tell. Muscle structure."

"He's just down on his luck."

She was trying to make him feel better. Sometimes she thought he was like a child. About eight or nine. His love of the movies, especially the cowboy thrillers and comic capers. The way he ate sweets by the bag. His simplistic method of analyzing complex issues.

"I was happy back there. I was born in 1910, during Halley's Comet. They said I'd be a little comet. Some of them old Southeast Oklahoma Choctaws come out of the woods when they heard I was born then, my mother's people. My father says they just stood and looked at me like I was a newborn elephant or somethin'."

"Did you know that Mark Twain was born and died during Halley appearances?"

"I did not."

He thought for a minute about that. They were snuggled down into their covers. The electric space heater had been turned off for the night. He could hear her breathing and thinking in the dark. Then her breathing and thinking were quieter, and he knew she was asleep. He went to sleep soon after.

In the morning he and Joseph went off on their route silently, in a state of stressful resignation. Donovan because he was holding the secret of their father, whom he knew his brother hated, inside. Joseph because he was looking forward to seeing Rucker, which he knew would irritate his brother.

Mrs. McCants was fully clothed today, which was good, because Donovan took Joseph up to meet her. He'd had enough of his sibling's questions about her state of dress and mind. Let the young man be introduced to all of this. He had hid it from him long enough.

"Oh, who's this?" Mrs. McCants asked. Holding a little spoonful of Post Toasties in front of the huge boy child, who leaned forward like a bald headed baby sloth in his high chair trying to suck in the cereal with prehensile lips.

"My brother Joseph," Donovan said.

"Well I am so pleased," the woman said, and miraculously, as she swirled around to shake Joseph's hand, her dressing gown flew open. This fabulous magician belatedly plucked it closed, but not before Joseph caught a glimpse of champagne bloomers and lace brassiere on tanned skin.

All the way down to the truck Joseph looked at the ground as if contemplating fate and reproduction. He had no more idea what to do with his thoughts than a little boy knew what to do with an automobile gear shifter. But there was much to consider.

At Rucker's he helped his big brother load up a three hundred, and they trudged up the concrete stairs. Rucker and Whitaker were at the top. Rucker reached out and grabbed Donovan's shirt sleeve.

"Go on and set that down, Bananas," Rucker said.

"Might as well," Whitaker said. He hardly ever spoke, but today his eyes seemed as lively as fireflies. Donovan, bent by the weight of the ice, his shoulder as cold as January in the High Plains, looked over at them.

"Whadaya mean?" Donovan asked. "Once I set her down, it don't get back up."

"Go on, set it down."

Donovan looked at his brother. Who shrugged. Donovan swung the tongs obliquely off his shoulder and let the huge block of ice smack to the concrete pad at the top of the stairs. It made a sound like boulder on boulder and jarred the hillside under them.

"You want it, you pick it up," he said.

"Won't need to. I have something to show you," Rucker said. He and Whitaker just grinned at him.

The brothers followed the pair back to the kitchen door, and in. Millie was busy at the range, baking. In the place of the huge ice box was a strange device. It was a round-shouldered rectangular metal box that stood upright. It had Frigidaire stamped on a metal plate.

It hummed ominously deep in its sheet metal, like some kind of big cat purring deep in predator bowels.

"There's your demise, boy," Rucker said. He had his hands dug deep in his pockets, his suit coat flung open, feet splayed. As if showing off a new non-existent oil field to a loaded investor.

"What is it?"

"What is it?" Rucker said to the room in general. Laughing. "Hear that hum?"

He opened the refrigerator door. A little fog of cold air spilled out. The hum was louder, as if they were getting closer to the motor buried somewhere in the box. There were shelves, just as in an ice box, and food on the shelves.

Donovan reached in and touched a bottle of milk gingerly. It was cold. He opened the little door on the top. More fog came out. There was no block of ice in there. Just more food. He reached in there, too. The shelf was very cold, and had whiskers of ice forming on it. He jerked his fingers away from the frozen wires as if they were hot.

"Refrigerator," Whitaker said.

"Boy, gaze upon it. Fill your eyes with it. That little box is going to put you damned ice men out of business," Rucker said. "Every last one of you that threatened to strike and hold up America's business."

Donovan looked around the room. At Joseph. At Millie, who had turned to observe his reaction. The whole world seemed attuned to his reaction.

All he could think was, He calls me boy one more time, I'm gonna clock him. But physically, all he did was nod as if in appreciation of this modern leap of technology.

"Get used to the idea, Bananas," Rucker was saying. "Times are going to be easy in the future. Everybody will have a refrigerated box. There won't be any need for big bohunks like you. You and the horse, you're on your way out. In ten years there won't be any of you around. People will sit around and take it easy, eating food from their refrigerators."

"Good." Donovan was having a moment of enlightenment. "Well good, then."

Rucker reached over to the long kitchen counter and ripped a banana off a bunch of them in a bowl. He handed it to Donovan.

"Have a banana, Bananas. Get your strength back. Look for other work lifting heavy objects up off the ground."

Rucker laughed the way he would at a competitor's misfortune. Whitaker was silent, observant, apparently the only one aware that the ice man might take this as offensive. He eased his coat open on the butt of a short automatic.

"You owe me fifty cents on that three hundred out there," Donovan said.

Rucker looked at him cockily. "You didn't deliver it."

Donovan looked deep into the man's face. He wanted to hurt this man in the worst way. He wanted to pull his ice blue eyeballs out of his head and pop them under his boot on the floor. He wanted to fold him three times and put him in that refrigerated space.

Right there he decided to pull the payroll heist.

Turning, he almost ran over Joseph as he left the kitchen. Went down the stairs and got in the ice truck. Joseph barely jumped in before the truck lurched up the street. He hadn't had a chance to talk to Rucker.

At home that night Donovan brooded for a long time. He got up and started making a fire outside. He liked it out there under the big-limbed coastal oak tree. Drinking beer and waiting for the wood to burn down to coals.

Wanda came out. "I got some pork chops today. I could pan-cook them."

"I'll grill 'em. Ought to be cooked over a flame."

"Careful. You might start a trend."

"Nah."

"Something wrong?" She had watched him brood around the house and then settle into the spring chair. He downed one beer after another, and not in the expansive way he drank when feeling good.

"Let's bust old Rucker."

After examining his eyes for flaw and doubt and uncertainty, any at all, Wanda came over and kneeled in front of him. Still she watched him so deep for a flinch, any sign of weakness.

"Let's knock him to his knees," Donovan said. His gaze didn't waver a bit.

"Let's strip him naked," she said.

"We'll need stuff."

"What stuff?"

"This ain't what you think. They'll kill you, and I mean it."

"I want a Thompson."

"We both ought to have one."

"I don't want to kill him, though."

"No, it's just for protection." As he talked she took his hands. Hers were shaking, he could feel them. "They'll kill you if you don't. You better be knowing how this works."

"We won't let them. We'll be alright."

"Wanda?"

"Yes?"

"What's it all about? The world. These people. You're smart. You read. I can't read for two minutes. What's it all mean?"

She had to think about this. It was a crucial moment. He wanted a synthesis. She did too. Something to make it understandable for him. She needed to make it seem that it was all worth it, this Robin Hood life they were entering, which on the face of it was addled and foolish. But wasn't it just a corollary of the turbulent thirties, an insane era disintegrating around her? And didn't that make it all right?

"It's all over in Spain. It's all over in Austria. Hitler's taking over everything. The emperor of Japan wants Asia. The dictators in South and Central America, they're in control. Nobody wants to do anything. What's Roosevelt doing? Nothing. England, she's by herself. Russia, I hate to say it, but the word coming out is not good. Everywhere it's dictators and extremism and fascism and fanaticism. Somebody has to act. There has to be a stopping point. What do we have here? Emily Post for etiquette and the Gibson Girl for a tease. Why do the scammers get to be rich and the women who work twelve-hour days get to be poor? What kind of world is that?"

"Why won't they all just take a drink together. Back off a notch. Shake hands and own up."

She smiled woozily. Just smiled at him. Nine year old boy. "Same reason we don't," she said. "Be too easy."

She just laughed and laughed and took that long-haired boy inside and fucked him so good that he forgot the coals and they had to eat indoors that night long after everybody else in the neighborhood had gone to sleep.

THE LAST COOKOUT

He wanted to take the Eastern girl on a real Western cookout before they went into this. The way they used to on the ranch. He planned it for a Sunday. He also took a Saturday off beforehand, but they used it to buy what they would need for the heist.

They went to a hardware store and bought rope and tape and canvas tote sacks. They went to a dance on a gambling boat off San Pedro and talked to a man from Kansas City who sold them two second-hand Thompsons. Picked them up from a little Italian at a seedy apartment in Culver City. They went to a gun shop and bought ammunition of three calibers. At a garment shop in Chinatown where nobody spoke the language he had new masks made for them of a proper fit, covering the entire head. In a department store downtown they purchased clothing they would not wear until that Friday as a way of being recognizable to no one.

Home again, Wanda immediately took to oiling the Thompsons up and down with a gentle hand. They were guns that had been well-used, and Donovan had told her that the worn-gray metal would have to be oiled so it wouldn't rust. So she oiled. She liked to wrap her hands around the knurled grips, which matched her hands so well they seemed like final justice after all. They went to the river and practiced with them.

"Am I a gun moll?" she asked him in the river bed, hugging a Tommy gun between her breasts as they walked along looking for a can to shoot.

"A what?"

"You know, a dame with a rod?"

She set him to laughing so hard he staggered around the dry river bed, kicking up dust as he tried to cope with the love he had for this woman. They shot cans happily that day.

Over a period of two weeks they had made plans, as intricate as if plotting a movie. In fact, in their innocence they took some of their plot points from movies and books. Pot boilers heavy on noir deeds. They carefully took their cues from the police characters, placing themselves in the shoes of the detectives who solved the crimes so they would be one step ahead. They jotted down notes and discussed alternatives, then carefully burned the notes. He approached it as if it were a construction job, she approached it as if writing a report.

"I want to go on a cookout," he said on Saturday night.

"Okay. We can load up the car and go to the mountains in the morning."

"Tonight. By horseback."

So they went up in Beechwood Canyon and rented horses at dusk. He had a lot of cast iron Dutch ovens and horse harness he had brought from the ranch, and they weighed down a rented mule with camp gear and food. It was dark when they started up into the trails above Hollywoodland.

They rode casually in a cold breeze, Donovan taking the lead on an old roan mare and she following on a little gelding with white feet. The mule followed, tied to Wanda's saddle by a rope. He let the horses pick the trails, and the couple spent most of their time scanning the Westside lit up and enjoying its Saturday night. They crossed over the divide and the San Fernando Valley came into view, the near communities enraged by light and, farther out, the citrus orchards and vegetable farms going to sleep in darkness.

Finally a flat ridgetop enticed the horses to a stop. Donovan got down and unpacked the mule. Scrounging firewood from a half-dead tree, he built a fire. Taking a blanket from the pack saddle, he spread it for her. They sat huddled together watching the fire chatter and make coals.

"All right!" he said finally. Hopped to his feet and started dragging Dutch ovens and food off the startled mule, which looked around suspiciously.

"What are you doing, crazy man?" Wanda shouted at him. He was by that time digging in the coals with a shovel.

"You like stew and biscuits and apple cobbler?"

"Oh yes." She was smiling, though what she was thinking about was Friday. Friday was their day. Friday could not be forgotten.

"You are looking at the Dutch oven king of Los Angeles!" he shouted. They were shouting, though they didn't need to. To penetrate the surrounding darkness, maybe.

"Cook it, Dutch oven man, cook it!"

Then he grew quiet. "You're thinking about Friday, aren't you?" he asked. Spooning food into iron kettles, shoveling orange coals under and on top of the kettles. Sparks flew up around him, and she drew her coat close around her neck.

"Maybe."

"You want to call it off?"

He stood there with a long stick in hand, pausing from his job of moving coals around. She shrugged. Slumped onto the blanket, enervated by heavy thoughts.

"Big responsibility," he said. He slid onto the blanket alongside. Took her hand. "Could get killed. Now's the best time to drop out. Forget about the whole thing."

"Yeah, I guess."

They leaned against each other and looked down into the valley. A sliver of Burbank burned crisply against the hunkering backdrop of the distant Verdugo Mountains. The firefly lights of individual cars slowly traversed the veinous Saturday night roads.

She turned to him in the aura of coals and said, "Surely you're not doing it just for revenge against Rucker and that bunch."

"Yeah. That's it."

"You know that's no reason to risk your life."

Quiet, he pored over the distant car lights, tiny crawlers in the night.

"He makes me mad."

She jumped up. Paced a circle around the fire pit. "See! That's not it! That's not what I want! We can't do that!" Her face glowing eerily.

"I got my reasons, you got yours."

She could see in his face—as set as his little pathetic brother's—that it was all he wanted. Vengeance. But in the end, what did she want? Justice and peace in the world? Those were weak lies told to assuage guilt over wars and stickups. Did she want to work toward that egalitarian world so promised by Lenin and Christ, or did she just want to take the bad man down a notch?

"I'm not doing this for that reason," she reassured herself out loud. "That's no reason at all."

"Do it for whichever reason you want. Or not at all."

"You're not going to do it without me."

"If it comes to that."

She could see in his coal-bright, coal-dark eyes that it was so. He was a murderous thing inside, a night animal, a hunter. He was looking at her across the deadened fire like a wolf come to the edge of camp from curiosity or hunger or just plain animosity. He was so bad, he was so good.

Finally he checked his pocket watch. "Time to put the biscuits on." He took a Mason jar from a saddle bag, unwrapped cushioning rags from around it. The flour and other ingredients were in there. He poured a little water in it from a bag. He mixed inside the jar with a long wooden spoon.

"My god, you thought of everything, didn't you. Was this going to be our last cookout?"

No answer. Realizing she wasn't as angry as she sounded, she got up and went over and hugged him from behind as he worked. "I'm sorry," she said. He bent to drop dollops of biscuit batter into the last little oven and put its lid on. Put coals on the lid. She was still holding him, riding his butt as he bent and swayed. Finally he said "Okay," and turned into her hug. "Gonna eat in ten minutes."

She buried her face in his neck the way she did that first time dancing. Why, they were almost dancing now as the food cooked in the old pots. But she was dead quiet.

"You're allowed to hate them," he said.

She looked up at him. She could see the reflections of the coals in his eyes as he peered down at her. He put his hands on her shoulders.

"I don't want to. It's not really about them."

"Sure it is. You started all this because of them, who they are."

"I know I did."

"It's okay to back out. I won't mind."

She put her cheek on his arm, an arm as firm as wood, a shirt smelling of wood smoke and horse sweat. The valley lights were in her line of sight. A civilization growing out there, the pulsing lights of vehicles carrying the nutrients of life out farther and farther every day, every week. Oh, to make it all right. Oh, to make the growth good and honorable and just.

"You want to kill him, don't you."

He shrugged. He'd thought about it in those terms. Decided it didn't matter either way whether Rucker lived or died. You couldn't kill all the oil men. What the hell. If you did, there wouldn't be any oil. Could you hate the oil men and love the oil?

"You hurt them worse by just taking their money and giving it to the poor," she reasoned.

"Good. That's what we'll do, then. Nobody's gonna get hurt. You ready for some stew and biscuits?"

She nodded against his arm. Was she sorry she said it?

And they ate as if they were starving. Because they thought they were.

THE GREYHOUNDS AND THE RABBIT

The green Buick lay in wait at the curb like a low-slung cat with bullet eyes. It had been freshly washed and waxed and it glinted in the winter Los Angeles sun. Even its big whitewall tires were spotless. Its license plate had been removed.

Inside, Donovan and Wanda sat low in their seats, bundled up in car coats with their fedoras pulled low over their brows. He was in the driver's seat, his hands resting in gentle curves on the steering wheel. She sat ramrod straight, her hands flat in her lap playing a nervous game of pattycake.

Until she realized what she was doing and with a grand effort willed the hands to lie still.

Two Thompson submachine guns stood on their noses on the floor between them, the thick stocks at hand. On the seat beside him, the Smith & Wesson. On the back seat a double-barreled shotgun and a canvas bag bulging with boxes of shells.

A woman on the sidewalk, huddled deep into her coat, clacked by the car on high heels, and she just happened to turn and glance in the windows as she passed. Something about what she saw, maybe the lovely woman in the fedora or maybe the shotgun lying on the seat, registered. She kept walking, but her face filled with thought processes.

At that moment the Pierce-Arrow pulled away from the curb across Wilshire Boulevard a block behind the Buick. As it lumbered into the clutter of Friday afternoon traffic the other cars around it, as usual, shied away from the big, square shouldered vehicle and left it in the slow lane by itself.

Donovan started the Buick and, without even glancing at her, looked in his mirrors and made a U-turn in the street. The car leaned hard onto its tires and righted itself, plunging into a stream of unwashed black Fords and Oldsmobiles.

Wanda grabbed the arm rest. More for reassurance than support. Her thoughts were a little scattered. She was thinking about the doll she had had as a girl, trying to remember what had happened to it.

He didn't speed, he didn't swerve around other cars. A police car passed going in the other direction and the pair didn't even glance at it. It may not have registered on their collective consciousness. They focused on the green car half a block ahead like a greyhound on an overgrown metal rabbit.

It was taking its time, more like a water buffalo. Two hats were visible through the rear windshield. A straw boater and a bowler. Every now and then the passenger would raise something to his face. An orange soda pop bottle.

The Pierce made a sudden left, darting across lanes. Wanda glanced hard left at Donovan.

"What are they doing?"

"I don't know."

"This isn't the route."

He slowed the Buick and waited for an opening and eased it left and around the corner, following the huge black car. Which speeded up, negotiating the narrow side street as if on a mission.

"I don't like it," Wanda said, reaching over and grabbing his arm.

"Maybe it's better. They stop off and get coffee or something, it'll be easier."

When the Pierce began to slow, Donovan slowed the Buick, half a block behind it. The car braked in front of an old multi-story building in a declining neighborhood. They were only a few blocks off Wilshire, it was more industrial than retail. The Pierce slowed so suddenly that Donovan had to pull up behind it. They were at the curb in front of what appeared to be an old hotel in the midst of remodeling.

There was sudden movement in his mirrors. Black cars came out of side streets, aimed right at the Buick. They screeched to a stop behind it.

The doors of the Pierce-Arrow popped open. Whitaker and Lewis popped out, pistols in hand. They aimed the guns at Donovan and Wanda.

Donovan gunned the Buick. Twirled the wheel hard right and took it over the curb, lurching past a startled Lewis. Who whirled and fired two shots as it passed. A bullet hole appeared in Donovan's window, another in Wanda's. She looked at it as if she had no clue what caused it.

Moaning deep in its guts, the Buick accelerated across a wide concrete patio, spun a 180 and faced back toward the street. The view was not encouraging. Four or five cars faced him, blocking the street, and from their doors men in plain clothes began to leap out. Guns drawn. Two bullet holes appeared in the windshield, one on either side of Donovan's head. Neither one of them later could recall hearing the sounds of the shots though they could see the recoil of Whitaker's automatic. It was as if the whole scenario was taking place in a vacuum.

Donovan jacked the gear shifter into reverse. Grey smoke boiled from under the rear tires as the car caught and bolted backward.

Across the concrete pavilion.

Up a broad expanse of curved steps.

Until the car banged into the front door of the old building, recoiled and came to rest, stalled. Pointing downward at the posse of men racing toward them.

"Get out!" he yelled.

That, she heard.

They slapped open their doors, grabbed guns, stumbled outside. Using the doors as shields, hats flying, they sprinted in halfback crouches to the building. The portico of which was being chipped at by bullets. At a glance backward he could see the figures in black coats converging.

He jerked the breached hotel door open for Wanda, who skidded inside on her hands and knees, her Thompson clattering across a marble floor. Donovan whirled and raised his Thompson and fired a long burst out into the street.

Scattering the men like protesters in a riot. They retreated and dove behind cars. There was quiet for a long minute. While Donovan sprinted back and reached into the Buick and pulled out the shotgun and the canvas bag. He tossed them across the marble floor to Wanda, and then he did something really stupid.

"Stay there," he said to Wanda. He turned and ran out the door and sprayed the cars again.

Running low and hard, he sprinted to the Pierce-Arrow, firing the Thompson until the windows of the car were destroyed and everybody behind the car ducked low. He jerked the back door open, reached in and grabbed a big attache case sitting on the seat, and ran with it back to the old building. Men on the other side of the car, not fifteen feet away, squared up and fired at his back as he retreated. Bullets chopped at the walls around him as he dove through the door and across the floor. Skidded to a stop against a marble fountain of a naked cherub. And kicked the door shut behind him.

They both looked up at the big wooden door as it splintered under a spray of bullet holes. Now the sound came back on in their movie. There was a cacophony of gun discharges and curses from outside, all of different tonality, and the door was holed like the top of a pepper shaker as they rolled to one side to avoid the barrage.

Wanda's eyes were as big as the hubcaps on the Buick. She turned to him—both lay on their sides behind the dry fountain, weathering the storm of slugs—and seemed to want to speak out, but couldn't. Her mouth just gaped. A bullet hole appeared in the throat of the cherub and a chunk of plaster chin fell off right in front of her.

"It was a setup."

Leaping to his feet and grabbing her heavy wool coat, he pulled her across the floor away from the door on her back. She struggled to get upright, but he dragged her, spinning this way and that on her butt, all the way across the wide foyer and into a hallway. He looked in all directions, slinging the machine gun around, but they were alone in the building.

"Some old hotel," he said.

Disheveled and angry, she swam around and got to her feet. Pulled her clothing back into place. One shoe was missing and she could feel that one breast had slipped out of her brassiere. She squirmed around and put it back in.

"What happened?"

"I dunno." He analyzed the building. He panted a little, but didn't seem at all worried. He had that patient look he got when about to fight. "They didn't mean for us to get this far."

"How did they know?"

"Get back in there," he said, gesturing toward the hallway.

He set down the extra weaponry and took his Thompson at port arms and ran back to the front door. Firing had stopped, and he carefully put his eye to a hole in the door where a .45 slug or bigger had passed through.

Wanda retreated a little farther into the hallway. Not far enough that she couldn't see him. She pulled their weapons and the attache case into a doorway and watched as he viewed the world through his knot hole. She started forward, worried what he would do, but without even looking at her he pushed her back with a gesture of his hand.

Wanda Kitchen sat down against the corridor wall of the dilapidated building and examined her feelings. Her gaze fell on the peeling, faded wallpaper of the opposite wall, a dull glaze coming across her pupils, her feelings shallow and filled with remorse.

She sighed, almost as she would at a small dose of daily disappointment, no more horrifying than a broken bottle of milk. They had already lost their hats and their composure, and she somehow knew they had just started. And they hadn't even had time to put on their masks.

THEY'RE NOT GOING ANYWHERE

Charles Rucker stood right out in the street surrounded by police cars that were unmarked save for the telltale spotlights mounted at the driver's side. He was yelling at two men half hidden behind the trunk of a car on the other side of the asphalt.

"You let him go right over and get the money?" he yelled. "We had them, and now they've got my money!"

One of the men, the nearest one, rolled over a little so he could see Rucker better. Whitaker. He stayed behind the car, though.

"Get the hell down. You want to get shot?" Whitaker shouted.

"They got my money!"

"They're not going anywhere!"

"Go in and get my money back!" Rucker yelled.

He was the only man oblivious or stupid enough to stand exposed in the middle of the street. Unlike the suave and immaculate oil share promoter he projected on a normal day, he was rumpled. His clothes were all pulled to one side of his pudgy body. Maybe one of his breasts had come loose, too. His self-congratulatory cigar lay smoking on the pavement where he had thrown it in disgust.

Striding to the car behind him, Rucker accosted three men in civilian clothes crouched on one knee. Their revolvers sagging. It was impossible to tell who they were, though all looked like policemen.

"Who's the copper in charge, here?" Rucker asked loudly. He didn't even duck down, though finally he bent over to address the men hidden behind the car. "Shouldn't we call for more cars? Get around behind them?"

One of the men looked up. Lewis, the big wide man with white eyebrows.

"Kind of an unauthorized operation," Lewis said, looking sheepish. "Got half the Red Squad here, but we call any uniforms in, we got ourselves a lot of explaining to do."

"Where's your captain!"

"The captain don't know about any a this. Don't worry, we got two men in the back."

Rucker stared at him as motionless as if he'd been frozen by lightning. Traffic on the street was being stopped and turned around by a couple of men in suits, and the other hidden cops looked between one another as if waiting for instructions. And not from this crazy man.

"Go on in and get him," Rucker repeated.

"Supposed to be a quick deal. Ball them up, shoot 'em down, plant the money on their asses, and get out before we draw a crowd." Lewis seemed convinced that the plan would still work if only he could go back in time about ten minutes.

Rucker peered at the men looking up at him and pirouetted on his heels. He strode over to the car where Whitaker remained on his hands and knees. His Florsheims clicked and clacked as he crossed the street, looking up and down at the roadblocks but not even glancing at the door of the old hotel.

"Where are the Pinkertons?" he asked Whitaker.

"I've got one of them over there directing traffic," Whitaker said. "You think you ought to get down out of sight?"

"Goddamn it! I want my Pinkertons over here where I can talk to them!"

"I'm in charge of this account," a man one car over from Whitaker said. He squenched around and sat on his butt facing away from the car and the hotel. He had a small, nickel plated automatic in his right hand and his bowler hat in the other, protecting it from rolling out in the street and risking a grease spot.

Rucker squatted beside him. Rucker was a big-barreled man who, when he got out of the upright position, squished into the full breadth of his clothing. His suit pants at his thighs seemed full to bursting. His shoulders hunched up into his neck and rolled his coat at the collar.

"What's the plan now?" Rucker asked the Pinkerton man.

"You're the boss, Boss," the man said. "There's two side doors, and we got a man at each. Saw what was happening right away. Back's covered. Up to you."

"We've got to go in."

"We?"

This insinuation, Rucker didn't like. He was eyeball to eyeball with the Pinkerton man, a tall, thin guy who seemed to be having trouble getting his entire body behind the car. He looked like he wanted to roll up and hide behind a tire.

"I'm an oil executive," Rucker said finally. "Not a cop. In fact, I shouldn't even be here. Be seen here. That wasn't the plan."

He stood. Motioned to Whitaker to come over. He was tired of walking around in the street. His bodyguard, bent double, trotted over. Keeping an eye on the hotel.

"Yeah?"

"I'm going home. Call me after you've gotten them." He turned to go, reconsidered. "And get my money."

"What do you want done with them?"

"Who?"

"The Okie and the Jew woman."

"What do you think?"

As he strode across the street one more time the front door of the hotel was shoved open. The barrel of a Thompson appeared. "Lookout!" a cop somewhere said ominously, and everybody but Rucker ducked.

The Thompson chugged out about a dozen rounds in short bursts, all aimed at Rucker. Who calmly, oblivious possibly, continued across the street. Slugs clanged into cars parked on the other side of the street, broke a window or two and chipped curbing. Rucker picked up speed and trotted around the corner house and continued toward another car he had parked down the street, a big Packard with side curtains.

The firing stopped as he went out of sight.

As he passed the cop directing traffic Rucker heard the driver of a bread van asking what was going on. Glancing over, he saw a short black man standing on the running board of the Helms truck, looking the situation over.

"Just turn around and get out of here," the cop said. A bullhorn in the background was broadcasting instructions for the people in the hotel to come out with their hands up. Lewis came running up behind Rucker, panting heavily.

"Whitaker says we could get his brother in here," Lewis said. Rucker seemed not to know who he was talking about. "That Joseph kid. Talk him outta there."

"Fine. Go find the brother."

"What's happening over there?" the Negro asked again. People in cars behind the bread truck were honking their horns.

"Just get the hell outta here!" Lewis yelled. "Fucking niggers!"

He commenced waving mightily, and finally the black man, Bony Fish, got back in his van. He managed to back up enough to make a U turn and go back down the street. Looking between his mirrors at the shot-up Buick in front of the hotel as he went.

FORCING KIDS TO SHARE

D onovan took the drum magazine off the Thompson and reached into
the canvas bag and took out a box of shells and started reloading
the drum shell by shell. Wanda watched, her eyes still glazed. He was
amazingly adept at thumbing the little copper-nosed instruments in, one
following the other.

"I can't believe what we've gotten ourselves into," she said.

"Shit. If I'd had my rifle I would have got him," Donovan said. "You
can't aim these goddamn things so good."

"Just this morning I was a little crazy, sure. But not a criminal."

"I knew I should of brought it. One shot in the lungs and everbody
woulda gone home. He's running the whole shebang, can't think why
he'd want to set something like this up."

"I don't have anything against Rucker. Personally."

"What's he got against us?"

They exchanged a glance.

"They'll have the other doors shut off," he said.

"Yeah, what does he have against us? The poor can be mad at the rich,
but what can the rich possibly have against the poor?" Wanda asked, some
fire coming back into her. Suddenly she was more angry than curious. He
liked to see that. He thought he had lost her for a while. Some people did
that in a crisis, shut down and quit.

"It don't matter, now."

He thumbed the last rounds into the drum and clapped it onto the bottom of the Thompson. Got up. Grabbed the shotgun and the bag of ammo.

"Let's see what we got here."

He stalked back into the hotel. She followed, seeing that this was once
a swell kind of place but now was not only peeling and grimy, it was

also covered with construction dust. The thin carpet was stained with past abuses, and when they stepped into one of the open hotel rooms their shoes carried in spots of grease or garbage. The room was empty, as were they all.

"Donovan?"

She stopped him in the middle of the hallway. Forced a hug on him, knowing this was not the time or place. That was the point. She was regretting a lot, and now she regretted that she had flipped his animal switch. He really did have that ferocious look in his eye, and all she wanted was a little justice. Now she was scared.

"We could turn ourselves in and confess," she said into his coat.

"Technically, we ain't done nothin'."

She brightened. "That's right. They ambushed us before we even had a chance to do our stickup."

But she looked down. She was holding the attache case.

"Oh yeah," he said. "Besides that, I shot up a lot of cars and maybe hit a cop. They'd trump some charge anyway. You could go on out. There's nothing you've done."

All she could do was stare into his big blue eyes. "How could you think I'd do that?" He shrugged, offering her the easy way out. "How could you think that?" she repeated.

It became so apparent. The ingenue socialist. The weak-kneed feminist. The lilly-white idealist. He wanted to kill somebody, and all she wanted was to demonstrate her commitment to world peace and good will.

"Love you," he said.

"Love you," she said. She smiled. He smiled. She'd never seen a man like him.

He shouldered his gear and took her hand and led her back into the bowels of the old hotel. He found a room that was somewhat defensible, a foyer that led to laundry rooms and the back door. He set them up in an entryway, possibly where the concierge once waited at his desk for a guest to call. He pulled an old metal cabinet around as breastwork so that he could fire back toward the front as well as turn to protect their rear.

Then he looked over at her. She had plaster dust in her hair and eyebrows. Her eyes had again lost their energy and light, but she was still functioning.

"You're a lollapalooza, ya know it?"

"You know, this was dumb. Why didn't we just sneak in the office on Thursday night and rob the safe?"

"We hold out till night, maybe we can do something."

"Sure," she said. Every bit of anger had gone out of her, and her manner was of resigned acceptance. Of whatever might come. She took the Smith & Wesson he handed her, nodding when he asked if she remembered how to put the blade sight in the back notch.

"Okay, hold on here. I'm gonna go out front and give them something to think about."

Really frightened now, she looked at him with pleading eyes. She might accept whatever fate came of her foolish actions, but she didn't want to do it alone.

She choked back a little threat of tears and nodded solemnly.

Donovan wended his way cautiously to the front of the dead hotel, wondering why the coppers hadn't stormed the building or at least inserted somebody in a window. He hiked up the long spiral staircase and found a second-story window that looked down on the street. It was in a larger hotel room, possibly a suite. An oak dresser left over from the salad days leaned hard to one corner because of a missing leg.

His view was of the intersection and indeed the entire block. The masterminds, as Donovan jokingly called them to himself, had retreated for a confab, leaving a few people to keep an eye on the front door. But the palookas had only gone around the corner of a little garage and were perfectly visible from up here. It was a bit cloudy in the afternoon, and the view was of a tight tableau of men in dark wool coats with their hands plunged deep into pockets as they talked animatedly. Crouching at the edge of the window, he wanted to take a shot at them but they were pretty much out of range.

Traffic was still being diverted, but as Donovan watched, a panel truck with ICE painted on it drove in and was guided to a parking spot on the lawn of a business. He rose to his feet. He realized that it was his ice truck.

There was some animation as Joseph was escorted into the knot of masterminds. Donovan couldn't see their faces from here, but he could recognize the angular Whitaker and the fat-assed Lewis. Joseph stood out away from the group as it focused on him. They gestured wildly at the little guy. His shy body would have been recognizable to his brother in a crowd of thousands. There was no Rucker, as far as he could see.

Finally Joseph started for the hotel. He walked quickly, stopping only to receive some shouted wisdom from the others. Donovan barely got downstairs in time to meet him as he came in the door hollering his name.

"Hello, little brother."

Joseph peeked around the door. Donovan stood in the hallway with the Thompson parked on his hip. Closing the door behind him, Joseph had that set look to his face.

"Oh, this is a real nice little mess."

"Come on in. Make yourself comfortable. Ya got your pick a the rooms." Donovan gestured generously around him.

He walked Joseph down the hallway to their little fort in the back. Where the brother stopped dead in his tracks. Wanda had the revolver laid out on top of the filing cabinet, aimed at the back door. She barely glanced at him.

"Oh, hello, Joseph."

"Jesus, what's this going on here?" Joseph asked Donovan.

"They set this trap for us. How they knew what we were up to, I can't figure out."

Joseph's expression was of disbelief. Wanda and Donovan exchanged a sheepish glance.

"We were gonna hold up the payroll."

"But we never got around to it," Wanda pointed out.

Joseph glanced at the attache case standing in the corner of the alcove. "They said you got it."

"Yeah, after they ambushed us on the road," Donovan insisted in a hurt voice.

"He went back and got it after that," she said defensively. They didn't like being called on the carpet like this.

The little brother glared at Donovan. He could hardly bring himself to glance at Wanda. "That Red talked you into this, didn't she?" He wouldn't even look at her when he said it.

Nobody answered. Joseph, angered, reached over and slapped Donovan in the back of his head. Hard.

Wanda was astounded. The older brother just looked more sheepish. If anybody else had done that, Donovan would have removed his head.

"Here's the history lesson for you, little fascist boy," Wanda said, clomping out in front of him. Angry again. "We were trying to remove some money from the evil folks and provide it to the good folks."

It took a while for that to sink in. When it did, Joseph took to laughing. He was a snarly little guy, a big teenager who had had his development curtailed somehow, and he didn't laugh often. When he did it only became obvious how seldom he did it.

"So you were going to start the revolution," he said.

"No, the revolution has already started. It started with some very smart people, who you've probably never even heard of. They were thinking very hard about how unfair life is for most people, and how that could be corrected."

"Right. Oh, right."

"The revolution has already happened, as a matter of fact. They even tried it here, briefly."

"Yeah, a hundred and fifty years ago. And it did just fine."

"Until it got co-opted by the capitalists. Who turned it into the hog trough."

"So I guess you just had to get it going again."

"They tried. They tried it in the Farmer's Holiday in thirty-four. They tried it when the Bonus Army marched on Washington, and the veterans ended up getting shot by their own brothers in arms. If Roosevelt hadn't gotten elected President we would have had our revolution by now."

"All right, you two," Donovan said gently.

"I thought you liked Roosevelt, you socialists," Joseph said.

"Yeah, but he kept the capitalists from collapsing under their own greed, and now they're sneaking back and working to undermine all he's done. If you got your history from books instead of Movietone News you'd know what I mean."

"All right!" Donovan shouted. "Goddamn."

He found a clean spot on the floor and plopped down against the wall. The Thompson across his lap. He had to move his ever-present ice pick to one side to get comfortable. He looked up at them proudly.

"We would of pulled it off, it hadn't been for somebody tipping them off."

"Good thing you haven't killed anybody."

"It wasn't for lack of trying. Had old Rucker in my sights, and missed him." He held up the Thompson in dismay. "Things ain't made for specific aiming."

"They tell me they'll let you come on out. All you have to do is give up the firearms and come on out."

Wanda grabbed her pistol again and waved it around for effect. "Oh, sure they are. They'll just forget everything and forgive us our trespasses."

"They want their money back."

"That's what it's all about, isn't it? The money? It's worth more than all their principles put together, not that they have any except get more money."

"It's theirs. They earned it."

Wanda turned to this little offensive half-man, a rogue child with evil intentions. A quiet and elfish demon. "That's all the principles they have, isn't it. Be allowed to earn all the money they want, however they want, and be allowed to keep it. There is no other principle for them, and all of human emotion and history be damned. They'll ride out the Hard Times and Armageddon too if only they have their money."

"It's a freedom thing. It's what America's all about, sister."

"It's what America's become, not what she was supposed to be about," Wanda said. "And don't call me sister."

She had grabbed the Smith & Wesson and taken to waving it around negligently, and the sight of it quietened Joseph somewhat. He still knew he was in the right, though. She realized that the pistol had become an impediment to what was a productive dialogue, so she slammed it back down on the cabinet.

"It's like you took that ice pick," Joseph said, motioning to his brother's favorite tool, "and you stuck it in the eye of the Constitution and everything. That's what you Reds are doing here."

"Hold on," Donovan said. Cocking his ear down the hallway. He got up.

There was the sound of a distant bullhorn. "Come on out," it sounded like it said. "Leave your weapons inside and come on out." Or maybe it said something else, the words ricocheting down the hallways like that. Maybe that was only what he expected it to say.

They listened for a while. Then the bullhorn said, "Joseph Daley! Are you all right in there?"

Wanda laughed. Donovan laughed. It all sounded so incongruous and foolish, this bullhorn business. Them balled up in the back of a deserted hotel just off the Miracle Mile of American business with a bunch of Red-hunting cops and Pinkertons outside. They both collapsed down against the wall.

"Offer's still good," Joseph said.

"Joseph, let me ask you this," Wanda said, reclined against the wall. "Your family lost its land, when something could have been done."

"That's none of your business. That's none of anybody else's business but our own."

"There were people starving to death in Oklahoma and Texas, and until FDR came in, the government just let them starve. And now you've got men like Charles Rucker bilking people out of their pennies on swindles like Beach Oil."

"Yeah, fine."

"It's one of the conundrums of our times. How do you force kids to share? I guess you sympathize with the swells instead of with your own family."

"You just shut up about my family!" A fine mist flew from his breath. He reached over and grabbed the revolver off the cabinet. Aimed it at Wanda. The tension and the convolution of the argument had apparently become too much for the little brother. "Now you all just go on out there and put an end to this mischief." He waved the gun between her and Donovan.

Who got up slowly and reached over and gently took the gun away from him by the barrel. Joseph looked about ready to cry. His little black eyes were puffy and red, and his chin stuck out the way a teenager's would in a tiff with his parents.

"Our father asked about you the other day," Donovan said.

"Yeah?" Joseph's nose dripped, and he rubbed the moisture away.

"He's doin' okay. Not great, but okay."

"I don't care how he's doing, Donovan!" Joseph leaned over and shouted up at his big brother. "I hope he dies and goes to hell! The way he treated her! The way he ran off like that!"

He whirled and stalked out of the little forted-up alcove and down a long hallway. By the time he got to the other end of it he seemed to sense that his brother had followed him at a distance. He turned and watched Donovan slowly come down the hall, scuffling his shoes along the dead carpet.

"I'm sorry there's nothing I can do for you!" Joseph yelled at his brother. "They said you could come on out, but oh no! I guess you're not going to do that!"

"They're gonna shoot us down, Joseph," Donovan said. Still sauntering toward him, sans guns, sans pretense. He was saying goodbye. "You go on and get out of here."

"They give me their word!"

"You take care, little brother."

Joseph waited until his brother had walked halfway the length of the hallway toward him and then turned and bolted for the front foyer. Afraid, maybe, that he would have to hear more about his father and mother. Or afraid he might be hugged. Afraid he might be loved.

There was the sound of his heels clacking in the foyer. The sound of the door. Opening. Closing.

Then the sound of the door crashing in. Donovan just had time to turn and run back down the hallway as the first cops raced toward him. They fired at his back until he turned the corner. And reappeared with the Thompson and sprayed them until two lay dying on the old carpet. The others retreated toward the foyer.

Donovan heard the sound of crashing wood behind him, and he ran back in time to see Wanda aim the pistol just as he had taught her and fire into the chest of a man coming through the back door. The man spun away, collapsed and crawled halfway out the door before he just stopped. His belly hung on the doorstep.

Other figures outside the door fired at them fleetingly before they turned and sought cover from the fusillade that Donovan unleashed on them. He fired until the Thompson stopped on an empty click, and he flung it aside and grabbed the shotgun and unloaded the first barrel into a cop who tried to sprint through the smashed door.

That cop limped one step and fell, coming down like a bundle of black wool at their feet. When Donovan looked over at Wanda she was dry-firing the Smith & Wesson, one savage pull after another aimed at the door. CLICK CLICK CLICK CLICK CLICK.

"Hey," he said. He took the pistol. From his pocket he fished a fistful of shells and expertly flipped the cylinder down and dropped five shells in and flipped it closed. A cartridge fell on the floor but he couldn't look away from her.

Wanda peered up at him, grief-stricken. And took the gun as he grabbed her Thompson and returned to the hallway. Peeked down it. Nobody down there except two bodies. Not even a sound, of man, or car, or bullhorn, or even a rat nuzzling ancient food from a cupboard. The rats knew to take cover.

Donovan turned to look at Wanda, who had taken cover behind the filing cabinet. He tried to give her the gun. It took her a long time to take it. "Now we've gone and done it," he said.

DO YOU WANT TO LIVE?

It was getting dark. Earlier in here than it did outside, where an adrenaline assault had turned into a grim and stubborn siege by men hunkered and only fractionally visible behind conglomerating shapes of cars and trucks.

Altogether depressing as Donovan and Wanda looked down on it from another second-story window. He showed her how to ease one eye only to the corner of the window, and she could see the frightened cops slumped behind the machinery made in Detroit by her union brothers. He knew the glint of the window glass would help conceal them, though the men down there didn't even seem to look up. Some were glumly eating meals that had been brought to them in tin plates.

"Wish they'd bring us something," he said. "I'm so hungry my stomach thinks my throat's cut."

His stale joke didn't go far. She turned away from the window in disgust.

"You okay?" he asked.

They had gone all through the hotel looking for another way out. Had snuck through dozens of rooms and offices. Been fired at once and sprayed with glass when they passed in front of a window on the ground floor. And now they were hunched and small in this last light as the wispy blue-green clouds above Los Angeles' beach side turned turquoise and then black.

She settled her back against a wall and scuffed a place in the demolished plaster refuse for her feet to rest. "You remember that time we went to look at houses in the San Gabriel?" She had a lump of plaster under her right leg that hurt, but she was too tired to move.

He stood at the window, looking at the pitiful but dangerous little men below. He didn't look at her, embarrassed that he had allowed them to get in this situation. Wanting to just break down and apologize.

"I loved them little kitchens. You could cook up a storm in there."

"I was thinking about that guy with the pox scars. The one who sold us the Buick."

"Yeah?" He moved a couple of inches and he could see the front end of their Buick, stranded on the front steps below him, a lot of bullet pocks in the hood and a flat tire. "What about him?"

"Do you think a guy like that, a salesman from the get-go, would ever take to unions? Wage regulation? Social security?"

Donovan shrugged. Who cared? He squirmed a little farther into his coat. It was cold throughout the dead hotel, as if it had a direct line to some of that refrigeration that was going to soon take over the world.

"Because that's the guy who has to get it," she said. "If he doesn't get it, America doesn't get it."

He didn't respond in any way. He was thinking of his brother. All of his brothers and sisters, so widely scattered and struggling. His father in that shack with that woman. His mother sitting up late at night after fifteen hours of cooking and cleaning up after boarders, writing letter after letter so eloquent in rage and hatred.

Did his mother not write to him because she thought a letter to Joseph would get to him? Or did she know that he knew of her infidelity as well as his father's, and not want to approach that knowledge in any fashion? Donovan had never told Joseph what he knew about the woman he knew as a saint.

"Maybe he will and maybe he won't," he said, knowing Wanda was expecting an answer.

He started picking up their gear, the weapons, the canvas sack. He shook a couple of .45 cartridge boxes, just to make sure they were empty, and tossed them aside. She didn't move, though.

"I don't want to go down by those bodies again. All right?"

"Yeah. Let's just find a better room."

"They forgot to make the bed in this one."

"Yeah." He laughed softly. "I'll call maid service."

Now a light from below slashed across the ceiling. He eased over to look. Two new cars drove in. Three. Four. They angle parked and more men got out of them quickly, energetically. Four from each car. They all carried rifles and shotguns and Thompsons.

"The Pinkertons are here," he said.

That got her up to look. She was familiar with the Pinkertons. Hired guns, goons, thugs with lead pipes, detectives, trackers. All dressed like the finest businessmen. Which they were. You needed a union hall trashed or an organizer beaten to death, you called the Pinkerton Agency.

"Is it time to give it up?"

She looked to him hopefully, then down at the courtyard. The new men had energized the old men, who got out from behind their cars and rallied around for an intense little conversation.

"You're kiddin' me, right?" He shouldered his weapons and headed back farther into the hotel. She followed, carrying her tommy gun the way a sleepy girl carried her doll. Dragging it along by one arm.

"What are they going to do with us, take us to the station house and drag us into court? All we do is plead self-defense." She trotted along behind him.

"We're never gonna see a courtroom. You didn't wonder why there ain't a bunch of uniforms and news reporters and such down there? They're gonna disappear us."

Trying to catch up to him all the way along the upstairs hallway, and all the way down the spiral staircase, she couldn't see why they shouldn't try. Humans couldn't be that cruel. There was an urgency to his step that got into her steps, but he had a big stride. They raced through the lobby, dance-stepped around the two bodies in the hall.

"Where are we going?"

"The kitchen. We can make a stand in there. Give us a chance, anyway." He glanced down at her hands. "Where's the money?"

"Oh shit. I left it up there."

He pivoted and went back toward the lobby. Which was by then filling with light from all the activity outside.

"Leave it," she said.

"That's our bargaining chips."

He ran up the stairs. Came back down with the attache case.

Just as he descended the stairs, the front door, what was left of it, smashed inward again. A big canister bomb, wailing thick white ropes of smoke, arched in and clanked in the lobby near the fountain.

Shots followed it, and the shapes of men dodging in through the fog.

The only light came in forced through doors and windows, and Donovan fired a ranging blast with the Thompson as he hit the lobby floor, the sound knocking hard on the walls. He skidded to a stop and leveled on two men awkwardly trying to bring their rifles to bear on him from behind the fountain. The cherub disintegrated under his bullets. The two men fell to their faces in fear or death.

Racing down the hallway, Donovan could see Wanda in the dim but growing light waiting for him at the far end. As he got closer she raised her Thompson and fired past him at somebody he couldn't see, and then he grabbed her as he passed and carried her along with him as bullets pounded the flowery old wallpaper behind them and plaster exploded into their faces.

The kitchen was a large room filled with old stoves and iceboxes and cabinets left over from the hotel's heyday, barely visible in the glancing lights that had bored into the hotel. They dove behind a stainless steel cabinet and scrambled for position and waited.

But even in the heat of the moment, in the midst of her fear, she had to grab his arm. "I love you. I'm sorry it came to this." He watched as two men ran by the door and down the hallway. Turned to look her in the eyes. "It's okay, Baby. We'll give 'em hell."

"Do you want to live?" a voice said softly.

Donovan whirled violently, kicking the cabinet awry as he screwed around to look behind him. Wanda pinched her eyes shut, fearing some sudden end.

What he saw was the old gas range, pushed halfway out from the wall, and a pair of glints in the dark space behind it. As Donovan watched, his Thompson gripped so hard his forearm hurt, a face appeared in the narrow space.

A black face.

Bony Fish.

Smiling big and white now.

"If you do, come on in here," the smile said.

With that, Bony pushed with both hands, and the range scraped out away from the wall, revealing a dark passage. Donovan and Wanda didn't even exchange the obligatory congratulatory glance. They scooted into the space like bats racing for the cave, dragging their various weapons and war paraphernalia, and of course the money, with them.

HE HAS A BONY FACE

It was surreal, like a painting out of France during those turbulent days when the art world was all akilter. Or like one of those badly made silent pictures where, with all the cheap sets, you didn't quite know where the play was taking place. Not that the talkies were any better, some of them.

Bony Fish had pulled the gas range back into place behind them, and as complete darkness overtook them they waited patiently and trustingly—what other option did they have?—until he squeezed by them and struck a match and lit the candle.

Together, with him, peering through the sulfur smoke of the match, they looked down this dark passageway, its dank walls glistening, greasy with something. It seemed to taper off, out of light, at the end.

"Old speakeasy tunnel," Bony chuckled, so pleased with himself. He stood, but kept his head low, almost short enough to stand upright. The tunnel was about five feet high and three feet wide, dug into the rock and reinforced with rough concrete slapped against the walls in places. "I used to wash dishes in this hotel, back when it was in full flower, so to speak. They would sneak the liquor in this way, cases and cases of it."

They looked at him with amazed eyes, filled with the revelation of hope.

Donovan and Wanda followed him, heads bent low, listening to his patter as he led them down the long, straight passage. It smelled like an overripe gas station, and they passed several seeps where they had to walk through puddles of oil and tar. It made sense. They weren't that far from the Tar Pits.

"You believe that? They would park a truck over the trap door and unload the booze right into the tunnel. Special trucks and everything."

About a hundred yards, Donovan estimated as they began walking up-hill a bit. The tunnel angled up, but they couldn't see much with Bony in front of them and the candle wavering weakly. Up some roughly made concrete steps they walked, quiet.

A sound. A door creaking open on loose hinges. A bit of light, a rectangle of normal darkness above them, so bright outside that it seemed like daylight against the final blackness of the tunnel. Bony blew out the candle.

They stepped up and out onto a wide concrete parking lot behind a warehouse. Turned to see Bony putting a latch on what seemed to be a cellar door in the weeds at the edge of the parking lot. Huge moving vans, parked for the night, loomed around them in rows as tall as apartments. The trio moved toward what Donovan guessed was the south. Away from a busy glow of headlights and car growls from the next street over. Away from the hotel looming next to the warehouse.

Bony had his bread truck parked at the curb a block away, and when he saw the coast was clear he waved them inside. They stepped up into the most beautiful smell they had ever been privileged to encounter.

As they slunk into the back of the van, amid racks of almost empty wooden shelves, Bony said, "Fresh or day-old?" He gestured toward a shelf of bread and cakes and donuts. "Well, I take that back. It's left over from the day's route, so it's all day-old."

Donovan took one of the rectangular applesauce cakes from a rack. Unwrapped it in a swift, unceremonious motion, kicked the wrapper out the door, broke the loaf in half. He handed Wanda the small half and swallowed his half in three bites.

Leaving them to their dinner, Bony started the truck and backed it up and pulled out onto the nearly deserted street. He went up one street, looked down to his left at a confusing jumble of car lights, where occasional traffic was still being stopped. He drove in the opposite direction two more streets, then a left, and another left, and made a right onto Wilshire Boulevard. From there it was only a right-hand turn and half an hour to Watts.

"How did you know to come get us in there?" Donovan finally asked. He and Wanda sat on the floor below window level, drinking from a water bag.

"Saw your car with the bullet holes in it," Bony said.

"How do you know my car?"

"Everybody along Central Avenue knows your car," Bony said. And he drove on with Wanda and Donovan eating steadily and wondering why everybody knew their car.

Where Bony Fish lived was in a section of Watts near the farm fields. They drove the final mile or so in silence. The bakery truck driver had asked them if he could drop them off somewhere, and they said no. They were likely to be discovered in their familiar haunts.

"Guess I could take you home with me for a little while."

"Good," Donovan said. "We'll figure something out later."

"Thank you, thank you," Wanda kept saying.

The Fish house was a small, square structure in a street of small, square structures. Even in the dark they could see that the neighborhood was well-kept but overwhelmed with the stuff of living. A tractor in one yard and a rowboat in another. Piles of leftover building materials, cannibalized car bodies and partly finished children's playhouses. The neighborhood might have been a decade old, or fifty decades old.

"One thing, now. Before we go in," said Bony, who spoke with a measured and formal tone. "What am I going to tell people? About that back there?"

He motioned in the direction of Los Angeles. Crouched in the back of the van, Wanda looked at Donovan, Donovan looked at Wanda, and they both looked at Bony.

"We got stranded on the highway—" he said.

"Just some friends come to visit—" she said.

"I don't know," Bony said.

"How about, you saved our butts from getting killed?" Wanda said. "And we followed you home?"

"Sure. Just give me those guns."

Wanda, in particular, clung to her Thompson. She looked down at its endearing shape. Where at one point in the night she was ready to leave it in disgust, now she could hardly stand the thought of parting with it. The wooden grips had come to fit her hands so convincingly.

"Don't you worry. I'm just going to hide them," Bony said reassuringly. He had heard the Bonnie and Clyde kind of stories and thought maybe this woman was that kind of desperado. Yet, her face gave off such a note of vulnerability.

Donovan handed his Thompson, the shotgun and the .38 over. Finally Wanda scooted hers across the floor of the van, and Bony gathered them all together somehow.

"What about that?"

Wanda looked down. She had the briefcase of money in her hand.

"We better keep that with us," Donovan said.

"I'll be right back, then." And Bony stepped out of the van and into the night.

"He wanted to put us in a tight, he wouldn't of rescued us in the first place," Donovan reasoned as they waited for the black man to come back. Yet they got to their feet tentatively in the back of the van to await what came next.

Bony's round face peeped back inside. He smiled. When not looking so serious he had an engaging smile, though not so visible in this darkness. Donovan and Wanda thought it was wondrous. "Here's what we'll do," he said. "We'll go on in there and see what happens."

So they did. It wasn't very late, and the house was still up. Bony went in, and the screen door slapped shut behind him, and Wanda grabbed Donovan's arm.

"Let me talk to these people," she whispered.

"What do you mean?"

"The Negroes. I know how to talk to them."

"I've been talking to Negroes since I was two," he said, whispering because she was whispering.

"Just let me handle it," she said as Bony came back to see what was holding them up. He held the screen door open for them.

The living room was full of Negroes. Big ones and little ones. Male ones and female ones. Light ones and dark ones. There was a pot-bellied stove crackling in one corner of the living room, and two big kids taking turns working at a butter churn in the other. They were being overseen by an old woman with a crooked back and the frizziest hair in the room.

"Lord a mercy," the old woman said when she looked up and saw Bony's friends. "Dare say you do got a surprise for us."

"This is Mr. and Mrs., um—" Bony started.

"I'm Wanda Kitchen, and this is Donovan Daley," Wanda blurted. As she spoke, a woman came in from the kitchen, which was hazy with smoke.

"I remember you," the woman said. "Club Alabam."

"This is my wife, Hattie," Bony said.

"Or you can call me Mary," Hattie said.

Bony looked a little confused. Donovan and Wanda looked a little confused. Then Bony's face opened in recognition.

"Oh yes, you called her Mary that night. This man certainly saved us some lost skin at that point in time."

Hattie, a serious-faced woman with konked-straight hair, wiped her hands on her long skirt and shook their hands. And proceeded to introduce their four kids, the grandmother, whose name was BaBa, and several cousins and friends. There were twelve people in the small room now that Wanda and Donovan were in.

"We thank you so much for your hospitality," Wanda began. "It's the forces of social change that bring us here, and we are so grateful to you. We couldn't do this without the support of people like you."

Twenty eyes stared at her. She might have been speaking German for all the response she got. As Donovan began to speak, the eyes shifted to him.

"Where'd you get that name, Bony?" Donovan asked, laughing his big laugh. "That's some kinda funny name for a man named Fish." Everybody laughed, as they must have done many times before when this came up.

So there commenced, entirely to Wanda's surprise, a complete conversation, with the family gathered around Donovan as he took over the butter churning chores, about the Fish family history from Georgia and Louisiana through Texas and on to California in the 1920s. The churn sloshed up and down in his skillful hands as he asked them questions about the profession of the maternal grandfather, who was dead, and what part of Texas they lived in, because he had traveled in Texas some. Turned out that Boniface was named after Napoleon, via the Louisiana sojourn.

"We have three generations of Bony Fishes," he said. "To back before the days of manumission."

He looked a bit like a Napoleon, the little black man did. A studious face on a flyweight body. Obviously, evidenced by what he had accomplished that night, he was something of a strategist, too. His wife matched him perfectly, her pumpkin face emphasized by the way she plastered every long hair to her head so they looked like the windings on a ball of twine.

"So we moved here to get away from it all," Bony finished his story.

"Lotta bad stuff out there on the roads." Donovan said. "You see any a that?"

A brief exchange of glances between Bony and Hattie. A look around the room at their loved ones. And friends. And friends of loved ones.

"That's why we migrated here," Bony said in his straight-laced tone. "To get away from all that. Being from Oklahoma, you would know about that."

Another patient silence as the room awaited Donovan's reply. Oh, this little Boniface was a strategist, all right. And was Donovan oblivious, or was his reply carefully calculated to suit the needs of the moment? It seemed so innocent.

"Not many colored up in the Panhandle, Bony. More Indians. But we had a cowboy on our ranch, black as lava on a summer night. Best roper I ever seen. Head or heels, he could flat throw 'em down, old Earl could."

Why, it was like the entire room let out its breath at the same time. Everybody but Wanda. The others relaxed into a chorus of yeah, yeahs, but she was still so startled by her man's easy nature with anybody of any social level. Apparently he was a man who could get into dire straits, or extricate himself from the same.

That provided her some hope that she would not die. Or at least not die in vain.

APPLESAUCE CAKE

Outside the abandoned hotel a marked Los Angeles Police Department car pulled up slowly to the front steps. On which rested the riddled body of the new Buick, cocked downward at a crippled angle. Most of the other car headlights had been turned off, so only the patrol car's dim six-volt high beams cut through the darkness and up the apron of the building.

Through the windshield of their turtleback Ford the two beat cops seemed transfixed by the sight of the flattened car. They assessed at some length the bullet holes in the fenders and in the shattered double doors of the hotel. They didn't even get out for a minute, as if fearful of entering such a fractured scenario.

Finally four men hurried out of the hotel carrying a body between them, hunched in exertion and clutching the dead man's clothing in tight fists, and deposited him in the open trunk of a car parked at the curb. They didn't even look at the policemen, who still seemed to have no inclination to get out of their patrol car.

"Help you boys?" said a voice, and the two cops jumped and looked left. One of the Red Squad cops approached the car from the rear.

"What's going on here?" the driver said. "We had a call of some commotion."

"Lewis, Red Squad," said the cop with his hand on their window. He held out his badge. "We got it all taken care of."

"We got a call there was maybe gunfire."

"We got it, I said."

The two uniformed cops exchanged a glance.

"Okay, then. What happened? Just between you and me?"

Lewis leaned in the window and began telling them the parts that he could. It centered on the amount of gunfire involved. As well as the mystery of the holed-up shooters. He was obviously taken with the uniqueness of the story. He put nothing in it about who was running the show. His unit was good about keeping secrets.

When the patrol cops backed out and left, the other went back inside the hotel. There was some degree of confusion in there. Men in fedoras and pork pies and derbies and boaters, their pistols drawn and their shotguns leveled and their coats unbuttoned for freedom of movement, went from room to room of the rundown hotel. Again and again. At first they searched hurriedly, randomly, running from floor to floor in high expectation, flashlight beams probing every nook and cranny. Then they searched it again methodically, room by room, coordinating their efforts and conferring on the details of closets and bathrooms and room numbers.

Finally Rucker hustled in the front, an unlit cigar forgotten in his mouth. He was without suit coat, without hat, his tie dangling without its gold nugget clasp. Yet even in the cold he was sweating.

"Hells bells," he said, hands on hips. "What am I paying you palookas for?"

He was in the lobby, the ceramic remains of the fountain scattered at his feet. Here and there shards—part of an elbow, a lip, a nipple--lay half-drowned in blackening pools of blood. Here and there spent cartridges lay in eddies of carnage, swept by the industry of human feet and glued in regions to the dried blood. The bodies had been removed.

Whitaker came pattering down the staircase fast, as fast as a man will come when looking for something precious lost to him. Pinkerton agents and Red Squad cops and Rucker employees gradually emerged into the lobby behind him.

"Nothing," Whitaker said. The normally calm man had a perplexed look about him.

"What's that mean?" Rucker said.

"The ice man's not here, the quiff's not here."

Rucker turned to the other men. "Pinkerton agent in charge?" he asked.

The tall, thin man he had talked to during the siege was standing right in front of him. He stuck out his hand.

"Roberts. Judge Roberts."

"You a judge?" Rucker asked, looking the man's neck over suspiciously.

"Just my name," the agent said.

"You were supposed to kill them."

"Dead," Whitaker said, as if the statement needed elucidation.

"Sir, our expertise is not in killing."

"What did we hire you for, then?"

"We did not, as my home office informs me, come to a financial agree-ment on that portion of this case. We were paid to be here at this…" He paused and scanned the room with the eye of a businessman evaluating a job gone over budget. "… event. Had the event been successful we would be under no further obligation. Unsuccessful, the same. The event is over."

"Damn you people. All right, then, Lanky," Rucker said, in the habit of giving the people around him nicknames. "What is your expertise?"

"Well. For one thing. Finding. Locating. Discovering. Searching out."

Rucker smiled. He smiled at Whitaker, who didn't smile back. He smiled at the growing circle of co-conspirators, who did smile back. Rucker took the cigar out of his mouth and looked at it. The chewed end looked like a rotten smashed plum. He spit tobacco fines.

"Okay, so search out."

"The home office—"

"I'll take care of it, goddamnit!"

Again the men split up. They went through the hotel one more time. Upstairs and down. As they did, making a pretense of working hard at what they knew from previous searches to be an impossible job, Whitaker and Roberts met on the stairs and conferred. Rucker listened in, expelling tobacco bits with the tip of his tongue the whole time as if the cigar were made of acid.

"They were on the ground floor when we came in," Roberts said, going back over what they had gone over four or five times already.

"Back in the back," Whitaker said.

"Balled up good and proper back there."

The two walked down the hallway, leaving their boss looking at his cigar in consternation. In the kitchen, Lewis was already there, opening cupboard doors, peering in the big pantry. He even opened the small top cupboards, moving aside a crusty old pan as if a little man might have been crouched behind it. He took the pan out and looked inside it.

The men clinked through spent cartridges on the floor as they shuffled around the kitchen looking for a clue in the pinpoint glare of flashlights. Whitaker pulled up in front of the Pinkerton man. Roberts, apparently an individual of some standing in the local community of background in-vestigations and dirty political tricks, had a habit of pulling his head back away from his companion the way a reared rattlesnake might.

"They disappeared," Whitaker said. He reached inside his coat and pulled out a pair of pliers and began playing with them unconsciously. Snapping the jaws closed, slowly and menacingly.

"Can't just disappear," Roberts said, ready to strike. Puzzled at the pliers.

"Surely right. But."

"So where do they go?"

"You tell me."

"There's two, a man and a woman."

"Correct."

"They were making a stand," Roberts said.

"You saw it. You were here. Not like you didn't see it."

"Two men bled to death right here on this floor."

Roberts and Whitaker scanned the floor, which was streaked with red where bodies had been dragged out. Shells scattered as Lewis continued to futz around, putting the pan in the upper cabinet. Even as he did he looked like he might take it down and look in it again, but he saw Roberts looking at him funny so he didn't.

Then Whitaker took a step toward the big stove against the wall. He squatted. Picked up a single round of ammunition. It was unfired. He put his pliers away.

"Thirty-eight Smith & Wesson," Roberts said.

"That's what she carried."

"The woman?" Rucker asked. He strolled into the room with his hands in his pockets. Cigar lit. "I can't stand it that that Red has got my money. But the worst is old Bananas. He isn't that smart. I just hate that."

But Whitaker didn't answer. He cocked his head, looking at the stove. It was angled out away from the wall at one end, just a bit. Maybe three degrees off parallel.

Whitaker eased over to that end of the stove and began tugging at it. Wiggling the heavy stove away from the wall. He did it with one hand, drawing an automatic from his shoulder holster with the other.

But there was no wall in the reveal. Just an empty black hole. Suddenly Lewis came alive, grabbing the stove, helping Whitaker see-saw it back and forth until it sat in the middle of the floor at the end of its umbilical gas line. The gaping hole behind it transfixed them for a second, like some empty space in history itself.

Roberts pulled his revolver from his belt. Lewis retrieved his shotgun from where he had leaned it. Rucker relit his recalcitrant cigar and took a puff.

"Old Bananas," he said.

Within two minutes Whitaker and Roberts and Lewis were heaving upward with their shoulders on the cellar door at the other end of the tunnel, a couple of men behind them holding their police flashlights on their sweating faces. Finally the hasp broke free and the old door flew outward and slapped against the ground like a broken gate.

Slowly Roberts' head emerged from the hole in the ground amid the weak, angled, addled light from flashlights. He sniffed the air as if searching with his crooked nose for guidance. His head and shoulders slowly followed the nose out into the night air, blowing fog from his exertions.

The other men extracted their weapons, nodded on cue, gathered themselves and burst upward behind the Pinkerton man into the deserted nighttime parking lot. To an onlooker, if there had been one, it might have seemed to be the denizens of hell escaping from an unholy air vent, one fallen angel among them sniffing the firmament for the sacred purity of oxygen.

Spreading out around the parking lot, bent double to look under the moving vans, the men moved through the darkness with a great weight lifted. They followed tarry footprints, spreading more tar themselves. The supernatural element of the couple's disappearance, the superiority that that implied, had been debunked, at least. They weren't up against the impossible odds of God or some other invisible hand that would work against them forever.

They heard a grunt. Roberts' lanky shape stood very still at the street curb. Examining something in his hand. The very stillness of him finally drew the other men. Even Rucker, who had braved the tunnel in a cloud of cigar smoke once everyone else had passed, emerging into the world like a smoking hot turd, eased up next to him with the ember of his butt glowing against his face like one of those newfangled neon signs pulsing on and off as he sucked.

"What is it?" Rucker smacked.

"Fresh," Roberts said, smelling the object he held in his hand.

"Yeah?" Whitaker said.

"My favorite, too."

"What is?"

The Pinkerton held out a crinkled object. Which they all bent to examine. Paper of some kind, they could see as they angled in close.

"Applesauce cake."

THE WRONG SIDE OF TOWN

Donovan and Wanda woke up facing away from each other, butt to butt, on a straw tick mattress on the floor of the living room of the little house. Wanda facing the wall. She had been awake for a couple of hours, soused in the imagery of men dying right in front of and all around her (part of it may have been a dream), but she could sense from Donovan's inert body that he was dead asleep.

Then she was thinking of her father. How he had brought them out of the tenements of Minneapolis and installed them in a small, rabidly anti-Semitic town full of the palest people in the world. And built their own world for them, and for other Jews who followed them, out of nothing but second-hand clothing and tribal determination. Built a little family so packed with ambition and neurosis that it had everything it needed to survive in America.

What was it about killing people with guns that made her think of her father? She couldn't link the two, though she woke up thinking about the horror of the one and quickly fell to grim memories of the other. Of folding clothes for hours at a time in the family's first store when she was a little girl, her bearded father, all in black, a top hat towering on his head, looming over her to make sure the sleeves were folded in and the collars squared. He would come back later and check to make sure she had uniformly placed them on the high wall shelves in perfect replication, making her go back up the tall ladder to correct any misalignments.

How had she forgotten those times so completely? Why had she remembered them now, as she lay agonizing over the face of a man running at her, gun in hand, until he drove his chest into the floor as she fired bullet after bullet into his bulky coat? What did the clothing store—a shelf-lined cavern with tables in the center heaped with blouses and trousers rumpled by persnickety sale customers and in the way-back a little nook where old Mr. Yupin the tailor kowtowed before the gentiles like a wind-up toy hinged at the waist—what did this have to do with that horrific siege?

Had it been deliberate, this forgetfulness? Had her sojourn in Los Angeles, and even her participation in the so-called heist, been a part of that forgetfulness? Was she forgetting her childhood by this violent methodology?

She lost her train of thought as she heard shuffling noises in Bony's living room. When she turned over she saw the black people, and she must have started, because Donovan jerked awake and saw them too. She grabbed his arm in alarm. Six, no, seven now, black people stood by their bed on the floor.

Watching the white people sleep, apparently. Seeing how they did it. Seeing if they looked any different than they did in their own sleep, maybe. Other than sleeping white, of course.

Wanda drew one hand from the handmade quilt covering them and twinkled her fingers at her audience. There were three children, a couple of teenagers, the mother of the house, and an old man who seemed completely bewildered by the sight before him. He whirled in a limping sort of way and went out the front door in a hurry, clunking a helpful cane on the floor alongside him.

When Wanda sat up, the others fled, except for one teenage boy who just seemed transfixed. If an angel had risen from that quilt, a particularly colorful handmade quilt with a starburst pattern in purple and yellow, the boy couldn't have been more happy.

"Morning," Wanda said. Which caused him to disappear too.

"What the hell," Donovan said, throwing off the covers the way he did every morning. He was shirtless, and he got up in his BVDs and trotted to the chair where he had deposited his clothes the night before. He was still pulling on his socks when the old man came back with an armful of skinny wood and, without a greeting, started a fire in the little stove.

"Little chilly out, is it?" Donovan asked the man. Who didn't answer. When he had the fire roaring he clapped the stove door shut and went out without a word.

"Little chilly in here," Donovan said to Wanda. He was slipping the scabbard for his ice pick onto his belt. That damned pick, for some reason it now irritated her terribly. It seemed so dangerous, so horrifying, and he didn't need it anymore. He wasn't an ice man anymore. He wasn't anything anymore.

"You might as well get rid of that, now."

Looking down at the pick for a moment, he seemed to be contemplating the validity of her thoughts about the tool. Finally he slipped it into its sheath as if it were as comfortable as a sock.

"There's still ice. The frigerators ain't taken over yet."

She emerged from the covers, still in her clothes. She tried to rub the wrinkles out of her blouse and trousers, without any appreciable success. Folding the bedclothes, she began piling them in a corner. She put Rucker's upper class leather briefcase on top of the blankets. The money and the misery made it seem very heavy today.

Hattie came in from the kitchen. Said good morning and asked whether they wanted flapjacks or oatmeal for breakfast. "Or we could go out back and see if the chickens done their job and get some eggs." It was very awkward, though she was friendly and smiling. The blacks were always smiling at whites, and Wanda knew it was a reflex, and that made it all the more awkward.

"Oh, thank you, Hattie, we'll go out and get something," Wanda finally said. She could barely speak, she was agonizing so over the shootout. The dead men would all of a sudden leap up, fresh in her mind, and she would have to deal with them.

This made Hattie all the more fidgety. She stared at Wanda as if she were crazy. Bony must have told her the story. The rest of the family, and other people, began coming in, sitting down, and watching. They hadn't been told the story. They made Wanda nervous. Everybody was nervous except Donovan.

"Heck no, flapjacks sounds good to me," he said.

So they had breakfast, with all these people sitting around watching. Donovan tore into his flapjacks and bacon—Hattie cooked it crispy just the way he specified—but Wanda could only pick with a lazy fork and mumble down a few bites. So many eyes on her.

"Where's that butter we churned last night?" Donovan asked, his mouth full.

"Oh my gosh, I forgot," Hattie said.

She brought a dish mounded with butter and sat down beside Donovan and they commenced a long conversation about chickens as he buttered his pancakes liberally. Something about speckled hens versus pure colored hens and whether one type laid eggs better than the other type. Country talk that Wanda didn't comprehend, nor why the conversation was happening.

She wanted to talk about repression of the colored people of the world. She wanted to say this here was proof there could be love between the tribes.

After breakfast, the other black people left to go about their business, except for the old man. Who turned out to be Bony's father. Hattie introduced him. He never said a word, but sat sternly, lodged in a stuffed chair in the far corner of the room watching the stove as if the wood might try to escape it.

"Where's Bony?" Donovan asked, slurping down the last of his half a dozen pancakes soaked in molasses syrup.

"He'll be back directly. He delivers half a day on Saturday."

Hattie started washing dishes, and Wanda offered to help, and Hattie refused to let her, so they couldn't even relate on the basic kitchen sink level. So the day progressed. At one point Donovan suggested to Wanda that they go for a walk and "talk things over." Despite the friendly surroundings, they recognized that their lives had come apart like broken toys and they needed to devise a plan to repair them. But Hattie remarked that it might not be wise to "just go walking around" in the neighborhood.

Apparently the word of their visitation had already gone out on the grapevine, and flaunting themselves in public in a Negro community could only send deeper shock waves. "We have to live here," Hattie explained. The old man nodded frontways and sideways in vehement involuntary agreement.

Finally Bony came home. Smiling. So Wanda knew something was wrong. He threw a Times down on the table. It flopped open to the bottom half of the page, to a small, grainy photograph of Wanda. The headline read "Radical Unionist Shoots Policeman."

"Jesus," Donovan said.

"Sweet Jesus," Hattie said.

The photograph, taken from one of her family pictures, was of a Wanda four or five years younger. But it was identifiably her. Strikingly her. Fascinatingly her. They all gathered around and stared and stared at it.

"What you got yourself into?" said a voice behind them.

The old man stood there leaning on his cane, looking at the photo. He was a grizzly old soul, pitted cheeks and discolorations about the forehead and neck. As if his skin had been absorbing deep bruises for much of his life.

"Where'd they get that picture from?" Donovan asked.

"From ransacking our house," Wanda said. She reached out and touched her own face, delicately, resigned. "My life is over."

A bunch of kids ran in, squealing and playing, and Donovan grabbed the paper and rolled it up so they wouldn't see it. Hattie took her father-in-law's elbow and led him to his chair. But he resisted, turned back.

"I can get my car. Drive you to where you want to go." The old man had worry lines crowding a face with half a century of worry already behind it.

"Don't you fuss about it, Paw Paw." Hattie sat him down and he commenced jiggling a nervous knee and swinging his head side to side. Locked in some perplexing internal rhythm.

"Wherever you want to go," the old man said loudly.

Bony took the couple outside, under a half-dormant elm tree that had very few leaves on it. It was sunny with that Mediterranean light that swelled up Southern California to a prideful postcard even when there was no heat in it. Behind the house a shed made out of second-hand boards leaned a little off-plumb, curios nailed to its walls. Antlers, muskrat traps, the head and half the splintered handle of an adze. Remnants of some other life the family had lived in some other, more elemental, region.

Bony stood them next to the shed, under the elm tree undressing for the winter. Yesterday it was cloudy, but it hadn't rained for what seemed like ages, and the sparse yard grass was as dry as straw. Donovan and Wanda looked down at the dry, struggling stolens as their benefactor talked.

"See, I will help you all I can. But now Hattie, she didn't know any of that stuff in the paper. Fact, I didn't know any of that stuff."

"It's true," Wanda interrupted. Head still down. "Some of it."

"They balled us all up in there, and we had to fight," Donovan said vehemently.

"Now Hattie's fine with whatever I say, but Daddy, he's stewing in there. He's a smart man, but he likes tradition. Keeping things straight and narrow."

"I understand," Wanda said. "The Red Squad, he's afraid of that."

"Not the goon squad, we see them down here occasionally. He's afraid of you."

"Me?" Wanda said.

"White people," Bony said finally. "You understand, this is the first time a white person has ever set foot in this house."

"See, that's what we're trying to correct!" Wanda said, perking up for a moment. "This kind of racial separation, class distinction, economic warfare. To where people of all backgrounds can...."

Bony looked blank. Finally Donovan shook his head sadly. "Got a right to be scared of white people," he said. "Specially us."

This set Bony to nodding. Wanda looked them over. She had thought she knew the social issues that roiled the world. Was it possible that they were even more simple than she thought? Was it possible that it was, and always would be, simply fear driven? As simple as skin color and eye color and the color of the paint they wore on their faces when they went to war?

"Look here, we appreciate what you did," Donovan said, looking Bony in the eye. "Can you give us a day or two to get on our feet? We'll lay low, find a way to get out of town?"

"We should go now," Wanda said.

"Naw, a day is all right," Bony said.

Wanda looked back and forth at them. In this light Bony's skin was horse colored, what they called a liver chestnut. Almost red, a tarnished penny. Donovan looked like second-cut pine lumber. A six by eight floor joist marred by freckles and scars.

"We could leave tonight," Wanda offered. "Go by the house and pick up some clothes and things."

They both looked at her as if she had gone daft.

"They're gonna be watching our place," Donovan pointed out. She remembered he had been a hunter, an outdoorsman. Sure. He knew how hunters lived, and he knew how the hunted would have to live.

"No need to hurry," Bony said politely. They could see he was lying.

"I've got to go see my brother," Donovan said. "See what's up."

"Good idea," she said. "Let's go now. We can leave our stuff—"

"By myself. Your picture...." He turned to Bony. "The pistol?"

Wanda's face looked pinched, as if by an invisible and mean hand. Bony opened the door of the shed and came out with the Smith & Wesson and hid it from anybody watching from the house as he handed it to Donovan. The two white people's emotions sparked across their faces. They were obviously locked in some kind of fear/hope seesaw. The Negro knew that seesaw. He went through it all the time.

"Careful. They'll be watching your brother." Bony turned to go in.

Wanda snagged Donovan's arm at the elbow. She pulled him around so she could look in his face.

"Please don't leave me by myself."

"Aw, Baby."

"I can go. I can cover up."

He tried to turn, but she wouldn't let go of his arm. Her grip pinched, and he started to pull free. She had fear all in her, her face so stricken and her body a little bent with the cancer of it. She needed to touch him, keep him a moment, he realized, so he relented. She appreciated it deep down, the terror just took her.

It made her remember an incident, in fact the incident that drove her from her Minnesota home. A young man had come into the family store begging for food at the beginning of the Depression, and her father had run him out, saying, "When you get work, come back." She had never thought her father could be so callous. There was no work. He just was never going to understand it. Sometimes people must be helped. Just because. Just because you're human and they're human. She had gotten on the train the next day, searching for people who recognized that the way she recognized it.

Putting his hand on her hand, Donovan stood that way for a long time in the skinny shade of the elm and she finally folded into his embrace. Letting her wind down, empty out what he thought was simple fear but was much, much more. Maybe it was her entire past that was passing into him, from the look on her face.

Finally she softened her grip, and she released him, and he hugged her, and he left.

ICING THE RUMP ROASTS

The trolley ride up Central and through downtown, and transferring twice, and going up Hyperion, was almost like freedom to him. The cold breeze blowing through the car from a couple of windows left open. The jolly way the sunny landscape flew by, and the way weekend passersby confidently strode the sidewalks outside. The average, everyday passengers who stepped on and got off the red car and hiked away from it as if there was nothing wrong with the world.

Donovan knew about where Joseph would be at three in the afternoon. In fact, the trolley passed the ice truck parked at a cafe. But there was a strange man sitting in the passenger seat, apparently waiting for Joseph to come out after a delivery.

Donovan rode the red car a couple blocks farther up toward Silver Lake before he stepped off. He quickly went around to the back of the Old World Meat Market, where the Ashkenazy family would be expecting the ice that would carry them through the weekend, and stepped quietly inside through a delivery door.

A little storage room behind the meat counters provided him a place to hide. He slipped in and could hear the owners up front, a man and wife, talking to customers in a staccato language and chopping bones with a cleaver. Donovan could hear the crinkling of the butcher paper as they wrapped the meat.

Joseph went by the door with two fifties dangling from tongs in both hands. Hustling. He would be having trouble keeping up, without Donovan.

"We prefer the hundreds," somebody said from the front, and Joseph replied, "I can't carry those big ones. I'll bring you four fifties. Be just as good." "Look at those rump roasts, you ever seen anything so beautiful."

"Awfully fine." "Where's your big brother?" "He had something come up."

Joseph made another trip in, laboring, and on his way out Donovan reached out with one big mitt and caught him by the arm.

"You got a second?" Donovan said softly.

"How are you doing?" Joseph asked, apparently not surprised at all.

"Not too bad, considering."

"I've got a Pinkerton man riding in the truck with me."

"I know, I seen him. I just want to get some of my stuff from the house."

"There's another one or two at the house."

"Uh huh."

The brothers studied each other's faces for a while.

"You've done some crazy stuff, but that was the be-all and the end-all."

"Any way you could buy a car for me? I'll give you cash." Donovan pulled out a bundle of bills he had taken from the briefcase.

"They're watching me every minute of the day and night. Shifts of them." He looked down at the money, though he didn't reach out for it. "How much did you get?"

"I don't know, we ain't even counted it yet."

"You haven't counted it? Wonder you and the woman didn't get shot."

"Little nick, is all." Donovan pointed to his leg. Indeed, there was a bullet hole in his trousers at the thigh. He hadn't said anything to anybody. "Didn't even bleed. Lucky, I guess."

Joseph snorted in that indignant way he had. "Lucky. I wouldn't say so. Her picture's all over the papers, and yours would be too if they could find one. And all for what? For that little communist bitch that talked you into all this mess?"

"Don't say nothin' about her. She's a peach. She's a bulldog."

Joseph snorted again. His indignation, possibly his primary personality trait, shot through him. At the waste of it all. All that money, and none of it available for use.

"I have to go. Old Lanky is going to be fidgeting out there."

"Okay." Donovan put the money back in his pocket. "They tell you anything?"

"It's some hush-hush kind of an operation. It's not the regular police."

"That Rucker's bought 'em off."

He started to step out of the doorway of the storage room, an involuntary move to get closer to his brother, but he saw a movement in the back door. Stepping back, he eased the storage door mostly shut. Dress shoes clacked on the concrete floor.

"What's keeping you?" he heard a voice say. "Just having a little talk with the owner," Joseph replied. "Let's keep moving." "I got customers to take care of." "Yeah yeah, I hear you talking."

In the little room among rolls of wrapping paper and boxes of packing tape, with barely room to turn around, there was a moment of claustrophobia. Donovan put his hand under his jacket and felt the cold butt of the revolver. He pulled it half out of his belt and put his thumb on the hammer. He was starting to like the feel of steel and wood designed into a weapon. How they were made into the pattern of the closed fist so exactly. In a certain situation this touch could be better than a hug.

Finally he heard the ice truck start up and pull away. Its gears grinding up through the register. That Double A was a good truck. Odd how, now that he had the money to replace it, he couldn't show his face. He opened the storage room door.

"Oop! Look at you!"

Donovan had the .38 half out before he recognized the owner of the butcher shop. Damn, the old man had sent a crazy jag of adrenaline through him in that split second, standing there in a bloody white apron with a big butcher knife in his hand.

"Your brother has driven off and left you!" said the owner.

"Mornin', Mr. Ashkenazy." He pushed the pistol back under his belt.

"It is good to see you, my friend," the man said, holding out his hand. Everybody on the route liked Donovan. Much more than Joseph, the tight-faced little tightwad.

"Yes, sir," Donovan said. Shaking the blood-smeared hand.

"Well, go, go. Or you will not catch him."

The owner waved Donovan out the back door and watched him, perplexed, as he walked nonchalantly to the trolley stop. How odd that the brothers' ice truck rolled on up the street, and Donovan just stood there waiting for a red car. As if the ice man had gone out of his mind and was lost, like an old man whose mind had finally burnt out.

THERE IS NO GOD BUT GOD

When Donovan showed up on the Fishes' doorstep, hiking from a Central Avenue trolley stop followed by a gang of little Negro kids frolicking on a Saturday afternoon, he had a big box of groceries in his hands and a smile on his face.

The blacks in the doorway smiled to put him at ease, he smiled to put them at ease. It was a purely smiling neighborhood for a white man to walk through. Only the kids who had followed him to the door didn't smile, being so fascinated as they were, remaining by his side as if to safely escort him up the street.

"You didn't have to do that, Mr. Daley," Hattie said, holding the door open for him and shooing the kids away.

"Sure I did." Inside, he put the box on the table. "And you call me Donovan, cause I'm gonna call you Hattie."

He looked around casually. The house was empty of the usual crowd.

"Where's Wanda?"

He tried not to sound worried. But inside, there was a little pang of anxiety, like a torn muscle in his abdomen from picking up a block of ice at the wrong angle. She was not where he expected to find her, and these were not times when the unexpected was welcome.

"Oh, out back somewhere."

Outside, Donovan circled the house, headed for the shed. These houses were on big lots, probably carved from farmland not too many years ago. There were still farms in the area growing celery and cabbage this time of year.

Behind the shed, an old green tractor with deeply corrugated rubber tires stood partly disemboweled under a leafless apple tree. Bony sat on an upturned wooden box, fiddling with a metal pan full of gear and brake parts. Cleaning them with a wire brush in a shallow pool of kerosene.

Beside him, watching, sat Wanda. Opposite her sat the inquisitive teen boy from the night before. They all glared through sun daggers at Donovan as he sauntered up.

"How did you do?" Wanda asked, flicking eyes at the teen boy to warn Donovan not to say too much.

"Couldn't get a car. We may have to buy one on our own."

"Do you know Henry?" she asked, smiling at the teen boy.

"How do, Henry," Donovan said.

The boy watched him quietly. "Say hello, Mr. Daley," Bony told him.

"Hello," the boy said.

"So you don't take a stand on the social issues?" Wanda said to Bony, continuing a conversation. "Not even civil rights?"

"I'm content to move a baby step at a time. Going to take a few years." He cleaned a brake linkage with a rag and laid it on an old overturned automobile wheel serving as a drying table. A pile of parts glistening with kerosene.

"But there are groups motivating for change, there are massive movements. There's change in the air, if people would just push for it."

"All I know is, I have kids to feed."

"See, all the greed and gluttony of the master class work against that." She waited. "You earn half as much as white drivers."

Bony kept polishing gears and bolts. The guts had been pulled out of the middle of the tractor, and it stood there waiting like an eviscerated elephant steadying itself.

"You done took a huge chance with us," Donovan said to Bony. He glanced at Henry, wanting to say more but not being able. "That's much appreciated."

"It's coming, Daddy," the teenager finally said. "Baby steps, sometimes they not the thing."

The boy looked shocked that his mouth had done what it did. Glancing at the white couple with a half-frown, he seemed to view them as both enemy and friend. Which is just what Wanda wanted from them. The Negroes. Fear us, for your own safety, but trust me to help.

"There! See?" She turned to Bony. "The young people, they're the ones."

"No, no," said a voice from behind them. "Don't you be messin' with our young 'uns."

Bony's father stood at the corner of the shed. He seemed absolutely abject at the sight of his son and grandson sitting with the white folks.

"I'm just talkin', Paw Paw," Henry said.

"Talk is dangerous, son," the old man said. "You don't know how dangerous that talk is."

Bony could seem to find nothing to say. Donovan wished he had some job to lay a hand to. Wanda caught the old man's eye. "Moses led his people to freedom, Mr. Fish. That's a human tendency that's been passed on down."

She was hoping to appeal to him through his religion. These people were notoriously mired in faith. That's how you found them and led them out. Appeal to their confining myths.

"The Lord knows his time, I don't know it," Paw Paw said, arranging his myths to his own liking. "I dasn't guess it. It's not our place."

"There are many gods, sir. The world is changing. I would advise you to pick one that facilitates that change."

Why, the old man seemed about to faint. He could have leaned against the grainy gray shed, it was so close to his shoulder, but he elected to bend over his cane and find heavenly support in it. Hovering at them like a wraith.

"That's blasphemous, young lady. There is no god but God." He looked from one to the other, as if his offspring had fallen into cahoots with cannibals. "There's my car. Take it. Please."

He pointed to an old car sitting in the opposite corner of the yard. Donovan looked over in dismay. It was a black rattletrap Model T, at least ten years old, that looked like it had been sitting in the yard so long its flattened tires had taken root in the dead grass and weeds.

"They'll be leaving in the morning," Bony said.

"That car run? I'll pay you for it," Donovan said.

"Ran a few months ago," the old man said, still offended that his religion had been assailed.

"Few years," Bony said. "It needs a lot of work."

Donovan went over and put his hands on his hips and looked at the car. Bony wiped his hands on a rag and went over and stood with him. They circled the car once, and went to work. Both handy men with wrenches, they spent the afternoon applying wrenches to the old Ford. Inside it, all around it, under it. They pumped up the tires with a bicycle pump. They became pretty well acquainted with each other, and even friendly, to a degree, exchanging tools and requests and diagnoses.

After the old man left to go to his own house, wherever that was, Wanda went in to help Hattie. Henry went in with her, possibly sticking to her ideas as much as to her personality, some inter-tribal fascination pulling him along.

She found all the women gathered in the kitchen, Hattie lying back in a chair with her hair dangling into the sink. A young hairdresser was concocting a konk out of a can of lye, a jar of petroleum jelly, a basket of eggs and a quart of milk. She mixed a smelly mess and smeared it tenderly into Hattie's thick curls, using rubber gloves to protect her hands. The smell made Wanda wrinkle and squint.

Hattie let out a low moan of pain. The other women paid no attention. Most of them had hair that had been straightened, some of it a deep reddish hue.

Going back into the living room, Wanda checked the stove. She pitched in a couple of sticks of wood from a box in the corner. She picked up a Negro-interest newspaper from the floor, the California Eagle, and sat down to her reading. One of the strange women stuck her head out of the kitchen to see if she was still there, then disappeared again.

It was twilight when she heard the Model T cough to life in the yard. She went out to look.

An odd sight. Bony sat in the driver's seat of the old car, trying to keep it running. It would hack and spit and fart and die. Donovan stood at the front, restarting it with a hand crank that he whipped up and down and jerked free as the engine kicked over. A fog of gray smoke pumped out the rear.

POP! Finally the car stopped altogether, and both men went over and looked under the engine cowling with hands on hips. Wanda saw Bony reach in and adjust something with a screwdriver, consulting with Donovan, who took the screwdriver and reached in and adjusted something with it.

This time Donovan jumped up into the driver's seat and Bony worked the starter. The motor chuffed to life the first time. The gray smoke started up, then dissipated, and the car sat there twitching and barking softly, born again and angrily into its new life.

"Get on in!" Donovan yelled to Bony. "Let's try 'er out!"

The black man jumped to the passenger seat, Donovan shifted and popped the clutch, and the Model T twirled around the yard and out the gate. Wanda ran to the fence to wave and yell encouragement. It was dusk as the old car chuffed out onto the dirt street and, its narrow tires barely raising tendrils of dust, disappeared around the block. Wanda smiled so big to see the men together.

Bony was scared to death. This Donovan was bellowing and waving his arms around, yanking the wheel right and left. Imbued with some kind of ecstasy of forward motion, he had forgotten who and where he was. Bony sat his seat like a city feller on a horse, holding on with both hands. Late afternoon strollers stopped to look as the car whipped onto Central Avenue.

On the Avenue on a busy Saturday night the Model T was the only one of its kind. The rest of the cars, new and driven by slicked and konked and derby-hatted Negroes so sedate in their sophistication that they positively glowed, roared by them like runners around a cripple. Yet Donovan persisted down the broad street, Bony knocked into silence beside him, the passersby rapidly swiveling heads in wonder from the crowded sidewalk.

"Thang runs good!" Donovan yelled over the motor. He blatted the horn at people standing on street corners, and it made a sound like WHEEE EW! WHEE EW!

What a sight they were, this black and white duo, the only mix on the street. An occasional white couple would speed by in an Olds or Willys, racing to some other city or to a jazz club, but everybody else was black. And here they were with no hats, no coats, on a cold and darkening evening with this white man whooping at children standing with their mothers bundled up in amazement.

"Getting cold, don't you think?" Bony yelled over at his crazy companion.

"Not me!"

"We better go home and adjust that magneto," Bony yelled.

Finally Donovan got it. Looked around him at what was essentially a separate city, an African city, a walled city entirely disapproving and shocked. He twirled a right hand turn, off the boulevard and into the neighborhoods. He took the back streets home, slowly, barely raising a stitch of dust behind them.

"I'll park it out here so we can sneak off in the morning," he said, parking on the street behind the house, where the racket of its starting wouldn't wake everybody on Sunday morning. Donovan's elation had subsided. Wanda was no longer standing by the fence to cheer him on. It was dark. He shut off the motor.

"How much you think that car's worth?" Donovan asked as they paused by the front door of the house.

"Daddy said you could have it." Bony was half a foot shorter than

Donovan, looking up at him boyishly on the dark front porch.

"Is four hundred enough?"

Silence from Bony as he studied the man. He remembered back to the incident at Club Alabam. He wanted to give him the car, but he knew Donovan needed to pay for it to feel good about what had happened since then.

"One hundred's plenty."

"Two hundred it is, then."

They went in, and Donovan got the briefcase from the top of the pile of blankets where Wanda had put it that morning. The house was full of people again, and he didn't want to open the case in their view. He took it outside, to the shed, where Bony had piled their guns on an old workbench. He took two hundred dollars out, looked the lovely money over again, and snapped the case shut.

When he got back inside he laid the money on the table. There was laughter coming from the kitchen, so he went in to see what it was about.

"Your hair is beautiful," Wanda was saying to the women. "Naturally. Why do you straighten it?"

Hattie sat in her chair, grimacing under an oilcloth skull cap designed to hold her konk in place until it finished cooking. "It's all the rage," she said. "You ought to konk your frizzy hair."

The Negro women were giggling and pointing at Wanda's Jewish explosion of kinks and curls. "Yeah, give it the congolese!" they laughed.

"Straighten out them kinks!"

"Make you a white girl too!" They laughed so hard they commenced hitting themselves and clapping to relieve the pressure.

"Oh, sure. Straighten my hair," Wanda said. Finally laughing along with them.

"You got any beer in that ice box?" Donovan said loudly. They all went quiet and looked him over. It was amazing how these white people would insert themselves and take over a thing.

Bony came in behind him. "We don't keep any beer, this is a dry house," he said.

"I'm a gonna get us some," Donovan said.

Bony and Hattie looked sternly at each other.

"Is that a good idea?" Bony said.

"I gotta have me a beer."

"Baby," Wanda said, "let's don't. Not tonight."

He pulled away and headed for the door. His pocket was full of money from the briefcase. His head was full of possibilities for that money. He needed a drink.

"Tell you what," Bony said, catching him at the door. He didn't reach out for him, just stopped him with his voice. "No use taking any more chances."

"Uh huh." Donovan stopped, his hand on the door.

"I'll go get you a beer."

Wanda and Hattie came in. "Honey," Wanda said to Donovan. "Baby," Hattie said to Bony. But he took the money Donovan offered, put his coat back on and went out the door. Wanda looking daggers at her man. They could hear the bread truck start up outside.

After it left, Donovan had an idea. They were standing by themselves near the stove as the hairdressing women talked in the kitchen. "Let's go count that money," he whispered in her ear.

Wanda shrugged. She didn't want to, but the idea had a certain allure. They put on their coats and went out, borrowing a flashlight from the table. Food was sizzling and popping in the kitchen, the family and friends in the living room played dominoes and checkers, and the snapshot Wanda had on closing the door was of a tranquility that made her envious beyond the telling. As soon as they left, a bubble of conversation burst open as if waiting for manumission.

They put the flashlight on a shelf in the shed and aimed it at the briefcase. Opened it slowly, reverently. It was still almost full of money. The bills weren't neatly done up, as from a bank. They were creased and soiled and varied, as if received from the hands of all degrees of people. Each denomination was tied together in bundles of similar size with rubber bands. By the time they finished they had counted $17,740. Plus a few silver dollars rattling around in the bottom of the case, which Donovan put in his pocket.

"Old Rucker rakes in some dough, all right," he said. "Jakes'll take a roll of the dice with a fast talker, I guess."

Somber, they stood staring down at the loot, all done back up in its rubber bands. It could have been a happy moment. All they had gone through to get it made them glum.

The sound of the bread truck returning home interrupted their thoughts. She sighed, looked at him in the thin light.

"Where to from here?"

A scream from outside stifled his answer. Not just a scream. A penetrating and prolonged and rising scream of anguish and agony. Donovan snapped the case shut and snapped off the light and grabbed a Thompson off the bench. The scream was interspersed with male shouts.

"Jesus," Wanda said. She started to run outside. He grabbed her. Held her still. He opened the door slowly, and they peeked out.

Two white men stood over a body on the ground, and other white men jumped down out of the bread van. Hattie stood screaming over the body, clawing at the men who held her back from it, her kids crying and clinging to her skirts.

The men shouted "Where are they!" "More hurt coming!" "You niggers don't mix in these affairs!"

"My god," Wanda said. Watching the men run into the house, guns drawn. They could make out Whitaker and Lewis among the last ones in.

Without a word, Donovan scooped up the guns. Handed a Thompson and the briefcase to Wanda. She took them lethargically, stunned, devastated.

"You take the old car," he said, grabbing her, shaking her.

He racked the receiver of the Thompson. A round snapped into the chamber. She realized what he was going to do. He had that look. There was enough light from the open door of the house, just yards away, to light up the anguish and anger in his face.

"No. There's women and children there."

A momentary pause. A flash of something across his face. Like a total and final loss of innocence and recognition of fate gone bad. For him, for them. For Bony.

They jumped the short back fence and ran for the Model T just before the other police cars arrived and the intruders burst out of the house and ran for the shed. The old car started on the first crank. With the noise of the other cars and the shouting, they were able to sneak out the back streets without so much as a shot fired.

As they drove north into the city of angels, perched on the bench seat of the rickety old car like mannequins in a diorama depicting an earlier era, silent as art work except for the putt-putting of the T, roaming the back streets and alleys, avoiding any sign of humanity, averting their eyes from the occasional late-night walker, they were almost glad to be alive.

CITIZENS OF THE CITY

They woke up squeezed together on a tiny bed on another wood floor. Clutching each other in sleep to keep from falling off the tick mattress.

He woke first and lay feeling headachy and damned. His arm around her neck was numb. It was cold, and there seemed to be no blood moving in his body. He had to move.

As soon as he did, she bolted upright as if she had heard that scream all over again. Her eyes jerked around the room, trying to shake free of an apocalyptic vision. What she saw was a cramped hovel, walls of unpainted boards, no furniture but a cheap dresser with a chipped porcelain wash basin on top.

Collapsing back into his arms, she let out a little moan and huddled into him and started to cry. She cried softly and relentlessly in a monotone of miserable memory. She lay on her side and cried until her face and the thin sheet were wet, and part of his shoulder too where he cuddled her head. It was half an hour before she sighed, resigned, at the end of a feral sob.

"All those people," she whispered, and there was something else. She could see into the future and see there would be no future for them. No issue. It was a simple statement of reality, written in gunsmoke and lead. She went back to sleep as if driven there by absolute necessity.

It was the only escape, this sleep, but Donovan couldn't manage it. Couldn't even imagine it any longer. He lay awake, thinking his tumultuous notions. Looking at the walls of the seamiest flop in Chinatown until she woke up again an hour later.

This time, she just lay there. They didn't say a word for a long time. Though they clutched each other like children, they hated each other and themselves with an adult fervor. Maybe even that fury was childlike, in that they hugged it inside as if fearful of being punished for it.

"You hungry?" he finally said.

She shrugged. She knew she was, but couldn't feel it. To be so close to Christmas and be so miserable.

He got up, so she did too. Brushed off the clothes they had slept in. Washed their faces in the basin of cold water. There wasn't a towel. They dried off on their shirttails. Her hair was in all directions and his three-day whiskers were an angry black attack on his face. They looked murderous.

On this Sunday morning the narrow dirt streets at this dim end of Chinatown were practically deserted. The couple came out of the doorway of the hotel, passing a Chinese woman who carried a brimming bucket of water through the tiny lobby, and looked down the winter street. It was a riprap of zigzag board buildings, chop suey joints and deserted shops, a couple of little people in the distance plodding across a street spotted with litter.

For a moment he thought his car had been stolen. There were a couple of old delivery trucks parked farther down, but no Model T. Then he remembered that he had parked it two streets over. They had to leave it, he realized. It was so old that Rucker's men or the coppers would soon recognize it.

He looked at Wanda in the crisp daylight localized between crooked stores and walk-up boarding rooms. She was a mess, her cheeks ruddy from crying, her blouse and trousers wrinkled. Lint and loose hairs clung to her.

"Hey, beautiful," he said softly. It was her glumness that sickened him. Her honey eyes seemed as dark as blackstrap molasses. The couple were saddled with the grief of what they had become.

She shook her head sadly. He took her hand, and they began walking. Away from the hotel with the faded, hand-lettered sign, away from where he had parked the car, away from the decrepit Chinatown slowly awakening to commerce and warming to a sun they hated for its exposure.

An hour later they stumbled up to a taco stand in Chavez Ravine where a Mexican with chin stubble and bleary eyes was just cooking the first batch of carne asada for the day. The man looked up, blinking rapidly to clear his own cobwebs.

"Six or seven a them tacos, por favor," Donovan said.

What the Mexican saw was a mismatched white man and woman who looked like they had just crawled out of a ditch after sleeping off a night's drunk. Their clothes were soiled and untucked. She carried a businessman's briefcase. He carried some heavy, angular objects done up in a sheet and slung over his back. To his wife that evening, the Mexican would swear the makeshift sack was an intaglio of the muzzles and stocks of guns, but she would dismiss that as unlikely.

"Si, senor," the sidewalk chef said, shoving more charcoal under his hot plate. He tossed onions and peppers in with the sizzling meat. Soon Donovan and Wanda's attention was taken up with the smell of the food. It was wrapped in corn tortillas, and they ate it, grateful just for the warmth in their hands. They left full, munching a last handful as they marched down Sunset Boulevard, and the world seemed bearable, though not attractive, again.

"So. What now?" she asked.

A two-story laundry with a sign in the window was to their left. It was Chinese lettering, but scratched just below it was "Room." He slowed, stopped. "We find a place to stay," he said. Putting his face close to the glass and peering inside.

He banged on the door. A Chinese woman with an infant in her arms finally opened it. She peeked out, looking from one to the other of them. Maybe it wasn't the neighborhood where whites roomed.

Leading them through the laundry, where huge washtubs sat empty so early on a Sunday, the Chinese woman clopped up narrow wooden stairs worn raw at the leading edges by years of travel. At the top she said something in Chinese and gestured with her head a couple of times down a hallway. They understood. The room to their left was hers, crammed full of bed, dresser and piles of clothing. They walked farther. Past a bathroom, to be shared, judging from the comradely hand motions the woman made. To a room at the end of the hall.

She opened the door for them. They squeezed by, the little girl watching with wondrous, half-hidden eyes seemingly carved into her face with a gentle knife.

"We'll take it," Donovan said. Nodding yes for emphasis, because he could see that she spoke no English. Wanda smiled and nodded too. He pulled a ten spot from his pocket and handed it to her.

"Mrs. Wong," the landlady said, pointing to herself and expending all her English.

Not offering their own names, they took their briefcase and clackety sack of guns inside, deposited them in a corner and closed the door. They looked all around them. There was a bed and a chair and three shelves on a wall. There was a tiny window to the back. Neither of them looked out. They knew what was out there. There was flypaper spiraling down at one edge of the window where flies would go to catch the light. There were about thirty flies glued to it and from their droughty state of decomposition they had been there for a while.

"It's something," she said. She had never been a negative person, never been depressed, and something of that resilience rose up now. At least, she could breathe again. They had a place. There was sunlight coming in the window and warming a narrow trapezoid on the bed. The dead flies and Wanda Kitchen, equal citizens of the city.

He sat in the chair, she sat in the geometric spotlight on the bed. For a minute or two they looked right past each other.

"You want to go get some new clothes?" he asked.

"It's Sunday."

"Right."

She fell back on the worn covers, curled, and was asleep within a minute. He crawled in too, up at the far end so as not to wake her. They slept all day. Curled like nautilus shells on a tiny beach. Unmoving. Barely breathing. Not dreaming.

They woke up for a while and then slept all night, too. As dilapidated as old machines in a deserted yard.

27

EDDIE'S MAN

Usually Eddie Whitaker's fan dancers and cigarette girls didn't turn out to be much, but this one was a little different. He turned in his bed and looked at her as she slept.

She had a real resilient face, sleeping there so sweetly after being up until three in the morning. She didn't seem the ambitious gold digger that Patricia had been, or the bubble headed ingénue that Shirley turned out to be. She just seemed…sweet. He wished he could remember her name.

Slowly he reached over and pulled the covers off her so he could see her tits. Turned on her side like that, her arms hid them for the most part, but she was pretty well endowed, and when he got out of bed she turned in her sleep and showed two fat brown nipples.

"Go ahead and get your beauty rest," he said when she peeked out of sleep at him, instinctively pulling the covers up to her chin and smiling at whoever was in bed with her. Her teeth were bad, but she didn't have to be at work until three, and he'd be back for a nooner if he could.

If there was one saying his father taught him, it was that you never messed with warmed-over coffee or woke-up pussy. In fact, as he got the Pierce out of the garage and waited for Rucker to come out of the front house he recalled that that was all his father had ever taught him. He hadn't talked much, old man Whitaker hadn't, and when he did it was about women or food.

"That fucking Bananas," Rucker said as he sauntered out to the car, which had had its bullet holes and windows repaired and was muttering in the cold so the heater could take the chill off. Rucker stood for a moment looking wistfully at the concrete stairway that the ice man used to attack with a three hundred pounder on his back. Whitaker didn't get it. His boss had a beautiful wife who cooked for him, a maid who screwed him on off days, a scam that brought in enough folding money to retire in Havana, and what did he like to do in the mornings? Watch that Okie tote ice up a hill.

"Get rid of those frigerators, and maybe he'll come on back," Whitaker said, holding the car door open for him.

Rucker muttered sardonically and got in the car. Touchy subject. They hadn't seen the ice man since Saturday, and then only a glimpse. They later learned that one of the Red Squad boys on backup had seen him and the Jew girl tootling out of there in a worn-out Model T, but hadn't known they were the perpetrators. One of the drawbacks of keeping only a few people in the know.

The Beach Oil office was two big upstairs rooms looking down on Wilshire Boulevard, and the boys were filing in already by the time Rucker and Whitaker trudged up the stairs. Carter was there, and Boise, and Bobby. Roberts, the Pinkerton man, along with a couple of his investigators, showed up shortly after. They all kept their overcoats on, fedoras and bowlers pulled down tight, because the radiator was just beginning to ping out a little heat.

Desks and chairs were supposed to be for the two girls who typed out oil shares and took in the money, but Rucker had told them to take the morning off. Whitaker put a Closed sign on the door at the head of the stairs. The boss ignored the whole crew and stalked back to his office with Whitaker and Roberts and shut the door behind them.

Rucker looked even more puffy on Monday than he had on Sunday, when they had spent all day hustling the goon squad and Pinkerton agents around town hoping to find Daley and his woman at one of their known haunts. A beat cop found the old car in Chinatown finally, but a search of the area and a stakeout until morning didn't turn them up. So the boss was not just sleep-deprived, he was angry again.

"Goddamn," the big man said simply. He sat behind his desk with both arms straight out on it amid piles of contracts and worthless share certificates. "Goddamn goddamn goddamn."

"We'll get him," Roberts said.

"Around somewhere," Whitaker said. The boss' anger came and went like a hailstorm out of rain. He'd be good for a while, and then right when you didn't want it, he'd be mad again.

Whitaker let his gaze float around the office for a minute as Rucker ruminated. The walls were decorated with travel posters from all over. Lots of palm trees, though how that could be exotic was difficult to see. There were two real fan palms, skinny and straight, visible from the windows of the office. Australia. That was where the bodyguard wanted to go. They didn't allow other races down there.

"You think we ought to bring in the regular cops? Get some more shoe leather on the street?" Rucker asked them. Mostly asked Roberts. Whitaker didn't mind. He knew his role. In fact, didn't want to get outside it. He was an escort, security, a man who conspired to remain invisible unless there was a need for sudden high visibility.

Roberts shook his head, took the cigar Rucker offered him. "Unnecessary. We have all the time in the world. What's the big hurry?"

"The big hurry!" Rucker shouted, pounding the desk with the flat of his hand. "Is the man has my money! Seventeen thousand dollars of it! That's five years' wages for most people! How fast can he spend it? That's the big hurry!"

The door flew open, and Rucker looked up angrily. When he saw who was standing there the anger left his face like a butterfly from a weed. He stood up as if the president had walked in.

"Morning, Daddy," he said.

An old man stood in the doorway like a middle linebacker, though much, much thinner. Gray tinged his hair and thick mustache, but the look in his dissipated face dispelled any notion of infirmity or weakness.

"My people down at headquarters tell me you've created quite a war zone hereabouts," the elder Rucker said. "They are having a hell of a time ignoring you."

Whitaker caught Roberts' eye, and the two of them eased out the door, squeezing by the old man. Who did not move an inch. They left the door open, though.

"Daddy, this sonofabitch stole my money," Rucker said miserably, groaning up from his chair. Whitaker peeked in the door to see what was happening.

"What steps have you taken?"

"The usual. We're on it. Matter of time."

"You want me to have a word with Chief Davis?"

"Hell, that's part of the problem. That Red Squad he set up is useless. What good is it? Lets these Jew radical unionizers set up shop all around town. All manner of riffraff coming to California and fooling it up."

Stepping in, the old man stood with his thighs leaned against the desk. He was quiet, let his son ramble on.

"I wouldn't be having this problem if the police did their job. Kept the

Okies and the Jews out of the city limits. Sent the Africans back. All sorts of discontent. What happened to that blockade they set up at the state line? Why don't they bring that back?"

He shut up. Seeing the look in the old man's eye.

"I told you once, and I'll tell you again. Let no man take from you. Let no government take from you. Let no woman take from you. Let no child or business or organization take from you. You take from them."

Rucker collapsed in his chair, which scooted toward the window from the weight of him. The wheels made a rusty screeching sound.

Whitaker snuck a quick look inside. He stood nearby, so he could intervene if necessary. One day a couple of months before, he had had to come in and pull the old man off his son. He was sitting on top of him on the floor, an old man in an ancient hundred-dollar suit, pounding the shit out of his much larger son with one steady, hammering fist.

Maybe Rucker was remembering the episode too. His voice receded to a whine.

"A man I trusted, a man who delivered ice to my door, a man my wife fed his breakfast half the time. Came into my house and stole from me, then came down here and held up my week's receipts."

"An ice man? A route man? Took from you?"

Again Whitaker, because of the ominous tone of voice, peeked in. But the old man was holding his ground at the front of the desk. Whitaker turned back to the front office. The other men had skedaddled out of there as soon as Rucker's father came up the stairwell. All except for Roberts, who seemed to know how to seem inconspicuous, and Carter, a little overweight office hanger-on not smart enough to get out of the way.

"When are you going to get some spine?" the old man said, putting his claws on the desk and leaning over as if to upchuck on his son.

Rucker looked up pitifully. "You want a cigar?"

"Give me some more of those oil shares."

His son hastily took a certificate off the top of a pile, began signing and dating it.

"What's that?" his father said.

"A hundred shares."

The old man pushed himself off the desk and stood straight as a rifle barrel. Just looking down at this son of his. The one who allowed an ice route man to take from him. He didn't have to say a thing. Rucker quickly tore up the certificate, dug down through the pile and came up with a thousand-note. Began signing and dating it. He ran out of ink and had a little trouble with the ink pot. His hands were trembling so badly that the pen tinkled around inside it looking for ink. Finally he got enough pumped up into the pen to finish the share.

Barely glancing at it, his father folded it once without creasing it and held it bellied out away from him, waving it as the ink dried.

"I'll talk to some people. We'll see what we can do about the ice man."

Whitaker was just turning again to make sure everything was okay, when the old man came out the door. Didn't even glance at him or Roberts, who was keeping to himself at a desk across the room. Whitaker touched the brim of his hat, just in case, though the man was already opening the outer door.

So when the boss came out, he was mad. Irate. He called Carter over. Carter was a tiny, frowning man with a very large head who hung around for chump change. If they needed a message or a package delivered, he was the man. He hopped over willingly.

Rucker slapped him across the side of his head. Carter managed to duck, so the blow struck him glancingly.

"Whataya do that for?" he yelled.

He made as if he were about to attack Rucker, so Whitaker came over and pulled him aside. "Get on over there," he said, motioning to Carter's former resting place in the corner of the room.

"He hit me," Carter said. "Man hit me."

"Get over there."

By this time Rucker was feeling better. This was something that Eddie Whitaker could never understand. Not the slap. He could understand that. Charles Rucker was a big, physical man who was a coward. He picked on the smallest man in the room. What Eddie Whitaker had difficulty with was why he worked for the man. He sat back on the edge of a desk in disgust.

"You know what I'm going to do with old Bananas?" Rucker paced the room, in a hurry to get from one side to the other. "I'm going to rip him apart. I'm going to pull his arms and legs off like a bug. I'm going to…"

He couldn't think of anything else.

"I'm going to do worse than you did to that colored boy," he finally said, and flopped in a chair. The other men slunk back into the office, having seen from downstairs that Rucker's father had left. They stood awaiting orders.

"Niggers are like the Okies," Lewis said, picking up the theme. "Boy was a knucklehead. You can't talk any sense into them. Clammed up like a damned oyster. Couldn't be helped."

Whitaker was remembering what they had done to the colored man. They had caught the bread truck at a stop sign and gone to the open door and pulled him out onto the street. He wouldn't say a word, wouldn't give the couple up, though they told him they knew Bony's address from the bread company. So they hit him with pipes and bats until blood flew out of his head.

But Whitaker could appreciate a quiet man. He hated to see Lewis and the goon squad mess him up like that, though he recognized that the cop had a grudge from the night at Club Alabam. Some things just have to happen. He hated to hurt somebody who liked good jazz and dancing that swing. But people didn't give you an option.

"How about this?" Whitaker said.

They looked over. Whitaker wasn't looked upon as a mastermind. He kept his mouth shut. That's why they brought in the coppers and the Pinkertons. Whitaker was Rucker's wheel man, he didn't operate in bigger circles. So when Whitaker spoke he surprised them.

"How about we find that brother of his. How about we look up anybody that knows them. What if we were to find out where the woman's from?"

Rucker looked over at Roberts, who he was paying a lot of money. "What do you think, Lanky?"

"We're already working on it," Roberts said. "Except her folks. That's a thought."

"You boys clear on out of here. Get on it," Rucker said. "I've got to get my girls back and get down to business. It's a hard life supporting all you Freddie-the-freeloaders."

The others went out, looking very purposeful for people who had no idea what their next step would be other than to get in their cars and drive around hoping for a chance encounter. And how probable would that be, finding a pair like that in a city already infamous for its odd couples and niches for them to hide in?

Whitaker went over and gave Carter a silver dollar and told him to get them some coffee and keep the change. He sat back down on the edge of a desk. Waiting for his boss to get over his encounter with his father. Once he did that, maybe they could do something.

28

THE PRICE OF A TACO

They had to go buy new clothes. They put the briefcase under the thin mattress of their bed. It made a big lump. But there was no other hiding place, unless they got really nervous and decided to stand it behind the door. There was no lock on the door.

"Let's just take it," he said. "I'm sick of looking at it," she said. Just before they left, Donovan got it out from under the mattress and stood it behind the door. Then they closed the door. He stopped once and looked back and she said, "Leave it, serve us right."

Wanda came out the front door of the laundry and started to walk down Sunset, but he stopped her. Rucker's troops would be driving around the area. He remembered a used clothing store down a few blocks, so they walked parallel to Sunset, one street over, until they got to the general area. Then they crossed over.

In a little store run by Russians, they bought a lot of off-color and off-size clothes for both of them, as well as a cardboard suitcase frayed at its corners. He bought a dented straw boater, because he had left his hat at Bony's. She bought a dime novel off a little shelf of books. Donovan had an idea. He bought a scarf and a cane leaning against a wall. Outside the store he had her put the scarf over her head, gave her the cane, bent her over and told her to walk like an old woman.

"What for?"

"Your picture is all over town," he explained. She tried to straighten up, but he put one hand on her stomach and one on the back of her head and bent her over again. The Russians watched in some puzzlement as they went through this pantomime and finally shuffled down the street.

"This is stupid." She could barely walk. They headed up a slope, and pretty soon her back hurt. "I can't walk around like this."

She straightened her back and walked quickly forward. They were on a shady sidewalk in a residential neighborhood. After she jerked the scarf off her head she tucked the cane under her arm and plunged forward, kicking dead leaves as she went. He had to hustle to catch up.

"Somebody could recognize you," he said. He grabbed the scarf out of her hand and draped it over her head. "Slow down!"

"No!" She turned on him, her face vicious. "It's stupid! I won't do it!"

She pulled the scarf off and tried to move on, but he caught her arm and held her. He went for the scarf, but she fought him off. She just seemed to have very little survival instinct.

"Stop it!" she yelled. "I don't care!"

Kids playing in their yard across the street, off school for Christmas vacation, turned to look at this angry couple. Sure that some bitter fight was about to erupt. He moved around in front of her and the pair leaned in at each other, she out of anger, he out of the perceived need to whisper.

"You want Rucker to win this?" he hissed.

"He's already won. He took our house, our lives, our car. He killed Bony. Poor Hattie, and those kids."

She started to cry again. The local kids were watching. Donovan got between them and her. "Come on. Let's go on home."

"Yeah, home," she said. Laughing. Straightening up and looking around and laughing through her tears. "I'm not living like this."

"Come on. Won't be for long." He let her stand there in the middle of the sidewalk and sob until she shuddered to a stop.

In the trees along the street some little winter birds flushed. Her eyes followed them to the next copse of trees. She was remembering good times when they had sat in their very fine back yard waiting for potatoes to bake in a fire. She was always amazed at how Donovan loved to watch those little diddly birds, as he called them, watching them so avidly as they disappeared into the branches and again as they came back out to flutter at insects. He said they reminded him of the ranch.

Finally he got her moving. He didn't try for the scarf again, though. She had thrown it down and stomped on it with her fine dancing feet. He picked it up when she moved on.

At the laundry six or seven Chinese women now labored over the tubs, slapping wet clothes and sheets around, running them through a big mangle that their landlady cranked. They talked loudly, as if competing in a talk contest. Kids played in a corner on quilted Chinese mats so very purple and red and yellow. A greybeard man pumped his knees at a big treadle sewing machine in the corner.

Behind the door the briefcase stood just where they had left it. Donovan looked at it in amazement, wondering why he hadn't taken it with him. He took some more money out of it. He put on a clean undershirt and shirt from the ones he had bought. He sat on the bed thinking about the colored boy.

The man had paid back his debt. Donovan had always shrugged off any idea that the man owed him something. But he felt he did, and he paid whatever it was in full.

"What's wrong?" Wanda asked. She worried when he went off into one of these brown studies.

"You want to change? I'll drop these clothes off to be washed."

Without a word, she changed her blouse and trousers. She hadn't been able to find trousers that suited her at the secondhand store, but she put on a yellow skirt that had looked half-right. And a white blouse. Now she thought she looked more like a Spanish dancer than a Jewish unionist. He plucked her clothes off the floor.

"Where are you going?"

"Get us something to eat."

"Why don't we just both go out."

He looked at her sideways. Hand on the door.

"What do you expect me to do here?" she asked.

"Read your book." He went to the suitcase and dug the book out of the bottom. As if she couldn't do it. He was becoming very irritating.

Alone in the room, Wanda bundled up in her coat and snuggled into bed. She could hear a loud burst of Chinese from downstairs every now and then. She took the book and looked it over. It was a reprint of An American Tragedy, which she had read in college.

She opened the book in the middle and started reading. Then snapped the book shut. What could she have been thinking? As soon as she read the characters' names she started crying, knowing how unnecessary an unnecessary death was. She closed it and curled up and went to sleep again.

Donovan was already in the bar by then.

He hadn't meant to go in. He was going to walk down to the taco stand they had eaten at the day before. But it was almost noon, and the door of the bar was open, and the smell of beer was already in the air. Really, he was going to walk by.

The last straw was that he heard a bar glass tinkle. Being jostled against other bar glasses. He loved that sound. He loved the sound of the brew going into the glass, subtle, seductive, easily distinguished from any other liquid.

It was a little, formerly-a-shoe-store cantina, with one patron slouched over a short bar and a Mexican in yesterday's dirty apron serving. Before long, Donovan had a drink. Before long, he had paid the other patron to go down and get them some tacos, and he had some more drinks. Beer, then tequila. Soon they were all laughing, full of drinks, Donovan demonstrating his few words of Spanish. Other men came in to have a lunchtime drink.

Then there was a sour mood, gathering momentum solely from a little something, a tone, from one of the men from a work crew with cement on their clothes. An insinuating tone. Mocking, somehow. Donovan turned on them suddenly. Snapping his fists out around him. Drinks flying.

The fight didn't last long. These were little men, the Mexicans. They could work any white man into the ground, but there weren't enough of them in the bar to wrestle down the drunken Donovan Daley. More came in from outside during the commotion and tried to help. They called him a puta and cabron. Donovan was finally bounced out the back door, bleeding and cursed. He didn't go back. When drunk he had just enough sense to think about preserving his life.

"Hey! Where's my tacos!" he yelled at the slammed door. Nobody opened it to answer him, so he whirled and zigzagged down the alley trying to focus on objects far enough ahead to keep his trajectory straight.

Feeling punk, he sat on a big rock for a while trying to remember where he was and why he was there. His shirt was torn in the armpit and back. He leaned over and threw up a hearty stew. Then he stretched out and slept for a few minutes lying there in the sun, his legs in the alley where a car could have run over them if there had been a car.

Wanda woke up from her nap starved, and scared. She stalked out the door and down the street, and would have walked right by the sleeping Donovan if she had stuck to her plan of walking down the alley. But she was in her old lady disguise. She was afraid to not wear it. Being a fugitive was such a stunting experience for her, a woman who had always courted public demonstrations. Having staged union walkouts and boycotts, making sure she got herself photographed for the papers, she didn't like skulking in greasy alleys and forlorn back streets.

She had slipped the bulky Thompson up under her coat. An old woman pregnant with weapon. All the way down Sunset, all the way up the little hill past the cramped immigrant shops, her cane knocked along sidewalks littered with candy wrappers and cigarette butts. She saw the world not through the clear lens of herself, but through the cataracts of self-recrimination. An abject killer posing as an old woman.

The taco vendor solicitously served her a meal, leaning to peek under the shade of her scarf. She ate three huge tacos, unconsciously straightening her back and letting the scarf slip. She finally noticed and covered up. Slumped over onto that odious cane.

On the way back she found Donovan stumbling along the street, having awakened from his stupor, heading home along Sunset. Cars dodged him and honked as he surged in and out of oncoming afternoon traffic. Playing some kind of stupid drunk game.

She had a good mind to let him die by roadster.

"You prick," she said instead.

She grabbed him by one arm and propelled him to the curb. It looked funny, an old woman with such strength. When he whirled on her, caught off guard, wondering who the hell she was, she struck him with her cane on the shoulder. It raised a little bellow of alley dust, and he jumped back.

"Oh, hi, Wanda," he said. Smiling that smile so big. For a second she just stood examining his saggy mug, hands on hips. Then she stooped over, pulled up her scarf and toddled off toward home.

"Let's get out of here."

They were only two blocks from the laundry, but it seemed to take all afternoon to get there. She steering him this way and that. He playfully pretending to veer into the street, running at pedestrians who ventured near. In the laundry the Chinese workers watched them stagger up the stairs, more curious and puzzled every time they saw the wild couple. Mrs. Wong shook her head sadly.

Wanda slammed the door and shoved Donovan down onto the bed. Stood looking down at him beaming up at her. Now his smile disappeared, though what was left wasn't a frown. Just some contemplative emotion drunk in its own skin.

"Sorry about your tacos. I had 'em."

"Not a good time for a binge."

"Twenty tacos, I got. For you."

"I got my own tacos!" she screamed. The Chinese chatter downstairs went quiet for three seconds, then started up again.

The source of her frustration went beyond the idea that they had ruined their lives with one foolish act. They had killed people. And gotten people killed. All for a drunken bohunk who wasn't even going to allow her a dignified exit. Wouldn't even give her a fanfare with some meaning.

"When you sent Bony out for beer. You got him killed," she said softly.

He stared at her with soggy eyes. She hadn't wanted to ever say it, because she knew he knew it. But here he was, drunk again.

"They was comin' for us anyway," he whined.

And collapsed back on the bed, his legs still hooked over the edge. Embedded deep in his drunkenness was a violent sense of shame. Of a worker with ambition, a citizen with integrity. A friend with loyalty. He lay there breathing heavily and trying to find enough sobriety to express his regret.

"They wrecked your tacos," he said, his mind for some reason unable to leave this area. After all, he had bought her food, the way he said he would.

"He died because of you."

How had this all happened? Not really believing in fate, she had to believe in evil. Were they, the two of them, evil? Wanda stared at the opposite wall, full of the possibility. What she really had to face was the idea that she had cultivated this violent man from the first moment she saw him. For her own purposes. Whatever those were. And now she had the consequences.

He crawled farther into the bed and turned on his side. "Fought 'em for them tacos. Them Mexicans." His eyes closed, and within a minute he was snoring.

After a while Wanda crawled in beside him. He didn't hear her. He didn't feel her arms around him. But she did put her arms around him.

Maybe if he could sleep off a drunk, she could sleep off a tragedy.

WHO TO KILL NEXT?

In his sleep in the first light of morning he said "…fucking Rucker" and then woke up smacking his lips as if trying to get food off them. He looked around, face beefy with hangover. The room was empty of everything but the bed and the dresser.

The first thing he wanted was Wanda. The next thing he wanted was the briefcase, which was also missing. The next thing he wanted was a drink of water, which he got out of the smelly basin they had washed in the night before, gulping like a horse at a trough.

And then the most compelling thing he wanted was to kill Charles Rucker. It was a fully visualized thought. He pictured himself beating him at the top of the concrete stairs where the man had watched him lug so many blocks of ice. He would also be happy to take him to Bony's house and slaughter him on the front lawn. He had butchered cattle back on the ranch in such impromptu places. Methodical, it would be, almost culinary.

He retrieved a Thompson from behind the bed where he had secreted them so they would be close at hand if needed. The other one was gone. Presumably with Wanda. He checked the chamber—loaded--and made sure the safety was on.

At that moment the door lock clicked and the door slapped open. Donovan flipped up the barrel of the Thompson. It was only Wanda, who instinctively raised her Thompson from under her coat.

Standing stock still, locked on each other, guns zeroed as if the best policy would be to kill each other despite the moment of recognition, they heard footsteps coming up the stairs at the end of the hall. She stepped in and closed the door most of the way and peeked through the crack. One of the Chinese workers, a beautiful smooth-skinned girl of about 15, slipped into the bathroom.

Wanda closed the door. "How do you feel," she said. "Okay, whatta ya been up to," he said. "Just getting some things," she said. "How come you took the Thompson," he said. "Never know," she said. "There's the pistol," he said, reaching around behind the bed for it.

After he had fumbled around for a few seconds she drew the Smith & Wesson out from inside her big coat pocket and laid it on the bed. He picked it up and checked.

"Good, you got the safety on."

"Yeah, I've got the safety on."

He didn't blame her for being testy. Although he didn't exactly feel guilty, he felt sorry for getting drunk and leaving her here hungry and scared.

"What did you get?"

"Phone book."

She pulled the book out from under her coat. He looked around the room to see if he had misremembered. No, there was no phone.

"I want to find out where Whitaker lives," she said by way of explanation.

"That's easy. He lives in the guest house behind Rucker's. He keeps him close-by, just in case."

"I wish you'd told me that. I want to kill him."

"Rucker?"

"Whitaker."

"I want to kill Rucker."

"Whitaker. He's the one killed Bony."

"Rucker's the boss. He ordered it. Besides, isn't he your capitalist demon man? Proletariat?"

"Bourgeoisie. I don't know why you can't get that right." She took a couple of Baby Ruth bars out of her other coat pocket and threw them on the bed. "I told you, the rich and the swindlers and the lords and masters will be what they are. You can't change that. But the Whitakers. They're hanging on for the paycheck, or the hope of rising up, or whatever it is we hope for. To be rich too."

"They're just the trigger men."

"Yeah, and there are a lot of them."

"Jesus," he said, stripping one of the candy bars and taking a huge bite. He studied the remaining two-thirds of the candy. "You're starting to sound like Pauline."

"'The fates lead the willing. The unwilling, they drag along.' Or something like that. Seneca. You can't change the Ruckers. So you change the Whitakers, then the Ruckers don't have anyone to carry out their fascist shit."

Chewing mightily, he turned his gaze from the candy bar to her. "That mean we're fate?"

"I'm forcing myself to think so." This despite the solid and once irrefutable fact that she did not believe in fate.

"So let's kill them both," he said.

"All right. They killed Bony. I understand how your sense of justice works, so I could consider—"

"It ain't no justice in it. He owed me one, now I owe him one. He took it serious, I take it serious."

Chewing. Smiling a bit in his realization of who he was.

She smiled too. She couldn't help it. He had such an honest sweetness about him when he wanted to kill somebody.

OLD JOE STALIN

They sat in Joseph's living room waiting for the little brother to bring them glasses of water. Eddie Whitaker was nervous. As if this Donovan, this strongman, might come back at any second to his house. Where they sat acting so calm. He almost reached under his coat to touch his pistol, just to remind himself it was there. Rucker, playing the knowledgeable boss, winked to relax him. But something about the ice man worried Whitaker. For one thing, they couldn't seem to ice him. It was almost like it wasn't meant to happen.

"There you go," Joseph said. He came in from the kitchen and handed one a glass and the other Donovan's coffee cup, which he had washed to make sure it was clean.

He sat in the chair across from the two intruders on the couch, who sipped their water politely. Set the glass and cup down. Were about to say something.

"You're lucky I had a spare key," Joseph said. "I don't live here anymore."

"Yep, we are," Rucker said. Not telling him that he and the police had been all through the apartment at least three times. "We're sure hoping you can help us get a lead on those two characters. Since you're our friend, we feel obliged to help out where possible."

"Trying to kill my brother, you mean?" Joseph said.

Charles Rucker just hated these fucking Okies. Stubborn, cunning, prideful, they had no more sense than the deer and the antelope that played in the fields of their homeland. Or so he imagined. He had taken the train through there as a young man on his way out from the east, passing through a huge dust storm carrying Oklahoma into Missouri, and Missouri into Georgia. The whole region was as destitute as a ragman.

Whitaker, who himself had come out from Kansas and could thus technically avoid the "Okie" label, knew Joseph's type as well as he had known his neighbors in his small hometown. They were all so perversely dedicated to whatever personality they had learned to be. That was a good trait if you could convince the boy that you wanted the same goals he did.

"Not true, son," Whitaker lied.

"Truth is," Rucker said, "that whole shootout came about because of the stickup he pulled. We don't have anything against your brother."

"Now, the woman...." Whitaker said.

"...on our hit list. We feel, the police feel, she was the mastermind behind all this. A puppet of old Joe Stalin and his ilk."

"Which is why we're here."

"Think you might be able to help us talk to her father? He's in town to see—"

"The Jew woman's father?" Joseph interrupted. "Why would you be talking to another kike? I thought you Bund people were out to get rid of them."

"Yeah! Yeah! That's the thing!" Rucker said, enthused by such talk. "You come on down to the police station with us, help us talk to her father. We find her. Get shut of her."

Joseph had to think about all that. He had no intention of talking to any more Jews. "What would I say?"

"You never know. You have inside information."

"Valuable insights. How to locate her."

"How she lived. Your brother and her. Something might come up."

"What about my brother?"

Whitaker watched the man angrily. Sometimes, fairly often as a matter of fact, people surprised you with how stupid they could be. He'd come to expect it, really. How a man would give up somebody he loved to get somebody he hated.

"Sure, he's in trouble. But get him a good lawyer, and who knows?"

So they got Joseph into the Pierce-Arrow and they all went down to Highland Park, smoking cigars and talking about the high desirability of oil shares in relation to this new Age of the Automobile. They drove by at least two brand new gas stations on the way, which Rucker used as evidence that the world was in thrall to oil. Or soon would be. Inside the stationhouse, Lewis and his boys had got the beat cops to clear out the interrogation room for them.

The four of them—Rucker, Joseph, Lewis and Whitaker—watched

the old man through the one-way glass for a minute before they went in. Whitaker could hardly believe how harmless this skinny little Jew looked. His bush of a beard straggling clear down to his chest. The man sat torturously straight in his wooden chair, not even looking around the room. He had the same damn stubborn look that the Okies did.

When they went in, David Kitchen didn't look up. He seemed to be in some meditative state. Or shock. Or nostalgia. Or resistance. Who could tell with someone that strange looking? Of course, he had been on the train a day and a night in getting here.

"Mr. Kitchen, these are some of the people who know your daughter," Lewis said. "We brought them in to try to jog your memory. Anything that would help."

"Then you must know more about her than I do," the father said in a deep, creaky voice.

Ah, Whitaker had heard about this at the Bund. The insidious Jew, the logical Jew, the sneaky Jew. Always so smart, so devious, turning things to their own end.

"Mr. Kitchen, I'm Charles Rucker," said the boss. Who didn't reach to shake his hand. "This here is Joseph Daley, the brother of her boyfriend."

"Boyfriend?"

"I hate to tell you this, but they were living outside the bounds of common decency. He may have led her astray as well as into infamy. This is a very notorious criminal she's with, and that's why we need your help."

"Save her from this guy."

Joseph squirmed at this. Rucker gave him a silencing glance. To let him know it was all part of their act.

"A killer. Killed several men."

"Ought to see the newspaper accounts."

"Bring her to her senses if she saw you."

The bearded man finally lifted his head and looked them all over. He had the strangest, dark, gold-flecked eyes. Just penetrating. A chill went up Whitaker's spine, clear up to his scalp. To be so close to this devilish enemy.

"So you feel my Wanda is corruptible," he said. He looked from eye to eye with those penetrating marbles of his.

This set them back a tad. It made Whitaker's skin crawl. The man had an odd tone about him, hard to read. Was he being sarcastic? Accusatory? Was it something from Jewry, or from Minnesota?

"We don't know, Sir. We don't know your daughter at all," Whitaker said.

"Let me tell you, then. My daughter is a heretic, an infidel, a blasphemer, a heathen."

They looked at him in shock and relief and, frankly, joy.

"Well, sir, we know all—"

"But my daughter is the most principled and honorable human being I know. I myself have drawn much inspiration from her in times of strife." The inquisitors' faces fell. Whitaker in particular felt very vulnerable and suggestible before this man. As if some fearful, hypnotic aura emanated from him.

"Uh huh, uh huh," Rucker said. They all were nodding, putting on the respectful faces of men who understood honor.

"My daughter left home to fight the forces of corruption and inequality at a young age, and I have not seen her for the intervening years. Despite my admonishment, she took to the battlefield of injustice and inhumanity. It's a losing battle, I tell her, but that's where she labors, on behalf of the common man, the person in need, the lost soul."

They were dumbstruck. It was as if he were talking some Old World language they had never heard and had no hope of learning. He couldn't have been more opaque if he had spoken Yiddish.

"Speaking of lost—"

"Do you understand? You wanted to hear some facts about my Wanda, is that not so?" the man said. "It's a fallibility of hers, this incorruptibility, this unflinching honesty. It's a philosophy beyond what we know as philosophy. It's action. I myself have thought about it often, how triumphant we would be if we could adopt her foundations. Though actions so often lead to trouble, to misery."

"Yes, sir."

"We picked that up."

"Only thing is, she's robbed."

"She's killed."

"Would you be willing to appeal to her to come on in, give herself up?" Rucker said. "This man's obviously corrupted her."

"According to the newspaper accounts you've shown me, she would be inviting a visit to the gallows."

"Well, we don't know that. You know how the papers are."

"They're pretty sensationalist, as an institution," Whitaker said. He found that his words, his speech pattern, changed as he talked to this man. He could see why people feared and hated them. The man had a magnetic affect, though he was as insubstantial and uncombed as a hobo off a train.

"They say she killed a policeman. What did the policeman do to her?"

"Now look here, you—"

Lewis was on the verge of taking the Lord's name in vain, but Whitaker reached over and put a hand in front of his face.

"Sir," Rucker said. "All we want to do is bring in this man. He's the real danger. She may have been pressured, by him, to go along for the ride. So to speak."

"Forced," Whitaker said, taking Lewis by the arm and pulling him to his feet. "Violation of all our laws. Abominations. Excuse us." He directed the burr-headed cop out the door and closed it behind them.

Outside the room, watching the interrogation through the one-way mirror, Whitaker let go of Lewis' arm. They peered into each other's faces.

"Okay, I getcha," Lewis said, his face a blush red. "My fault."

"Just let us get what we want out of this sheenie, and we'll send him back to Minnesota."

"Send him back on a board, I got anything to do with it."

"Send him back safely so he can report on the honesty of our proceedings," Whitaker said. Still for some reason talking in his new syntax.

"Send him off to Germany, let old Hitler take him down to size, is what I say."

"You calmed down?"

"Yeah, fine."

The two men grabbed a pot of coffee and china cups and took them into the interrogation room. Poured coffee all around. The old Jew didn't touch his. He was so thin he was like a refugee from some bankrupt farm or something, Whitaker thought. His beard covered skin painted onto a bone canvas.

"This here's Joseph," Rucker was saying, "we brought him here in case you two might put your heads together and see a way to help us out."

"A good name," David Kitchen said. "I'm pleased to meet you, Joseph."

He reached his hand suddenly, and, out of reflex, Joseph took it. Why, it was like handling a little bundle of wheat straw, the hand was so dry and emaciated. The man was like one of those space creatures drawn in the pulp science fiction magazines. Joseph had seen Jews before, around Hollywood, but they were of the hefty, forward type. This one seemed somehow more insidious.

"Hello," Joseph said. He shook his hand free of the scarecrow's claw.

"So your brother is in trouble."

"Yes, Sir."

"This is a lamentable position for both of us, I'm afraid."

"Right, right."

Whitaker looked at Joseph hard. The young man had gone into some shy, terrified state of being right in front of them. Witched. Mesmerized.

"Does your brother love my daughter?"

"Sir?"

"Are they in love, these two?"

Well this Joseph just balled up like a bug in front of a spider. His eyes opened wider and wider until he seemed not to be considering the question. Shitting his pants, possibly. Whitaker thought he might faint from a lack of breathing.

"I believe so," he exhaled. "I believe he does."

"Well."

Joseph stared into the man's face, a face he considered goddamned and preposterous. This was a question he had never considered, possibly because he didn't know what love was. Was this the factor that he had never understood in the couple's relationship? He had thought it was just impulse, a carnal collision. Were they in love? The idea sounded so far-fetched, and indubitably true.

"As I said," David Kitchen said, "I have not communicated with my Wanda in years. I do not have a single notion where she might be at this time."

A commotion outside. They looked to the door. In came several people. Uniformed cops escorted in a reporter with a notebook and a photographer lugging a huge Speed Graflex with a flash on top.

"Mr. Kitchen?" Lewis said. "Do you mind if we take a picture of you? For the newspapers?"

The old man looked shocked at the thought. "For what purpose?"

The photographer heaved his camera to his eye. The old Jew stood as if to leave. Lewis reached to push him back. Thus, when the flash bulb popped, the image it froze was of a gaunt, bearded figure reared slightly backward, away from the gentile's intrusive hand. Which was visible, though they cropped it out of the eventual photo.

"For posterity," Rucker said.

THAT'S WHAT THEY WANT

It was Christmas Eve. The first thing Wanda did that morning was to don her festive old-lady disguise and shuffle out onto Sunset to get a newspaper. When she came back to the room five minutes later she was running, the hell with the pretense of aging. A Times was coming apart around her as she ran.

"Move, move!" she yelled at a couple of laundry customers, parting them with her cane like a sword fighter in one of those Fairbanks swashbucklers. Leaping up the stairs, her yellow skirt swishing right and left.

Donovan nearly jumped out of his clothes when she blew into the room, panting and slapping the Times. He had the .38 stuffed into his waistband, but hadn't been an outlaw long enough to think to whip it out.

"Jesus," he said, peering into her stricken face.

She pointed at the headline. FATHER APPEALS TO FUGITIVE MURDERESS.

"That's my father. He's in Los Angeles."

Donovan read it aloud: "Daniel Kitchen, father of fugitive murderess Wanda Kitchen, appeared in Los Angeles, can you believe this, to appeal to his daughter to give herself up to authorities," interspersing the news with commentary. "The concerned gentleman, owner of a clothing store chain, goddamn them all to hell, arrived by morning train from Minnesota specifically to ask the woman becoming known as the Dark Angel to think of the family name before she killed again."

When Donovan looked up at her, Wanda was breathing even more heavily than from her run. That was done. She was panting from some deeper stress.

"They're going to find us," she said in a voice that reflected an onslaught of trepidation. She couldn't even think about her long-lost father.

"Your dad," he reminded her. "He came here for you."

"They'll find us, Donovan! They're not going to stop!"

"There's a million people in this city. How they gonna find us?"

"My father came all this way." She said it with a note of last-ditch wonder. "I haven't seen him in so long."

"Bastards brung him in."

"I wish I could see him. Oh," she said in her constricted throat. She seemed in a walking dream, trying to dream her way out of it. "I so wish I could see him."

"Says right here," he said, pointing to the paper, "he's staying at the Roosevelt."

"I know! But that's what they want!"

"The bastards. The goddamned bastards."

They collapsed to sitting positions on the bed. She kept looking at the photo of her father, his funny stance, as if he were retreating from a blow or some unpleasantness. He looked so good. Not at all the ogre who drove her away from home with his demands and strictures. His eyes, as much as they were visible in the photo, seemed trapped, almost pleading.

"I want to meet him," Donovan said. She couldn't pull her gaze off him. Her father. Then Donovan. "I want to meet your father."

She smiled so big.

That afternoon they bought their fifth meal in a row at the taco stand and stood chewing the stringy carne asada in a nearby vacant lot. They circled each other, bending their necks to gnaw at the ends of the tacos, looking at each other warily. Each afraid of what the other might say.

"You sure?" she said finally, wiping her hands on her skirt, which was getting dirty now with salsa verde and melted Mars chocolate. They looked out of place, out of sorts, standing ten feet apart as if fighting, in the wan winter sunlight gone green way out toward the unseen ocean. They had their coats tugged up around their ears to ward off the cold and any prying eyes.

"I want to meet the man. I like the looks of him."

She stepped through his shadow and hugged him. The man who got along with everybody. On dirt and asphalt streets on all sides of them, kids ran in and out of houses and played stickball and cowboys and Indians, their voices quacking across the weedy lot, their vocal gunshots PEUW PEUWing off the little houses.

"I love you," she said.

"It's Christmas Eve, you oughta see your dad." He kept pounding that logic, knowing it made no sense. The risk. But that was all he could see ahead of them now. Risk. So why not? It was the naivete of the novice fugitive, the man who deep down felt he couldn't be found and killed, who wanted to meet his girl's father. He somehow isolated the gut feeling of the one from the logic of the other.

So it happened that at eight in the evening, dead dark at this time of year, an ice truck backed up the service ramp at the back of the Roosevelt Hotel in Hollywood. This wasn't unusual. A Christmas Eve party was jumping to the sentimental swing music of a big band somewhere inside the voluminous building, and they would need ice.

A man with his tam o'shanter pulled low over his forehead got out of the darkened cab of the ice truck. He went around to the back. As he climbed the steps to the service dock, and came under the lights, he appeared as a small man almost engulfed in his leathers. He cased the area nervously, lifted the canvas flap at the back and tonged a fifty pound block of ice and skidded it to the tailgate. Nobody was on the dock. He swung the ice to his back and stepped lively to the nearest door.

Inside, Joseph toted the block along a zigzag corridor to the kitchen. Cook staff and dishwashers on the left and right hustled here and there, and farther into the maze-like area cooks labored at huge gas ranges, skidding dishes across a stainless steel counter. Joseph dodged between them and opened one of the commercial ice boxes.

Shoved the block inside.

Looked around just as casually as he could.

Joseph was exactly the kind of man to be here. Small and somewhat childish in the face, he would no more draw attention to himself than a waiter would. A cook glanced over at him and dismissed him immediately even as Joseph took off his leather serape and dropped it in a corner.

A cop on stakeout in the hallway, looking for a frizzy-haired Jewish woman or a bulky Okie with a tommy gun (the outlaw images had built so suddenly that they frightened even the big, physical beat cops), let him pass without question. Joseph had on his nicest coat. He almost could have been a partygoer.

Emboldened by his success, Joseph toddled up some short steps and walked right through the big open atrium in the center of the hotel, where a classy crowd of white people was dancing very little and drinking cocktails very much to a Tommy Dorsey look-alike band. A clinking, laughing atmosphere prevailed, and Joseph nodded to one reveler after another as he shoved through the gay crowd. From where police were positioned at front and back entrances, and even from where Roberts and Lewis were standing in the open area downstairs, pretending to be part of the crowd, they couldn't see Joseph.

He took the stairs up at one end, to the mezzanine floor, where he stood at the balcony with half-drunk couples tippling pink and green drinks in glasses shaped for martinis and manhattans. The little teetotaler looked down on the dancers below for a second in indignation, hat pulled low, more to calm himself than to seem inconspicuous, and walked to the elevators. He rode up alone to the fourth floor and knocked on the door of room number 1106.

The door opened a crack. Joseph talked softly to someone inside who never showed more than an eye and cheekbone. He listened for a second, then spoke again. The door closed.

Joseph hurriedly retraced his steps. Retrieved his leathers from the kitchen. Stood and listened politely as the head chef told him they desperately needed more ice for the bar. And went back to the truck.

He was standing by the rear of the truck when Mr. Kitchen came out of the hotel. Joseph nodded once and lifted the canvas flap for him. The old man peered inside the truck suspiciously for a moment, his beard protruding forward as if to dust the worn floorboards before he went in.

"It's okay, Father," a voice said softly from inside.

He stepped onto the tailgate and into the van. Joseph lowered the flap behind him.

A flashlight was on, and in its wan glow Wanda stepped forward and gave her father an off-balance hug, splashing through meltwater. Over her shoulder as he hugged, Mr. Kitchen could see a bulky figure sitting on a huge block of ice draped with leather to ward off the chill. Donovan nodded politely at him for the duration of the brief hug.

"My god, Wannie," Mr. Kitchen said.

They pulled apart, but Wanda could not catch her breath. She wiped away tears. "It's been so long. I missed you," she said.

"Six years, your mother tells me. I had lost track."

"I wanted you to meet Donovan." She turned to allow her man in the picture. Donovan stood, stooping under the roof of the van, and held out his hand.

"Pleased to meet you, Sir," he said. Taking the frail hand and looking down at it in surprise. He let it go, for fear of injuring it.

So the three of them stood apart, Donovan stooping slightly. "Oh, Father," Wanda started. But she was still sniffling, and couldn't go on.

"Your mother and your siblings send their love," the old man said. "And your friends, and Rabbi Goldstein. We have heard of your troubles, the news of which travel far. The investigators have asked many questions of us."

"Father...."

"Wannie, I know you could not have done such a thing. Those ridiculous policemen, they told me such foolish tales of horror. Killing a policeman with shots to the chest from a revolver, how—"

"Father—"

"We'll find an attorney, the best attorney. The stores are doing well, I can afford any and all—"

"No, it's true, Father. I killed the policeman. Maybe more than one. Corrupt policemen. And others, too. Other people."

Such a silence. It followed their emotional outburst in the cold, confined space like an empty room discovered in a busy household. The bearded man now looked not only thin and pale, but diseased or damaged as well. Maybe he had slumped some in the last few seconds. He pulled his coat tighter. His breath huffed visibly in the ice van.

"How could that be, Wannie?"

"It just is. I didn't come to—"

"But we raised you well. We thought. How are you capable of such immorality?"

"Maybe in its perversion it's a form of morality. That's how I explain it to myself."

"But a policeman."

"The Red Squad. The goon squad, is what they call them. They beat up communists, denounce Jews, meet Okies at the border and turn them back. They are in league with the Ku Klux Klan, the Bund, the Black Legion, the German government. They murder, they intimidate, they blackball. They apprehend black and yellow people and make them disappear."

"Even so."

"Yes, even so. But they ambushed us. This stupid stock swindler, they're in his pocket. The Pinkertons too."

"The Pinkertons are after you? My God in heaven."

"Everybody is after us."

There was a sudden pounding on the side of the van. Donovan and Wanda grabbed their Thompsons from behind the block of ice. Snapped off the safeties.

They could hear Joseph talking to somebody outside. "The cook wants some more ice," the somebody said. Another male voice farther away mumbled something. "Soon as I'm finished with that," Joseph said. "Gotta have it, and how," the other voice said.

Mr. Kitchen looked down at the machine guns, paralyzed by his indignity. Wanda gripped his hand tightly with her free hand to quiet him. Both Thompsons were aimed at the back flap of the van. If it opened, there would be more death, the old man realized in horror.

Finally Joseph whacked the side of the van again.

"All right," Wanda said, letting out a tightly held breath.

"My lord, Wannie," Mr. Kitchen burst out. He was entranced by the Thompsons. He could not look away from their horrifying designs.

"I know it. That's the way it is, though."

"This is against all our principles." He looked at Donovan. Even in his black wool suit and his beard and his little homburg her father looked like a tiny man, an escapee from the north country, from many north countries.

"There are different principles now," Wanda said. "Different rules of engagement."

"But our liberty depends on...." The little man seemed stumped, unable to finish. He looked to Donovan for help.

"Liberty don't work as good in practice as it does in speeches," Donovan said, "and that's a quote, pretty much."

"Is that Nietzsche? Schopenhauer?"

"Will Rogers."

"Ah yes." The old Jew—in fact, he was only fifty-two, but he had been through a lot en route—seemed unimpressed with the cowboy/humorist's philosophizing. "You are from Oklahoma, I'm told."

Donovan looked to Wanda for an explanation.

"The newspaper stories," she said.

"I must reprimand you for allowing my daughter to drift so far from our value system." He stared at Donovan as if it was all his fault. "But then you are a gentile, and ignorant."

"You can't help who you're born to, Mr. Kitchen."

"Quite right. Your mother determines who you are, your father what you are. I'm so ashamed."

"Sir, this is the best woman I know. She done good all over town until this come up. Some of it was kind of an accident, matter of fact."

The flashlight flickered and dimmed as its battery argued with itself. They became more shadowy and less substantial as their imprints on the walls of the van subsided. It was as if they were drifting away from life even as they spoke.

"Course, if they hadn't done made us mad...." Donovan added.

It seemed an impasse. The old clothier had no thoughts that he could express to the young cowboy. Who seemed to him to be somewhat cavalier about the whole thing, as if it were a lark and a duty to risk so much. This survivor of the pograms of the Old Country could at least understand that, his only point of reference to this man from Oklahoma.

"I just wanted to see you," Wanda said to her father.

"They're using me as bait."

"We know."

Mr. Kitchen sighed. It was a huge exhalation for such a frail-seeming figure. Their breath filled the van like smoke in a burning house.

"I should go. For your sake. I don't know what else..."

Father and daughter hugged. He didn't reach for Donovan's hand again. Peeking out of the flap, he stepped onto the loading dock, took Joseph's hand in assistance, and clopped into the hotel in his thick, old-world shoes.

"Father!" she yelled, thinking something more could be made of this situation. But he was gone.

"Bye, Daddy."

Wanda couldn't figure whether he left so precipitously in order to protect them, or because of some enormous unease around them and their guns. Or because of the obvious disparity, this incongruity between Old World chaos and New World disorder, connected though they were by the unbreakable chain links of history.

Donovan reached over and pounded on the side of the van, and they could hear Joseph get in the front. The old truck whinnied and started. It began moving, rocking under them as its narrow tires passed over irregularities in the street.

To keep their balance, they collapsed onto the big block of ice, completely enervated. But though they reached out and put their hands against the walls to steady themselves, the ice slipped this way and that underneath them. It was a shifty kind of world all around at the moment. They felt they were sliding through it as if on a vast lake that had frozen under them and then broken up without warning.

They took each other's hand and slid from one side of the truck to the other so comically it might all have been a child's game they were playing.

BANANA SPLIT

Joseph pulled around to the back of the laundry, stopped on the upslope and jerked the hand brake that stood up from the middle of the floor. The truck jiggled as Wanda and Donovan jumped out of the van. Looking in his mirror, the younger brother could see them pulling their machine guns from the back.

Donovan ran up to the window. Joseph cranked it down. His big brother's face was stark white from moon glow in the black night air.

"Thanks, little brother."

Wanda came around too. She looked reluctant to say anything. This night changed her thinking about Joseph, but only at the surface.

"No trouble," Joseph said.

"Yeah, you could have gotten caught with us," Wanda said, pushing to the window. "I hadn't seen my father for so long."

"Sure."

She could see that Joseph didn't even like thinking about the Jews. It must have been all he could do to go to the old man's room and speak in a normal voice. She had no idea why he had done this. Because his brother asked, is all she knew.

"It's Christmas tomorrow," Wanda said. "You two should go see your father."

"Oh no."

"I got plans for the morning," Donovan said.

"That's not for me," Joseph repeated.

He rolled up the window and put the old truck in gear. He gave a little dismissive wave to this weird couple, who, Wanda realized, were the closest to him in all the world. He let out the clutch and gunned it up the hill and turned out of sight onto Sunset.

"What plans?" she said, in their room.

"Tell you later."

That night the couple tried to make love, making a big production out of it, showing each other their stuff, but it was no good. They fought their thoughts. Neither could come to orgasm, and finally they fell away from each other exhausted, heaving like railroad laborers laying track. It was a while before Donovan felt able to get up and turn off the light, and after he did they lay a little apart until the cold room drove them together, their hearts still racketing like hot little motors looking for the company of other motors.

For the first time she doubted her once bedrock hypothesis: That the sex force was a world force. Her force. She could find no momentum in it at all.

In the morning he told her his plan, and she reluctantly agreed to it. They dressed, slipped their guns under their coats and tiptoed downstairs at daylight, briefcase in hand. Donovan found a car with a key in it a couple of blocks away, and they borrowed it. It was an old Hudson that, once it started, hacked every now and then and belched out a smoke bomb behind them.

"Must be Buster Keaton's car," Donovan said, trying to get her to smile. But she didn't, and they drove looking straight ahead into a Christmas Day so gloomy it seemed draped with gray, year-old, weatherbeaten bunting.

The car barely made it up the hill to Rucker's house. It was even grayer up here, and cold. Not a tree seemed alive, not a bird came out to play. The couple parked on the deserted street and sat in the Hudson a minute staring straight ahead, then got out and walked up the concrete steps he had trudged so many times with ice on his back. He stopped her at the top.

"Here's where he always was, making fun of me when I come up with a three hundred."

"I remember."

They kept on to the back of the house. Donovan warily glanced back at the guest house where Whitaker lived, but there was no sign of life there. He ran back there, motioning for her to stay put. He pulled the tommy gun from under his coat and went around to all the windows of Whitaker's house, but not a light was on.

Opening the kitchen door of Rucker's big house, they walked right in. They listened to the house. It smelled so good, like baked goods and coffee. She thought Donovan looked so cute there with his chin tilted up and his tommy gun cradled just so. He gave her a little Christmas Day smile. She returned it.

There was the tinkling of children's laughter. She gave him a puzzled look. "I didn't know he had kids." There was so much they didn't tell each other, she realized. So many complicating details. "Who cares." They didn't even lower their voices. She realized he was standing there angrily looking at the new refrigerator humming. Pulling himself away, he proceeded into the hallway. Down past the den he had invaded twice before. Into the living room.

Around a splendid ten-foot fir tree that almost touched the ceiling, the Rucker family was opening presents from a huge stack. There was Rucker, in his silk robe, grinning around an unlit cigar. There was his wife Lilly. And three kids, the oldest about eight, all in pajamas. There was Millie, the maid, sitting to the back and watching. A little boy was just unwrapping a train set from a box as big as himself, when the oldest girl caught sight of the newcomers.

Rucker and his wife looked up too. There was a period of awkward silence. A lovely fire in a huge fireplace crackled nervously. The room was very hot. Donovan recognized that something had to be done, so he stepped forward, leveled the Thompson at Rucker's chubby face and cocked the slide.

"Don't nobody move," he said, remembering his movie lingo.

Nobody did. "It's Christmas, for Christ sake," Rucker said for some reason.

That set Wanda to giggling. She realized they had no real plan at all. "Everybody up," she said, waggling the machine gun at them.

Everybody stood up except the little boy, who clutched his train set and ignored them. Finally his mother grabbed him up, and he started screaming. "I want my train set! Leggo! That's my train!" It was an era where the youth, fanned on by Shirley Temple and her little-foot-stamping roles, spoke out.

"What's this all about, Donovan?" Lilly asked.

"Well, Lilly," Donovan said, shocked that she remembered his name. "We have some business with old Rucker, there." He waved his Thompson.

"What business?" Rucker said. The kid was wailing so loudly that it was hard to hear. Then the youngest girl, a little blondie, started to cry.

"Be quiet!" Rucker yelled.

"You shut up!," Wanda screamed at Rucker, startling everybody. "You killed our friend."

She was suddenly frothing. She could hear Bony and Hattie talking softly and lovingly in their kitchen, their children all around, and this man had destroyed all that.

All crying stopped, but there was some general snuffling. The mood was a shocker in this setting. A new Schwinn bicycle stood in one corner, and a hobby horse with a ribbon around its neck leaned against it.

"Good, good, let's keep calm here," Donovan said uncharacteristically. Looking up at his big broad face she realized how much she wanted Rucker dead. She had a wonderful idea.

"Lilly, you and the kids... and you," she said, pointing to Millie....

"That's Millie," Donovan interjected. "Morning, Millie."

"Hi. How are you today?"

"Millie.... You all come with me."

The little group gathered together, very stressed. The kids oblivious, more irritated at being interrupted at the high point of their year. The boy looked back longingly at his train set. It was a nice five-piece Lionel. "Okay, go get your train set," Wanda said. "And you girls, go ahead and get a toy."

The girls didn't move from their mother's side, and Wanda remembered her own childhood. How girls seemed more attuned to the reality of life. But the boy retrieved the train, struggling to drag the big flat box along the floor.

"Sorry, Lilly," Donovan said. "You was always good to me." He was glad he hadn't had to yell or threaten. And shocked that Wanda had.

Wanda herded them through a door and into the den. Lilly moved slowly, aware now that something very regrettable was about to happen. "Please," she said, but she went in with Wanda, who nodded reassuringly and shut the door behind her.

"Who are you?" Millie asked, retreating to the far side of the den behind the desk, feeling obliged to stick up for her employer as much as possible. Though she was terrified now.

"Don't you read the papers?" Wanda asked.

Millie and Lilly looked at each other. "This is the woman radical. Who shot those policemen," Lilly said matter-of-factly. "But I don't know why she's here."

"You'll find out," Wanda said, turning an ear to the door. Finally she opened it a crack and looked out. She could hardly believe her eyes. She quickly closed the door.

Donovan had Rucker down on his hands and knees and was riding him like a horse. Rucker wasn't moving, Donovan was just sitting up there talking to him.

"Set us up to kill us, didn't you," Donovan said.

"Now that's not the way it was."

Donovan prodded him with his knees the way he would a horse. "Come on, you son of a bitch. You can admit it. I'm gonna kill you dead either way."

"Wait just a second. Money, that's it, isn't it? I've got more. Right in there where you took that other money from. My desk. You started all this by stealing from me. I had to do something."

"You started it by making fun of me coming up the steps with that ice. Calling Wanda a Jew."

"Which she is, no harm in saying it. Come on, now. That was just funning. You know I admire a man that can carry three hundred pounds of ice."

"Nice try. Here's the deal, though. Here's the damn deal." He grabbed the back of Rucker's collar—his hair was too short to hold—and pulled hard. "You killed my friend Bony. That was a good man, and you killed him."

"Who?"

"The man that snuck us out of the hotel."

"The nigger? I had nothing to do with that. I wasn't even there. They told me about it afterward, honest."

"He's not a nigger. He's a Negro."

Donovan, angered by the memory, took the Thompson by both stocks and jabbed the barrel into the back of Rucker's head. Which popped forward and then swayed side to side, just like a horse's, to try to get away from the gun.

He tried to pull the trigger. He had his finger hooked solidly against it. He knew from previous use of the weapon precisely how much it required. There was a tipping point, and all he had to do was move past that.

But his finger wouldn't apply the foot-pounds. It just froze there like a finger holding a coffee cup. Something about the back of the man's head, maybe, how it just seemed some guy's head. Not Rucker at all. Just another man. Any man.

"Goddamnit," Donovan said.

Disgusted, he looked around the living room. At one end a huge dining table sported bowls of Christmas nuts and fruit. Oranges and bananas.

"Giddyup," he said. Rucker wouldn't move, so Donovan took out his ice pick and gave him a couple good jabs to the ass. The man started whimpering and moving, and Donovan steered him by his coat collar and slowly rode him over to the table. He dismounted and went over to the fruit bowl.

In the den, Wanda kept waiting to hear the shot. But instead of a wait of gladness, it was becoming a lump of horror deep inside her expectant soul. They shouldn't be here. She had somehow leveraged Donovan into this plan. He was a good man, willing to take on the difficult tasks. He was doing what a good man would do, under certain definitions of good. At the last moment, after he explained his plan, it was just understood that he would be the one to kill Rucker. And now she was sorry.

"I read all about you," Lilly said, causing Wanda to start half out of her shirt. The hostages were all backed into the far corner of the den by the desk. The little boy was on the desk. His mother had helped him get the locomotive out of the box, and he scooted it back and forth across the scattered papers, its little interconnected wheels rattling along.

"Yeah?" Wanda said.

"I like your causes. Women's rights. Better working hours. Wages that a woman could live on."

"Sure you do."

"You think because I'm married to Charles Rucker I don't care?"

"You know how he makes his money?"

Lilly didn't answer. Maybe she was pondering how to phrase her reply without offending. Maybe she just couldn't think of anything to say. Maybe she didn't know.

"He makes his money," Wanda said, warming to the topic, "off the backs of little people. Swindling them out of their hard-earned wages by selling them worthless oil stocks. The oil wells on that property were emptied out years ago. He takes people out there and shows them dead oil pumps, and they buy oil that doesn't exist."

"I have my hands full here. With these kids." She stroked the hair of the youngest girl, who was sitting in her lap now. "It's hard to keep up."

"Too busy buying a mountain of presents for everybody. You know there are thousands of kids in this city who are lucky to have an orange for Christmas morning?"

"We give to charity. We help out."

"It's not that. It's the whole setup. The rich get richer, the poor get poorer. If you people have any say about it. And you're the only ones to have any say. If the poor people try to say anything the goon squad shuts them up, quick-smart."

Wanda started pacing in front of the door, marching with the Thompson up on her shoulder like a soldier on the parade ground. Lilly looked sorry she had said anything. This intruder, like the little black locomotive, was on a fast track, back and forth, back and forth.

"See here, you people live the American Dream. It's not a dream to you, it's real. But to the rest of us, that's all it is. Illusion. It's been created to give us hope that we'll be rich too. Rich is what it's all about, correct? But there's misery out there. There's hunger at night. There's a depression, for god's sake."

This angered her so much that she jerked open the door and yelled out, "Kill the bastard!"

But she couldn't see anybody in that field of view. Nervous now, she waved the gun threateningly so that the family backed even farther into the corner behind the desk, the little girls really crying now. She got the door open and stepped out, blinking in confusion.

"Aren't you going to do it?" she asked. The sight before her was too difficult for her to digest, much less comment on.

Donovan said. "You want to shoot him?"

Wanda came out and closed the door to the den. "I thought you were going to." She felt deprived, unfulfilled. She studied Rucker, down on the floor. His pants off. She couldn't understand what had happened. Her heart was beating so hard she couldn't think.

"This is good enough," Donovan said. "I couldn't goddamn do it."

"Fine." She hardly heard him. She turned away. She didn't want to see any more. Ashamed she had called for his death.

They went out the way they came in. As they passed through the kitchen, Donovan turned and fired a full burst into the offending refrigerator. The slugs chunked into the door, and the machine wheezed, sniffed and began to hiss out of its butt at them. They left in a hurry, afraid it would explode.

At the sound of the gunfire Lilly ran out from the den. Stopped dead. In the middle of the living room floor, half buried in the pile of used Christmas wrapping paper, her husband lay on his side. He was naked from the waist down, his hands and feet tied tight with red and green ribbons. His mouth was crammed with wrapping paper, and a banana, still in its peel, protruded about a third of the way out of his ass like a little yellow handle somebody could pick him up by.

Lilly quickly closed the door. "Stay in there a minute!" she yelled to the others. She took the papers from her husband's mouth. He was crying softly. She started untying his hands so he could move, but he just lay there. Crying softly.

The banana was barely visible now, as if it were working its way in. It wiggled like a little tail as Rucker sobbed, so she did what any good wife would do. She reached down and, with one hand braced against an ass cheek, pulled the banana out.

ALL THE FATHERS

Joseph was now living in their house. Donovan and Wanda pulled the Hudson into the alley behind, and they could occasionally catch a glimpse of him moving here and there through the back window. He must have been cooking his breakfast.

The cop on surveillance was in an unmarked car on the street in front, down a block. About as unobtrusive as a fire truck. They had seen him when they came in. He was slumped down in the driver's seat, his fedora tipped almost to his nose. Probably thinking about his family enjoying Christmas without him.

Donovan tapped on the kitchen window while Wanda waited in the alley. Joseph unlocked the back door. "Merry Christmas," Donovan said. "You too," Joseph said.

So as Joseph scraped his eggs from the skillet to a plate—Donovan shook his head no at the offer to share—his older brother tried to talk him into visiting their father. Joseph chewed eggs and chased them with coffee. He declined the invitation with some indignity.

"Come on out with us," Donovan pleaded. "Do you some good to be with family on Christmas day."

Joseph looked out the window at a skinny tree that had lost its leaves. Other trees in the neighborhood were still bright green, but the ones in his line of sight were as naked as forks on a table. He shook his head. No.

"I'd like this family to be together again. To be something." Donovan had practiced his approach and thought it was sound. "What our father and mother done to each other don't mean we can't be a family, any way we can manage."

"I'm not dealing with that man by any means."

His brother had that set to his mouth, in fact his whole face, so Donovan knew it was hopeless. But he kept trying. Maybe he just needed to say some things.

"Ain't right we don't act like family. Example. When you helped us out with Wanda's dad, that was a great thing you done."

Joseph shook his head. He didn't even like to think about the Jews. What was this big thing about the Jews, anyway? Why were they so almighty important? Why were people always talking about them? How come they deserved so much attention? He just resented the whole thing.

"Wanda and me, we're going on out there," Donovan continued. "We'd like you to come with us. Buy you lunch someplace. There's a lot of good Mexican food out there."

"I don't like Mexican food. I don't like Mexican anything."

Donovan studied him. It wasn't hard to figure his little brother. Some part of him had hardened and, like concrete in a dam, blocked some other parts of him. The family breakup was ugly, but it shouldn't do that to a person. A person ought to be able to walk away whole and alive and be able to have emotions that didn't stab him. Their separate upbringing, his and Joseph's, had created a rift in itself. Donovan was years older and was sent out to work with the ranch hands. He inherited their rough acceptance of anything. Joseph was the youngest, and he had to stay indoors to help his mother. He got her dictatorial intolerance.

"All right, then. I got to get on."

"You want me to get you a car or something, let me know."

"I thought you couldn't."

"I can sneak away."

"We got one. I appreciate it, though."

"Where'd you get it?"

Donovan got up. Held out his hand. Joseph shook it without getting up. The older brother didn't answer his question, not wanting to disillusion him further. The cop was still sitting in his car when Donovan left. Asleep now.

On the drive out to the San Fernando Valley Wanda and Donovan were quiet. Thinking their separate but equal thoughts. She thought about her family, the people she was sure she would never see again. Christmas at Rucker's reminded her of the stifling religious rituals she had gone through. A little precocious all her life in a misbehaving kind of way, she couldn't stand to stand still and watch men anoint and appoint each other. She hated it when the men used ritual to tame the women. But she had loved family gatherings where they talked about honor and tradition and patriotism. That's what she thought of now. The higher principles, the ones she didn't have anymore.

He was wondering where they would eat. Everything was closed. It was Christmas, after all. He hated the thought of not having good eats on Christmas.

He had lost the directions to his father's house, but together they recalled enough of the twists and turns to get them into the right lemon grove. As the Hudson lumbered along the dirt roads, down between endless rows of citrus trees, emitting noxious fumes, he strained to see through the gloomy morning. The place didn't look the same. Some trees had been taken out, another row of houses started in their place. They drove into a clearing and looked around in some confusion.

Where his father's little shack and shed had stood only weeks before there was a small pile of lumber disassembled from the buildings, old boards blackened from years of rain, the crooked nails still protruding. Even the weeds in the yard were dilapidated, dead and dried and flattened from traffic, though there was no vehicle there to match all the tracks in the powder dust.

"I wonder what happened?" Wanda said.

He got out and walked around the pile of boards, as if he could conjure an explanation and a father out of it. But it was only a reminder that a pair of lives had camped out here. He flipped a board over. The inside of the wood was the same color as the outside. There wasn't even a foundation. The shack had been built on dirt.

Donovan sat on the seat of the car, the door open, his legs outside, thinking about possibilities. Thinking about his father's woman, and what Joseph had said about Mexicans, and how he hoped the pair were looking after each other this Christmas morning. Everything tied together if you looked at it long enough, for good or for ill. But it didn't mean it made sense.

Wanda got out and came around and leaned on the open door, looking down at him. "You have any idea where he would go?" This big strong man looked confused for the first time.

"I don't know." He felt very emptied out. All the fathers of the world could have been gone, from the size of the emptiness.

On the way back, after detouring through the rapidly growing housing project his father had shown them the last time, they actually found a little café open. It was Greek, of all things, but they ate Christmas breakfast, lunch and dinner there all in one meal. Back in the city, after they parked the Hudson where they had found it, Donovan and Wanda got on a trolley car in silence. They paid their fare with a dollar bill because they had no change. Disgusted and too distracted to care, they carried the Thompsons right out in the open. Let somebody say something.

"Christmas presents," Donovan said when a couple of passengers looked down at the big guns.

"Here, look at this," a man in the back said. "I got one too."

He pulled a revolver out of his waist band and showed it to Donovan. Who handed over his Thompson for the man to examine. Another, up front, stepped back beside them. He pulled an automatic from a pocket of his coat. "Have a look." The three talked for a minute about the calibers and capabilities of their weaponry, and Wanda had to interrupt them as their stop approached. The men exchanged weapons again, somewhat reluctantly, it seemed.

"Ah, the sweet society of shooters," Wanda said sarcastically as they exited the bus. They pulled up their collars as a wet west wind came upon them.

"You're the one wanted a Thompson," he reminded her.

Getting off just down from the laundry, they trudged up the shallow hill as if it were Mt. Kilimanjaro, sneaking in the door furtively and almost angrily, passing among the Chinese workers bathed in steam, the men shirtless like Buddhas from some other kind of holiday.

Or the ghosts from a horrible Christmas past.

CRYING IN THE RAIN

Damned if it didn't rain that night. Just streamed down in a slobbering drumbeat and knocked on the roof all night. It was the rainy season, but who expected it?

Sometimes, after months of steady sunlight sifting down from a blue sky cluttered only with the smoke of wood fires and dust rising from the unpaved roads of far-flung subdivisions, the feeling that Whitaker had was that it was never meant to rain. That somehow the land out here, cloaked in low-slung chaparral forest, dry despite shadowing the ocean, could just thrive without it. The water for trees and lawns and humans just popped up from the faucets so fluidly that its source never entered your mind. It wasn't like Kansas, where the family farm lived by the rain and the lone hand pump that he, as a kid, had to work and work to coax up a bucket of water and was always reminding him where the stuff came from.

Whitaker and Lilly stood on the front porch of the guest house behind Rucker's place. Waiting for Rucker to compose himself. The big man had stood there blubbering for five minutes, ever since Whitaker had gotten home. Rucker wiped his whole face thoroughly with a yellow silk handkerchief and again tried to talk.

"I want that son of a bitch caught, I want him strung up by his thumbs, I want his nuts removed, I want him…" Rucker couldn't seem to think of anything more, and he suddenly sobbed and went to the yellow hanky again and let out a lengthy double whinny inside it to clear his nose.

Lilly said, "Honey…" to start to comfort him, but the big man shook her off.

"No! He's a danger to society. It's a wonder he didn't kill me, he would have if I hadn't been so skillful in putting him off."

"The man's got moxie," Whitaker said, and Rucker just whirled on him.

"Where were you? Where were you all this time?"

"Told you, I was at Trisha's parents' house."

"I pay you good money. I provide you a house. You could leave the cigarette girls alone for a couple hours and do your job."

"You said I could have Christmas off, so I—"

"No! That quim of yours is sleeping in a home under my ownership, and you're distracted from your job!"

Whitaker reached over and closed the front door so Trisha wouldn't hear this. She had retreated as soon as Rucker came over and started up. She understood crazy and had the good sense to get away from a grown man crying in the rain. The others stood on the porch for a few seconds watching the rain pour down the way it did out here at rare intervals, washing all the smoke down with it. The Pierce would have to be washed again if they went out in this, and he had been looking forward to a nice evening off.

"You sleep in our house tonight," Rucker said.

"He won't be back tonight, Charles."

"Well he could be, Eddie," Rucker said sarcastically. "I mean, he comes and goes as he pleases, apparently."

"Trisha's here, and—"

"Yes, that's right," Lilly said.

"Stop it! Please!" Rucker started sobbing again, his big white face raised to the rain clouds in theatrical pleading. Lilly and Whitaker waited for him to subside. Wipe his nose. Sigh heavily. It took a while.

"I'll take her home," Whitaker said.

"No!" Rucker raised his hands to the heavens. "That would leave me unprotected!"

"Sure, she can stay over here by herself, then."

"She can walk home, for all I care."

"I'll take her home," Lilly said.

"But that would mean the car would be-"

"I'll take the Olds. That leaves you two cars to make your getaway in if the ice man comes back with another banana."

Rucker struck her immediately. A good resounding clap upside the head. Lilly had known he would, yet she said it anyway. She was tiring of his sissy theatrics and took the slap unflinchingly the way she took all the others. With an antic sense of optimism. She knew she would someday be rid of him, and each slap was payment on that promise. Maybe the ice man would take care of it, in point of fact.

Everybody looked away from everybody else. Whitaker was just about to chuck this job. But he realized how good he had it. Soon the ice man would be caught, the sobbing would stop, and they could get back on track to making a ton of money here.

So he went inside and talked to Trisha. She was in the bedroom, looking very big-eyed at all the commotion. Trying not to hear it. As soon as he opened the door she started taking off her blouse, she was very motivated that way. But despite the fact that she had the sugar tits in her hands as in a sacred offering, he had to explain to her what was going on, and she buttoned up and accepted the ride home from Lilly, who didn't seem at all afraid of the bogeyman returning.

Of course, he spent a nearly sleepless night on Rucker's living room couch. Eddie Whitaker was not a man who normally gave even the slightest expressions of opinion. His face was a veritable concrete pavement of emotion. Yet he wondered if he were allowing his frustration to show as Rucker and Lilly and Millie and the three kids periodically wandered the house checking the locks on doors and windows. Asking him if he'd heard anything. Asking him if he was sure the cops were out front.

Odd, at eight in the morning, woolly headed from lack of sleep, he was standing out at the top of the concrete stairs with Rucker as if waiting for the ice man to return. Odd, because they didn't get ice anymore. There would be no ice man. And odd because if the ice man showed his face Rucker probably would turn tail and run. It was still raining hard, yet Rucker stood there watching runoff sluice down the crease of his fedora and splash off the concrete steps.

At the office, Whitaker and Roberts started calling people in, and by ten there were twenty men: the goon squad, Pinkerton and various Beach Oil employees they were going to use. The place was a little crowded, with the girls manning the phones for a special after-Christmas stock promotion. There were six or seven men in Rucker's office, the rest leaning in at the door so they could hear.

"I want that whole area searched. Fine tooth comb and all that," Rucker was saying. He looked highly authoritative again. He may have been sitting tenderly in his chair, or that may have been the imagination of Whitaker, who had heard the banana tale from Lilly and almost burst out laughing.

"We could use some police help."

"They're alerted. Once it's in the news they have to jump in. There's an APB out on those two."

"No, I mean extra help. Big help."

"You'll have to call the chief."

"He owes me. I want you boys to scout the union halls, the synagogues, niggertown, over there where the Japs and Chinks live, everywhere."

Damned if an irate stock holder didn't come in then and interrupt them. "Is Charles Rucker in there?" he yelled from the back of the little crowd. A rotund business type, typical Beach Oil investor looking to get rich off a hundred-dollar buy. "Tell that son of a bitch I'm not getting my dividends!"

Whitaker got a nod from the boss, and the meeting was interrupted while he took the investor out to the stairwell and talked to him. "You'll get your dividends," he said at first. "Darned if I don't want my money back," the man insisted. "You promised me a 200% return by now, and I haven't even got my initial back."

So finally Whitaker had to sap him just to shut him up. He caught him pretty good and knocked him down the stairs, and when the man landed he was there standing over him. "Whatdja do that for?" was what they always said, and that was what this one said. They would come up here asking to get sapped, they'd get sapped, and then they would struggle to understand why.

"The sap?" Whitaker answered. "Because I've busted up a couple of good automatics pistol-whipping people. Not worth it."

"I don't get it," the man said.

"Okay, get this." Whitaker put the sap away and reached inside his coat. Extracting the pair of pliers he carried in there. As the investor got to his hands and knees, the gunman reached down and grabbed his left ear with the pliers. He gripped it until he could hear the flesh squashing.

"Ah ah ah ah!" The investor stopped all motion, his face wrinkled into a picture of pure pain. Whitaker pulled him to his feet with the pliers and jerked him toward the door. Blood ran down the pliers and onto his fist.

"All right, mister! All right! Ah!" He was whimpering like a baby.

As Whitaker let go and stepped back, leaving a path open to the door, the man's eyes spilled over with tears. "Whatdja do that for? What kinda operation is this?"

By the time the lug toddled out the door Whitaker was back in the boss' office, wiping his hands on an old towel. Rucker was handing out assignments.

"Lewis and me, we're going over to the brother's ice route," Whitaker said, his heart rate already low and steady.

"We've talked to him twice," Rucker reminded him.

"No, we're really going to talk to him this time."

"I'm with you. Good idea."

As they all filed out, the boss stopped him to make sure there were a couple of uniformed cops out front watching the office. There were. And one out back in the alley. On his way to his desk Rucker grabbed a banana off a phone girl's desk and threw it out the window into the street.

Whitaker took the Pierce and told Lewis to bring his own car. They found Joseph's ice truck in the hills not that far from Rucker's place. It was parked in what had become a relentless rain, its ice logo barely visible in the subdued light. When the little guy came out of a driveway after a delivery he opened the flap to toss his tongs in, and the two grabbed him from inside and dragged him into the van flailing and scrabbling.

There was just enough light seeping in from around the edges of the flap for Joseph to see Lewis' leering face right in front of him. Whitaker leered from the other side. Sat down on the ice behind him but kept a hold on the back of his shirt.

"What the hell are you doing in my truck?" Joseph yelled, skidding around in the ice chips and slush as he drew himself to his knees.

"You're going to tell us where your brother is," Whitaker said. He had his automatic out, resting on his knee.

"I don't know. You know that."

Lewis lashed out with a fist that caught Joseph on the side of the head and knocked him against a panel of the van. Both men jumped on him and wrestled him to his back on the floor. They sloshed around in the ice melt, Joseph as slippery as a trout, hindered by the bulky leathers. They pinned him down. When Joseph stopped thrashing around and looked up, Whitaker was on top of him with a knee in his chest.

"Go ahead and bash 'im," Lewis said.

Whitaker made a movement with his right hand. "You never want to hurt your hands in these matters," he said. A pair of pliers appeared. Joseph just looked up at them in some puzzlement.

The pliers descended quickly and took a bite of Joseph's right cheek. Whitaker improved his grip and squeezed the fold of skin he'd captured. A look of pure pain appeared on the little guy's face and he stopped squirming because that just made the pain worse. Whitaker tightened down, and the flap of skin burst inside the jaws of the pliers. Joseph's legs shot straight out in shock and he let out a prolonged squeak.

"Before we leave here, you're going to tell me, you little fruit."

Suffused in pain, all Joseph could do was say "Aaah! Aaah!" Whitaker gave a quick twist, and part of the skin of his face came away with the pliers. Joseph squalled and thrashed. His head racked right and left.

Lewis had to put his knee up against his head to keep it from racking away. Whitaker slowly opened the jaws of the pliers and took a grip on his lower lip. Joseph's teeth clacked against the nose of the pliers as if he were trying to bite them. Joseph could see the fist holding the pliers right in front of his face. He saw the fist tighten down. The pain from the pinch of his lip was so intense it blinded him. Not just with tears. With pure fear.

Again Whitaker gave a quick twist, and part of Joseph's lip came away in the jaws of the pliers. Whitaker flipped the tool with the jaws open. A chunk of flesh flew out and whacked against the wall of the van.

He looked down at the little brother. Whose face was covered in blood. The stubborn little bastard spit blood with every harsh breath. Even Lewis was a little stunned. He looked at Whitaker sideways. Mr. Calm, as the goon squad called him, was still calm. But there was a torturous look about him that Lewis had never seen before. But then, he'd never seen the man not get his way before.

"Mr. Rucker wants his money back. And he wants it right away," Whitaker said.

Joseph whipped his head side to side, both to deny he knew where his brother was and to get away from the pliers.

"Hold his head," Whitaker said to Lewis. Lewis did. It took everything they had. Joseph purely hummed in his determination to not be held still, heels and elbows thumping the floor of the van, but they jammed his head tight with their knees.

This time the pliers grabbed the skin just beside Joseph's right eye. "I've found that this skin here is very tender," Whitaker said as he clamped down on the pliers with both hands. This time Joseph screamed. He hadn't wanted to, he'd said to himself that he wouldn't, but he did. It spattered out of him like blood. In the dark little truck it was huge.

"Damn," Lewis said. He could picture the scream being heard up and down the street. He saw a greasy rag on the floor and crammed it in the brother's mouth. Whitaker gave a twist, and the pliers tore a patch of skin away like a bandage off a wound. Blood poured into Joseph's eye.

"Damn, Whitaker," Lewis said. "Maybe he don't know."

Whitaker was starting to allow the possibility. Below him, Joseph's face twitched with pain, hardly visible under the blood. He was baying like a hound through the rag. One eye was shut, blood pooling inside it. The other opened and closed in terror, trying to keep track of his torturer.

"Shit," Whitaker said. He stood up in the truck, disgusted. He had blood on his trousers. There were blood spots freezing like little blisters on all the blocks of ice.

Sweeping aside the canvas and jumping down from the truck, blinking around in the bright light, Whitaker swiped something off his face in disgust. Looked at it. It was just sweat. He held the canvas open for Lewis, who jumped out and quickly made for his car in some degree of haste.

Whitaker closed the flap, and his last view of Joseph was of a curled-up, boy-like figure snuffling for air in the bed of the truck. A watery stream of blood and ice melt ran to the edge of the tailgate and dribbled to the street. Blood on asphalt always had a funny, clotted color, he'd noticed.

"Watch him," Whitaker called out to Lewis, who looked severely uninterested in doing so. Whitaker got in the Pierce and drove it off in a disgusted hurry. Lewis hunched down in the seat of his car and, without any enthusiasm, watched for Joseph to emerge.

It took a few minutes. Joseph opened the flap gingerly and peeked out with one jaundiced eye. He looked like he had been hacked about the face with a machete. Gobs of blood clung to his leathers. He had taken a hunk of ice and touched his face here and there to try to deaden the pain, but flaps of skin and lip hung in the dirty water and made it look even more grotesque. Some bits of ice stuck, also. His face looked like a fresh–cut roast dragged from the meat counter.

Yet, he had that set look to his face. That stubbornness born of something even more animalistic than torture. Nobody knew where he got it, where it came from, even his brothers. Family probably. The rigors of family. He looked around, trying to remember where he had been in his route. Oh yes, the next delivery was to Mrs. McCants' house. He had been looking forward to that.

He slowly, tenderly tonged a twenty-five, dragged it out the back, hesitated for a moment, crying in the rain, and lifted it free. The block of ice nearly hit the asphalt. The pain seemed to have robbed him of his strength. It felt like a two hundred. He got it against his leg and hobbled with it up the driveway to the house. The kitchen door was at the side, and he stood there leaning against the jamb for a second before he knocked.

Mrs. McCants jogged to the door in her robe, and her face just fell from a full smile to a downcast mouth of agony. "Joseph? What happened?"

she screamed. She couldn't even look at his face. She looked behind him, as if he might be followed by cannibals.

But she made him drop the ice—it had blood all over it anyway. Pulled him inside. She cleaned him up the best she could and called the doctor from the hall phone, all the time watching the ice man sitting as still as wood on a kitchen chair and trying to get his breathing regular. She took her son and got the car out of the garage and drove them all down to Los Feliz, the boy looking backward at the man holding a bloody towel to his chin in the back seat. As if trying to keep his head from rolling off his neck.

She tried to drive carefully, but at every lane change and pothole Joseph lurched and wavered on the seat, conscious still of not messing up her car. He hadn't said a word the whole time. He couldn't think of a word, and probably would not have been able to get it out. Yet if pain had elements of expression in it, he would be at the element that expressed ... satisfaction.

Yes, satisfaction. That's just how stubborn he was. If he could smile, he would. The bastards couldn't hurt him. He was a goddamned Daley.

WISDOM AT THE TEMPLE

I don't want to," Donovan said. "We'll need that money." In bed, Wanda held her little Sears & Roebuck necklace watch up close and peered at it. She loved that watch, shaped like a heart. He had bought it for her along his route one day. "It's six-twenty. It will be dark soon." She couldn't believe that neither the watch nor the chain had been broken in all their struggles.

She pulled out the little stem and wound it angrily for a minute. The watch made a sound like an angry insect as she wound it.

The room's tiny window was on the south side but it gathered only a slim angle of light this late in the day. The sun was going down, leaving enough afterglow to highlight his face as he stood there. He had been looking through the gloom at the tattered trees and rundown back yards for ten minutes.

"It's only half an hour away," she said. "She'll be there."

"I ain't goin'."

"I'll go, then."

"You can't go. I ain't lettin' you go."

Lying back on the pillow, she put her hands behind her head, propped up so she could see him. A kind of calm had come over her after their last escapade. Not killing Rucker—and seeing him with a banana up his backside, too—had freed up her agony somewhat. Released it like a laugh. Or a scream. Like her screams for Donovan to kill the man, which had surprised even her. And it hadn't come back. She felt free to escape, now. Just to get out of this entire universe. But there were things to be done, first.

"Tell me about this mine we're going to."

"The Old Soldier."

"Yeah, tell me about it."

"Told you. It ain't been worked much, just the vein exposed. Layin' out there to be taken."

"Gold."

"And silver. Some lead. Other trace minerals, but gold's the big one. They smelt it all out later. It assays out to $100 a ton if we can get down to the good stuff. That ain't a lot, but it's a living."

"Ton of gold?"

"Ton of ore."

She studied him. His face in the winter evening looked much older than she remembered. Even ten minutes ago when they lay together on the bed, not saying much in their disagreement, just resting, he looked younger. He always looked so boyish in bed. Maybe it was because during their first few times lying together, just that few months ago, he was so sweet and eager and grateful. A boyish machine created for love and destruction.

"What is it you find so attractive about digging dirt when it's a hundred degrees out?"

"Hard to figure it myself. Looking for that gold. Prospecting up and down the washes. Getting' your shirt off and swingin' a pick. Taking your haul into town. Looking for something precious."

"So what would I do down there?"

He turned from the window, happy in the thought. "Oh, we'd go places. That's so close to the Mexican border, we'd take a week off and go down there to Nogales and have us a party in a cantina. We'd ride the horses down California Gulch and splash in the water."

Donovan sat on the bed and encircled the calf of her leg with big strong fingers. She smiled at him. Such a goofy character. He reminded her of the movie cowboys, Gene Autry and Roy Rogers. They didn't say a lot, but just provoke them a little bit and out they came with silver six-guns a-poppin'.

"And there's a little town where there's dancing of a Saturday night. Have a couple beers."

"Or ten."

"I told ya. I'm done with that."

"Then I'm looking forward to digging in the dirt with you. But you've got to do this first. For me."

He smiled. The briefcase lay open on the bed, full of its money. Wanda looked over at it explicitly. It was a hateful little pile of money, having cost them so much. She took a stack of bills, tens and twenties, and put it in a number ten envelope. It was a pretty thick stack. The envelope was full to bursting like a white shirt on a fat man.

"That's too much," he said.

"We really should take more. That's nothing." The briefcase was still mostly full. She reached and took another stack out.

"We'll need the rest of it." He grabbed the bulky envelope and jammed it into his left-hand coat pocket.

"Thank you for doing this. I'm sure she'll be there."

"It's their meeting night. And with Christmas and all."

She put the other bundle back into the case and sat up and took his hand. There was still a guileless smile in her every now and then, and she used one now. But it went away quickly with a thought.

"Aren't you taking a gun?"

He patted his right-hand coat pocket, which wobbled with the weight of the .38. "You stay in here, all right?" She looked so fragile at this very moment. And felt fragile. It was her understanding that their life had become about guns and stealth and fragile moments full to bursting with violent surprise. And death. Approaching and receding, approaching and receding. She had almost welcomed it, but now it was about to shatter her.

This act would redeem them somewhat, she thought. The bad would recede a little bit again.

He didn't think so. To him, there was no redemption. They had gone too far. There was just moving forward. Action. Escape. No matter how far she had gone, though, or how much she harped at him, he just loved the sight of her. Sitting there on the edge of the bed looking almost content. Who couldn't love somebody who had such gentle anger. No matter what she had become. Maybe he had to now, whatever she was. Because of what he had become.

Why, he loved her all the more.

So, even though it was dark when he went out and walked down Sunset and caught a trolley, he pulled his dented boater down over his eyes. He took a back seat and hunched his shoulders up to hide his neck and chin. There were only five other people on the red car, and three of them were Negroes who probably didn't read the white newspapers. But he was still careful. Anybody could drop a nickel in a pay phone.

Donovan got off at Azusa Street with two of the Negroes and followed them right to the church. It was a fairly new residence with PENTECOST TEMPLE carved expertly into a board above the front door. Negroes, and the occasional white or Mexican or Oriental person, hurried inside dressed in their Sunday finest. Donovan stayed outside for a while, hat tugged low to ward off the yellow glaze from a small porch light.

A persistent hubbub of voices emerged from inside, swelling and ebbing, and finally it drew him past his uneasiness and tugged him in. The congregation was a sight that surprised him, though he had heard of this. A crowd was packed upright, body-to-body, in a house with all its interior walls removed, and they all faced a chunky black man on a platform in the middle. He was gyrating and calling out, they gyrated and called back.

"Do you bring the holy spirit with you to this house of God tonight!" the preacher yelled.

Some of the replies that Donovan could isolate were: "Ah yes we do!" "Spirit got me, sure!" "You tell it, preacher man!" Many of the worshipers spoke in strange tongues, all pizzicato and onomatopoeia and glossolalia as they gyrated and flailed, their arms thrown up and waving about.

"Holiness!" the black evangelist shouted.

"Holiness!"

"Belliness!" "Monumess!" "Congeress!" The speaking in tongues meant nothing to anybody else but the speaker and God.

Inside the door, Donovan hesitated. First, it wasn't his kind of meeting, as if any meeting was. Second, apart from a few bright faces in the crowd, everybody was dark-skinned. Third, he finally spotted Hattie Fish, and she was way over on the other side of the melee.

He began pushing his way through worshipers energized by the wound-up and highly vocal preacher. Bodies bounced off bodies as they leaped and clapped. A chorus of chants and wails. It was a dance macabre, an a capella riot. Occasionally someone fell to the floor, gabbling and thrashing, and the black bodies made a little space and danced around that fervent believer until he finally got up again.

Suddenly the evangelist yelled "Soul kiss!" and everybody turned to the person closest and pressed their lips on his or hers. Whether male on male, female on female, black on white, brown on yellow, everybody coupled for the kiss. A huge black woman in a flour-sack dress grabbed Donovan and smashed her face into his. Her tongue went down alongside his tongue and around his teeth. He tried to draw back, but she had him gripped in a sweaty embrace so sexual his face heated up like a rock in the sun. When she drew back he could see that it wasn't him she was kissing. Her eyes were raised and glazed and gone to another realm.

He had been God for a moment, and now he was nobody again. A chill went through him, wisdom at the temple, and he was sure the hair on the back of his neck was standing upright.

A chorus of babbling tongues broke loose and the entire congregation raised its arms heavenward and spoke to God in two hundred unknown languages, because that was how many worshipers were in that house. It was a panic of chaotic beseeching, and a sour stench of sweat and after-supper bad breath filled the overheated space.

Again Donovan pushed toward Hattie, whom he caught sight of now and then through the waving arms. He moved around a man giving a thousand rapid genuflections, past a woman doing the boogie woogie. When he glanced up he saw the preacherman gazing down on him in a trance-like focus, but then the little black man lifted his arms heavenward and let loose another stream of exhortations and hallelujahs.

"Hallelujah!" the crowd shouted back as he reached Hattie. "Hallelujah, oh Lord!"

She was a statue in the swaying forest of arms. The tall, thin woman had her hands on her heart, her gaze fast on the ceiling. Sweat dotted her forehead and upper lip. Overheated in a long white cotton coat, transfixed by something within, she was as still as a post in a windstorm of swaying trees. Where the others were loud, she was absolutely silent. Was it prayer or was it rapture? Was she lost or was she found?

"Hattie!" Donovan yelled over the din from all sides. He reached out to touch her arm, needing to announce his presence because she saw no one. "I wanted to say I'm sorry! Me and Wanda."

It might have been in one of the other foreign tongues around her, for all Hattie Fish seemed to understand. She did not move, she did not acknowledge. Her meditation was deep, the rapture complete, her agony her ecstasy.

"I won't ever forget what old Bony done!" Donovan yelled in her ear. "For me! For Wanda and me!"

Suddenly Hattie broke free of her study of the ceiling. She looked abstractly at the crowd around her. Not acknowledging Donovan, just coming free of something.

"Bother the Beelzebub in the bathtub of hell I say and bring me new ghosts of spirit to apricot the lord's fruit all of a sudden now LORD HOLY!" Hattie replied. "Galilee lalilee balilee fa le la la la."

Several nearby worshipers took up her assorted words and made them a chant. "Galilee fa le la la la!" they shouted.

"Hattie, I'm sorry!" Donovan said right into her stock-still black face, worried that she might never acknowledge him. He took the thick envelope from his pocket and, moving close to her so nobody else could see, shoved it into her coat pocket.

Still she didn't move. He slowly backed away into the congregation, bumped and jostled on all sides by their flung-out butts and elbows. Dodging and ducking, he pivoted and pushed back the way he had come, circumventing the platform where the holy man on the dais exhorted his people with one demand after another.

"Repent of all thy sins!" the man yelped as Donovan pushed out the door. "Lo, ye can make it right, yes ye can!"

Outside, in the cold air of the deserted yard, its grass stomped flat and muddy at the edges from the day's rain, Donovan caught his breath. The cold hit his sweaty skin like an ice flake on the tongue on the Fourth of July. His heart was throbbing as if he'd been in one of those footraces he had excelled at as a kid. When he turned and walked down the street the hum of the transported voices accompanied him a little ways, but the hurt had not left him by the time he got on the next trolley car.

He was the only traveler, and he sat way in the back. As far from the conductor as he could get. As far from any conceivable voices as he could get.

ALL FACES BREAK EVENTUALLY

Sucking air violently, Donovan slept on his back, knees up, one limp hand folded across his chest. The bed covers seemed a relief map with a couple of high mountain ranges. Wanda slept clenched in next to him like a grub deep underground. This was the ultimate defense against bad lives. Good old violent sleep. The cold and damp had inhabited the room the way a three hundred pound block of ice inhabited an ice box, and the two blankets they had been allotted barely warmed them.

Under the covers her bottom hand was caught under her, captured under her cocked leg. Her other hand was balled into a little fist that she inserted between her chin and him. Her breaths were tiny and shallow.

She was dead asleep, but she was the one who heard the noise.

It was a tink, like a drop of water hitting the bottom of an empty galvanized bucket. Wanda backed out of slumber and away from him. Uncoiled quickly and listened very very hard, face entirely focused. In the dark the act of listening so forcefully was terrifying. The next time it tinked, she reached under the bed for her Thompson, which had become almost a part of her waking clothing. She got up clutching its two grips.

Another pebble hit the windowpane. Tink. She saw it bounce away. Slowly she eased over, the long, second-hand nightgown with big flowers on it sighing as the hem swept along the wood floor. Standing back from the glass, she squinted out into the darkness until features began to materialize. A dim light in a distant window. A glow of the city on the southern horizon. A figure in the alley moving sporadically in front of a white wall.

"Donovan," she whispered forcefully. She put her tongue hard on her palate and snapped it off. "Donovan! Donovan!"

Wanda jabbed at his thigh with her fist and he finally snuffled out of a totalitarian blackness, a dry husk of a dream. Startling her with his energy, he lunged to the window in his undershirt and heaved at it until the bond where it was painted shut broke and the frame banged up against the sash. He grabbed her gun and leaned his head out in increments.

"It's Joseph. Somethin's wrong." She could see that he wasn't quite alert enough for this, but he started putting on his clothes. She did too.

Downstairs, they unlocked the door to the laundry and let Joseph in. Donovan leaned in close to him. The three white bandages on his face shone in the moonlight.

"What happened?"

Joseph looked backward out into the dark for intruders, hunters, ghosts. He closed the door. Then drew a long breath. It was darker in the Chinese laundry than it was outside, the big tubs and pressing boards as angular as coffins in moonlight. It could have been a morgue, it was so spooky.

"He hurt me."

Wanda took his arm and walked him inside. There was a little light, thrown in through the laundry's window from someplace, and they bent close and peered at him in disbelief.

"They got me in the truck." He sounded like a harelip. His voice was distorted from the wound to his lip.

Donovan went up the stairs in a hurry. Wanda guided Joseph up behind him. The little ice hauler seemed so tender and tentative now, fumbling for the banister with a flopping hand. They hadn't turned a light on, and at the first room on the left the landlady opened the door and closed it just as quickly as they passed. When they got into their room Wanda pulled the shade down over the window and turned on the light.

"Oh, Joseph."

Donovan came around from behind and peered at his brother's face. It was a patchwork face. The bandages on his cheek and eye were big, and the little one just under his lower lip was spotted with blood from talking. Black catgut ends protruded from horrifying stitchwork. But his face had that set to it.

"Sons of bitches." Donovan said simply. He straightened up, looked at Wanda. She knew immediately that things would now get worse.

"Pliers, they used," Joseph said, almost in amazement. "Regular old toolbox pliers."

"Who was it? Rucker?"

"Eddie Whitaker. And that cop, with the white hair."

"Working for Rucker, though."

Wanda reached up to the bandage on his lip. "Let me look at that. It's bleeding." For some reason she felt very tender toward the little fascist. The fact that Joseph was here, and Rucker's crew wasn't, meant that he had sacrificed for them. Joseph closed one eye in pain as she tugged away the loose bandage.

"Sons of bitches," Donovan said again when he saw the torn lip, a hole spaded out of the flesh, its purple edges crusty with old blood and bubbling new bright red clusters along the cornrow of stitches.

"Mrs. McCants helped me. She took me to the doctor, right in her own car," Joseph said in his mumbly voice. He looked over. Donovan was tossing the Thompsons onto the bed. Pulling out all the boxes of ammunition they had and piling them up. "The baby was right in the car. Mrs. McCants, she's got the cutest little old kid."

Wanda followed Joseph's eyes. To Donovan's eyes. There was a stare in them, a blind stare. Just to look in there now was horrifying.

"No, Donovan," she said. "That's the end of it." He was checking the loads in the drum magazines again. "We've got to get out of this city. Look what's happening." She dabbed at the lip with a tissue. She shook her head continually, lost in regret and an expectation of even greater horror.

Now Donovan had that set to his face. It was the middle of the night, but he had lost all traces of sleep. The blood rushed uphill and awakened his skin, his whole head vibrant. He wasn't even going to answer her. He couldn't have explained how he felt, but his body, even in the cold room, had gone sweaty. He felt swelled up, gorged, choked on a vast and overheated anger. It hurt him, it was so filling.

"Just regular old pliers," Joseph said, almost in admiration.

"Donovan, no."

Joseph leaned away from her dabbing at him and said, "Like you'd use to tighten a bolt." He seemed entirely fascinated with the concept.

Donovan pulled on his coat. Stood in front of his brother, the damned stubborn little guy who mistrusted everybody but white people, even though he was at least a quarter Indian and most likely some part slave. The goddamned little maniac. He loved him so much.

"You sure they didn't follow you here?"

"The cop went to sleep. He's still sitting in his car out in front of the house."

"Lewis?"

"Lewis?"

"The white-haired cop?"

"That's the one."

"You both wait here."

"What?" Wanda said. "I say let's get out of here."

"The ice truck down there?"

"I parked one street over. I sat in it a while to make sure nobody--"

Donovan gingerly gripped him on the shoulder. "You did good, little brother."

Taking the truck key out of his pocket, Joseph handed it over. The two ranch boys seemed automatically to know what needed to be done in this kind of situation. "Regular old pliers, you believe it?" Joseph asked everybody.

But Wanda wasn't paying attention. She held the blood-spotted tissue in mid-air, fighting her way into Donovan's eyes. "Can't you please just leave it alone? Can't we just get in the truck and drive on out of here? Now? Arizona? Anywhere?"

"You look after Joseph right here."

"Please? Go mine some gold? All of us?"

"Don't go nowhere."

He went out the door and down the hall, past the landlady, who peeked out again at the noise. She ducked inside her bedroom again when she saw the Thompson dangling from his hand. This time he could hear the door lock click. It may have been the look on his face rather than the gun.

Wanda tore off the whitest part of the bandage and stuck it back to Joseph's lip the best she could. He went over and slumped on the bed, the pain breaking down his strength. She began to pace. It started with some nervous steps to the door to look out, and back to the window. She moved faster and faster, gesturing with her hands to the door in some kind of un-spoken conversation with the long-gone Donovan. Joseph wasn't paying attention at first, then the energy of her movements got to him.

"In Oklahoma?" he said tentatively.

She stopped dead still, listening. To him, to the universe out there where Donovan was. Finally realizing that she was listening for the sound of shots in the alley, trying to figure what they would sound like this far away.

"Yes?"

"I had a friend. Raymond was his name. Before I came here, he told me, 'Don't you notice how different you are from your brothers and sis-ters?'"

Over by the window, Wanda fought the impulse to look out into the darkness. Her man Donovan had such an energy about him that others anticipated it even in his absence. Like dynamite that's out of sight, but you know it's there. You can almost hear it hissing. You anticipate its shock wave.

"That's when he told me I was from a different father than my brothers and sisters. Everybody in town knew it."

This got Wanda's attention. She looked over at this boy. He wasn't looking at her. He was staring down in his lap.

"It just means…."

"That means my mother is no saint. You're the only person I have ever told this to. Even my friend Raymond, I vowed I would never see his face again. What kind of a friend would tell you that? I came out here to live with Donovan just to get away from him."

"So your father had reason—"

"He had no reason to do anything! He was a cheater too! Raymond said that's why my mother did it. To make him sorry. Is it possible a mother would do that?" His hand flew up to hold the bandage that popped free from the force of his words. Blood blossomed and seeped between his fingers and down his chin.

For once Wanda was not angry at his anger. What a strange turn of events, that the accepted underpinning of these lives was not what it seemed. Mothers and fathers, all in a jumble.

"I've heard of it happening," she said.

So he shut up. As if hearing the information he feared most. Wanda thought it made so much sense. The brothers so unalike, the father so adrift, the anger so almighty. The whole family was lost, like stories she had heard of people in the tallgrass prairie where there were no reference points even in the daytime and you would become disoriented from the sun swirling in your head.

She sat on the bed next to him. This made him very nervous. She moved away a bit. Neither of them said anything for a while. They both glanced down into their laps.

"I'm sorry, Joseph. There are no guarantees on families. I can tell you that for certain."

"You know what else?"

"What?"

"I'm the one told Rucker about your heist."

It took a while for this to penetrate Wanda's exhaustion. It took a while for her even to engage him. It was a form of disbelief. A refusal to believe even as she saw how much sense it made.

"I saw Rucker's appointment book at your place. I saw the plans you drew up. Donovan finally told me what was up."

"What did you do, Joseph?"

At the saying of his name his eyes teared up. His little rigid face quivered. It was as if she had invoked some icon or totem. It was just his name, but it was all he had now as a touchstone to the rest.

"I'm sorry. I told Rucker about it. Just so he could avoid it. He already knew Donovan had been in the house, because their maid saw him one night. I knew there wasn't any use talking to you two, all those guns you bought and everything. I didn't have any idea he would try to ambush you. He told me he was our friend. I didn't want my brother to get in trouble."

They sat a while longer. He stopped crying almost immediately. It must have been three in the morning, but she was too tired to go look at the watch she had left on the dresser. She was stunned, waiting for her man to come back, though she knew that the business he had in mind would take much longer than this. She hated the thought of what he was doing, she hated him being gone, she hated everything right now.

"When did you get to be a Jew?" Joseph finally asked. He didn't look at her when he said it. He touched the back of his finger to his lip and pulled it away to see if it had blood on it. It did.

Wanda laughed despite herself. It was a little more maniacal than comical, her laugh was. The boy was going out beyond his boundaries today.

"You get to be a Jew when you're born of a Jewish mother," she said. "That's the way. You can convert from something else, but it's hard."

"They don't want anybody else in?"

"It's not a club, Joseph."

He nodded. Apparently he had enough information. He seemed thoroughly subdued and not at all racist for the moment.

"What will Donovan do?" she asked.

Joseph nodded some more. "He's going to hurt somebody. It's the way Father taught us. The Daleys can bust up each other's faces, but if somebody else busts our faces... That's all she wrote."

There was silence. "Serves them right." she said after she thought about it for a while. And why not. All faces break eventually, don't they?

Again he touched his lip to see if he was bleeding. He wasn't. The stream had coagulated into a hardening lump. He wished he'd brought a bottle of whiskey to give his violent brother. The thought of him drunk and loose with those two torturers made him feel good. He didn't connect it with Rucker so much, because he hadn't been there.

"Darned tootin' it serves them right," he said.

In a little implosion of negative, painful energy Wanda crawled up to her position on the bed. She curled up, this time facing in the other direction, toward the window. She pulled covers up and over. After a long while of sitting with his head hanging, Joseph gave up and fell back on the bed and crawled up to the head too.

They went to sleep there, turned away from each other like figurine bookends on an empty shelf, the light still blazing over them.

THE DOUBLE A IS A VERY FINE TRUCK

It felt so good to be at the wheel again. He hit the starter with his toe and got rolling. The bubble gas gauge showed almost full, and he felt like honking the aooga horn the way he had when he first bought the truck from a dairy out in Riverside. Celebrating up and down the street even though the truck was seven years old when he got it. Donovan stopped completely at the next stop sign even though there was nobody else out this deep into the night. He wanted to shift through all the gears. Up into first, double-clutch into second, double-clutch down into third and finally let it slide into fourth. The old Ford growled like a big cat at every ac-celeration. It would only go forty, and when he hit thirty it howled in its power train until he let up.

A block from Joseph's place, his and Wanda's old place, he shut it off and coasted to a stop. He reached down and set the hand brake even though it was a level street, a habit from his ice man days, which seemed so very long ago. He opened the narrow little door and squeezed his knees out the way he always had to. On the sidewalk he stood in appreciation of the ICE sign they had painted themselves on the panels on both sides. He shook his head, remembering how that was the only thing they could think of to paint there. Just plain old ICE.

At times like this, fingering the ice pick on his belt, Donovan had a very deep calmness come into him. A ranch provided a childhood filled with the violence of livestock and brothers and nature, and from it came the autonomic system to deal with crisis. As ingrained as a swallow reflex. He felt as at peace as any man could be who wanted to kill. He had forgot-ten his hat, though, and felt very much outside the bounds of civilization.

Walking a block over and a block up, he held the Thompson out away from his flapping coat. It was the darkest part of the morning, and not a car moved in the residential parts of Hollywood. Even if anybody saw him they would just think he was an actor carrying his prop to an early-morning shoot on a Cagney film.

He recognized Lewis' Chevrolet parked on his street, one of the un-marked cars the goon squad used. He came up from the side cautiously, out of the mirrors. As he drew alongside, the machine gun ready, he could see Lewis' head slung back on the seat, his mouth drooped open and eyes draped closed.

Quietly, Donovan set the Thompson on the sidewalk. Walked around behind the car to the driver's door. Jerking it open, he had Lewis by the hair and was dragging him out onto the street before he was fully awake. The big man spun around and, groggy, jerked away. He stood leaning like a lightning-struck tree, blinking at Donovan standing six feet away.

"You," he said. And charged. Accustomed to bulling people over, he ran right at Donovan. Who put one foot back for leverage and lowered his head into Lewis' chin. Like a linebacker, he lifted the cop and deposited him on his back in the middle of the dark street.

He was on him immediately. Hitting and hitting. His fist crunched bone and tooth. "You hurt my brother," Donovan said. Hitting and hitting and hitting and hitting.

Lewis neither answered nor moved. Ready to do more, Donovan was surprised at how limp the copper was. He frisked the wobbly form and got the automatic out of his shoulder holster.

"Son of a bitch, hurt my brother that way," Donovan said, talking to the limp form on the concrete. He put the automatic in his pants pocket and pulled the Smith & Wesson from his coat pocket and thumbed the hammer back. It made a tiny click as simple as the single tick of a pocket watch held to the ear. Oh, it was sweet, that sound, the whispered pre-amble to a shout Donovan's pounding blood wanted to hear.

"No, that ain't good enough for you," Donovan said, though the man hadn't moved so much as a twitch all this time. He lowered the hammer and put the pistol back in his pocket and went around the car and came back with the tommy gun. He racked back the slide and aimed it from the hip. The barrel almost rested on Lewis' crotch, and a burst would cut up the length of him.

Donovan stood there a minute and finally remembered to take off the safety. He stood there another minute.

Finally he lowered the Thompson in disgust and cussed himself. "God-damnit, what's wrong with you?" he asked. The cop was stirring now, his eyes fluttering open. Donovan leaned over him as he sat up. Lewis flinched back as Donovan came into focus. Donovan punched him in the nose as hard as he could, leveraging and rolling his shoulders into the punch. Lewis collapsed again.

"Get that set and you'll be back at work in a week," Donovan said as he walked away. "Or maybe two."

By the time he got the ice truck rolling the horizon glowed with the potential for sunlight. Cars and trucks here and there woke up and got on the streets. Coffee smell seeped from houses. Los Angeles was a hard working city, and it got out early.

But for some reason—these moods of uncertainty, he was having all too many of them—he had lost his enthusiasm. He paused too long at stop signs and got honked at. He dallied on the hard streets, babying the old truck along. It was sprung so tight it virtually leaped from the earth at each bump. But that wasn't it. He just had lost momentum. For the same reason he hadn't killed Lewis, who he knew had tortured Joseph and maybe killed Bony, he was driving more and more slowly as he headed into the seething sunlight.

Up in the Franklin Hills he parked on a side street four blocks from Rucker's house. He got out and, once again, looked back admiringly at the truck. The Double A was a very fine truck. Certainly, the ICE lettering wasn't the best, since the brothers had done it with a three-inch brush and a can of ice-blue paint from the hardware store. Certainly, it wasn't as sleek as the Buick that had been shot to pieces. But it was as sturdy as a brick and would haul three tons if you loaded it right and it had carried the brothers through their ice venture and made them a good living during the Great Depression.

Fine. Donovan found himself walking very slowly around the block toward Rucker's street. The winter sun was up into his face, and he could feel hunger cutting into his energy stream. But that wasn't it. A moment of indecision later, he veered off into a little copse of native coast oak trees in a vacant lot on the crest of the hill. He needed to think about this. He was a block from Rucker's. He could practically look down across a couple of yards and see the back of Whitaker's little house from here.

Flopping onto the ground by one of the massive oaks, he tried to think what it was he should do. What the hell was wrong with him?

He leaned against the ancient corrugated tree, rubbing his back around to find a comfortable spot, pulling the tommy gun out from under his coat because it was pressuring his belly. Was it that he had seen enough of this business? Was it that he felt he could still escape, go to Arizona, go back to Oklahoma, or to Australia or Argentina, and still have a life? Was it that Wanda was too important to throw away in a binge of revenge? Was he afraid?

For a long time he sat there, the butt of his jeans soaking through with the morning dew. The more he thought about it, the less he knew. Finally he got up, made sure his revolver was still in his pocket, checked that his ice pick hadn't fallen out of its sheath, put the Thompson up under his coat. And walked back toward the truck.

But he came to a stop at the screech of tires nearby. He was at the edge of the street, and he ducked to his right, bursting quickly through a thick privet hedge with a rattle of dry leaves. He could just see the top half of his ice truck around the corner.

And now police cars slamming to a stop around it. He could just see their tops, too. There must have been five or more.

It was another of those Keystone Cops moments. He could see the caps of the coppers bailing out of the cars and bobbling around as they ran to and fro in a virtual comic frenzy. But he knew he wasn't going to laugh.

38

MAN'S ON THE MOVE

It was way too early when Whitaker woke up, the cigarette girl's blubbery tits virtually wrapped around his face like hot water bottles. He was suffocating, but that wasn't what woke him. Somebody pounded at the front door. He slowly extracted himself from a pile of flesh and down pillows. Out his front window he could see the silhouettes of men haloed by the headlights of cars parked in the long drive.

"Man's on the move!" Rucker yelled.

They piled into various cars, mostly police cars of the men guarding Rucker's property, and sped to Joseph's house, where Lewis sat on the doorstep nursing another broken nose. In fact, much of his face was broken. He whined his story out to them, spitting out a broken incisor.

They searched for Donovan, couldn't find him. Searched for Joseph, couldn't find him. Leaped in the cars and rushed back toward Rucker's place hoping to catch the Daley boys there. Whitaker became a passenger in a police car driven by a rail-thin copper he didn't know well. They parked down the street a ways from Rucker's. No conversation. The car heated up from sunlight and smoke from the cop's mentholated Spuds. "You palsy walsy with this Rucker, are ya?" the copper finally asked.

Whitaker didn't answer. He looked out the car window. On the sidewalk lay a dead cat. There was nothing uglier than a dead cat, he thought, with its lips all snarled back exposing its fangs and its fur gone flat and messy. "Ya are, I'd like to get me some a them oil shares, if you can do it," the copper said.

At that point there was a choppy call on the radio. One of the wide-ranging police cars had come upon the brothers' truck parked down the hill a few blocks. The copper flicked his butt out the window and toed the starter. They left the dead cat to a long line of ants marching lockstep to the feast of its eyes.

The ice truck was just sitting there. When they all bailed out of their cars they aimed weapons, prepared for anything.

Somebody yelled that he saw something move in the truck.

There was a trigger-pull instant of hesitation. A glance exchanged.

Somebody fired a shot.

Everybody jumped at that opportunity. Let loose a veritable explosion, like a string of firecrackers equating to one major eruption. They had pistols, rifles and shotguns, so the holes that appeared in the truck varied quite a bit in size. Bullets and slugs and double ought buck whanged into the old vehicle for a full minute, back, front and side. Sheet metal popped and gaped, glass shattered and splashed onto the asphalt. Whitaker didn't even bother. Just watched.

Nobody actually ordered them to stop, least of all Rucker, who pulled up half a block away in his Pierce and took it all in with a maximum of satisfaction. Finally the shooting tapered off to a couple of flat pops. They almost started up again, because they saw something move, but it was only the Model A settling askew on a deflating tire. Cordite hung in the still air as thick as bar smoke, its smell heavy and chemical.

"All clear?" a police sergeant yelled, hoarse with excitement.

At this point there was some shouted discussion among them. Of who and when and how to approach the vehicle. It was as much a stress reliever as it was tactical. There was mention of the tommy guns known to be in the hands of the revolutionaries.

After the firing stopped Whitaker pulled his pistol and went for the ice truck. He ran side to side, looking for a target, but could see nobody in the vehicle. There was a general movement in that direction as men in their winter coats came out from behind their cars with weapons aimed. They shuffle-stepped in, courageous en masse. There was the sound of pleading as a policeman shot in the crossfire rolled around on the ground with a leg wound on the other side of the A.

"Nothing," said Roberts, who had been in the Pierce with Rucker and had fired a couple of shots just for fun. His head was poked in the cab through the shot-out window.

Others lifted the canvas and looked in the van. Coming out looking genuinely confused, the way they had in the abandoned hotel the night the couple disappeared. There were blood stains in the back, so it was very worrying to not find anybody in there. They slowly reloaded, almost comically perplexed, and holstered their weapons. Then they realized something and jumped back in their cars and rushed off to Rucker's house.

It was there in the long driveway, as the cops searched the grounds with unusual fearfulness, that Whitaker stood by the front of the Pierce, drawing in a little sketch book he kept in his suitcoat, and wondered at the foolishness of all this. Though the previous week's storm had blown through and left the sky as sunny as a Long Beach whore, there was still a grimness to the scene before him. There were so many men in long, dark coats that the scene was black and gray instead of blue and yellow. Everyone tried to reassure Rucker that all would go well.

"No telling how long that truck's been there."

"He's high-tailed it out of here, for certain."

"Your family's gonna be safe, I assure you."

"Damn fools," Rucker said. "My family's been removed to safety. I'm not worried about them. I'm worried about me."

The boss waved at Whitaker impatiently, and the bodyguard tossed his sketch book through the open window of the Pierce and sauntered over. Looking as concerned as he could manage under the circumstances.

"Find him? Just find him?" Rucker said. He waved away the other men, turned to Whitaker with that look on his face. The bodyguard could see that he was about to cry again.

"Eddie?" Rucker asked him.

"Yeah?"

But Rucker didn't have anything else. He didn't have a real question. He had seen what the ice man had done to Lewis. He had seen how fearful the coppers had been on finding the ice truck empty. Whitaker saw it too. Everything was understood between them.

"You want to go see Daddy?"

"Yes, please."

Whitaker went to his porch to pick up his overcoat. Rucker took a deep, fluttery breath. He walked to the Pierce, stopping at the door to look in the window.

His bodyguard's sketchbook had fallen open on the driver's seat to the current drawing in charcoal pencil. It was a pretty good representation of the iceman's boxy truck. Surrounded by black-cloaked men aiming weapons at it. Over it all, not a sunny sky, but a cloud-banked storm and torrent of slanting rain. The artist had taken liberties. Had put his own noir twist on the day, for whatever reason.

The truck had a hundred irregular pencil-point bullet holes in it. This only reminded Rucker that the ice man could still be in the neighborhood.

Maybe the man had left the vehicle there to taunt him.

Rucker let out a little sob and got in the car.

39

CENTRIFUGAL THOUGHTS

That evening Donovan and Wanda walked right past the taco guy, whose name was Roberto, she had learned during her last meal there, and went to eat at a real restaurant. Fine, it was a little hole in the wall over in Chavez Ravine. Japanese food, and well after the normal dinner hour so that nobody was likely to see them.

Wanda was still shaking from her reunion with Donovan, though. He had come home completely unlike himself. Had tapped so lightly on the apartment door that she thought it was somebody else and stood ready with her tommy gun. He had muttered a beleaguered hello, to her and to Joseph, who, in the glare of daylight, sat on the chair in the corner as far from the armed and dangerous Jew as he could get. Threw his Thompson on the bed in disgust and jolted backward from the force of her delirious hug.

Now, trying to get her fingers to properly grip the chopsticks, which she had used so many times successfully in the past, she finally gave up and dropped them in the noodles and just stared at him from underneath her camouflaging scarf. Sweet Jesus, he was avoiding her gaze.

"What happened?'

He didn't answer. She assumed he didn't want to admit the enormity of what he had done. She assumed the worst, and was almost happy to think it.

"Fine. I don't want to know. Just tell me the plan to get out of here."

No answer.

"What happened?"

"Ice truck's dead. Shot to hell and gone."

"Were you—"

"No."

"The copper?"

"Free and clear. Layin' there snoozin' on the street."

"Whitaker? Rucker?"

He didn't even reply. Say how he had hidden in the hedge like some small, trembling prey species. Had practically crawled down the hill through people's back yards. Rat-like.

Finally she worked up the initiative to try the chopsticks again. Maybe it was the hunger. Still shaking, she was able to get a drooping gang of noodles up and into her mouth. The miso heat slithering into her body gave her a little energy. Enough to eat another big bite, and another after that.

So he started in with his fork. The waitress had had to hunt all over the place to find one. These were the first gaijin ever to set foot in here except for the beat cop looking for his monthly payoff. She watched him closely as he stabbed down into the big bowl trying to nab the slippery noodles.

"Here's the deal," he said as he chewed. "Let's go. Let's beat it on out of here. We've had it."

She paused in mid-bite, a long drool of noodles dripping out of her face. She tried a noodle-infested smile. Getting out of there sounded so good to her. She clipped off the noodles and swallowed.

"I finally got you convinced?"

She smiled at him, he smiled at her. Suddenly they picked up momentum, eating so fast they flipped miso droplets around the table. They splashed into their food as if they hadn't eaten all day, which was more or less true except for the paper sack full of fruit pies and apples and soda pops he had bought on his way home to her.

When they left, the Japanese cook came out to clear the table and turn off the lights. He bowed lightly to them at the door, thanking them for the five-spot Wanda had thrown on the counter. Outside, she linked arms with him and got him over to a side street so they could walk home with some peace of mind. Wanda was mindful of the old days, of last summer, when they had often come out of their double late at night, satiated with sex and food, and padded around Hollywood like prospective film stars admiring their future domain. It was like that. Hugged in so tight against each other that they could barely swing their legs, paying no mind to the rest of a wacky world gone to prejudice and injustice and war.

Joseph jerked awake when they came in, rustling through a field of food wrappers on the bed. "You eat, did you?" he asked. "You didn't want to go," Donovan reminded him. "We're getting out of here," Wanda said.

"Good news to me," Joseph said.

They hurriedly gathered their guns, stuffed the suitcase full of their second-hand clothes and grabbed the briefcase from its new hiding place under the bed. But then Joseph just flopped there on the edge of the bed like a child. A child with a savaged face. His bandages had spotted reddish-brown as he opened his wounds in fitful sleep, as if he were starting to rust at the surface like a sheet metal toy left outdoors.

"You all go on," he said.

"You got to beat it with us," Donovan said.

"They'll know," Wanda said. She had decided to not tell Donovan about Joseph's confession. If she wanted to be forgiven of her sins, she could forgive the baby fascist of his. "It's not safe for you now."

So Joseph, who had just wanted a good invitation, got his boater off the wood floor and put it on his head. Something about the straw hat made him look even more the sulky teenager, up too late at night.

"Where we going?"

"Arizona."

They stole the same old burgundy-faded-to-lavender Hudson Essex that Donovan had taken before. It had been moved, but the key was still in it. It was about midnight when Donovan maneuvered it down the back streets through Echo Park, avoiding major thoroughfares. Wanda felt so vulnerable. The car barely pulled some of the hills, as if it were overloaded as well as worn out.

"We're not going to Arizona in this," Wanda said, looking around sadly. The gray velour interior was ripped and soiled. One door was indented from a wreck, and the bud vases, once a selling point to an upscale buyer, dangled loose. "Probably belonged to some investor who jumped off a window ledge in twenty-nine."

"This is a 1930," Donovan pointed out. He knew his cars, model and year.

"He probably jumped out the window right after he bought it."

"I don't think there was that many people, total, that jumped out of windows," Joseph said. "That's just the commies talking."

"Yeah, there's not a depression, either," Wanda said sarcastically. And Joseph seemed chastened, as if understanding something he had never understood before about the economy of speech.

They parked in front of her old apartment building. It seemed the same. The weeds along the side and back were dead at this time of year, and they leaned crooked and dehydrated in the headlamps.

"I'll come with you," Donovan said.

"Sure."

"What are we doing?" Joseph asked.

"Looking for Pauline," Wanda said.

"That Red?"

Wanda gave him a pointed look and got out and walked back on the dirt drive. It was as dark as black except for a little light in a downstairs laundry room. Confident of Pauline, she went up the stairs to the back apartment and knocked lightly, Donovan waiting to one side with the Smith & Wesson hidden behind his leg. Finally the door peeked open a slot.

"Wanda," a man's voice said.

She stepped back rapidly. The door opened halfway. Donovan aimed his gun, holding his breath for the shot. But it was only Mike, the union president.

"Is Pauline in?"

"No."

"Where is she?"

"She had to go down to that dress shop we're striking on Olive Street. There was talk of trouble." He looked her over nonchalantly. Her dirty second-hand skirt, her unsettled face. "How are you doing?"

"Fine." She took a long look at him, too. It had only been a week since she had seen her boss, but he seemed almost a stranger. He was a stranger. She had no idea he was sleeping with Pauline. "You?"

"Can't complain."

He looked at her so hard she knew he knew everything. Hell yes, he knew everything. Everybody in the state of California knew everything.

"Where on Olive?"

"You'll see them outside. Having to picket all night because they've got three shifts going in there. Seamstresses fainting from exhaustion. That kind of thing. We're trying to force a vote."

"Uh huh."

She turned and left. Union business was so far from her mind now. She could barely remember what it was all about, this other format of the clashing humans.

They drove downtown in silence. A wet wind blew palm fronds and paper trash into the streets, and occasionally a swirl would edge the old, top-heavy car to each side. Its weak headlights barely cut into the night, as if the darkness were denser than usual, and Donovan leaned over the wheel to guide it around debris. The sky seemed overcast, though Wanda couldn't see that high. The only other people out were a few swells in new Cadillac V-8 coupes and Packard convertibles careening home from the last parties of the night.

"They think they're so swellegant," Wanda said of the partygoers. This was hardly a bubble out of what was once a vast, boiling vat of indignation, though.

"What do we want from this Pauline?" Donovan asked.

"We can't drive to Arizona," Wanda said. "They'll be watching the highways. I'm going to see if she can arrange something. Truck, train, anything."

"Are you sure?"

"Who else can we trust?"

Wanda saw the picketers a block away, women walking small against the street of tall brick office buildings. About ten of them made their little circle with homemade placards in front of a lit doorway. It was a narrow building with concrete façade. The seamstresses looked so heroic to her. They stamped their feet mightily to keep warm as they walked.

Donovan drove on by and parked half a block down. "You see her?" he asked. Wanda was twisted around in the back seat. Looking out the little rear window of the Hudson.

"I think that's her in the door."

Donovan twisted around to look. Joseph seemed not interested. Wanda supposed that the idea that Jews and Reds and immigrants and unionists were involved in this operation had dampened his spirits even beyond the mood his injuries had imposed. Every now and then he would reach up and touch his face as if to make sure it was still there.

"That shop has a back door on the alley," Wanda said.

Donovan put the car in gear, and it groaned away from the curb. Except for a few office lights burning high up in the taller buildings, downtown Los Angeles was dark and foreboding at this time of night. A mist had started to accumulate on the windshield of the Hudson, and the wipers didn't work.

A narrow alley. The wind shot down it. Twice he had to get out and move overturned garbage cans. "I think this is it," Wanda said. He stopped the car behind a door with light seeping under it. Off-cuts and remainders of cloth overflowed from a row of garbage cans.

"Wait here," Donovan told Joseph.

Getting out, he and Wanda approached the back door cautiously. "Leave that here," he said, and she returned the Thompson to the back seat. At the back door, cockroaches resting in the sliver of light on the doorstep scooted in and out at their approach. Donovan opened the heavy door and Wanda dance-stepped over and around the roaches.

The dress shop was a long, open hall with room for forty or fifty seamstress tables mounted with manual sewing machines in two long lines along the walls. A wide aisle in the middle was where off-cuts and seconds were thrown on the floor, waiting for a cleanup man to sweep them out. There were only two women working, one on each side, one in the front, one in the back. They sewed so rapidly, their machines whirring away, they seemed to be trying to make up for their striking comrades.

When Wanda sauntered by, the working women didn't even look up, though she knew them by sight and they her. At the front of the hall was a little foyer, and she could see Pauline standing lit up against the dark of the outside doorway. The strikers and their signboards passed in and out of the frame as they made their silent rounds on the sidewalk.

"Hi, Pauline," Wanda said.

Pauline whirled as if the devil had spoken in a woman's voice. "Jesus," she whispered as she backed cautiously into the foyer. "Wanda."

"How have you been?"

"How you been?" Pauline glanced at Donovan, back at Wanda. As Donovan followed her glance he noticed something that he hadn't before. Wanda had lost a lot of weight. She looked gaunt, in fact, now that he saw her through another's eyes.

"You know," Wanda said.

"I know."

"How's the walkout going?"

"Good so far."

"Where's the owner?"

"Disappeared a few minutes ago."

"Good."

She took Pauline's arm and pulled her back into the darkest edge of the foyer, where the light from the hall didn't hit. Pauline looked around wildly, as if afraid of this friend who had become a renowned revolutionary.

"We need your help. To get out of town." She kept her hold on the woman's arm. It was a vice grip on the last vestige of friendship.

"I don't know...." Pauline didn't seem such a vitriolic and cocksure Red anymore. She cowered farther into the shadows. "All that stuff in the papers."

"Sure, sure. We were set up, though. Trapped. Ambushed."

"Still. It's my neck."

Donovan didn't say anything. Even when Wanda looked to him for support. Something about this Pauline he had never liked. She seemed to be a Red when she was up in front of a meeting, he had warned her, and some other color the rest of the time. He didn't give a damn about the Communists, but if you were going to be a Red, be a Red, had always been his take on it.

"We need a ride east. In a truck or something," Wanda said.

Pauline thought this over. Thoroughly. At some length. The strikers made a complete circle before she replied.

"There's a union bus going out day after tomorrow. Morning. Headed for Phoenix. But they might check us, too."

"We could get in the baggage hold or something."

"Look, I can't talk too long here." Pauline stuck her head out the door for a second. "Where can they meet you?"

Wanda and Donovan looked at each other. They had just left their place. They had no place, not one place, to go.

"1620 Running Spring Road. Out in Pomona."

Wanda had no idea why she said that. Donovan didn't say anything, but he had even less idea why she said that. He didn't even know where she was talking about.

"1620 Running Spring. Pomona," Pauline repeated.

"It's a new subdivision. It's on your way out of town. We'll be there day after tomorrow. What time?"

"Ten in the morning. Maybe eleven."

"Sure. Pauline, I—"

But there was a sudden commotion of yells. Wanda shrank back at the zoom of a motor. Two motors. Now screams. The three fell back against the foyer walls.

Wanda peeked out. In a misting rain two cars braked hard at the curb and men in dark coats and white hooded masks leaped out of them. One of the men lashed out around him with a billy club. A woman was knocked sideways and fell to the sidewalk.

The women picketers fell back toward the door, their circle in disarray. Signs were knocked to the sidewalk. Another scream. Abbreviated, as if chopped off in the middle.

"Ku Kluxers," Pauline said as she spun and fled back into the hall.

Donovan started to follow, but Wanda grabbed his arm. From the moment when she saw that club hit the woman's shoulder, some dangerous excitement overtook her and the veil between violence and benevolence fell away. When he whirled to see what she wanted, she was already through the door and outside. She picked up a dropped sign and attacked the first big man she saw.

"Well shit," Donovan said.

He ran out, gathered his springs under him and plowed into a masked man trying to jerk the placard from Wanda. The sign went flying—TEN HOUR WORKDAY FOR WOMEN—and Donovan drove the man across the sidewalk and whanged him into the side of one of the cars. The man collapsed.

There was general panic among the women, who were bounced and beaten from one edge of the sidewalk to the other. And panic among the assailants as Donovan began hitting them. They were fairly easy prey, with their hoods skewing and blocking their vision, and he jumped from one to the other fisting them in their eye holes. He had the element of surprise, they expected no real opposition.

Three of them were on the ground when he was met by a frontal attack from two hooded men. He wrestled with them far longer than he wanted to. Off to the side someone yelled, "It's the Dark Angel!" That man pulled a pistol out from under his coat, and Donovan just managed to pull free and close on him before he could get it up and aim at Wanda. He shoved the gun up in the air and shook the arm hard. The gun boomed and went flying.

Three of the men finally ripped their hoods off for vision and converged on Donovan. He whirled and whirled, hitting, but they dragged him down. Wanda struck at their backs with thin placard wood and she saw a sap raised. She leaped for it but it veered down out of her sight and made a sound she was familiar with.

Donovan saw it coming. Pinned, there was nothing he could do. It just came right in and disappeared from his vision.

And then his vision disappeared. That's all he remembered.

Until the sound of women's voices brought him to. He woke up thinking that of the three men without hoods he had seen two of them around. He didn't know when or where, and it didn't matter, but his thoughts were all transient and inefficient. He went right on thinking them anyway for a while, as if he had the right to a little leisure thinking.

He sat up in a gaggle of garment workers down on their knees around him on the sidewalk. The attackers were nowhere to be seen. Pauline was nowhere to be seen. The cars were nowhere to be seen.

Wanda was nowhere to be seen.

Apparently some minutes had passed. They didn't speak much English, the women. "You sit," one woman kept saying. "Goot. Goot," another said as she dabbed at his temple with a rag that came away spotted red. He had to blink water out of his eyes as he looked up at them. In his confused state he thought they were spitting on him, but he finally realized it was a light rain falling down through the street lights.

Struggling to get his feet under him, Donovan pawed at the women for support. He lurched a bit, but their strong arms held him up. His thoughts were really homeless but finally were able to focus on one object.

"Wanda?" he sputtered at the women? "The woman with me?"

They just shook their heads and pointed down the street. Farther downtown.

He lurched back into the shop. He ran through it and through a knot of jabbering dressmakers in the aisle. He skidded on fabric fragments on the concrete floor. He fell. He got up, skating right and left. Finally he made it to the back door.

In the alley he leaped into the Hudson and mashed the starter. The old thing wheezed to life, and Donovan double-clutched it and lurched down the narrow passageway. A garbage can caromed away as the car banged into it, and he made a hard right on a numbered street he couldn't identify in the rain.

He had no idea what he was doing, and he kept looking in the back seat. "Joseph? Joseph?" he kept saying. His little brother was gone too. He could see almost nothing through the water now sheeting off the windshield, and he drove wildly among the tall buildings looking for black police cars on black asphalt. But there were no cars at all at this black hour.

Driving madly, as the buildings got shorter and shorter, the street ending at a wood fence, Donovan suddenly felt as if the blackness had inhabited him. He lost all his energy, it had spun away in centrifugal thoughts of Wanda. He wheeled the car over to the curb and his head just fell to the steering wheel as if somebody had sapped him again. The engine clattered softly, but the overriding sound was of the rain galloping on the steel roof of the car. The world was patched with blackness savaged by slashes of rainfall glinting in the headlamps as it heaved itself at the glass.

He wanted to cry, but his eyes were dry as Mojave stream beds. He wanted to get out in the rain and scream, but he couldn't move his legs. Finally he shut off the rackety motor and lay down sideways on the seat and, careful of the painful new knot on his head, went off into a very violent sleep punctured by pain. And dreams. And then painful dreams.

DADDY'S BOY

Mr. Rucker senior lived Hancock Park-adjacent in a two-story Victorian with a Southern gothic look. All these houses were mishmashes of architecture. The Rucker mansion was rundown, the only house on the block with furniture in the yard and an untrimmed jungle of trees, and Whitaker thought the whole setup was a good artistic representation of the family's life.

A ruin in the midst of riches. A fiction in the heart of fact. A neglected mansion looming in the mid-morning darkness of a pounding rain in the colorful land of citrus.

Whitaker was standing on the back porch because the old man had ordered him outdoors. He said he wanted to talk to his son alone. Rucker had wanted him to stay, the bodyguard could see by the worried look on his face, but the old man got what he wanted. He had been out here in the cold for ten minutes. It occurred to him that the eviction had something to do with the unseemly nature of their interaction, the father and son. As with sexual matters, they didn't want others to see them at it. But he could hear them talking through the screen door even over the rain.

"You've got to get the Chief on it," Rucker's voice whined.

"There will need to be incentives," his father boomed. "No man works for nothing, every man pays for his mistakes."

"Oh, there would be definite incentives."

"He'll want to see your bona fides."

"We'll handle it discreetly."

"Eddie!" the old man yelled.

Whitaker went back inside. The den of the mansion was as big as Whitaker's whole guest house, and father and son stood in front of an ornate marble fireplace that sported a tiny stick fire sputtering moistly.

When Whitaker had arrived, the old man had sent him outside to gather fallen twigs from the back yard, gave him a match and a wad of the Examiner and ordered him to build a fire. It was hard to start and its heat was practically suffocated by the stone cold house.

The floor of the den was as cluttered as the yard, mostly with broken bicycles, for some reason. Daddy Rucker had never been seen riding a bicycle, but the room was piled with 19th century bikes, unicycles and tricycles, some with wooden wheels. Parts had been cannibalized from some bikes, taken to other more unfortunate bikes, but never attached. Whitaker always thought of the old man as shrewd until he saw him in his home environment, where he seemed addled, abandoned. It was a womanless house. Whitaker never knew where the wife, Rucker's mother, had gone.

"Beach Oil shares," the father said to Whitaker.

"What about them, Mr. Rucker?" Whitaker asked innocently. As punishment for kicking him outside in the cold.

"I want some."

"Anything on the radio about the ice man, Eddie?" Rucker asked him.

"Haven't heard a thing."

"You let me know, goddamnit."

"The boys are on it."

Rucker and his daddy looked at him as if he had just assessed them with taxes. This was a common tactic of Rucker's, to take the heat off himself by putting his bodyguard on the spot.

"Well goddamnit, why don't you do something?" Rucker said.

"Charlie." The old man's voice scissored through his son's shrillness. "I'm sure Eddie has done everything humanly possible. And if you want to stay here for a few days…."

"We have hotel rooms. Where he can't find us."

"Eddie…. Those Beach Oil shares?"

"They're in the car, Mr. Rucker," Whitaker said.

"Of course you're welcome here without the shares, but that would be a nice gesture. Really, you need to think more globally, Charlie. The hirelings out on the street can only do so much, they need a general to formulate a precise plan of attack."

"See, the Chief, he could—"

"Forget the Chief. You're already making trouble for him. All this publicity, and now the public is afraid of these outlaws. How does he keep things on the QT after all you've done?"

The old man's voice snapped out and bit like the tongue of a bullwhip falling on his son. Who shut up immediately.

"Are you going to get those shares for me, Eddie?"

Whitaker left for the car. When he came running back out of the rain the old man was slapping his much larger son about the head with a limp hand. Rucker cowered and shrugged off the lazy biffs, but he dared not retreat too far or the father would pick up the nearest object for better results. Once Whitaker had seen him chasing his son down the driveway and lashing out at him with a bicycle handlebar.

"Got 'em," Whitaker said. It was important to be matter-of-fact about these spankings, because he didn't want to laugh out loud. Then the father might attack him, and that would mean one old dead man on the floor. His pride was at the tipping point.

"Good man," Rucker's father said, leaving his beating as nonchalantly as he might leave the watering of a shrub. He took the two thousand-share notes and began filling them out on the mantle. He handed Rucker the pen, and the son signed his name to them, squinting closely in the dim light.

"Someday these will assuredly be worth real money?" he said. It was more of a demand than a question. "Hopefully sooner than later?"

"Absolutely," Rucker said, combing his hair back in place with spread fingers as if a breeze had ruffled him. Whitaker could not figure out this relationship, nor the father's preoccupation with the worthless oil shares. Unless the son simply hadn't let him in on the scam, in which case he was scamming the old man too.

"That's daddy's boy," the old man said, snagging the shares from his son's hands.

"We got her!" a voice yelled from the back porch.

A figure lurched into the doorway. Lewis, with his bandaged face. Then another cop, and another. Some of the Pinkertons sidled up too.

"We got the Dark Angel!"

Rucker practically ran to the back door. When he threw open the screen he knew from the ecstatic look on Lewis' face that he wasn't bullshitting.

"You got her?" Rucker yelled.

"She's out in the car."

"How did you get her?"

"Last night. Some of the Kluxers was bustin' up a garment union strike, and there she was. We had a couple boys in there, and they recognized her."

"All right." Rucker turned to his father triumphantly. The old man wasn't smiling, so Rucker turned back to Lewis. Whose face was bandaged so tightly it looked like it had been put in a cast.

"Old Bananas?"

"I beg your pardon, Sir?" Lewis' nose honked from being swaddled in bandages.

"The ice man, you got him too. Right?"

"Nuh uh. See, he might of been there, but these guys didn't know. All they knew was they'd seen the Jew woman's picture in the paper."

"Shit."

"Goddamn shame. Some guy was there with her, but they didn't know."

"She's here?" the old man said ominously. "At my house?"

"Yes!" Lewis yelped. He slapped his thigh with his hat in delight, but stopped when the pain caught him midway.

"You think I want to be involved in your shenanigans, you idiot? You brought that woman here?"

They all fell silent, and then they all fell out the door. Hasty goodbyes were said, but none by the old man. Who slammed the screen and the door behind them. They heard the lock click.

Sure enough. Rucker just stood at the curb beaming in a light rain. They had the Kitchen woman trussed up and lying on the back seat of one of the goon squad's Chevys. Through the rain-beaded window he could see that she was gagged. A man in the front seat had reached over and was holding her down by the neck.

"There's my girl," he said admiringly.

"Oh, that's her," said one of the other cops, wanting to get in on the good feelings.

"Did they get the money?" Rucker asked Lewis. Who shook his sore head.

"She didn't have it on her."

"No, she wouldn't have it on her! There was a lot of it! It was in a briefcase! My briefcase!" Now he was prancing around in the rain. Didn't anything ever go right?

"Nobody said nothin' to me about any money," the strange cop said.

"You sure your buddies in the Red Squad aren't hiding something from you?" Whitaker said softly to Lewis.

"Yeah," Rucker said, whirling on Lewis.

"Sure I'm sure," the white-haired cop honked. "They wouldn't do that. They're good boys. You don't mess with niggers and Commies lessen you're high-minded."

Through the car window Rucker caught Wanda's eye as she squirmed around on the seat to see what all the talking was about. He calmed himself and smiled a beatific smile down upon the one frightened eye.

"Well then, you'll just have to mess with her."

CIGARETTE GIRLS

Hung over from a drug-like sleep, Donovan woke up with a headache. It was full daylight, which he hadn't slept into for months. Maybe this was what unconsciousness felt like if you could be conscious of it. Just too much to bear inside one small skull.

When he stepped from the Hudson he was surprised to feel rain still falling. One of those Southern California rains difficult to figure out. Sky bright, clouds high. The street was running with clear water, so it had probably poured not long before.

He lifted up his face for a little wash. He held there a minute, rain pricking his skin and beading in his hair and brows, and then rubbed the accumulated cool liquid into his eye sockets. Still he felt a tightness in his lungs. His thought was that this was the first time for months that he had slept without Wanda. That thing in his lungs, it could have been fear.

Unrefreshed, dizzy from moving his head around in the rain, he got back in the car. He was parked at the dead end of the street, well out of downtown. He could turn and see the stumpy buildings to the west, though. All around him old board fencing hid old board structures being used to lean old rusty tools against. From one garage protruded a dilapidated buckboard. Another had a metal Dr. Pepper sign on it showing a bunch of cowgirls on a fence.

There was no traffic at this end of the street, so he got out and pissed against one of the battered fences. He bent and looked closely, but he couldn't see any blood in it.

He got in and started the Hudson. A good car, the Hudson, he thought. They would be making these forever.

A weird city. You couldn't leave a tip on a bar without somebody stealing it, yet there were the briefcase and two Thompsons on the back seat where anybody could have grabbed them while he was asleep. The suitcase was upended in the back, he could see the top of it. He made a u-turn and headed home.

Home, he thought, was the apartment above the laundry. But as he drove up on Sunset, his boater pulled low, he saw several police cars squatted around the building, one straddling the sidewalk. Coppers had all the Chinese workers outside, where they chattered desperately with much gesturing. A small crowd of shopkeepers and unemployed men had gathered to watch.

He kept on going. Only the top of his hat visible from the outside.

Donovan passed the day getting food and gas—amazing how adventuresome that was when you were wanted by the law. He felt bad about the Hudson. But if he took it back he would have to return to the neighborhood of the laundry. That could be dangerous, and he would just have to steal another car anyway.

He drove through Rucker's neighborhood, but there was no sign of him or his family at the top of the driveway. He parked down by the reservoir and read the newspaper microscopically for any indication of Wanda's capture, but there was nothing. He fell asleep.

So it was nightfall before Donovan, reeling with guilt and worry, found the Palomar Ballroom over on Vermont near the Bimini bathhouses. With its huge, arching neon sign and parking lights, it was lit up like a cruise ship. Cars eased in and out of the lots.

He parked the Hudson in a residential neighborhood down off 3nd Street and walked over. Entering the Palomar through the huge kitchen, where ten cook staff worked frantically in storm fronts of steam and smoke, dissecting entire cows for the stoves, he eased into the ballroom through a swinging door. Waiters banged him aside, rushing out with steaming piles of food. He got up the nerve to move into the edge of the crowd.

The Palomar was a hot spot, everybody from the corrupt mayor to working stiffs coming here for an evening of catchy jazz and fried beef. They ate and mingled at long, smoky tables, like one big happy family in their second-best suits and dresses, stumping out smokes on broad ashtrays and turning to plates heaped with steaks and pork chops. A few people danced to a small orchestra playing sentimental popular tunes. The shiny brass of the horns glinted in the awkward lighting.

Cigarette girls. That was what Donovan was interested in. There were two of them working the room, dressed in their Chesterfield costumes, bare-legged and leggy, trays of smokes and chewing gum suspended from their necks. Both girls were working the far side of the ballroom, chatting and flirting with customers, and finally they both migrated his way.

The one on the right, the more buxom one, was the girl Donovan had seen at Whitaker's place a couple of times during deliveries. Somebody had mentioned she worked here.

Realizing he was in for a long wait, he sat at a table where single men gathered and occasionally got up and danced or went to a table of single women. He had done this himself in the past, though never with such a sense of impatience as tonight. The table was centerpieced with their hats. He ordered a steak dinner, returned greetings from a couple of the men, and watched the cigarette girls.

"Nice figure on that one," one of the men said as Whitaker's girl passed, saying "Lucky Strikes, Camels, Chesterfields?" as she went. "Light up your life, boys."

Donovan turned half away. He didn't know if the girl would recognize him from his deliveries to Rucker's. He didn't smoke much, but when he did he rolled his own. He had bought tobacco earlier in the day, so he poured a furrow and licked the edge of the cigarette paper, sealed it, lit it, ordered a beer, started to drain it, and stopped and pulled it from his lips with a pop.

It wasn't in his nature to nurse a bottle, but he needed to be sober.

"Where you from?" his persistent neighbor asked. Donovan suppressed the impulse to swing around and strike him in the forehead with his fist. He didn't want to talk to this irritating drunk. "Guess you're in the ice business," the man said, nodding at the ice pick on his belt. "Not a real friendly feller, are ye." Donovan stolidly glared straight ahead and took the occasional small sip of his beer.

Finally the man got up and left and sat with another table of men across the polished dance floor. Donovan's food arrived, its steam adding to the thick haze of smoke in the joint. He began cutting on the steak and potato. He realized how tense he was. It was an effort for him to not lash out at people. He ate so quickly he almost choked on the chunks of food.

It was Wanda. Every woman he saw reminded him of her. He had picked up his share of cigarette girls, fan dancers, taxi dancers, bubble dancers, dime store clerks, motion picture extras and closing-hour waitresses. California held half a nation of wandering women living on the margins of enterprise. Now he wanted every one of them in the ballroom to be Wanda, but not one had that spark in her eye or hop in her movements.

He thought of that night when she had bailed him out of jail, and he'd smelled like vomit and looked like shit. Or the other way around. How she went to court with him a week later and and made up some cockamamie story and got him off with a fine. Once they had gone out with friends of hers and ended up sneaking off and necking so hard in the back of their '38 Dodge that the back door was kicked open. He thought of the time she had accompanied him to his father's shack in the lemon groves, hoping for the best right along with him. And how brave she had been, holed up in that old hotel with the Red Squad baying at the door through megaphones. There was a distinct vision of her spraying the corridor behind him with a tommy gun as he sprinted for his life, her eyes half closed, hanging onto the gun for dear life.

What made Wanda different from, say, the cigarette girl, whose name he didn't know? Just watching the woman work the ballroom of the Palomar, he could see that she was nothing like Wanda. The little union organizer was an entire ethic, a complete ideal, in herself. Her concern was for other people, for the world, for history. He had been so stunned by this when he first met her. A socially conscious person who didn't care where she stood in society. All the virtues you would want your friends to have, your parents to have, your kids to have--she wanted the world to have. A peacemaker who would go to war for her beliefs.

Where the hell had she come from? He didn't even know the forces of nature or culture that produced such a creature.

A long night, it was, thinking of her. He was still a little puzzled why she would stay with a mug like him. He'd never be able to figure that one out. It was obvious why he loved her. She was beautiful, smart and a burning fire on the long, wet Great Depression night. What did he have to offer in the deal? He was bringing a punching bag mentality (which he was trying to resist tonight), a tendency to go on benders (also on hold), and a murderous ice route with a second-hand truck (the route now abandoned and the truck shot to pieces).

As he ate his second piece of pineapple upside down cake and watched the late-night crowd filter out of the club in twos and fours, Donovan realized that he had been lost in this relationship from the beginning. He had been getting through on native energy and bombast. All he was looking for, until they decided to rob Rucker's payroll, was somebody who would help him clear a little pathway to tomorrow. Notoriety had never occurred to him. Riches never tempted him. Even his gold mine was more about the search than the gold. He was built of vengeance, a faulty vehicle, and he realized that his biggest hope over the years was that he would once again have a family gathered around him. Wanda was the start of that.

It was late. The Palomar emptied out slowly. Finally the cigarette girls had sold all they were going to sell to this sparse crowd, and they turned their trays in at the hat-check counter. They put coats on over their skimpy costumes, flipped off their high heels and put on flats. Just as they were saying their goodbyes to the help, Whitaker came in the front door, all in a rush.

Donovan turned half away and pulled his boater across his forehead. He got up and sauntered to the rear, his hand on the .38 in his coat pocket. He pushed back through the kitchen, quickly sidestepping exhausted dishwashers sucking on cigarettes. He got outside as fast as he could.

By the time he peeked around the front corner of the building, Whitaker was helping the cigarette girl into Rucker's black Olds. Donovan sprinted away from the club, keeping the building between himself and Whitaker, coat flapping, head pounding with a new headache. He was able to get the reluctant Hudson started. He jerked it out onto the road. Located the Olds before it got lost in the motley dark.

The skies had cleared, the night allowed far-reaching vision. So many of the cars were black, but Donovan's eyes were excellent. The Olds made only one turn, a left, and didn't go far. To a tall brick block of apartments over on Franklin, where Whitaker left the car double-parked on the street while he escorted the girl inside.

Donovan found a parking spot on the sleeping street and left the car running. Finally he had to turn it off. Whitaker must have been getting a quickie. He trotted out fifteen minutes later and dove into the Olds and took off again.

This time it was a darting race down into Hancock Park, with Donovan pressing the old Hudson to keep the other car in sight. By the time he parked it among the big houses of actors and businessmen a block past Whitaker's car it was misfiring badly. In the rear view mirror he could see the man get out and rush inside one of the mansions.

Donovan got out. The rain had quit as if it meant it. The street was littered with leaves so wet it was hard for a lingering wind to lift them clear of the asphalt. To his right lay the big house, and he approached it cautiously, his shoes squishing through puddles.

All the other houses were regal, electric light bursting forth, their white hides glowing even in the dim street lights. This glum house needed paint. Its landscaping was old and diseased. A divan sat in the front yard, sagging under the weight of the water it had accumulated.

Donovan glided to the near side, his hands gripping his Thompson. Peering in each window as he went.

The interior of the house was darkened, a window occasionally reflecting other neighborhood lights and jolting him as he passed. He worked halfway around it before he came to a window of the den. There was some hint of light in there, but he had to press his face to the glass before he could see clearly.

An old man whom Donovan had never seen before stood with his back to a little fire fidgeting in a grandiose fireplace. There seemed to be no other light in the huge house, and the man rocked back and forth on his heels, alone, as if savoring a good life he once had known.

A noise of a car grinding and starting. Out back. Donovan launched himself away from the window. Ran full steam around the corner of the house. Through a huge, deserted back yard. To a long curving driveway.

Just in time to see the brake lights of the Pierce-Arrow pause at the street end of the driveway, then pull out onto the street and disappear down the block. Donovan got to the street just about the time the car passed his parked Hudson. It raced on to the next intersection and turned right, two heads silhouetted through its rear window.

Donovan slammed himself into the Hudson. Turned the key and toed the starter. There was dead silence. He redid everything. Hit the starter and arched his back digging his toe into the floorboards.

Dead.

His head hurt too much for him to pound the steering wheel, but he did, jarring tornadoes of pain all the way up to his frontal lobes. Then he just sat for a while. Hurting all over. The rain started up and stopped twice in the minutes he sat there contemplating his misery.

When he got out he was in the mood to make somebody pay. He went around to the back of the house. He opened the screen door, forced open the locked back door with his shoulder, and stepped into the flickery darkness of the old house.

Oddly, the old man was still standing there before the dwindling but persistent twig fire. He faced it now, though, so his back was to the door hinge that squeaked and to Donovan when he stepped into the center of the den.

"You forget something?" the man asked. And turned.

He just stared at Donovan, the features of his face clouded in this darkside of the fire. The ice man, Thompson hanging from one hand, walked toward him.

"Who in Sam hill are you?" the man asked, and as Donovan got closer he could see that the old man was much smaller than he had seemed from outside. And older. A little gaunt and grim, as could be seen as he turned his way and the firelight snapped off the side of his face and pomaded hair. His impulse had been to knock the guy flat, but he was just an old man.

"Nobody you'd know. Where's Rucker?"

"Who?" the old man said, full of instinctive survival skill.

"You know who. Was just here."

"Which one?"

"You're his daddy, ain't ya."

The two perused each other for a moment. Old man Rucker, one to appreciate and court predominant forces, looked down at the tommy gun almost admiringly. Donovan, always one to see the blood lines, read Rucker in the hooky nose and almond eyes.

"What do you want him for?"

"I'll bet you don't even have electricity in this house."

"The police will be back shortly, so you better scoot."

"Can't afford it, can you."

So the old man attacked. He was a crafty old fellow, dedicated to holding fire when superior forces confronted him, but this intruder didn't have the right to insult him. He went right for the Thompson, and got so far as to get a grip on it before Donovan jerked it away and pushed him off with an almost gentle shove. Rucker's father ended up whirling around out in the middle of the room, turning back to the fire so that his old-style wool coat and yellow cravat showed their age and deterioration.

"I'll have you sent up. I'll have you put away for good."

"Where they keepin' her?"

"Keeping who, you vermin, you criminal?"

"The woman they caught."

"I don't know a thing you're talking about, mister. And I'll tell you what, I'll telephone the authorities this very second."

"You can't even afford a phone, I'll betcha. Look at this mess."

The old man actually looked around the room at the piles of old bicycle parts, the stringy curtains, the fireplace that hadn't had a decent fire in it for weeks. As if seeing its meanness for the first time. The little mess of wet firewood somebody had deposited on the floor and which was now making puddles on the hardwood. And back at the machine gun, wistfully.

"You wish you could," Donovan said, reading his mind. For some reason he could read this old creature's entire history, and he did not feel sorry for him one bit. Besides, he was Rucker's kin.

"In a second I will."

"Good luck to ya on that one."

"I'll tell you where she is. They've got her hidden away and they're going to kill her for her crimes against society."

This shut Donovan up. A rage redder than fire came over him, and it was all he could do to refrain from wadding this little man up and cramming him in the chimney.

"They'll have their way with her and she'll tell everything she knows and you won't be able to do anything," Rucker's father said. He knew he was on the right track with this man.

Donovan was dumbstruck. The rage gradually drained from him. It was replaced promptly by a grim, heavy negativity. The old man's imagery made him realize how hopeless their situation was.

"Then they'll find you and do the same."

Nothing in Donovan now. He had no comeback, he had no violence for this man taunting him. All was grim and vastly unapproachable in his mind. He would like to murder somebody, but the energy required made it an academic matter.

"Just like you, ain't he," Donovan said. Idling to the door. "Full of bull with them fake oil shares."

"Fake what?"

"Oh, you think them dead oil wells is on the up and up?"

"Beach Oil? Sound as the Bank of America. What do you know about it?"

Donovan opened the back door. He could see he had accidentally tagged the old man. He paused at the screen door for effect. He had never acted in his life, but he was going to give it a try.

"I'm Okie. I don't know much. But I know oil."

And out he went into the cold, dripping neighborhood. Where the actors and the directors and the studio bosses lived, he supposed. The history of this old father, cold and broke, was hidden to him. Yet it fit into the altogether seamy history of the City of Angels just right on a black and deranged night like this one.

YOU GOT YOUR NATIONAL PRIDE

She was on the chair and Lewis was on the bed. She was tied upright in a corner like a poorly wrapped Christmas present. He was stretched out like a fish on a slab of ice.

His hugely bandaged nose was very white and structural like a tent, with buttresses of tape running outward and around his head. She had a thick rag tied across her mouth, muffling her breathing.

His eyes were closed in rest. Hers were open wide in unrest.

Wanda thought the big cop looked concrete-like, what with his arms and legs pulled in tight to the central core. Like one of those hefty Soviet statues of Lenin that she had seen in photos. What one would look like if it were pulled to the ground. He uncrossed and recrossed his outstretched legs. He appeared to be sleeping but he was wide awake.

Hearing the toilet flush down the hall, she feigned sleep. The door opened and the other goon came in. She didn't know what good it did to pretend to be asleep. Mostly she just didn't want to look at them when they were looking at her. Maybe it was more fear of what they could see in her than what she saw in them. Maybe it was that their eyes were so indifferent, and any blend of intelligence and indifference was frightening.

"Where the hell are they?" the second man said, and she looked at his eyes. So did Lewis. That was all he moved, though, and neither one of them looked at her.

The second man must have been an outside detective or something. She knew most of the goon squad by sight, and she didn't recognize him. He was skinny, more like an accountant in a little fedora pulled down snug over a narrow head. He wore voluminous trousers that didn't match the tight fit of his suit coat. In all the time she had been in this room he had never taken off the hat.

"Weren't they supposed to be rolling in here by now?" the lanky man said impatiently. Wanda realized suddenly that this man, and maybe Lewis too, were very afraid of something. Maybe it was this situation. Maybe it was a situation that was shortly to develop.

And then she saw it, saw into their tension. The second man, all Adams apple and hat, turned to her. Looking at her for the first time since he came in with his narrow, naked eyeslits. The look in there.

He was afraid of her. They were afraid of her. They were afraid of being with her. Which was even more scary. Because it meant that ultimately they would somehow have to find a way to get rid of her in order to disassociate themselves.

"We're going to have to get her some food," he said.

"Why don't you run out?" Lewis asked.

Lewis sat up and looked at her, as comical as Charlie Chaplin in that movie a couple years back when he got stuck in the gears of the factory machinery. The nose tent bobbed and wobbled as he spoke, the bandages anchored to his upper lip as they were.

"Don't know if we should."

"Hell with her, why doncha go get us something?" Lewis said. "I'm empty."

"They'll want her tip-top. We always deliver in tip-top condition."

"Ah! You Pinkertons. Ya got a high opinion a yourselves."

So. He was one of the Pinkertons. Agents hired to do the dirty work of people with money. Lanky man slowly turned to Lewis, giving him the sign to shut up. "And the police don't? Even when they've gotten their noses punched in?"

Their voices even said they were afraid of her. The tension in their throats. This hefty Lewis, he was a brute, even then struggling to think of some half-witty comeback. Scouring his brain. He was in it for the power surge, for the ride on the water of whatever stagnant ideology he adhered to. But the Pinkerton man, he was in it for profit. Not money, profit. Such a huge, scary difference in temperament and outlook was required for that. A man would beat his mother for ideology, but for a profit he would sell her.

"You gonna get us something or not, Roberts? There's a café right over there on Hollywood Boulevard. Steak and eggs for sixty cents."

"I'd take some flapjacks, I would."

"You want me to go, or you want to?"

"I love to put an over-easy egg on top of a flapjack."

"Aw, that's disgusting. Egg yolk sogging up a pancake."

"I'm just worried if I'm not here when they come…. Who knows what that crazy Rucker's liable to do?"

Wanda tried to think what her chances were. If they turned her in she would have a trial, at least, but she didn't think she would make it that far. A trunk, a drainage ditch behind an orange grove, that was as far as she would get. Lewis was a cop, after all, and he wasn't turning her in. The other man, who knew what justice system he worked in? It was the knowing of some things and the not-knowing of other things that scared her. Which meant they were all terrified of each other. The system was out to punish her for her sins against it. She wasn't going to get breakfast or court.

"The John Henry Lewis and Joe Louis fight is coming up. You think he can beat him?"

"I don't know. Nobody's gonna whip that colored boy now," Lewis said. "It's got all out of hand."

"That Lewis any kin to you?"

"Naw, I don't think so. It don't matter, Joe Louis ain't goin' down to no pug."

"Louis versus Lewis, with Lewis listening in. Ain't that something."

"Just breaks my heart, them lettin' the niggers in to boxing."

"Still," Roberts said, sitting on the bed and lighting up a smoke, "it's a world championship or it's not."

"But these colored boys, they get a foothold, pretty soon they'll be playin' baseball in the bigs."

"Joltin' Joe, though, he's already been king of Yankee Stadium. That Schmelling fight, you listen in? That one was a dilly."

"Did I? Say, I wanted to see him put that nigger down for good."

"What? You can't be rooting for the German. Not against an American."

"He's Hitler's man. Nothin' wrong with that, is there?"

"You got your national pride to think of."

"Roberts, he's a Negro. Where's that gonna stop?"

"How do you think? He beat Carnera, he beat Schmelling, he beat Baer, he beat Braddock. What are you going to say, he doesn't deserve it? Put them all in there together, maybe they'd whup him."

"Fine by me. Got so I don't even listen to the fights anymore. Rather hear about Seabiscuit. Now there's a story. Hell with the niggers."

For a while Wanda listened in. Distracted. The argument in a way made no sense to her and was outside her entire sphere of interest. At this moment. Still, the men fascinated her. Arguing world history and human justice in the nutshell of a sporting event. It was telling how they could sympathize more with a horse than they could with a man of another race.

"Let the better man win," she said, tonguing out the gag far enough to make her words understandable.

They slowly screwed their heads around from where they were looking out the window of the hotel. They looked her in the eye. Maybe her words hadn't been decipherable. They just looked at her in some consternation.

She tongued out the gag again. Her tongue hurt from the effort. "Afraid of a little black man?" she gabbled.

Roberts turned back to Lewis. "Would you rather eat flapjacks or steak with those eggs?"

Wanda closed her eyes. She determined right then that she wasn't going to cry or beg or reveal a goddamn thing to these fools. In a moment the mood took her, and she thought back all the way to the beginning. It was all Donovan's fault. The dangerous boy had corrupted her. He took anger and injury wherever he went.

No. Head sinking to her chest, she realized it wasn't so. She had jumped at the chance to right the world with an ugly twist. My god, she had forced her moral imperative on him, turned him like her own little private army to the task she had so naively selected. Wanted him to kill people, and he had. She killed people herself. She was the dangerous one, a little nihilistic demon.

Listening morosely as the two goons talked about her in the background, calling her "the Jew woman," "the Jew" this, "the Jew" that, Wanda felt she was in a dark room with historical horrors lurking all around. That family legacy still defined her from its distant past, and she had defiled it. The horror in this room befitted the shame and remorse she felt.

And, of course, hiding behind that was her pride. In what she had done. She had done the wrong thing, but as in the best moments of her life, she had done something. It could have been right. It could have. As Donovan would say, the hell with them. The hell with them all.

She looked up. The two men were now vehemently arguing over whether eggs should be eaten on top of flapjacks. Who knows, they might come to blows over a topic this significant.

WAYS TO MAKE YOURSELF FEEL BETTER

Donovan woke up curled into a tight ball, his flesh as cold as chilled dough. He stared in studious consternation at a sloping surface upholstered in a kind of cloth he hadn't seen before, right in front of his face. It worried him, this odd piece of furniture.

He didn't know where he was.

When he sat up and looked around he remembered. He was on the back seat of a car. Parked in a little pocket of orange trees at the edge of Hollywood, one of the last groves left. Groggy, he remembered how he had walked up and down the streets of Hancock Park for half an hour the night before and finally found a car with the keys in it—what was the world coming to when everybody was taking their keys out at night? Coincidentally, it was an almost new green Buick just like the one he and Wanda had driven to its death. He had pulled it between rows of citrus trees in the early morning after cruising all over the city looking for signs of Wanda.

Chilly, the night was, after the rain storm had passed. He blinked the bright out of the daylight and shrugged off the extra clothes he had taken out of the suitcase and piled on himself for warmth. He opened the door and got out and took a whiz.

A couple of workers were on tall ladders at the end of a row of trees, picking Valencia oranges into long bags hanging from their necks. They didn't even look at him. Okies, by the haggard looks of them. Maybe they were used to the playboys and it-girls from Hollywood parties drifting in here late at night and sleeping off their gin fizzes. When Donovan got back in and slammed the door, one of the workers glanced over and then went right back to dropping oranges into his bag.

He didn't like not knowing where to go. He not only didn't know where

Wanda was, he also had lost Joseph. He was a man who found a direction and marched to it. This was agonizing.

Starting the car, he backed out of the oranges, the tires slipping in the soggy soil. Drove slowly toward Pauline's. What made the loss all the more maddening was that Wanda had disappeared so unexpectedly and completely. Recalling how frightened she had been when he left her alone, he hated the thought of her being in danger without him. He plowed the Buick inside the apartment complex and parked downstairs from Wanda's old unit. As he got out, the landlord, a blimpy man in overalls, came out to intercept him.

"Don't allow parking there, fella," the man said just before Donovan decked him.

As he climbed the stairs Donovan could see the man rolling around in the dirt, wrestling with his pain, trying to reorganize his jaw. He pounded on the apartment door. Again. Again. He went back down the stairs. The man was still rolling around like a burnt worm. Donovan was tempted to drive over him but swerved around at the last second. He was building a mood for the day.

At the union hall he parked in the back alley. It was the middle of the morning. He rested with his head out the window in the sun for a minute. Warming up the concussion a bit. Not that his skull felt any better as it expanded in the heat.

The hall was empty but he heard noises in a back office. He found Pauline and Mike fucking loudly on a desk, flesh slapping flesh so hard they didn't hear him, and he backed out quietly and let them finish. It took a while. He cooled his heels out front, looking at union handouts, and then came in noisily, heels pounding the wood floor, to allow them to gather themselves.

"Morning," he said.

"Donovan," Mike said. The Irishman's face was like a big raspberry from his exertions, and Pauline flung her hair back in hurried rearrangment as she buttoned her blouse.

"What happened to you last night?" she asked, glancing at Mike.

"I got decked," Donovan said. "What happened to you?"

"I beat it out of there. That's what you do when the KKK arrives. They mean business. Where's Wanda?"

"That's what I came here to find out."

A grim look from Pauline. "Okay, the girls told me that rough bunch packed her off. I haven't heard a thing."

"She's wanted, you know," Mike offered. "Have you called the police station?"

"Sure, I'm gonna call the coppers," Donovan said. He looked this pair over. They just did not appear to be the zealots for humanity that their positions suggested they should be. Their faces were distrustful. The office had a disused quality to it, as if nobody got asked in, and there was a smear of dampness on the desk.

Right there he saw the difference between Pauline and Wanda. Wanda wanted to do good despite what it might cost her. Pauline wanted to engage in an ideology that served her needs at the time. It wasn't about the world at all. If he went back to the Pentecost House trance meeting next week he might find her there instead, speaking in tongues with her hands waving around. Or a Bund rally. Or the Chamber of Commerce. There were so many ways to make yourself feel better than you really were.

"Best thing for you is to not go to that rendezvous tomorrow morning," Pauline said. "Just get out of town. Use the back roads."

"Good advice," Mike said.

"You sayin' you won't be there?" Donovan asked.

"The bus will be there. We won't be there. It's all set up."

"We'll do what we can. Unless you want to cancel."

"We'll be there," Donovan said.

"This is risky business, you understand."

"I appreciate that."

"Don't do it. She'll turn you in."

"She what?"

"She'll rat. They'll make her do it."

"She would never rat."

"Up to you."

"I'll be there," Donovan said. "She'll be there too. If she's…She'll be there."

"I'm sure she will."

"Yep."

The two fuckers nodded and nodded. Affirming what he already knew about them, about the world. That compared to Wanda? It wasn't worth her effort.

HURT HER

The radical revolutionary sat slumped in her corner chair. Her mouth gagged, eyes shut, head nodded forward, jungle hair over her face. If she was faking sleep she was persistent. If she was asleep she wouldn't wake up because of the actions of the men by the door. Every move they made was on the quiet, on the QT, on tiptoe. As if they were afraid of disturbing her.

The door opened. Whitaker preceded Rucker into the hotel room, and the two hirelings, Lewis and Roberts, talked softly in greeting. No, they hadn't heard from anybody else. No, the police hadn't been snooping around. There was no trouble. They were hungry, was all.

Whitaker eased the door shut.

When they looked around, she was staring at them.

To Whitaker, who was expecting something else, she had the most peaceful look about her. Scared, alert, but peaceful. If that was possible. With her, it seemed so. She had put them through so much, and he knew that the peaceful face could hide so deeply a raging heart.

He used it himself, the happy facade of calmness. You could hurt so much more deeply utilizing the outward appearance of peace. There was universal respect for the smile that masked violence, and in fact didn't the world operate on this very principle?

Rucker began doing a little dance. He jittered over there toward her in a floor show manner, his arms out for balance like Fred Astaire in a flicker. Enjoying himself so very much. He even stopped down by the foot of the bed to fake a little tap-dance, sweeping around in a complete pirouette for her benefit. This wasn't surprising, that he would flaunt his power so. What was surprising to Whitaker was the Kitchen woman.

Her eyes actually crinkled into smile, her face around the gag showing laughter. Though when she laughed she was muffled by the rag. She threw back her hair and huffed through it loudly.

That wasn't the reaction Rucker was looking for. "Oh, you think my dancing is funny?" he asked. It was a shame, Whitaker thought, that the man was so delicate. He had a real genius for cruelty but lacked the physical prowess.

She couldn't answer, of course, she was in such paroxysm. It was the fear. She rocked helplessly, puffing out muffled laughter, her head falling to her chest. Rucker was just what Donovan had always said he was. Ludicrous.

Even Whitaker had to smile. And when Rucker looked back at him for validation he didn't try to hide the smile. Goad the man. It was time for his boss to show what he was made of. Where would that go?

"She's tough, right?" Rucker asked his companions. Lewis and Roberts also were in observational mode. Giving the addled oil scammer his head.

Rucker whirled back around to Wanda. "Here's the deal, lady. You want that gag out of your mouth?"

Wanda shrugged. She was trying to catch her breath.

"Say, give us a break here. We're just trying to help you out."

So Wanda broke down in laughter again. She was just racked with it. Finally crying with it. Shaking her head sadly. Something had come over her. Whitaker could see it, and it froze him up. He had been at this point a few times in his life. Desperate times. Hard times. Men feared him when he went there.

Rucker bent down, the better to get in her face.

"The deal is, we just want to find out where old Bananas is. You promise not to yell, I'll take that gag out."

Wanda shrugged.

Rucker motioned with his head for the others to come over. The three men sidled closer, didn't seem to want to have anything to do with the woman. To touch her or even be near her. Rucker stood there waiting. Finally Roberts, who figured his contract called for it, reached over and untied the handkerchief gag in the back.

"No screaming, or you go back again," Rucker said. "This hotel is empty anyway. We've reserved the whole top floor."

But Wanda was looking at Whitaker. As if she knew that whatever significant action taking place here would be taken by him. She licked dry lips. She looked like she was preparing to say something. Instead, she dissolved again into laughter.

When Rucker slapped her the tears went flying. He hit her pretty hard. Harder than he usually hit his wife. The boss was mad.

"There, how do like them apples?" Charles Rucker had never had the power to exercise the peaceful face. His eye flesh had a greedy crinkle, too needy for peace. "You little thief. Where's my money?"

"You're the thief," Wanda said.

"You took my money."

"I took back the money you stole from the people. And only a little bit of it at that."

"Can you believe the gall of this woman?" Rucker turned to engage his henchmen. Who shook their heads. No, they couldn't.

"That was my money," he said.

"For the moment. Just the way it was your victims' money, until you cheated them out of it."

"Can't everybody have the money."

"So now I have it."

Wanda Kitchen was a vision of pure defiance. The tears of laughter were still there, drying on her face, but there was no mistaking that she had gone to another level of interaction. Whitaker had the distinct sensation that she may have been waiting for this very opportunity. Some little final victory. Her irises were absolutely golden, which seemed almost eerie, as if they were backlit.

"Goddamit," Rucker said. "Fact is, the money was in my hands, and you took it. You and that hack ice man."

"So you use the act of possession as the rationale for stealing? To justify your greed?"

"I want something, I go and get it."

"Even if it's mine."

The oil scammer did a little dance of frustration. "You're the one stole from me!"

"You're the one stole from all of us."

"Jesus Christ. Are you crazy, sister? None of that money ever belonged to you."

"I'm using 'us' in the public sense. As in, We the Public are being scammed, and I'm part of the public."

"You're as daffy as the duck."

"Lewis? You got any of those Beach Oil shares? What do you think, Lewis? Have you ever seen the company return any money on those investments?"

"How would I know, I ain't involved in the company," Lewis said triumphantly.

"Have you ever seen any returns? You yourself?"

Lewis looked blank. Rucker looked nervous. Whitaker, having as much fun with this as he could, marveled at the woman. Hell, she was right as rain. He'd never bought any Beach Oil shares, and he never would. The ones he had been given as bonuses were sitting on his dresser at home, where anybody who wanted them could take a few. They never were going to be worth anything. Why Rucker would even argue that point, he couldn't see. Why didn't he just get down to business.

"Donovan Daley," Whitaker said softly. "Where is he?"

Everybody turned to the woman. Focused again.

"I don't know," she said to Rucker. "Maybe looking for a nice banana for you."

"Hurt her," Rucker said, backing off.

Whitaker's fist caught her unawares, so it was more solid than he thought it would be. It struck her square on the cheekbone, and her head rocked to one side and then wobbled groggily. He didn't even have to hit her again. She was out on her feet, though she was sitting down.

Roberts was looking at him funny when Whitaker glanced over at him. That didn't make him feel any better. He hadn't hit many women, and they usually had some inkling that the blow was coming, so it was never as solid as this. He might have broken her cheekbone.

"Fucking Christ," Roberts said. He was no stranger to hitting women, either, but he had never watched one being hit. There was no anger in him, as preceded his own slaps at his wife, so this one was viewed cold. It didn't seem right, somehow, when you had to look at it acted out.

"Again," Rucker said.

"She's out," Whitaker said. Irritated. They had spent all morning trying to explain the death of several coppers to the powers that be, and now this.

"Hit her again."

"You want her to come up with information, you don't want her unconscious."

"All right, then."

They all stood back away from the woman a step. Remembering perhaps moments when they had been struck and had been out of body for a few seconds. They knew the feeling.

Gradually Wanda came around. She scanned the rug by the bed for a while, then rose to meet the men. There was an instant where Whitaker could see fear in those eyes, but she erased that and gave them defiance.

"You liked that, didn't you?" she asked, gazing right into Whitaker.

Well that was a goddamned lie. He didn't like hitting women. It had to be done sometimes, that's all. So he hit her again. This time she had the forewarning and she jumped her head back and the fist only landed on her nose. But he waded in on her, connecting three or four good shots.

Hands grabbed at his arms, and they pulled him off her. As he got back his objectivity he could see that she was out again. She had a glass jaw, for a woman. The fairer sex, he had found in the past, were not easily knocked out.

"All right, all right," Rucker said. "Unconscious, remember?"

"Jesus," Roberts said again.

She was dripping fluids from mouth and eyes when she came around. This time she wasn't so cocky. But Whitaker could see the defiance, more canny now, more experienced in setback.

"Just tell us," Rucker said.

Wanda made not one motion. She was hunkered down. People did that in these situations. The stubborn ones. The others just blabbed until they were empty, truth or not. The ones who had some idea, some concept, driving them, those ones hunkered down for the long haul.

Whitaker took out his pliers. He kept them in his inside coat pocket. Anybody who knew him knew they were there. As soon as Wanda saw them, saw him flex the jaws open, she understood.

"Remember Joseph? I'll bet you've seen him lately," Whitaker said. "Remember what he looked like?"

Wanda had thought about Joseph last night in the middle of thinking about Donovan. She remembered how amazed the little brother had been at the application of the pliers.

She shook her head. She wasn't going to have the energy to talk, she realized. Her jaw hurt, anyway. Her gesture of negativity, in fact, was a demonstration to herself more than an answer to Whitaker. She didn't care about him anymore, she was signaling herself, marshaling her resolve.

At once, without waiting for that quim Rucker to say a thing, Whitaker grabbed the back of Wanda's head and forced it forward. He snagged a piece of her cheek skin in the pliers and clamped down.

She screamed. He had forgotten that she would scream, and he had to let go and muffle her with one hand. She was huffing and puffing mightily, coping with the pain. Blood curtained down her cheek and neck.

But she wasn't talking.

"Pull her shirt off," he heard Rucker say.

Lewis jumped to that. Of course, the blouse couldn't be taken off, tied down as she was. So Lewis ripped the buttons off and jerked it down, pulling her brassiere straps off her shoulders and jerking it down too. Her breasts bounced up and free.

"Get her nipple," Rucker said.

Whitaker just looked at him. "She won't milk properly after," he said.

"Grab it. She won't ever be milking."

But Whitaker balked. What it was, he didn't know. He wasn't going to mutilate a woman's private parts. Something about it offended him. Maybe the reputation it would leave him with. Beat their faces, all righty. Punch them in the gut, fine. But he wasn't the kind of man who would damage a woman to where she couldn't have your kid.

Wanda sobbed softly, sucking air and shaking her head from side to side almost ritualistically. As if physical activity could dull the pain.

"Give me the pliers," Rucker said.

"Arcadia," Wanda said.

"What?" Rucker said. He took the pliers from Whitaker, almost sorry she had said anything. He felt torture was a good thing, and he might even be able to carry it out.

They all looked down at the woman, thinking she must be burgeoning with confession. What they would have known, if they could have known, was that she was thinking how her father had made her rake yard leaves every fall. And how hard she tried to get every last one. But couldn't, and her father punished her with an admonishing look even if a new leaf had just fallen from a tree. And how she hated it.

"620 Standing Bear Lane," she said. "Arcadia."

"What's that?" Rucker asked. They all backed off, looking at her breasts. One little sketch line of blood from her cheek ran to the left one, then angled off to her armpit.

"Donovan."

"Arcadia's way the hell out," Lewis said.

"She's making it up," Whitaker said.

"Goddam. Goddam, goddamn, goddamn." Rucker handed the pliers to Whitaker.

Who had never seen a Jew bleed before. Had never seen a Jew's tits. Had never seen a Jew cry. It just hit him all of a sudden. The Jews were human, despite what some people said about them. They weren't supernatural.

It gave him cause to believe that they could be eradicated after all.

Now Wanda said something. Muffled, it was, because her head was down and she was leaking fluids again.

"What?" Rucker shouted.

She pulled her head up. "And don't call me sister."

WE'RE ALL FRIENDS HERE

In Joseph's confused little world, which seemed addled and sadistic to him at the moment, one and one didn't add up to anything any more. The proper world, the one around him and his family and their beautiful prairie ranch, had long ago been upended and whirled and left in an unrecognizable not to mention irretrievable shambles. And it was getting unspeakably worse. Maybe the rest of the world was still all right. It looked all right out there. He was left in his head with the shambles-world.

Yet, here was a wonderful sight. Mrs. McCants drove the car with the forthright resolve of a simple mathematical equation, amounting to what could be construed as a one-and-one simplicity. He held the baby in his lap as they, the three of them, sped through the neighborhoods of palms and bougainvillea and citrus.

Mrs. McCants, which is all he ever could call her—never Tildy, as she asked him to do—by the good fortune of her no-good cheating husband, owned a handsome Cadillac with plenty of room in it. A monster of a car. He rode with his head thrown back in luxury and the baby scrambling in his lap and clawing at the closed window. Every now and then the chubby little boy would pause in his activities and peer at Joseph as if to say, Who is this person here?

And well he should. Joseph's face just got more and more hideous every day. The torture wounds were healing in that brown, crusty way that skin tears heal. He retained only one bandage—on the wound beside his eye—but the protruding scabs and stitches were even uglier. Chock full of doubt, he was self-conscious even of the baby's gaze.

And of course, who was this Joseph who was stealing around with another man's wife? How could this man, this person who was so damaged by his parents' infidelities that those stitches would never heal properly,

be so sporting? He pondered the question very briefly, and the only answer he could come up with was that consequences sometimes dictated
scenarios that the man himself never would.

It was out of his hands. He was helpless. The woman was all his.

He looked over at her as she drove to the union hall and just couldn't
bear the thought of his earlier principles. They seemed so... limited...
now. For two nights she had tended his wounds and tucked him into her
bed like one of her corn shuck dolls. Then introduced him to breasts
whose enormous, mounded nipples only recently had been withheld from
the baby. Introduced him as well to other pleasures he wouldn't even talk
to himself about. And was careful of his damaged head while doing so,
cradling it so gently as she rocked him back and forth until she'd had her
fill.

Yes, he had to endure her lengthy, prosecutorial treatises about her husband's malfeasance, but he went to bed in the smell of perfume and woke
up to the smell of biscuits and eggs. And when he went out to the kitchen
pulling up his suspenders she would have a smile on her face and her robe
would flop open for his eyes alone. He accepted her attentions in amazement the first night and then ecstatically the next.

And so, apart from this mess concerning his brother, he rode along in
the sunny Cadillac in an accepting and self-congratulatory manner.

The car eased into downtown Los Angeles traffic, a hundred hunch-
back sedans beetling around it. Joseph guided her to the alley behind the
union hall. He tried to jump out, but she grabbed his shirt and hauled him
back in and kissed him on the healthy cheek. Right in front of the little
boy. Gently, so as not to pop a stitch.

"I don't know if that's...." he said, eyeing the boy.

"He's not even two years old," Mrs. McCants said. "Besides, he likes
you."

Joseph touched his lip with the back of his finger to see if she had
drawn blood. No, he was okay. Still, when he smiled his face hurt like
jumping Jesus.

The back door of the hall was locked, so Joseph walked all the way
around to the street and went in the front. Some kind of ILGWU activity
was getting ready to start, with a few men and women waiting in the hall.
He went searching through back offices and finally found Pauline, whom
he'd met a couple of times through Wanda. She had called her a member-
ship organizer. He knew her in his own mind as a provocateur.

She stopped her business and waved a couple of other people out of her office when she saw him. Saw his face. People were peering around corners looking at his face.

"What happened to you?"

"Never you mind. I'm looking for my brother."

"Sorry." She said no more, despite the fact that Donovan had been there only that morning. "I don't know where he is."

"If you see him," Joseph said, warily looking around as dreaded unionists passed along the passageway outside the office, "can you give him a message for me?"

"Sure."

"Tell him I saw Rucker's Pierce-Arrow at the Daylight Hotel on Sunset Boulevard this morning."

Another man came into the office. Mike, whom Joseph had never seen before. The office grew quiet. The two men looked each other over suspiciously.

"It's all right," Pauline said. "We're all friends here."

"I was driving around with a, with a friend, looking for him. And that's where I saw the car. And maybe a couple police cars. At this hotel. I know Wanda Kitchen is a friend of yours, is why I tell you this."

Mike exchanged a glance with Pauline, and she waved him out the door.

"Your name's Joseph, isn't it."

"Yeah, I'm—"

"Joseph, I've got information for you."

"All good and well."

"Donovan's going to be at 1620 Running Springs Road, in Pomona, tomorrow morning. We're getting him out of town."

"What's there?"

"Never been there. That was the arrangement, that's all."

Joseph, miles friendlier with women now that he had one, went to Pauline and shook her hand. "Thank you. You saw Donovan, then."

"This morning. I just wanted to make sure who you were."

"Where is he now?"

She shook her head. "All I know is where he'll be tomorrow morning."

Joseph nodded. Some relief was coming in. Coming in gradually.

"You see him again? Tell him I'll be there too."

"I'm thinking he won't be back."

Joseph looked down at the floor. It was brightly waxed hardwood, barely used and hardly scuffed compared with the floor out there in the union meeting room. He could hear the clopping of shoes out there now, people getting ready for something subversive.

"I reckon she's at that motel. You tell him that. You're her friends. You Reds, you socialists. I never knew what a Jew was."

He waited, but Pauline had her mouth tightly pursed. She was going to let him say what he had to say.

"All this is for her, a Jew. All because of her. I don't know how that happened."

"I suppose that's right."

"I hope he finds her. She's a good one. You tell him that if you see him before I do. I don't care who she is."

In the alley Joseph got into the Caddy and flopped into his seat as limp as an empty suit, sweating like a day laborer. His unburdening had taken a lot out of him, and Mrs. McCants could see by his face that he hadn't found anybody he wanted to find. Now he was suffering somehow.

"It's going to be all right."

She had a big smile, an expression generous with its intensity. But her eyes were full of sorrow. She was a Scot, and the Scots, as much as any nationality, knew how to mix the smile with the sorrow. They, like the Okies and the Jews and the Negroes and the Mexicans and all the rest, had come here to this city for specific reasons. She squeezed his hand and started the car.

A HOTEL IN CALIFORNIA

A ll she knew was she was in a hotel in California, because that was what they had said. She could see the tops of a couple of other buildings out the window. They had rented the whole floor, so it wouldn't do her any good to scream or make a racket. That's what they said. They had put the gag back in anyway.

Wanda was beaten sore. Her head hurt in two or three places. Her face throbbed. Her breasts had been exposed for a long time, and she shook from the cold. Finally Whitaker had come over and pulled her clothes up and covered her. It was odd that he, the torturer, of all people, was the one so reluctant to mutilate her.

She almost smiled up at him, the monster.

Rucker had called somebody on the phone and told them to go out to Arcadia to check the address she had given them, so she knew she hadn't bought much time. Spent it thinking about her family. It would be snowing in Minnesota, most likely. Her brothers and sisters would visit her parents. Her father would say a prayer for her. Hanukkah was probably over, but she didn't even know the date of it this year. She had lost track of all the old things.

And Donovan, what was he doing? He seemed like such an illicit pleasure, such a happy tragedy, now. What a galloping fool of a Robin Hood he had been, taking from the rich and ending up giving a good part of it to the victims of the couple's misadventure. Of course she loved him, but what was love in this atmosphere of flight and violence?

What a disaster their alliance had turned out to be.

She could not think of one sensible decision they had made in the last month. Their choices had grown more and more calamitous, in fact. If they were learning anything they were learning tragedy on a grander scale.

Still. Wasn't it grand at this scale? Wasn't it a source of satisfaction as her chin fell to her chest in exhaustion? Maybe they had righted a wrong figuratively, at least. Even if it was only in their own minds and not recognized as such by anybody else, wasn't that something? Wasn't lashing out better than wallowing? A gesture, if nothing else? Wasn't the self-gesture important to the laws of the universe?

There was a knock at the door, and she didn't even raise her head. That's how far inside herself she was. She was trying to mark the time, to estimate when she might be in for another beating or cutting. That was taking up a lot of her energy.

But after the three men went out the door she heard a woman's voice say, very distinctively, "1620 Running Springs Road." That brought her chin up. That brought her to her senses. Had she dreamed it?

"Pauline?" she said softly, indistinctly, through her gag. She could have sworn it was Pauline's voice. "Pauline!" she shouted as best she could.

Dead silence. Even the men's voices fell away. There was a sound of rapid footsteps, but there was nobody in the room and the door was closed. She hadn't imagined it, that sweet woman's voice among all the quarrelsome, impatient men's voices, but it was gone.

The door opened, and in came the three. They walked across the room and stood over her. The drive to Arcadia couldn't have taken this little time, though maybe time had slipped away during her bouts of insensibility. Maybe that's how the body managed the pain, it glossed the hours so as to fool you.

"You're a very bad girl," Rucker the scammer said.

He wagged his finger at her. But he was smiling. Maybe everything was all right.

"Very naughty," Whitaker the torturer said.

"I heard Pauline," she said through her gag. Her jaw hurt so much and the gag was so tight that the words couldn't have been effective.

Roberts reached to untie the gag. Her head sagged and rebounded as he worked at the stubborn knot, which had gotten tangled in her hair.

"Pauline!" she screamed when the gag came free. She screamed it because it was her last hope for discovery.

That set the men to laughing. Indeed, as she looked up, she would have been something of a comical sight to torturers. Not to ordinary people, who would have fainted at the sight of her bloody, bedraggled head. But any torturers who happened upon her would have gotten some joy from the result of the plier arts, the fisticuff persuasions. There must have been some kind of appreciation of this craft passed down through the generations, keeping it alive in the hearts and minds of certain people. And the fact that she was a Jew, the ultimate object of the torturer's art, would have been the cherry on top of the malted.

Oh please, Pauline, she thought. Please get help. I'm here, your comrade in arms, your friend.

"All lies, what you were telling us," said Rucker, doing his little dance again. "But everything's under control now."

The men didn't even think enough of her now to hit her in retaliation. Roberts and Rucker turned away to do some planning under the window at the other side of the room. While Lewis, Lewis of the sainted goon squad, the police brigade ordained to bring the communists and the Negroes and the Chinamen and the Okies to heel, Lewis reached over while the other men weren't looking and loosened her shirt again.

Her clothes fell down to her waist, and he sat on the edge of the bed and watched her breasts as she began to shiver again. Quivering with a chill as much of desperation as of cold.

But she wanted Donovan, and now she felt she was going to see him. One way or another. And she could be wrong, she had been wrong before, but that would be some consolation.

NEW YEAR'S DAY, 1939

What a sparkly day, full of sunshine and glancing little breezes that wiggled loose the few deciduous leaves still hanging from the new trees sprigged upright in the new housing development. The leaves fell to the bulldozed ground and lay curled on their backs like thin little mummies. The normally grotesque mountains to the north were soft-shouldered and cuddly in this wan light, and far back in there were peaks topped with snow, as lovely as a rack of ice cream cones.

Donovan woke up in the back of the stolen Buick, alert immediately. A rectangle of sun hit him in the face when he looked out and he had to squint to see anything. Light seemed to ricochet off the fresh paint of a hundred new houses. Everything so fresh. There was no reason to believe the sunshine wouldn't bring a day that would be good for outcomes.

It was one of those new subdivisions ground flat from undulating land, jerked out of the soil, muscled into shape, in the San Gabriel Valley. It could have been anywhere in this part of the state, but this was primo in the world of developments. The ground so smoothed and zippered with the tire tracks of heavy machinery, the mountains jumping out of the alluvium just five miles away like part of an advertisement. The houses so stripped down in their loneliness, the ones at the ends of streets just sticks in various stages of assembly, accumulating themselves as they marched along.

Last night, Donovan had spent the late hours touring the neighborhood. Munching on cold foods bought from town markets on the way out, he felt he was "casing" the area, as Wanda would have put it in her detective phase of skulduggery. Yeah, she would have admired his foresight in coming to Running Springs Road early to "get the lay of the land."

It was a bare-naked streetscape like many others out here. He remembered it. The two of them had come to look at the model homes, and now the homes were full of people, and the yards, some of them, were green. Stick-like saplings had lost their first year of foliage already. It didn't take much to make a place livable for human beings, who seemed less discerning than rabbits or birds.

There was no running spring, and probably wasn't one for miles around, but somehow the name must have fit for Wanda. Maybe there had been a spring at one time, dried up now and capped with asphalt. She had seen no cynicism or irony in the name, unless it was the delicate irony of dreams. She had been sideswiped by the place, seduced by her own nesting instinct.

He didn't really expect her to come. She probably wasn't free to come. He had brought extra food for her, in case she did. He had even bought a new white silk blouse from a small store, on a whim, for no reason other than he had seen it in the window. In case she did, they would laugh and cry so very much about the weird predicaments they had left behind, and they would be off to Arizona in the union bus. Hidden among the workers, or in the luggage hold, or on the roof if they had to. Wherever it was, they would laugh just the way they had so many times, on Muscle Beach, at the movie about Robin Hood in his tight pants, kicking up their heels at the clubs.

If she didn't come, he wouldn't get on the bus. He would turn around and drive the stolen car back into Los Angeles and look for her until he found her. If she didn't come, he knew, he would have some tough moments. But he set those thoughts aside. She would come.

Without a watch he couldn't tell the time, but from where he was parked he could see the last of the cars pulling out of driveways as the working men, owners of the new houses, left for their jobs. He was one street over, just for security purposes, but there weren't many fences up yet and he could see through to 1620 Running Springs Road.

It was a small yellow and white house, just the way he remembered it from when Wanda had gone through and admired every bit of it. The streets in this neighborhood ran straight, then curved around a large chunk of hilly ground in concentric semi-circles. Maybe it would be a park or school someday, but now it was still raw dirt dumped there from the foundation diggings of the houses around it. 1620 was on the curved part, one street over.

After the cars left the driveways, Donovan lay back in the driver's seat and rested. His head was threatening to throb again today. He rolled the window down for fresh air. It was cold air, but it was just right for an overheated head. He closed his eyes.

But immediately there was noise from the neighborhood. Far down the last row of houses hammering started up as a crew framed walls and porches. A couple of houses over, a woman popped wet laundry before she hung it on a line. And now a single car eased down Running Springs Road. It turned left at the next intersection, then nosed down his street toward him.

A Thompson lay on the seat beside Donovan and he reached over and got it even as he scunched down out of sight. He took off his boater and threw it to the floor. He sat lower as the car, a black Cadillac, approached.

Barely high enough to see the driver, Donovan tightened his grip on the tommy gun. Ready to rise up with it.

Goddamn if it wasn't Mrs. McCants. She was paying attention to her driving and didn't notice him, and then as the car passed him Donovan saw Joseph sitting in the back seat.

Throwing his door open, Donovan jumped out into the street and hollered. Mrs. McCants' head swiveled this way and that, trying to locate him. Joseph saw him pass, and got his door open and jumped out. He had a baby in his arms.

"Goddamn, Joseph!" Donovan yelled as his brother jumped out.

"Hullo, big brother."

"What the hell you doin' out here?" They trotted around each other in happiness.

"Looking for you, you big oaf."

Donovan tossed the Thompson back into his car and thumped his brother on his shoulders. This, he hadn't counted on. He tickled the baby in its armpits. He was feeling exuberant now.

"Your face is doin' better," Donovan observed.

"Took the last bandage off last night. How did you get your car back?" He indicated the Buick. At first Donovan didn't understand.

"No, it's a different one."

Mrs. McCants parked the Cadillac at the edge of the street where the asphalt feathered off—there were no curbs yet—and came over. She took the baby from Joseph's arms. Donovan just looked between the two as if not understanding basic biology.

"You two go on, now," Mrs. McCants said. "I'm taking the baby down the road a ways."

"Hello, Mrs. McCants," Donovan said.

"Donovan. Happy New Years."

"What?"

"It's New Years Day, 1939."

"Well, happy New Year, then."

Joseph went to the car and took out a rifle and a bottle of water. He leaned the rifle against the Buick and set the jug down. He went back to the car and opened the trunk and took out a large roll of what appeared to be cow hides.

Mrs. McCants gave him a motion to her cheek. Joseph leaned over and gave her a gentle peck there. He pecked the baby. The baby pecked him back. Mrs. McCants pecked him also. Donovan watched all this with some fascination. It was excellent diversion, and he was tempted to hop with joy.

She walked back and got in the car and situated the baby and drove away.

"She's been a big help," Joseph said, in answer to his brother's quizzical face.

Donovan grinned. Sure, he got it.

"What's that?" he asked of the roll of cowhide.

"I'll show you, but we better hurry up. They could be here soon."

"Who could?"

Unrolling the hides, Joseph separated out three different ice man leathers. "I don't know." He held one up to his chest.

"Is Wanda coming?"

"I don't know. Now look at this. I found the biggest, longest leathers I could."

"Is she all right?"

"I don't know. See, you put these on, one over the other, and they'll stop a bullet."

"A bullet?" Donovan dipped his chin at him.

"Yeah. I have the feeling they're not coming here to give you a smooch."

This may have been the first time he had heard his little fascist brother's sense of humor. He never knew he had one.

"I thought you didn't know who was coming."

"I don't."

"You sure these'll stop a bullet."

"I tried it last night."

"With that?"

Donovan toed the old rifle parked against the car. It was a single-shot

.22, by the looks of the size of the hole in the end, its stock and bolt worn raw with use.

"It works. I borrowed it from a fellow."

"What makes you think there's trouble?"

Joseph had to think about this. Actually, all he knew was that his brother was going to be out here. And he knew that Rucker's Pierce was parked at a Hollywood hotel along with some police cars. And that Wanda was missing. And that Pauline knew the address too.

"A lot of people appear to know that you're going to be here."

"Wanda wouldn't tell."

"I didn't say she would."

The two ranch boys turned slowly to take in the neighborhood. They could have been mistaken for city boys now. They could have been mistaken for California natives, if there was such a thing. But they were ranch boys, and they knew what to do.

"Where do you want to lay up?" Donovan asked him. They were both looking at the piles of dirt in the park area.

"Looks good enough to me."

"Running Springs is the next street over. That's a long shot with that .22."

"You got anything better?"

"I got another Thompson. Only a few shells in it, though, and they don't aim good."

"Give it to me."

As Donovan loaded up his brother with Wanda's tommy gun and the .22, he tried to figure all this out. But there were too many unknowns. You were best just moving on forward.

"We'll just wait and see, then," he said.

After Joseph went to the dirt piles, which put him even farther from 1620, Donovan went back to the Buick. He put on the leathers, one over the other, and his coat, which barely fit over them. He awkwardly got in the back seat, where all his weapons and Rucker's briefcase lay, leaving the door open and his feet reclining out. He could barely see out, as encumbered as he was. Two houses down, the housewife carried out another load of laundry and popped it and hung it on the line. Then there was no sound on the street. It was like a desert, this new city-in-the-making. Yet Wanda had loved it, the promise of it. She had foreseen tall trees and small children, she had foreseen big family gatherings and neighborhood socials. She had loved the little kitchen of 1620, and now somebody lived there and cooked in it. A car had left its driveway this morning. It was all coming true.

A shape turned off the main road and moved slowly down Running Springs Road. Donovan squirmed around so he could see glimpses of it as it passed behind the houses on both streets. When it pulled up in front of 1620 he saw that it was an old square Dodge school bus, repainted white. The lettering above its windshield read GARMENT WORKERS.

Sitting up a bit, Donovan could see a single driver and three people in the back. Even from this distance, he could identify Wanda, Rucker and Whitaker by shape and posture.

He got out. He got the Thompson. He grabbed the briefcase. He walked between two houses on this street and two houses on the next street and slowly approached the white bus. Walking right up the street toward it, looking this way and that. There were no other vehicles in sight.

The bus's door was on the other side, but he didn't have time to go around there. Two of the figures in the back of the bus stood up and jerked the other one to her feet.

"I see you've got my money!" Rucker yelled. His voice plenty loud enough to carry through the glass.

Donovan didn't reply. He walked right up to the bus. He could see the big man clearly, stooped slightly so he could see out the bus windows. He could see Wanda, who had a gag across her mouth and blood on her face. He could see Whitaker, who held a pistol to her head.

"You want to trade?" Donovan asked.

"That thought occurred to me!" Rucker yelled.

Donovan looked up and down the street. Something was wrong, and he couldn't think what it was. Nothing else moved. There were no other cars coming in, as he had half expected.

"Wanda?" he yelled.

Wanda twisted this way and that, muffled shouts barely escaping from the bus. But Rucker and Whitaker held her tight.

"Send her out!" Donovan yelled. "I'm putting the money right here."

He bent to lay the case on the street. When he rose back up he caught a glimpse of window reflection and realized the driver had opened the bus door on the other side. He saw a man's head, and another, hunching out of the bus in a hurry.

Suddenly many men's heads popped up into the bus windows. They had been crouched down in hiding, and they raised guns all at once. They fired as Donovan jumped forward. They got in one round each, at least two of the slugs hitting into the leathers at Donovan's chest.

Donovan bent and raced toward the bus. Slid halfway under it, leathers flapping. A volley of shots shattered the bus windows from the inside, and he ducked under the line of bullets. Ran his hand up under his leathers. No blood.

Extracting the Thompson, Donovan fired a burst at the legs of two men who had jumped down from the bus. As their legs broke the men collapsed into his line of sight, squirming in the dirt along Running Sprints Road. He killed them with single shots.

All firing stopped for a moment.

From under the bus he could hear a jumble of footsteps and voices from inside. Then, gunshots. Holes appeared here and there in the floorboards, and Donovan rolled away awkwardly, the leathers hindering his movement.

As he did, two more men ran out of the bus door. One went one way, the other the other way. He concentrated on the one at the rear of the bus, firing a long burst as the man swept his pistol under the frame and fired several shots at Donovan without even seeing him.

The back tire popped under Donovan's withering fire, and the slugs that tore through it also tore through the man. It was Lewis, and as he went down, still firing wildly under the bus, Donovan recognized him and put a good burst into his skull.

As Donovan rolled around on his back and turned to deal with the other man, a heavyset lug in a black coat, he saw him twirl heavily. A little pop sounded as something hit into him, and the man twirled again as if a bee were in his clothing. He saw Donovan finally and raised a shotgun, but another pop sounded and his head jerked back and he fell as if sapped.

No more firing. Joseph's aim had been true from the dirt pile. Not much creaking from the floorboards, now.

"Send her on out!" Donovan yelled from under the bus.

"We're going to kill her if you don't give it up!" Rucker shouted.

"You started it!" Donovan shouted back. "Your money's right out there on the street, but you started it up!"

"I don't even know if the money's in there!"

"Come on out and see!"

There was more creaking and mumbling, as if the people inside were shifting position and arguing.

"Donovan!" Wanda shouted very clearly. "There's five more of them!"

There was a shot. Silence. Much creaking of floorboards toward the front of the bus. Frantic, Donovan slid out from under the bus opposite the door. Leaping to his feet, he fired at the men through the windows. Even as he repositioned for a second volley he saw a small hole appear in a window and a man inside whip backwards away from it.

"There's somebody else out there," he heard Whitaker say.

"Get out there!" he heard Rucker say.

"Donovan!" he heard Wanda scream. Then another gunshot, another from farther away, another hole appeared in the window. Another shot, another, near, far. Glass fragmented. Floorboards squeaked. It was maddening because everybody had ducked out of sight.

48

WANDA'S RATIONALE

The view outside the perspecting line of windows was bleak with squandered sunlight. She saw only glances of it as she squirmed away from Rucker's hand and the foul rag he shoved farther into her mouth. For a moment there was a photogravure of Donovan as he ducked in and out of the frames of light and the others inside the bus fired jerkily at him, but he quickly bowed low as to an audience of fools and disappeared below the horizon of the windows.

For that moment she had seen him staring up at her as if in the midst of a quick little eternity of their own. And then the eyes fled.

She shut her own eyes and squirmed mightily. She bit at the rag and the hand. She opened her eyes. Rucker clung behind her, out of sight, like an abusive lover. Again there was firing of the close guns, firing of the far guns. The pop pop of small rapid objects hitting through the glass on one side and sometimes out the other. A bullet from somewhere whacked into a body and one of Rucker's men made a brief herky-jerky dance and slumped from view and complained to himself down on the floor before he went quiet.

Wanda could only think back to the original decision to be Merry Men. Was it hers or was it his? She hoped it wasn't his because now after all this she would take the responsibility gladly. Felt the full justice of it and was fine with that as long as she could bear it away from him like a clean body hauled from an accident and laid to rest. The accident would always be there, but the responsibility would be all hers.

Another window blew inward and a man near her whirled away as from a bee in his hair and Rucker spun her and shoved her forward and she stumbled on the men lying in the aisle and the ones collapsed in the seats with the legs and arms protruding to trip her. Snoozing out of breath, out of life. She scrambled over and through the arms and legs, remembering that first time she had seen Donovan in that café and the men he had hit squirming on the floor. She recognized that it had been her and it had been him. That was Wanda's rationale, that it was all their doing, the both of them, but she didn't want him to think that.

"It was me!" she shouted through the soggy gag, through the odious hand that again clamped her tight. "It's me!" That was all she needed to say to him, the man in the photogravure, that was all she needed him to hear as another outburst of explosions went off and her gaze curtained down and the world blotted. That was all.

49

THERE'S YOUR HOUSE, BABY

Donovan sprinted to the front of the bus and met a man coming around the fender. The man discharged a shotgun into his chest, and the charge knocked Donovan back a step as if he had run into a post. He fired a burst into the man, and ducked away from a spray of glass that erupted out of a bus window. He could feel the bullet pass through his hair and on.

Then the faint pop, and as he whirled and clicked on an empty chamber with the Thompson he saw another tiny hole appear in the window and a man behind it falling away. Donovan dropped the gun and pulled the .38 from one pocket and the little automatic he had taken from Lewis from another pocket. Firing, he watched a man in the bus come toward the window and fall away again as Donovan fired two, three, four shots through it. The window finally collapsed from the frailty of its supporting webs and the man bounced back and tipped forward and fell out of the bus almost onto his feet.

So Whitaker came out from behind Rucker and Wanda and leaped over bodies down the aisle of the bus right in front of Donovan and they fired at each other steadily with pistols as they ran. Bullets hit into Donovan's cloak and burned along his cheekbone and Whitaker stumbled and fell out the door. When Donovan ran around to meet him Whitaker was already running dead away from him down the row of houses.

Into the bus the ice man jumped and up the steps and ran the aisle toward Charles Rucker who had slumped with Wanda onto the floor, almost hugging each other. Rucker had a trickle of blood coming out of his hair, but he raised a big automatic and Donovan shot him twice, three times in the face and neck until he slopped over.

Wanda was looking up at him from the floor with astounded eyes as he fired, and he thought she was all right. "Stay right there," he said. He whirled and ran the aisle again and out of the bus.

He just caught a glimpse of Whitaker rounding the first house, rounding 1620, with a terrified housewife standing in the front yard next door with a dishtowel to her mouth. As soon as Donovan rounded the house Whitaker was waiting for him with the briefcase of money in one hand and the gun in the other and fired steadily and calmly at the onrushing ice man. Who fired back once, twice. Then stopped and also tried to fire calmly, since that was the smart thing to do.

Whitaker jammed or came up empty and he turned and fled, working at the gun as he ran. Then whirled again and fired one shot. Which Donovan didn't really feel so much as hear rip inside. He took two more running steps before something gave way and he fell. His face landed in the dirt and there was a moment of bewilderment before he got up and fired once at Whitaker, who was running dead away, and then he clicked on empty too.

So he wallowed around and shucked off his protective leathers and pulled the ice pick, remembering what Wanda had said about the man long ago, about the man who was most responsible for all this terror and all this world. Struggling to his feet, he ran after Whitaker for a few steps until he fell again as if he had tripped over a rope. He looked down and saw the blood coming through his trousers at the thigh. He put the ice pick back in its sheath and put his thumb hard on the bullet hole and looked up.

Whitaker had disappeared. The bleak row of houses was like a veil that had been pulled down over its humanity and he swung his gaze side to side in an attempt to make sense of it all.

There was a long curvature of houses on the next street paralleling Running Springs Road. And on the next street too. Whitaker could have gone behind or into any one of them. The new houses sat out there like matchboxes in a vast shell game, and Donovan didn't have the strength to pick and choose and gamble away his time.

There was a shuffling behind him and Donovan spun on his butt and raised the ice pick in self defense, but Joseph skidded to a stop and stood there looking down on him. Not happy at all, was Joseph, which was odd considering there seemed to be no more men in dark coats firing guns at them.

"Help me up, will ya?" Donovan said.

"Maybe you ought to stay there a minute."

But Donovan reached out his hand, and Joseph took it. As his big brother hopped around on one foot trying to regain his equilibrium, Joseph looked down at the discarded leathers. They were shredded with bullet tears.

Up the bus steps again. Hopping this time, but in a hurry. To the middle of the bus holding onto the seatbacks for balance, surging over bodies, one finger on his wound which was starting to hurt like hell and fill his shoe with blood. It squished with every other step.

Wanda and Rucker lay cradling each other. Eyes closed. Wanda's face was hideous with injury. When Donovan shook her they both opened their eyes.

"You hit?" he asked her.

"I think so," Rucker said.

Donovan took out his ice pick and gently inserted it into Rucker's chest just under the sternum and withdrew it. He inserted it again a little higher and felt the heart's muscley resistance to the thin point. He kept it in there a second, feeling for the thickest part of the muscle as it twitched against the point.

He shoved it as deep as it would go.

When Rucker relaxed completely Donovan took out the pick and put it back in the sheath. He pulled the big man's arm until he slumped off of Wanda. She fell into the ice man's arms. At first he tried to revive her, and her eyes would open but not comprehend, open but not comprehend.

He picked her up, stumbling between the seats on his bum leg, and Joseph met him at the steps and helped get her down. The blood poured out of him and the wound twitched uncontrollably.

Outside the bus, on the thin new lawn of 1620 Running Springs Road, gone a little winter-brown, he lay Wanda on her back. He and Joseph kneeled over her looking for wounds as she struggled motionlessly within. There was a little intermittent pulse at her neck, and the brothers began the search for wounds to stop.

"There's one here," Joseph said after Donovan tugged off her bloody blouse. "And one there."

Joseph gently touched two small holes in Wanda's stomach and neck, oh so gently feeling at the clammy little body. He reached around her back, and slid his hand up and down her, and looked at his hand. There was no blood on it. The slugs had fragmented inside. They were ignoring the most obvious, the execution wound in the side of her head.

The brothers exchanged a look of brotherly love and fear.

When they looked back at her she was looking at them. She said something through inanimate lips and they leaned close.

"It was me," she whispered again, and Donovan jerked back upon understanding what she meant. Closing his eyelids tight and shaking his head no, he violently disagreed. When he opened them all he could see was a stormbank of his own tears. He wiped at his eyes with bloody knuckles.

"No!" he said. "No!"

The golden eyes were open but the golden eyes were not gold. They had fallen open a shade dark. A film like cataracts had already come in behind the irises. Her little neck watch and its chain had puddled in a low spot on her throat.

"There's your house, Baby," Donovan said. He turned her head so it faced 1620. She didn't move after that. She just looked continually and longingly, he thought, at the house. The necklace slid down her neck and dangled into the dormant grass.

Finally he got his good leg under him and stood up. He looked down the street. The carpenters at the ends of the streets had gathered to see what was going on. Out on front porches and lawns stood women drawn by the gunfire and subsequent silence. All looking at Wanda Kitchen as if in gratitude, their arms crossed over chests in the cool air.

A car swooped in. The brothers recoiled, groping for weapons, their nerves damaged by their experience, but it was the Cadillac.

Mrs. McCants got out and ran over. The baby boy was clawing at the window and crying and the mother ran to a stop as sudden as a wall. She stood with Joseph and looked down at the mangled body. Donovan whirled away. He hobbled briskly between the two rows of houses, all the way to the green Buick, his fingers tight against his thigh. When he came back he sat Wanda up and slid the blood-soaked blouse off her and put the new white blouse on and buttoned it. He was crying, and it took a while. Every now and then he would stop to wipe away his tears with bloody hands.

"We should go," Joseph said. He had his fingers jammed down on Donovan's thigh to stop the bleeding.

But after Donovan wiped his eyes the last time he saw that he had cross-buttoned it, so he unbuttoned the blouse and redid it. He tidied her hair using his fingers as a comb and straightened her legs and left her lying with her gold-gone-to-gray eyes facing the house she loved.

They got in the Cadillac, and Joseph drove fast. Just as they swerved out of the subdivision, going east, a flatbed truck loaded with brand new refrigerators turned in. Making deliveries. Donovan watched it pass them, the machines roped in so tall and solid and shiny, heading for one of the kitchens of Running Springs Road. Maybe 1620.

He took the ice pick from its sheath, worrying it out from under his good leg as he pressed one hand to the hole in his other leg. The pick was crusted with blood and Donovan rolled down the window as they passed some farm fields and backhanded it out the window as far as it would go.

THE GOLD IN MOUNTAINS

Springtime in Arizona on the border was a holy and healing time, day after day. Donovan Daley sat at the entrance to the mine tunnel where he could soak up the morning sun. He rolled a smoke with tobacco from a Prince Albert can and lit the wrinkled paper and took a long suck and looked down at the can for a long time as if trying to remember something else but unable to grasp what it was. He sat on an overturned galvanized iron ore bucket and had a cigarette with his face upturned and his thoughts outward.

Two Thompson submachine guns stood propped on their butts against the rock wall beside him. A gouge in the mountain at his left shoulder went back about ten feet, far enough to shade the end wall of hacked rock. A young horse and an old burro and a middle-aged pickup truck stood in a cleared area around a one-room shack made of deconstructed boards and half-rusted corrugated iron roofing salvaged from abandoned claims in the area. There was no sound except for the racket of a cactus wren arguing with itself in the catclaw and ocotillo on the hill above him.

When he finished his smoke he dropped the butt and said, "Time to go to work."

On cue, his father came out of the little house with his gloves in one hand and a gallon water bottle slung from a piece of rope in the other hand. Behind him came Henrietta, the Mexican woman. She too had gloves and a water bottle.

They stood over him where he sat propped against the mountain. Up in the sun like that, they were difficult to see.

"How's the leg today?" his father asked.

Donovan looked down. He hadn't even checked his own leg this morning. There was a bandage bulge along his thigh under his dungarees, but there was no blood seeping through today.

"Good."

"A wonder, the way you worked yesterday. You trying to kill your-self?"

"You two sleep all right?" Donovan asked, not wanting to address the question.

"Good," his father said. "You read Joseph's letter?"

He had a folded sheet of paper in his hand. Donovan didn't take it. "I read it last night."

When he looked up he was crying even though he didn't feel he was crying. Every morning for the last month he had a moment like this, when some sight or sound or just an unexpected thought or unsolicited word in a letter brought tears to the surface. Not like crying, more like his soul was leaking.

"He and that woman bought a house."

"That's what he said."

Henrietta came close and pressed up to him and put her arms around him, the way she had gradually come to do in the time of the tears. She smelled nice, as of fruit or flour.

"You be fine," she said.

"You suppose he'll visit?"

"Said he would."

Donovan wiped his face clean of the seeping tears. Shaking his head at his torturous thoughts and memories. Of her. Always of her. Of their times and places together. Not her words. He didn't dare recall her voice.

"You be all right, Donovan," the Mexican woman said again in her wild border accent and off-kilter English acquired from the Daleys. "You be good again."

"Yeah."

Donovan got to his feet. The leg felt fine. Henrietta followed his father into the short tunnel they had dug over the last month, and as they re-trieved picks and shovels leaning against the walls Donovan stopped just inside the opening where the rock was overhead but the sunshine was still on him. It was odd. He could feel the cool filter out of the mountain rock, but the sun fairly scorched his back.

He knew he wasn't long for this gold. Despite it being his dream, there was something distasteful about the way it hid in the mountain and tempt-ed him. There was something unsavory about the way gold had looked so good on Wanda, and now there seemed to be no one or nothing that gold would look good on again. He had dug some, and it looked as black as oil.

"We be good," he replied to the backs of the two figures stopping at the dead end of the tunnel that contained, as they all knew, gold in bankable quantities. He didn't even follow them in today.

It was but a minute before the sound of them chopping at the mountain echoed out of the hole in the ground like a blind man's cane tapping on a sidewalk. They would find something, the sound implied. But Donovan knew what it would be.

51

A NEW HOUSE

Under a palm tree in a long line of newly planted palm trees lining the entryway to a growing subdivision in a long valley speckled with subdivisions sat a large black and green town car splayed with the shadows of fronds drooping far above it. A man sat in the back seat, right in the middle, barely visible through the small windows of the Pierce-Arrow, looking straight ahead as if his driver had left him for some errand and just never came back.

Distracted perhaps by a distant noise, by palm fronds pattering in a slight breeze, Whitaker glanced out and then returned his gaze to the briefcase open on the seat beside him. Looked and looked as if satisfying some disturbing hunger. He had only taken out enough money to get by living on sardines and crackers and soda pop after he left Rucker's service, so the case was still nearly full of bills. He couldn't seem to get enough of looking at the money and greeted it each morning in just this way.

Rolling the window down on the shadowy side of the car to alleviate the heat, he moved away from a trapezoid of spring sunlight that had been creeping toward him on the seat for several minutes. And smiled without parting his lips or putting any energy into his eyes. It was a tightly zipped smile, but at least, after a month of living in the car, he was starting to relax into his future.

He had just decided to buy a new house with the money. He wanted a new car, too, but since he had been able to appropriate the Pierce there was no need to hurry that one. No hurry at all, since he was enjoying how it felt to sit in the back seat, as if he had a driver who was running errands, though he didn't, and how it felt to wallow in the gaze of passing motorists hurrying to view the new homes.

Why shouldn't they be envious? Surely they could see that he was a man satisfied with the way his life had gone.

Not that he wanted a house here. This valley living wasn't for him. He wanted a place in the hills, the rolling hills, the oak hills, where he could get away from the idea of Kansas and the Depression.

He was only here because it was another random place to be on the way to a place that was not random. A place he desired and would soon identify and then occupy. Where he could let out the artist in his soul and maybe even make a living with his talented hands. That was why he had come here, that was who he really was, not that man who carried guns and bag money and fake stock certificates.

Though he still had the gun. It was on the seat on the other side. Unlike before, when the automatic was a positive force for improvement, he resolved now that he wouldn't use it until he had to. It was an emergency measure now, a preventative, a prophylactic. To protect his new house when he got it. Theoretically, someday he would be able to get rid of it, but he knew he wouldn't.

Here's what he wanted the house to be, he thought. Yellow. Inside and out. And he wanted all the latest radios and refrigerators and washing machines. And he wanted another cigarette girl like... whatever her name was. Trish. Like Trish, but not Trish. He would buy her anything she wanted, with the money from the briefcase and from when he started selling his drawings, so she would be happy

That was the important part. That everyone around him be happy. He wouldn't hit them if they were happy. He wouldn't shoot them. He wouldn't strike them with a sap. He would use the pliers to repair the new house he would get.

Then, once he was sure his past was lost and forgotten, he would be happy too. As long as he found a house that was suitable and in the hills and yellow. In a nice town with nice folks and nice cars where he wouldn't stand out except for his art. And if that didn't work out, he thought as he sat in the back of the car and took out his pliers for the sake of reminiscence, he could be a mechanic or a dentist or a refrigerator repairman.

Because you can be anything you want to be in America as long as you pay your dues and have a pair of pliers. He crawled over the seat back and got behind the wheel and started the car and followed the train of curiosity seekers to look at the white model homes in the valley up ahead.

What the hell, he didn't have to live in the hills.

Donnie Dale had one previous novel published, *A Hunter's Fire*, and has written for the movie and television industries.